YOU NEVER BELIEVE ME

YOU NEVER BELIEVE ME

AND OTHER STORIES

Davis Grubb

St. Martin's Press
NEW YORK

For Susan Grubb

With special thanks to Ruth Cavin, editor

Design by Glen M. Edelstein

Library of Congress Cataloging-in-Publication Data

Grubb, Davis.
You never believe me: and other stories/by Davis Grubb.
p. cm.
"A Thomas Dunne Book."
ISBN 0-312-02997-7
I. Title.
PS3513.R865Y6 1989
813'.54—dc19 89-30084
CIP

First Edition

10 9 8 7 6 5 4 3 2 1

CONTENTS

FOREWORD

Davis Grubb, 1919–1980

My brother was born in Moundsville, West Virginia, a rather sleepy Ohio River town that was a stopping point for our grandfather's steamboat in the 1880s. Dave remembered being taken, when he was ten, on a trip from nearby Wheeling to Cincinnati on the great stern-wheeler *Queen City*. For more than two hundred years our family has lived in that part of the Ohio Valley, and in setting and spirit, it has been the source of Dave's novels. Our father, an architect, came from a prominent Wheeling family.

Dave's childhood was rather typical for a small town in the 1920s, except for occasional summer trips to Chautauqua, New York, a cultural center on Lake Chautauqua where he met F. Scott Fitzgerald, Thomas Edison, Paul Whiteman, and received a dime from John D. Rockefeller.

Of his work, Davis has said, "I have never wavered from a resolution made at the age of seven that I would become a writer. My earliest influences were the tales of old men in my river town." After a rather uninspired high school record in Clarksburg, West Virginia, he studied art for one year at Carnegie Tech, in Pittsburgh, where, for extra money, he stuffed Brazilian hummingbirds and finally left after being told he was color blind.

He began to write fiction seriously after a stab at radio announcing, copywriting, and a year at NBC as a fifteen-dollar-a-week page. He broke into print with a half-hour radio play, and that launched him on a long career of short story writing. He published over fifty short stories, most of these in *Colliers*, *American Magazine*, *Cosmopolitan*, *Good Housekeeping*, *Saturday Evening Post*, *Ellery Queen's Mystery Magazine* and in many anthologies. Three of his stories were seen on *Alfred Hitchcock Presents*. His "Horsehair Trunk" was used on radio and later on television. "The Siege of 318" was produced after his death on ABC's *Dark Room.*

The writers who influenced Dave included William Blake (whose poetry he especially loved) and then Rebecca West, Robert Graves, William Faulkner, John O'Hara, D. H. Lawrence, and Thomas Wolfe. He was not only an avid reader but a book collector as well. Dave was also a very funny man, and knew many comedians. Lenny Bruce was a good friend.

Our mother's beliefs and experiences had a great influence on him; she became a child welfare worker in 1936 after the death of our father, and many of Dave's characters came directly from her job experiences. He traveled many miles with her in the hills of West Virginia, and packaged surplus food for the poor in the late thirties. All of this, plus a belief in God (but not the formal church that he railed against in his last novel, *Ancient Lights*) surfaced in his work.

Dave published eleven novels:

Night of the Hunter (Harper & Row, 1953. Twenty countries, currently Penguin Books, 1982). The story is about a little boy who holds a secret, and a soft-voiced preacher with a bloody history who stalks the child through a moonlit night at a place called Cresap's Landing.

Nelson Algren said of this book, "As compelling a story as I've come across"; Walter Van Tilburg Clark said, "A moving and darkly disturbing book. There is power, poetry, imagination here."

Hunter was sold to Charles Laughton and Paul Gregory for a film. It was released in 1955, featuring Shelley Winters, Robert Mitchum, and Lillian Gish, and is considered a classic. It is in the permanent collection of the Museum of Modern Art.

RCA released an LP of Laughton reading an abbreviated version that Dave had written. Dave also wrote two songs for the movie score, and presented a series of pencil sketches as the basis for several scenes to Stanley Cortez, the noted cinematographer, who followed them. The book itself had been written in Philadelphia in six weeks while Dave was working as a copywriter at the Al Paul Lefton Advertising Agency.

A Dream of Kings (Scribner's, 1965). A civil war novel peopled again with family characters and stories. (Our Grandfather Cresap ran away from home at twelve to join the Confederacy, but was sent home because of his age.) Dave returned to this period twenty years after writing an as yet unpublished novel, *The Scallop Shell. A Dream of Kings* tells of a young man's growth to manhood in a West Virginia river town and of his rediscovery of a first love after soldiering with Stonewall Jackson.

The Watchman (Scribner's, 1961). This novel revolves around a prison (which was, indeed, in our home town, Moundsville). Dave renamed the town Glory for his later books. *Time* said, "The latest of the author's marrow-chilling tales of good and evil—a mixture of poetic rage against cruelty in man, a song in praise of physical love, a cry of despair at the blows dealt to the innocent young."

The Voices of Glory (Scribner's, 1962). The voices of nearly thirty people—the men, women, and children living in the twenties in the West Virginia river town of Glory. As Orville Prescott said in *The New York Times*, "Davis Grubb's *The Voices of Glory* is an overwhelming novel. It overwhelms with torrential eloquence, with tempestuous emotion, with drama and melodrama and pathos. There hasn't been anything like *Voices of Glory* ever—although some may be reminded of the poems in Edgar Lee Masters' *Spoon River Anthology* and others may be reminded of a play, Thorton Wilder's *Our Town*. But those works were efforts to distill in a brief space the essence of human experience. His almost Dickensian quality does not make the people of Glory any the less striking as individuals or their stories any the less dramatic. He is a born storyteller."

Twelve Tales of Suspense and the Supernatural (Scribner's, 1964). Dave always wrote with the camera in mind so it is not surprising that three of these stories were seen on television.

A Tree Full of Stars (Scribner's, 1965). This is a Christmas story. It was based on a family, again from Moundsville, who kept their Christmas tree lit all year. Strangely, this enraged some people in town. The family was finally forced to leave.

Shadow of My Brother (Holt, Rinehart & Winston, 1966). A

young boy is brutally murdered in a Southern town while five people watch. The author goes back three generations of the Wilson family to build a narrative of terror and evil. Lillian Smith said, "*Shadow of My Brother* is . . . one of the best novels ever written on the mind-in-depth of a white racist. Davis Grubb knows of evil and sweetness in the human heart as few writers understand it."

The Golden Sickle (World, 1968). The old inn where most of the action of this story takes place was actually run by members of our family, and Dave played there as a child. He loved the books about pirates by Howard Pyle, and here he tells of the Ohio River pirates.

Fools' Parade (World, 1969). The plot centers on a convicted murderer who has served forty-seven years in Glory Prison and has earned $25,452.32, saving his earnings in the "Work and Hope Savings Plan" at the local bank. His problem is how to get his money from the bank. The story, set in 1935, was made into a wonderful movie by James Stewart and George Kennedy; they filmed it in Moundsville. Dave went back for the filming and took his dear friend—a Lhasa Apso named Rowdy Charley.

The Barefoot Man (Simon & Schuster, 1971). Miners, their women, strikebreakers, and a character based on Mother Jones make up the cast of this novel. One critic said, "Grubb's new novel is perhaps the most searing and convincing work to come out of the American agony in the thirties since Steinbeck's *The Grapes of Wrath.*"

Ancient Lights (Viking, 1982). This was Dave's last novel and, in his opinion, his finest. Actual work on it began in Moundsville, where he was working on a grant from the West Virginia Arts and Humanities Foundation. It is his biggest book—540 wonderful pages filled with so many people and places it is impossible to describe in a few words. Let me quote:

Stephen King: "I found *Ancient Lights* exhilarating, hilarious, amazing—and sometimes shocking, with its image of Christ as a happy-go-lucky bumpkin from Weirton, West Virginia. It's an authentic by-golly-damn tour de force. Grubb, like Heller in *Catch 22*, is inventive, clear and full of a febrile imagination. His language throws off sparks; it coruscates. I absolutely loved it and envy the people who will read it." *The Chicago Tribune:* "A river of a book, powerful, brilliant in its moments of religious light and insight." *The New York Times:* "*Ancient Lights* is the kind of book you put down again and again, think about for a while, and then resume reading in pursuit of the author's manic vision."

Dave died on the eve of his sixty-first birthday, six weeks after delivering the manuscript of *Ancient Lights* to Viking. He is buried on a hill overlooking the Ohio River and Moundsville—or "Glory," as he would say—among the people he wrote about so well.

—*Louis Grubb*
New York City, 1989

YOU NEVER BELIEVE ME

"I exist, therefore I am" is all very fine. But I say "I exist, therefore so do you." It is this insisted-upon existence upon which "understanding" of immortality hinges.

—Davis Grubb, notebooks

It was not that Nell hadn't done everything she could. Many a windy, winter afternoon she had spent reading to the child from *Pilgrim's Progress* and Hadley's *Comportment for Young Ladies* and from the gilded, flowery leaves of *A Spring Garland of Noble Thoughts*. And countless times she had reminded the little girl that we must all strive to make ourselves useful in this Life and that five years old wasn't too young to begin to learn. But none of it had helped.

And there were times when Nell actually regretted ever taking in the curious, gold-haired child that tragic winter when Nell's brother Amos and his foolish wife had been killed. Eva stubbornly spent her days dreaming under the puzzle tree or sitting on the stone steps of the icehouse making up tunes or squatting on

---

*Dramatized for the television series *Alfred Hitchcock Presents* under the title "Where the Woodbine Twineth."

the little square carpet stool in the dark parlor and whispering softly to herself.

Eva! cried Nell one day. Who are you talking to?

To my friends, said Eva quietly, Mister Peppercorn and Sam and—

Eva! cried Nell. I will not have this nonsense any longer—you know perfectly well there's no one in this parlor but you.

They live under the davenport, explained Eva patiently. And behind the pianola. They're very small, so it's easy for them.

Eva, hush that talk this instant! cried Nell.

You never believe me, sighed the child, when I tell you things are real.

They aren't real, said Nell. And I forbid you to make up such tales any longer. When I was a little girl I never had time for such mischievous nonsense. I was far too busy doing the bidding of my God-fearing parents and learning to be useful in this world.

Dusk was settling like a golden smoke over the willows down by the river shore when Nell finished pruning her roses that afternoon. And she was stripping off her white linen garden gloves on her way to the kitchen to see if Suse and Jessie had finished their Friday baking. Then she heard Eva speaking again, far off in the dark parlor, the voice quiet at first and then rising curiously.

Eva! cried Nell, hurrying down the hall, determined to put an end to the foolishness once and for all. Eva! Come out of that parlor this very instant.

Eva appeared in the doorway, her round face streaming and broken with grief, her fat dimpled fist pressed to her mouth in grief.

You did it! the child shrieked. *You* did it!

Nell stood frozen, wondering how she could meet this.

They *heard* you! Eva cried, stamping her fat shoe on the bare, thin carpet. They heard you say you didn't want them to stay here! And now they've all gone away—*all* of them, Mister Peppercorn and Mingo and Sam and Popo—

Nell grabbed the child by the shoulders and began to shake her—not hard but with a mute, hysterical compulsion.

Hush up, Nell said thickly. Hush, Eva—stop it this very instant!

You did it! wailed the golden child, her head lolling back in a passion of grief and bereavement. My *friends!* You made them all go away!

All that evening Nell sat alone in her bedroom trembling with curious satisfaction. For punishment Eva had been sent to her room without supper and Nell sat listening now to the even, steady sobs far off down the hall.

It was dark and on the river shore a night bird tried its note cautiously against the silence. Down in the pantry, the dishes done, Suse and Jessie, dark as night itself, drank coffee by the great stove and mumbled over stories of the old times before the war. Nell fetched her smelling salts and sniffed the frosted stopper of the flowered bottle till her trembling stopped.

Then, before the summer seemed half begun, it was late August. And one fine, sharp morning, blue with the smoke of burning leaves, the steamboat *Samantha Collins* docked at Cresap's Landing. Eva sat, as she had been sitting most of that summer, alone on the cool, worn steps of the icehouse, staring moodily at the daisies bobbing gently under the burden of droning, golden bees.

Eva! Nell called cheerfully from the kitchen window. Someone's coming today.

Eva sighed and said nothing, glowering mournfully at the puzzle tree and remembering the wonderful stories that Mingo used to tell.

Grandfather's boat landed this morning, Eva, said Nell. He's been all the way to New Orleans and I wouldn't be at all surprised if he brought his little girl a present.

Eva smelled suddenly the wave of honeysuckle that wafted sweet and evanescent from the gangled blooms on the stone wall; and she sighed, recalling the high, gay lilt of Mister Peppercorn's voice when he used to sing her his enchanting songs.

Eva! called Nell again. Did you hear what Aunt Nell said? Your Grandpa's coming home this afternoon.

Yes'm, said Eva lightly, hugging her fat knees and tucking her plain little skirt primly under her bottom.

And supper that night was quite pleasant. Jessie had made raspberry cobblers for the Captain and fetched in a prize ham from the meat-house, frosted and feathery with mold, and Suse had baked fresh that forenoon till the ripe, yeasty smell of hot bread seemed everywhere in the world.

Nobody said a word while the Captain told of his trip to New Orleans, and Eva listened to his stern old voice and remembered Nell's warnings never to interrupt when he was speaking, and only to speak herself when spoken to.

When supper was over, the Captain sat back and sucked the coffee briskly from his white mustache. Then rising without a word, he went to the chair by the crystal umbrella stand in the hallway and fetched back a long box wrapped in brown paper.

Eva's eyes rose slowly and shone over the rim of her cup.

I reckon this might be something to please a little girl, said the old man gruffly, thrusting the box into Eva's hands.

For me? whispered Eva.

Well now, grunted the Captain. I didn't fetch this all the way up the river from N'Orleans for any *other* girl in Cresap's Landing!

And presently string snapped and paper rustled expectantly and the cardboard box was open at last and Eva stared at the creature which lay within and Eva's eyes were shining and wide with sheerest disbelief.

Numa, she whispered.

What did you say, Eva? said Nell. Don't mumble your words.

It's Numa! cried the child, searching both their faces for the wonder that was hers. They told me she'd be coming but I didn't know Grandpa was going to bring her. Mister Peppercorn said—

Eva, whispered Nell.

Eva looked gravely at her Grandfather, hoping not to seem too much of a tattletale, hoping that he would not deal too harshly with Nell for the fearful thing she had done that summer day.

Aunt Nell made them all go away, she began.

Nell leaned across the table clutching her linen napkin tight in her white knuckles.

Father, she whispered. Please don't discuss it with her. She's made up all this nonsense and I've been half out of my mind all this summer. First it was some foolishness about people who live under the davenport in the parlor—

Eva sighed and stared at the gaslight winking brightly on her Grandfather's watch chain and felt somewhere the start of tears.

It's really true, she said boldly. She never believes me when I tell her things are real. She made them all go away. But one day Mister Peppercorn came back. It was just for a minute. And he told me they were sending me Numa instead!

And then she fell silent and simply sat, heedless of Nell's shrill voice trying to explain. Eva sat staring with love and wonder at the Creole doll with the black tresses and the lovely coffee-colored skin.

Whatever the summer had been, the autumn, at least, had seemed the most wonderful season of Eva's life. In the fading afternoons of that dying Indian summer she would sit by the hour, not brooding now, but holding the dark doll in her arms and weaving a shimmering spell of fancy all their own.

And when September winds stirred, sharp and prescient with new seasons, Eva, clutching her dark new friend, would tiptoe down the hallway to the warm, dark parlor and sit by the pianola to talk some more.

Nell came down early from her afternoon nap one day and heard Eva's excited voice far off in the quiet house. She paused with her hand on the newel post, listening, half wondering what the other sound might be, half thinking it was the wind nudging itself wearily against the old, white house.

Then she peered in the parlor door.

Eva, said Nell. What are you doing?

It was so dark that Nell could not be certain of what she saw. She went quickly to the window and threw up the shade.

Eva sat on the square carpet stool by the pianola, her blue eyes blinking innocently at Nell and the dark doll staring vacuously up from the cardboard box beside her.

Who was here with you? said Nell. I distinctly heard two voices.

Eva sat silent, staring at Nell's stiff high shoes. Then her great eyes slowly rose.

You never believe me, the child whispered, when I tell you things are real.

Old Suse, at least, understood things perfectly.

How's the scampy baby doll your Grandpappy brought you, lamb? the old Negro woman said that afternoon as she perched on the high stool by the pump, paring apples for a pie. Eva squatted comfortably on the floor with Numa and watched the red and white rind curl neatly from Suse's quick, dark fingers.

Life is hard, Eva sighed philosophically. Yes, oh, yes, life is hard. That's what Numa says!

Such talk for a youngster! Suse grunted, plopping another white quarter of fruit into the pan of spring water. What you studyin' about Life for? And you only five!

Numa tells me, sighed Eva, her great blue eyes far away. Oh, yes! She really does! She says if Aunt Nell ever makes her go away she'll take me with her.

Take you! chuckled Suse, brushing a bluebottle from her arm. Take you where?

Where the woodbine twineth, sighed Eva.

Which place? said Suse, cocking her head.

Where the woodbine twineth, Eva repeated patiently.

I declare! Suse chuckled. I never done heard tell of *that* place!

Eva cupped her chin in her hand and sighed reflectively.

Sometimes, she said presently, we just talk. And sometimes we play.

What y'all play? asked Suse obligingly.

Doll, said Eva. Oh, yes, we play doll. Sometimes Numa gets tired of being doll and I'm the doll and she puts me in the box and plays with me.

She waved her hand casually to show Suse how really simple it all was.

Suse eyed her sideways with twinkling understanding, the laughter struggling behind her lips.

She puts *you* in that little bitty box? said Suse. And *you*'s a doll?

Yes, oh, yes, said Eva. She really does. May I have an apple please, Suse?

When she had peeled and rinsed it, Suse handed Eva a whole, firm Northern Spy.

Don't you go and spoil your supper now, lamb, she warned.

Oh! cried Eva. It's not for me. It's for Numa.

And she put the dark doll in the box and stumped out the back door to the puzzle tree.

Nell came home from choir practice at five that afternoon and found the house so silent that she wondered for a moment if Suse or Jessie had taken Eva down to the landing to watch the evening packet pass. The kitchen was empty and silent except for the thumping of a pot on the stove, and Nell went out into the yard and stood listening by the rose arbor.

Then she heard Eva's voice. And through the failing light she saw them beneath the puzzle tree.

Eva! cried Nell. Who is that with you?

Eva was silent as Nell's eyes strained to piece together the shadow and substance of the dusk. Nell ran quickly down the lawn to the puzzle tree. But only Eva was there.

Off on the river the evening packet blew dully for the bend. Nell felt the wind, laced with autumn, stir the silence round her like a web.

Eva! called Nell. I distinctly saw another child with you. Who was it?

Eva sighed and sat cross-legged in the grass with the long box and the dark doll beside her.

You never believe me— she began softly, staring guiltily at the apple core in the grass.

Eva! cried Nell, brushing a firefly roughly from her arm so that it left a smear of dying gold. I'm going to have an end to this nonsense right now.

And Nell picked up the doll in the cardboard box and started toward the house. Eva screamed in terror.

Numa! she wailed.

You may cry all you please, Eva, said Nell. But you may not have your doll back until you come to me and admit that you don't really believe all this nonsense about fairies and imaginary people.

Numa! screamed Eva, jumping up and down in the grass and beating her fists against her bare, grass-stained knees, Numa!

I'm putting this box on top of the pianola, Eva, said Nell. And I'll fetch it down again when you confess to me that there was another child playing with you this afternoon. I cannot and will not countenance falsehoods.

Numa said, screamed Eva, that if you made her go away—

I don't care to hear another word! said Nell, walking ahead of the wailing child up the dark lawn toward the house.

But the words sprang forth like Eva's very tears.

—she'd take me away with her! she screamed.

Not another word, said Nell. Stop your crying and go up to your room and get undressed for bed—this instant!

And she went into the parlor and placed the doll box on top of the pianola next to the music rolls.

A week later the thing ended. And years after that autumn night Nell, mad and simpering, would tell the tale again, and stare at the pitying, doubting faces in the room around her, and then she would whimper to them in a parody of the childish voice of Eva herself: You never believe me when I tell you things are real.

It was a pleasant September evening and Nell had been to a missionary meeting with Nan Snyder that afternoon and she had left Nan at her steps and was hurrying up the tanbark walk by the icehouse when she heard the prattling laughter of Eva far back in the misty shadows of the lawn.

Nell ran swiftly into the house to the parlor—to the pianola. The doll box was not there.

She hurried to the kitchen door and peered out through the netting into the dusky river evening. She did not call to Eva then, but went out and stripped a willow switch from the little tree by the stone wall and tiptoed softly down the lawn. A light wind blew from the river meadows, heavy and sweet with wetness, like the breath of cattle.

They were laughing and joking together as Nell crept soundlessly upon them—speaking low as children do, with wild, delicious intimacy, and then bubbling high with laughter that cannot be contained.

Nell approached silently, feeling the dew soak through to her ankles, clutching the switch tightly in her hand. She stopped and listened for a moment, for suddenly there was but one voice—a low and wonderfully lyric sound that was not the voice of Eva.

Then Nell stared wildly down through the misshapen leaves of the puzzle tree and saw the dark child sitting with the doll box in its lap.

So! cried Nell, stepping suddenly through the canopy of leaves. You're the darkie child who's been sneaking up here to play with Eva.

The child put the box down and jumped to its feet with a low cry of fear as Nell sprang forward, the willow switch flailing furiously about the dark ankles.

Now scat! cried Nell. Get on home where you belong and don't you ever come back—you hear me?

For an instant the dark child stared in horror, first at Nell and then at the doll box; its sorrowing, somnolent eyes were brimming with wild words and a grief for which it had no tongue; its lips were trembling as if there were something Nell should know that she might never learn again after that autumn night was gone.

Go on, I say! Nell shouted, furious.

The switch flickered about the dark arms and legs faster than ever. And suddenly with a cry of anguish the dark child turned and fled through the tall grass toward the meadow and the willows on the river shore.

Nell stood trembling for a moment, letting the rage ebb slowly from her body.

Eva! she called out presently. Eva!

There was no sound but the dry steady racket of the frogs by the landing.

Eva! cried Nell. Come to me this instant—do you hear me?

She picked up the doll box and marched angrily up toward the lights in the kitchen.

Eva! screamed Nell. You're going to get a good switching for this!

A night bird in the willow tree by the stone wall cried out once and started up into the still, affrighted dark. Nell did not call again—for suddenly, like the mood of the autumn night, the very sound of her voice had begun to frighten her.

And when she was in the kitchen, Nell screamed so loudly that Suse and Jessie, long asleep in their shack down below the icehouse, woke wide and stared wondering into the dark. Nell stared for a long moment after she had screamed, not believing, really, for it was at once so perfect and yet so unreal. Trembling, Nell ran back out onto the lawn.

Come back! screamed Nell hoarsely into the tangled far-off shadows by the river. Come back! Oh, please, please come back!

But the dark child was gone forever.

And Nell, creeping back at last to the kitchen, whimpering and slack-mouthed, looked again at the lovely little dreadful creature in the doll box—the gold-haired, plaster Eva with the eyes too blue to be real.

FIFTY OF THE BLUE

DRUNK: Have to have a drink before the fight.
BARTENDER: What fight?
—Davis Grubb, notebooks

Aunt Cynthie whispered some of it to me once—how both men had come back from the war on the same autumn day: Jason Beam, proud and spotless in his Yankee blue and riding a fine, shimmering sorrel mare and Grandpap, nigh barefoot, in ragged, rebel, linsey jeans and a borrowed homespun coat. They had passed each other on Jefferson Avenue without speaking that day, thirty years before, and had not spoken or even nodded, except in the courtroom, ever since. Jason had learned his law in a fine school in the North and Grandpap had got his from a dog-eared Blackstone during his years on the river, under the yellow lantern in the pilothouse of the *Beulah Curtis*. Grandpap was always called the Captain.

Jason Beam ran for county attorney that autumn of his return. The people had elected him and he held the office for more than a quarter of a century. Yet never once in all that time had he ever defeated Grandpap in a case. It got to be a joke with the people of Cresap's Landing. And, whenever Grandpap went to court, folks would flock from miles around to watch Jason Beam pit his school-learned skill against Grandpap's hard, shrewd mother wit.

When Jason Beam retired as county attorney and ran for judge that autumn, some people claimed he wanted to escape this humiliation and be able to sit safely by and watch some other poor boob cross foils with the Captain. At any rate, he was elected, and not a month later the sheriff arrested Dred Booher.

Grandpap and Willie Showacre were playing billiards in the game room that afternoon when Sam Kidd, the city jailer, came puffing up the tanbark walk.

Where's the Cap'm, boy? Sam said.

In the game room, I said.

Sam went in the house and directly I could hear them talking.

Sher'f Sigafoose arrested him not ten minutes ago in the billiard room down at the Brass House, Sam was saying. Claimed he was runnin' a faro game and locked him up. Now he's down in the jailhouse hollerin' his head off fer you, Cap'm. Claims you and him was pardners on the *Beulah Curtis* durin' the War and he wants you fer his lawyer. Judge Beam got wind he was a reb somehow and a friend of yourn, and he's called a special session of court and is fixin' to try him right away.

Is his name Booher? Grandpap said.

That's it, Cap'm, cried Sam. Dred Booher! Little ol' white-headed feller with a jaw full of Maryland twist.

I heard Grandpap rack his cue and fetch his gold-headed cane from the umbrella stand. Come on, Willie, he was saying when he came out the front door. We'll have to see about this. . . .

Word had got around fast that Grandpap was going to defend the gambler. And when we arrived at the courthouse, the people of Cresap's Landing were already standing around outside.

Dred Booher was a little round man with a stained white mustache and trickles of brown juice in the creases of his leathery cheeks. He was sitting on a cot with his head in his hands, staring at the floor of his cell when Sam Kidd let us in.

Deed to God, Cap'm, he said, hopping to his feet and grabbing Grandpap's hand, I don't recollect when ever I was so glad to see a mortal man!

Dred, said Grandpap, what have you been up to now?

Aw shucks, Cap'm, growled the old man sheepishly. It warn't nothin' but a friendly little game of faro between gentlemen. I come in on the mornin' packet about two hours ago and was figurin' to come up and pay you a call as soon's I could git me enough coppers together fer a shave—

You needn't explain anymore, said Grandpap, taking a long stogie out of his silver case and gingerly clipping it.

Then—then you mean you'll take my case, Cap'm? Dred Booher said.

Dred, said Grandpap softly, scratching a kitchen match on the stone wall, we stood together on the texas of the *Beulah* the night the ironclads hit us, didn't we?

Y'damn if we didn't now, Cap'm! said Dred, cracking his fist in his horny palm. Lord, sometimes of a night I can hear it yet—them dern minnies thwackin' through the paddle box. Y'damn, Cap'm, if we hadn't skeedaddled for the Red River that night, I reckon we'd all gone up.

Storekeepers, corner loafers, and big farmers from downriver in the bottomlands had got wind that the Captain was tangling horns with Jason Beam that afternoon and they'd piled up on the worn benches of the little courtroom like sinners at a tent meeting.

Grandpap's mouth went white under his mustache when Judge Beam stalked into the room, lordly and swollen with petty dignity, straightening his black string tie and fussing grumpily with the lawbooks scattered across the long table.

Bailiff! he growled, never once glancing at Grandpap. State the defendant's name.

Dred Booher, yer honor, squeaked the bailiff.

What are the charges?

Defendant was arrested for running a faro game in the billiard room of the Brass House, said the bailiff. The rest of the fellers that was playin' all got away.

Does the defendant have counsel for his defense? Judge Beam asked.

Grandpap stepped forward. I am representing the defendant, he said quietly.

Dust motes spun in the shafts of sun that poured from the tall, quartered window. There was no sound now in the little room except for the damp rustle of tobacco pokes and the uneasy shifting of farmers searching for space to spit.

How does your client plead? Judge Beam asked, leaning back in his big chair.

My client pleads innocent, said Grandpap.

Bailiff, said Judge Beam, produce the evidence in this case against Dred Booher.

The bailiff dumped a pile of poker chips onto the table and slapped down a greasy deck of cards.

These hyere was found right smack dab on the billiard table where they was a-playin', yer honor.

The people of the county all looked at Grandpap. Everybody wondered how he was ever going to get out of this one. Grandpap was slumped down a little more in his chair, drawing on his stogie.

Our contention here, he said at last, is that the evidence introduced is insufficient to prove that the defendant was actually gambling. Gambling, I believe, is a procedure by which money is exchanged illegally by means of a game of chance. And there is no actual money here among this evidence.

For a minute the judge's round face looked as if it could scarcely contain the triumph that swelled behind it. Thirty years before he had ridden home from the war on a proud sorrel mare and met Grandpap limping up the dusty road in defeat. But that had been a long time ago. And Jason Beam had never beaten Grandpap at anything since.

The court rules, he boomed triumphantly, that these chips *are* money as much as if they were silver dollars bearing the glorious eagle of the Union!

Grandpap's great white head sank a little lower and he was silent a long while.

In that case, he said softly, my client has no alternative but to plead guilty to the charges.

Judas priest! somebody whispered hoarsely among the mob. Beam's got him at last!

The judge reared back in his chair, looking as if he had just won Second Bull Run singlehanded.

Fifty dollars' fine, he growled. Or thirty days in the jailhouse.

For a while nobody moved. The people of Marshall County that loved Grandpap sat gawking and stunned. I turned and ducked out through the courthouse doors, out into the golden sunlight that swirled and swam through my tears. I sat down on the dusty curb by the brass cannon.

All of a sudden people came mobbing out into the yard, hollering and shouting. Willie Showacre ran over to me, gasping with laughter. He collapsed on the grass beside me. I stood up and clenched my fists.

How can you laugh? I said. You his best friend! Ain't it bad enough him bein' whipped by his worst enemy without his best friend laughin' about it?

Whipped! said Willie, rolling around in the grass in a fresh spasm of laughter. *Whipped!* Why, Lordamighty, boy, this here's the best one yet. They're laughin' at Jason Beam clean down the river to Paden City. The Cap'm just got through payin' Dred Booher's fine. With fifty of the blue!

BITTER ALMONDS

Tomorrow is a dream I may miss. I may not live to be in the audience, yet may be among its starry audience.
　　　　　　　　　　　　　—Davis Grubb, notebooks

But, you see, it just couldn't have been murder. Because Miss Ruth Ann Hawk was more than just the wealthiest lady in Glory, she was the best loved. And when she dropped dead on the pavement in front of the Palace Furniture Company on Pike Street there wasn't a living soul within twenty feet of her. It was a pleasant September morning in the year 1932—two months before election time—and for Sheriff C. D. Pancake to call Miss Ruth Ann's death murder was to put his coming election square on the line. He had a little less than two months to put up or shut up or he was through. Moreover, there were witnesses to her death. Maybe not the most reliable, but at least sober, and sane. I mean the unemployed whittlers and watch-traders who were sitting just across the street from where it happened. They had seen her walk, falter a moment, and then collapse on the pavement.

Mound County, West Virginia, had never had a better sheriff than C. D. Pancake. Nor a more popular one, even if Glory was a river town and C.D. was a mountain man from clean across the state in the town of Romney, Hampshire County. Feelings be-

tween people from those two extreme regions weren't always
neighborly. Still C. D. Pancake had a quality about him that
people instantly felt confidence in. He didn't say much. His favorite expression was: Them that talks much—lies some. Folks
liked that. Mound County had never had a more popular sheriff
than C.D. But then Glory had never had two more popular citizens than Miss Ruth Ann and her brother Abel, the town's only
dentist. The Hawks had struck it rich during the Sistersville oil
boom back before the war but Miss Ruth Ann had inherited
most of the fortune. Which is not to say that her brother Abel
wasn't well off. He had made more sets of dentures than old
Doctor Bruce had birthed babies in our country. He was a quiet,
kind-faced man in his middle sixties, spare and lean and graying
at the temples and generous to a fault. Nobody, however poor,
ever came to Abel's little office with a toothache that got turned
away. Even if it was at three in the morning. Even if they didn't
have a penny and had to pay Abel for his services with barter: a
peck of sweet potatoes or a gallon bucket of handpicked raspber-
ries. Moreover, Abel was C.D.'s closest friend. Neither Miss
Ruth Ann nor Abel had ever married. Abel had his work and
Miss Ruth Ann had her social activities and that was enough.
Miss Ruth Ann donated a public library to the town which was
probably the best in the state. She was, naturally, head of the
library board and saw to it that the library was stocked with all
the best books, some of them a little too modern and even
shocking to the town, but nobody ever complained. She also
paid to have famous concert artists like José Iturbi and Lily Pons
come and perform in the high school auditorium every winter.
As for Abel, nobody had ever known a dentist to beat him.
Dentistry was his obsession. He would spend six weeks on a simple set of dentures where most dentists would spend three. He
worked on a set of dentures like Cellini at his masterpieces. A set
of false teeth made by Abel was as perfect as any piece of jewelry
to come out of Tiffany's. Every little imperfection in the original
teeth was duplicated, from a tooth that was a little whiter than
the one next to it to the yellow tobacco stains of an inveterate

smoker. Those dental instruments of his were the tools of a master craftsman.

Miss Ruth Ann was two months from her seventieth birthday the afternoon she dropped dead. She was, as always, dressed expensively but tastefully, wearing all the latest fashions from Stone and Thomas in Wheeling. And despite her age, she was a pretty creature with quick, black eyes and the sweet, full mouth of a girl. And now she was dead. Suddenly. Abruptly. And to anyone with a reasonable way of thinking, naturally. For it was common knowledge in Glory that she had a heart murmur. Her death was shock enough for the town. But for C.D. to call it murder—this was almost too much.

C.D., for all his popularity, wasn't much of a talker. Except for summer evenings when he'd call on his best friend Abel Hawk and they'd sit in the white wicker rockers on Abel's ivy-trellised porch and talk philosophy sometimes till way past midnight. Mostly modern thinkers like Ben Lindsay and Bob Ingersoll. Abel was a Cornell graduate, but C.D. had educated himself. He had done it mainly by sending away for those little two-bit Haldeman Julius Little Blue books. C.D. was dead set against capital punishment, for example. While Abel staunchly defended it. You'd think it would be the other way around— C.D. being a lawman and all. Yet there it was, his unyielding conviction that it was cruel and unusual punishment and a violation of the Constitution for the state to take a man's life for a crime. Any crime. Even murder. And since the state penitentiary, with its fairly busy gallows, was located in our town, it was a subject fairly close to C.D.'s heart. He attended every execution, went home in silence and stayed indoors for two days. Not drinking. He never touched a drop. Just getting over what he had seen.

Well, after they had taken poor Miss Ruth Ann's body off the pavement in front of the Palace Furniture and hustled it off as quickly as possible to Charley Peace's Funeral Parlor, C.D. arrived on the scene. I mean the place on the pavement where she had dropped dead. He got out of his old Whippet roadster and sat on the running board a long spell staring at the place where she had collapsed and died. Just looking. And thinking. After a while he saw something on the concrete which the chief of police and Charley Peace had missed. He stared at it a minute and then got up lazily from the running board and walked over and picked the thing up and looked at it. A sack of unshelled almonds. They were in a white paper bag with the name of the place of purchase—Candyland—printed on the paper. It was nothing unusual. Candyland was no more than a dozen yards back up Pike Street on the corner across from More's Opera House, and everybody knew it was Miss Ruth Ann's custom to visit Candyland every Saturday afternoon and buy a sack of unshelled almonds just like these. C.D. put the paper bag in his jacket pocket and looked around the pavement some more. Like many mountain men he had the eye of a falcon. Nothing much ever missed the eye of C.D. Pancake. Nor did it now. Two tiny objects he spotted a few feet back from where he had found the paper sack of almonds. He stood a moment staring down at them, then stooped, picked them carefully up, held them in the palm of his big hand for an instant, studying them, pondering them, then fetched a plain white courthouse envelope from his inside pocket, put them in it, sealed the envelope and put it into his inside pocket. Then he took out his Yello-bole pipe and the oilskin pouch of Buckingham tobacco, filled his bowl, tamped it in good and lit up. Now the unemployed loafers across the street on the steps of the county courthouse knew when they saw this that C.D. was doing some heavy thinking. For most of the time he went around with that pipe champed between his even, yellow teeth, but cold. No tobacco in it. Just clenched there. The only time he ever lit up was sometimes during those long debates on Abel Hawk's front porch or when he was doing some very hard thinking. Presently he got back into his roadster and drove over to the funeral parlor and asked to see Miss Ruth Ann's body. Charley Peace and his boy Junius were both there with Abel Hawk, pale and shaken. The county coroner, Wade Belcher, who had finished his postmortem, had filled out his sheet for the county records and was getting ready to leave

Charley and his boy to go to work on Miss Ruth Ann's dead body.

Charley Peace was almost as popular a man in Glory as C.D. or Abel Hawk. Old Doctor Bruce brought Glory citizens into the world and in due time Charley Peace buried them. Moreover, Charley owed a good deal of his reputation due to the way he could straighten out the face of a convict just hanged and scarcely cold. It wasn't always easy, either. Once in a while a victim would be torn clean off his head if the hangman hadn't calculated the ratio right between the weight of the man and the length of the drop. Usually, however, it was a clean break of the neck. Though now and then a man would hang there for ten or twenty minutes strangling before the prison doctor came with his stethoscope and pronounced him dead. In which case there would be considerable discoloration of the face. Nothing that Charley Peace couldn't deal with, though. And the next morning there would be a viewing of the body and usually there was a line of people clean down from Charley Peace's place to the Grand Theatre on Seventh at the corner of Lafayette Avenue. I tell you Charley Peace was more than just a mortician—he was a showman.

When C.D. appeared and asked to see the corpse, Wade Belcher was more than a little offended.

I've already made out my report, C.D., he said. Why is this necessary?

C.D. just puffed a little harder on his Yello-bole and the sweet fragrance of the tobacco helped kill the acrid odor of formaldehyde in the room.

Just want to check something out, Wade, C.D. said. Nothing personal.

So Charley pulled the muslin sheet down from poor Miss Ruth Ann's naked corpse and stood back while C.D. stood there staring at her face. After a moment he went to the far end of the slab on which she lay and studied her face. Then he opened her mouth, with some difficulty, since she had already begun to stiffen, and fetched a pocket flashlight from his vest and studied the inside of her mouth for a full three minutes. Then he took his pipe out of his teeth, laid it on the little steel table beside the embalming slab and went back to the body and lowered his nose close to Miss Ruth Ann's still gaping mouth. He sniffed four or five times, straightened up, put his Yello-bole back between his teeth and looked at Wade. His pipe had gone out. He fetched a kitchen match from his pocket, scratched it into flame on the seat of his britches and still stared at Wade.

Wade, he said. What did you report in that file yonder as the cause of this lady's sudden death?

Simple coronary thrombosis, Wade said, a little ruffled, a little offended, because he could read in C.D.'s cold, blue, Hampshire County eyes something that he didn't like. It is well known that she had a heart murmur. I see no cause for you coming in here this way and questioning my opinion, C.D.

C.D. nodded.

Do you have a different opinion of what killed her? Charley asked. Do you disagree with my opinion?

I do, said C.D.

You could have heard a pin drop in the room for the longest while.

Well, what is your opinion, then? Wade snapped at last.

Murder, C.D. said. First degree.

Abel was so shocked at this pronouncement that he faltered away from the group and sat down suddenly in a straight-backed chair.

Wade Belcher's face was livid with outrage.

Why, that's plain craziness, C.D., he said.

Is it, Wade?

Why, sure it is. How could it be murder? There were witnesses, fifteen or twenty at least, that will swear in any court that there wasn't another living soul within twenty feet of Miss Ruth Ann when she dropped dead.

That is so, Wade, C.D. said. That is quite true.

Then how could it be murder? Wade asked.

C.D. did not answer right away, puffing slowly on his pipe, thinking hard.

Can you produce the murder weapon? asked Charley's son Junius.

C.D. hesitated a moment more. Then he reached in his jacket pocket and took out the sack of almonds.

Here it is, he said simply. This sack of almonds from Candyland.

Charley Peace stared, the boy stared, and Wade Belcher stared. Abel leaned back in his chair, his face livid with shock.

But why? Why, C.D.? he sobbed. My sister was the most beloved woman in this town. Why?

He paused, an asthma attack coming upon him.

You know, C.D., he said, what a scandal this will bring down upon our family name.

C.D. looked at his old friend with a kindly light in his eyes.

If you loved your sister, Abel, he said, you surely want to see justice done over this. And I vow to you that my decision hurts me a lot more than it does you. We've been best friends for a long time, Abel. You know I'd never deliberately do anything to shame your family or hurt you. Believe that.

He paused and walked to Abel's side, laying his big hand on his friend's shoulder, racked and shaking with sobs.

Abel, you are a master craftsman, he said. Not just a small-town dentist. An artist of your breed is worth ten of me. Yet I have my job to do, too. And my conscience. So, for the sake of our friendship, if for no other reason, let me alone to do my duty.

Nobody within living memory had ever seen or heard C.D. allow himself such a display of emotion. I don't think anybody, for that matter, had ever heard him do that much talking in so short a time. Wade Belcher stood with the sack of almonds in his hand, staring at C.D. and shaking his head.

Every Saturday, he said, for years now, Ruth Ann Hawks has gone to Candyland for her sack of almonds. Sacks like this one.

He hesitated, striving to control himself, for it was more than outrage now: It was bafflement.

And yet you claim it was this bag of almonds that caused her death?

I do, C.D. said.

C.D., Charley Peace exclaimed, getting in his angry say. This opinion of yours isn't going to go very well with folks who were friends of the deceased here. And that takes in almost everybody in the town of Glory.

C.D. turned his gaze on the undertaker then; his eyes blue as the ice of a frozen mountain stream.

I was not elected sheriff for the purpose of maintaining my popularity, Mr. Peace, he said. I was elected to see justice done.

He paused, puffing slowly on his pipe.

No, he said, I did not run in a popularity contest last election. I ran for sheriff. And this decision of mine may cost me the election come November. But I am not concerned with that, Mr. Peace. Not a whipstitch worth.

But—but this is just a plain sack of unshelled almonds, cried Doc Belcher, from one of the most reputable confectioners in the state of West Virginia.

He paused for breath.

C.D., are you claiming that Miss Ruth Ann here was poisoned?

That's right. She died by reason of the ingestion of a very small but lethal dose of cyanide.

You mean that one of these almonds contained poison? cried Charley Peace. That someone in the store where she bought them—?

No, C.D. said, I haven't got it all figured out yet. Give me a day and a night. But the poison was not in the almond.

Then, in God's name how could you say it was the almond that killed her?

I have told you all I know now, C.D. said, moving toward the door. It will take me about thirty-six hours to figure it all out. I think that by then I'll have my proof. I think by then I'll be able to make my arrest.

And before any of them could say another word he had turned and disappeared through the door, leaving only the fragrance of tobacco in his wake and the sound of Ruth Ann Hawk's brother

Abel sobbing, his face in his hands, in the straight-backed chair across the room.

C.D. had said it would take him thirty-six hours to figure out the means which had caused the poisoning of Miss Ruth Ann but he was wrong. It only took him the rest of that afternoon. Just after supper he knocked on the front door of Abel's office to tell him his discovery, thinking how relieved he would be to know that his sister's death would be avenged. At least, that's what he told Miss Ella Hankins, the county clerk, when he locked his office and headed for Abel's house. Abel let him in, his red eyes searching C.D.'s face.

C.D., Abel said, I want you to know that I was the one living soul in that chamber of death today who believed you. That Ruth Ann was murdered.

Thanks for that, Abel, C.D. said quietly, laying his hand on his friend's shoulder. I appreciate it more than I can say.

The only difference, Abel said with a chuckle, is that when you arrest whoever did it, and prove in court how they did it, when he's convicted and goes to the gallows, I'll cheer for joy! We differ only in that.

We do, Abel, C.D. said. You know my feelings about hanging.

Abel's face grew livid with outrage at the thought of his sister's murder.

My only regret, he said, is that we don't have outdoor public hangings like in the old days! But I know one thing—when they lead that bastard to the death chamber—I want to be there.

C.D. said nothing, just crossed the room and sank into an easy chair in Abel's parlor. The Yello-bole appeared in his hand then, the oilskin pouch of Buckingham, and soon he was puffing away, harder than ever.

Abel, who had recovered remarkably since his breakdown in Peace's funeral parlor that morning, sat on the settee opposite him.

Have you got it figured out, C.D.?

Just about, Abel, said the sheriff. Just a few pieces to fit into place before I'm sure. Before I make my arrest.

There was a long silence then, broken only by the puffing of

C.D.'s pipe. C.D. seemed to be troubled, so troubled that he bit down on the Bakelite stem of his pipe and winced with pain.

Damn, he said. This tooth—I think you call it a front molar, Abel. The tooth I bite down on my pipestem with—it's been troubling me lately.

Well, let's step into my office and take a look at it.

Are you sure you feel up to it? C.D. asked gently. It's been a hard day for you, I know. Maybe tomorrow—

Tonight, Abel Hawk said. This very minute. I'm funny, C.D., I guess. When something hits me hard, real hard like Ruth Ann's death this morning, it doesn't usually hit me really till two or three days later. Tomorrow I might not feel up to looking at that tooth of yours.

He rose.

Come on, he said. I'm chipper as a squirrel.

Are you sure, Abel?

Never more certain, C.D. Come on.

When C.D. was in the chair with the white towel around his neck and his mouth opened wide so Abel could look at the tooth, the latter was not long in seeing the trouble.

Abel smiled and nodded.

Nothing complicated about it, he said. You've champed down on that pipestem of yours for years. The upper bicuspid—it's almost hollow with damage but I can easily clean it out because the nerve's dead.

And what then? C.D. asked.

Then when I've cleaned out the bad part and filled it, Abel said, I'll put a nice porcelain cap on it. Good and sturdy. And you can bite down on that pipestem till Doomsday and it'll never bother you again.

Again? Never again? asked C.D. softly.

You know my work, C.D., Abel said. Of course I'll want you in for a checkup in six months.

Fine, C.D. answered, while Abel injected the gum with novocaine and stood by waiting till it took effect before pulling down the drill. It didn't take long. It didn't hurt either. I mean the drilling didn't hurt. Everything else about C.D.'s heart and mind did hurt though. But he let Abel fill the tooth and cap it with the porcelain.

Now, Abel said, at last. Clean as a whistle. Here—rinse your mouth out with this Lavoris and spit in the bowl yonder. And, incidentally, stick your pipe in the other side of your mouth for a day or two. Till that porcelain sets good.

C.D. did as he was told and sat back in the chair, staring at Abel's pale face.

Incidentally, Abel, he said quietly. You're right when you say that once I bite down on this bicuspid it will never bother me again.

That's right, old buddy, Abel answered. You can champ on your pipestem as hard as you want.

I know, C.D. said, getting out of the chair. Just the way Miss Ruth Ann bit down hard on that almond shell this morning. I found a piece of that shell and a fragment of paper-thin porcelain on the pavement right where she fell.

Abel paled a little, but he was cool. Very cool.

I don't know what you're getting at, C.D., Abel said.

Sure you do, Abel, C.D. said. You hollowed out one of your sister's bicuspids sometime last week, I judge.

That's so. It's in my record file. But what are you getting at, man?

I'm getting at this, C.D. said. I've got Exhibit A for the prosecution in my own mouth this very minute. You put a shell of very thin porcelain over that bicuspid. But not until you'd filled the big cavity with enough cyanide, fifty or a hundred milligrams I'd reckon anyway, enough poison in that hollow tooth to kill three of Miss Ruth Ann's kind. Or one of mine. Knowing that she'd bite down hard sooner or later, probably on one of her Saturday almonds, break the porcelain cap and release that poison into her mouth. Like you figure I'll do once I'm safely away from here, with my pipestem. And you—God help you, Abel Hawk—with the alibi that you were nowhere near.

He paused.

Come off it, Abel, C.D. said. Whilst you were filling this

tooth of mine I could smell the cyanide plain. It's the scent of bitter almonds. You probably used solid hydrocyanic acid.

Abel said nothing, a foolish, helpless look on his face and some tears in his eyes.

I'm running some risk, C.D. said. But that's part of my job. I'll go to Wheeling tonight and have Doc Quimby at the Ohio Valley General Hospital remove this tooth real easy. *Real easy.* Carefully.

Abel broke into sobs.

I had to do it, C.D., he sobbed. I—I got into a financial investment hole that would have meant prison for me. And I was about to get caught. I'm one of the directors of the bank, you know. And I was the only beneficiary to Ruth Ann's considerable fortune. It would have saved me—her legacy. And then when I knew you'd figured out my—my modus operandi—I had to put you away, too, C.D. Not that it didn't clean break my heart to even think of such a thing. But it was my life or yours—

C.D. broke in here.

But how did you know I knew, Abel? he asked. That it was you who'd done it. And how you'd done it. And that you'd have to kill me off the same way.

I know you pretty well, C.D., Abel said sheepishly. All those nights on the front porch. It don't take many nights like we'd spent together to get so you sense things in a man.

He paused.

I read it in your face like a headline in the *Glory Argus*, he said. The minute you walked in that front door an hour ago. That you knew it was me that killed Ruth Ann. Though I didn't know you knew how I'd done it. Otherwise I wouldn't have expected you to hold still for me to do the same thing to you—

In God's name, man, why didn't you just go to her and ask for a loan to cover whatever trouble you'd gotten into.

My sister, Abel said, was very wealthy. Very generous. But also very moral. And she'd have asked me why I needed thirty thousand dollars within twenty-four hours. Before the bank auditors came. And I'd have had to confess to her that her own brother, as director of the Glory Farmer's and Merchant's National Bank, had embezzled—God, C.D., can you blame me?

I'm not in this job I hold to censure or forgive either one, Abel, C.D. said then. Not even my best friend. All I know is I have the evidence. And I'm afraid I'm going to have to take you in.

Abel shook his head and walked towards the door. He smiled.

You wouldn't do that, C.D., he whispered. You're my friend. You wouldn't arrest me. See me tried. See me hanged.

I don't think you know me as well as I always figured you did, Abel, C.D. said, sadly drawing his service revolver from his hip and holding it pointed toward the floor. Abel shook his head.

No, he said. I do know you. You'll give me a chance to make a run for it. Because you're my friend.

He passed across the threshold backwards, still smiling at C.D.

So long, old buddy, Abel said. I know you. My touring car's right outside. You'll let me go.

C.D. shook his head.

Abel, don't make me stop you, he said. Christ, man, don't hang me on that cross.

I have no choice, cried Abel Hawk, and turning, ran for the frosted glass windows of the front doors which led to the porch, to the sidewalk, to the Nash touring car parked in front. C.D. let Abel get as far as the running board and open the car door before he called out his last command to halt. When Abel moved again, C.D. promptly, and without emotion visible to any who saw it all—shot him twice in the back. Abel Hawk stood poised upright for a moment, almost as if posing for a snapshot, one foot on the running board, his hand on the handle of the open door, his head held high, and for a moment C.D. thought that both his shots had missed. But they had not. Neither of them. An instant later the sheriff was kneeling at the curb, holding the dying man in his arms.

The perfect crime, C.D., Abel whispered, a baffled look on his face. I was so sure I had it all doped out. The one perfect crime.

No, C.D. said. You didn't. You were wrong, Abel.

He paused.

There is only one perfect crime possible in the state of West Virginia, Abel, he said then.

There—is—one? Abel whispered. There is—a perfect crime?

Yes, said C.D.

Lord, Abel said with a smile. How I wish we could argue this out all night up on the porch tonight—you and me, C.D. But it's too late. It is too late, isn't it, C.D.?

Yes, said the sheriff. Too late, Abel.

But there is one? Abel whispered, his voice failing fast now, and C.D. feeling the seep of blood through his sleeves on the arms that held Abel up. There is a perfect crime? Now then tell me, old friend, what is that one perfect crime?

Hanging, said C.D. Or any other killing by the law.

He held Abel there a goodly spell after he had died, his head lolling against C.D.'s badged chest like a child who had fallen asleep. Then, still without apparent emotion under the eyes of the small crowd that had heard the shots and gathered there, C.D. lowered the body to the brick sidewalk, went back in the house, and called Charley Peace to come and fetch Abel Hawk's body. Then he went to the courthouse, presented the evidence to the prosecuting attorney and the chief of police, and went calmly home.

C.D. Pancake won the election by a wide margin in the 1932 Democratic landslide that November. He hung around the noisy, smoke-filled, booze-reeking suite of rooms which the Mound County Democratic Committee had taken in the Stonewall Jackson Hotel that election night. C.D. tarried around just long enough to hear the final returns, to know if he had won again. Nobody knew why. Because of what he did a half an hour later. Maybe he just stuck around the suite long enough to find out what the people of Mound County thought of him now. Or maybe it wasn't that at all. Maybe he just sought out the surge and clamor of a drunken, celebrating mob to drown out certain old voices, endless discussions on a porch, in white wicker rockers, on soft autumn nights. Because the minute he was certain he had been reelected, C.D. left the suite, took the long marble

stairway down into the hotel lobby, pushed slowly out through
the revolving doors, walked thoughtfully to the courthouse, got
the county clerk out of bed, and, when the latter arrived, irri-
tated and still half asleep, C.D. dictated to him his statement of
resignation as sheriff of Mound County, signed it, had it nota-
rized and went slowly home to bed.

It was almost three years later before some distant kin of Miss
Ruth Ann and Abel Hawk came to Glory to tend to selling
Abel's and Miss Ruth Ann's houses. Meanwhile, in the interim,
nothing had been touched, nothing moved, nothing changed.
Except that many's the soft cool dusk of a September evening or
the starry hush of an April night when folks would be coming
home from the movies and a soda or a claret phosphate after-
wards at Candyland that they would walk past the vine-covered
trellis which covered the front of Abel Hawk's front porch and
they would hear the steady, rhythmic tread of a white wicker
rocking chair moved by someone alone on the deserted porch.

And cutting through the redolent and frail perfume of honeysuckle and swamp rose and sweet shrub which also spread their
fragrance there, they would smell on the light river breeze the
scent of Buckingham tobacco wafting out through the green
cloak of ivy growing there. And the scent of that would linger in
their senses long after they had hurried past toward home. Ill at
ease. So troubled they'd sometimes be a long while falling asleep.
And having not the slightest notion why.

THE STAINLESS STEEL SAVIOR

Walking on the street in Manhattan—a veritable merde gras!

—Davis Grubb, notebooks

Chano didn't get one every week, and sometimes a month would pass by without one coming in. But Chano was a patient man. And like all violent men, very calm, very cool. For this was his mission in life since the death of his baby sister, Esta Mae. He now regarded himself as a bringer of Peace, as a savior for teenaged girls like his sister. Already he had brought Peace to five—and talked six others into going home on the next Greyhound headed South.

This brisk October night he sat on one of the long, hard benches in the Manhattan Bus Terminal. He sat there every night, appearing each day at sundown as though he were some sort of civic guardian; as though he had to punch a time clock at that hour of dusk. He turned and gazed with cold, black, and unemotional disinterest at an old, dirty wino sleeping at the other end of the bench, his empty fifth of muscatel beside him. Winos were not his business. His business was saving—or getting back home—young girls.

Chano was lithe and slim with an air of fearsome inner
strength about him; skin drawn taut and tan over the high, fine
cheekbones of his almost Slavic face. He resembled Jack Palance,
the film actor, though this meant nothing to him since he never
attended movies. He lived in a neat, sparsely furnished one-room
flat in the East Village and had no television. He hated films—
especially war films. He considered himself a man of infinite
peace. Yet, if the New York City district attorney or chief of
detectives had made any connections between his five Peace
Givings to the five girls and the five well-dressed, well-heeled
Negroes found dead with them, it would have been called
murder. So inside he knew it couldn't last much longer—his
mission. Five or six more at the most, and the pieces of the
puzzle would fall into place in the minds of the law.

The bus terminal on Eighth Avenue in Manhattan is a vast,
sepulchral chamber. Its morguelike stillness is shattered every
now and then by the dispatcher through several loudspeakers announcing the arrival or departure of a bus and informing those
departing at which gate to line up.

None of the guards or attendants ever paid any attention to
Chano. And this despite his costly, hand-tooled boots, his skin-
tight black chinos, his homespun cotton Mexican wedding shirt
with intricate embroidery and bone buttons, and the motorcycle
helmet he wore. He seemed to know the trick of making himself
unnoticeable; sitting there waiting, watching, listening. His
hands—long and slow and strong, sheathed in white chamois
gloves—were tucked into the pockets of his black leather bike
jacket or resting on his knees. Sometimes he would hold those
long hands up, flexing them as if keeping them always ready. His
hands were flat as ax blades. And when he got up to go to the
washroom or saunter into the coffee shop for a doughnut and a
Coke he would move noiselessly from the bench as if he were
weightless; gliding to his feet with an infinite and somehow un-
canny ease. Then he would return to his bench. Waiting.
Watching. For the Lost Ones who came to the city, to the
Dream of America, the hope, the gateway to Glory and Glamour
and Riches beyond imagining. And when he walked across the

sterile, vast chamber it was like the movement of a great white shark in southern seas, a gliding progress that gave him the appearance of being not made of flesh and bone at all, but rather of soft, costly, and faintly tanned leather stretched taut across an intricate and obedient framework of light stainless steel. And there was always a little smile playing about his thin, colorless lips, as if from the satisfaction he felt in his mission. Yet, be it known, he dreaded it when he saw one of Them come in with her cheap little luggage and her too short dress. He dreaded it, but he knew his duty, and he would make his Move.

He reached his gloved right hand to his jacket pocket, took out a pack of Tiparillos, gave it a toss, and caught the tip of the little cigar neatly in his lips. He never missed. He lighted up and slowly inhaled, exhaled, that flat, humorless smile on his lips.

Abruptly after an ear-piercing feedback, the loudspeaker, in its listless, mechanical voice, announced the arrival of the midnight Trailways from Savannah.

He stared. His heart fell. Because he saw her. She was perhaps a little past seventeen. Yes, she would be the next one. He already sensed that. She carried an imitation-leather suitcase in her right hand, her beauty kit in the other. Over her right arm was a beige wool coat with a collar of imitation fur. She wore a plain tweed skirt and a white shirtwaist blouse and a red and blue striped kerchief round her black hair. She had a waist that a man with middling large hands could encircle with the thumb and forefinger of each, and the blouse did nothing to diminish the size of full, mature breasts.

He could almost smell the Avon cosmetic on her. In profile her face was that of a madonna by a lesser Flemish master, but in full face it was pretty and full and self-indulgent. He waited, hopefully, prayerfully, for a couple of parents to search for and find her in the crowd and come and take her away. But he knew better. Neither kith nor kin came forth. He had known there would be none.

Yet he knew, as well, that there is always Someone to greet a pretty girl. And that Someone Chano could not yet see but could sense, with that jungle sense men pick up in rain forests

like those among the Mekong; he could sense the eyes of that
Someone already fixed upon her. She stood a moment, scared to
death, but game. She had come this far; there was no returning.
She would die before she would hear the laughter and teasing if
she returned. She picked up her luggage from where it rested
beside her patent-leather high heels and, spotting the coffee
shop, headed for it. They always went to the coffee shop, Chano
thought. She took a stool at the far end of the counter. The
waitress, knowing the type, knowing the tip would be small, if at
all, took her time wiping down the dirty plastic countertop and
asking for her order. She ordered, as he watched, just what he
knew she would order, what they always order—an egg salad on
white toast and a cup of black coffee. He stared, a sadness in his
black, slitted eyes—his dark, almost Levantine face fixed upon
her; eyes not blinking, lest in that interval he might miss the
Move.

When she had finished half her sandwich and all of her coffee
she ordered another cup just as the tall Negro in the faultlessly
tailored, immaculate Petricelli suit, two-inch heels and soles on
tan shoes, and a wide-brimmed pearl gray hat, entered the coffee
shop. They never come on too strong, Chano knew. They always take the stool one stool away from hers and pay her no
mind. He ordered a Pepsi, drinking it "genteelly" from a Dixie
cup and sipping it slowly and thoughtfully. He was not ready for
the Move. He knew his business.

Chano knew his business even more. The girl finished, and
fumbling a little leatherette billfold from the pocket of her coat,
asked for the check. She was holding forth the dollar bill when
the Negro moved. He reached up and took the check from the
waitress's fingers and put a ten-dollar bill on the counter. The
waitress, at his instructions, kept the change. At that instant,
the girl, her composure shaken, turned to him and thanked him,
then looked quickly away. He could see the flush of red at the
corner of her face. The Negro sat smiling at her for a moment.
Then he reached into the breast pocket of his jacket, pulled out
a billfold and took from it a white business card, which he put
before the girl. She stared at it for a moment, then picked it up

and studied it cautiously, thoughtfully, and finally seemed set at ease by it. By it, and by the innocent and ingratiating affability of the black. It was a practiced, unforced politeness. He had that gift. That was why he was in the business. They all had that gift. And southern girls, and the girls Chano always spotted and saved from themselves in the bus terminal were almost always from Baltimore or points South, could tell a good Negro, one you could trust, one whose grandmother may well have given breast to her own mother.

Chano's gloved fingers lay white and flat on his slim thigh. He flexed his fingers back and forth, getting the feel, getting them ready. And even from that distance he could fairly read the business card. He had seen so many. Gotham Night Club Hostess Employment Service, Big Apple Photographer's Model Studios, Empire City Masseuse Academy, Miss Ada's Go-Go School. He did not need to see. For a moment his mind worked on two levels: never for an instant taking his stare from the girl and the Negro, yet remembering Esta Mae, for there was much of this new girl that made him think of her: the figure, the taste in clothes, the round, go-to-hell face.

Chano's family lived in a town called Hundred in West Virginia. After serving in the Marines in Vietnam, three years of it, he had spent two years bumming around New York City, mostly in the East Village. Two sturdy young blacks had jumped him one spring night at 123rd and Broadway. It was their mistake. He had taken away the cheap, one-shot .38 caliber gun and broken the arms and legs of both men and sauntered off, leaving them groaning on the pavement. So the three years in Nam plus the two in Manhattan meant that he had not seen Esta Mae since she was eleven. He then had come home to find that his darling baby sister, apple of his eye, had become a woman. He was hardly home for a week when she announced her intentions to quit her job at King Kong Variety, a small notions store, and take her savings and buy a new coat and an expensive beauty kit and a one-way Blue Ridge bus ticket to Pittsburgh, where she would take a Greyhound nonstop to Manhattan. Somehow Chano could not bring himself to tell her the facts about Manhattan. He knew that such dreams as were fomenting her thoughts to riot would not change.

Ain't it jist glorious there? she asked him once.

He had not answered.

He had looked at her with his black, Mongoloid eyes. He was quite silent. Chano's silences were worth reams of cheap sermons. And that look meant one of two things, fondness or a warning. Yet Esta Mae, despite her knowing which, still left.

She wrote a postcard home every day. Then her mail began to arrive in scented envelopes on expensive stationery. Then the mail began to arrive erratically and on plain envelopes from a Walgreen's Drug Store. Within a year she was back to postcards, perhaps one every six weeks. And increasingly her handwriting, so neat and elegant in high school, began to become scarcely legible, with words scratched out and others erased until the paper tore through and the words were scrawly and out of line. Towards the end, the cards—there were only two that last month—seemed smeared with something vicious and nasty, causing the ink to smear.

Two years after her departure, almost to the day, an official brown envelope arrived—registered mail—from the city offices of a man named Halpern. The letter was not devious, consoling, or equivocal. It stated that a certain Esta Mae Colfas, during a period of eighteen months, had been arrested on four counts of prostitution, and that in the past four months she had been arrested for use or sale of dangerous drugs, namely heroin, and had been discovered in an abandoned room at 93rd Street and Columbus Avenue dead from an overdose of barbiturates. The letter inquired what disposition the family wanted to make of the deceased girl's body. Chano's parents had wanted the body sent home for an open-coffin funeral. Chano knew better. He forbade it. He knew his parents expected her to look perhaps a little older, but much the same as when she had left. Chano knew better about that, too. He had seen them after a week of lying dead in condemned tenement bedrooms. Rats are not particular about what they nibble.

He said little for the next two weeks. He went to New York by plane that autumn and began his Mission. The Stainless Steel Savior had been born.

His mind now thinking of this, harking back to the slow, numb horror of it, and yet watching every move of the new girl and the black in the coffee shop.

They were both up now and so was Chano. They passed within five feet of him, he as inconspicuous to them as the cigarette machine against which he leaned. The black was now gallantly carrying the beauty kit and the suitcase towards the exit to Eighth Avenue. The girl had slipped into her cheap little coat, for the October night was chilled by a wind whipping in from the river. He could hear them—the deep-throated liners announcing arrivals and departures and the little tugs whistling like popcorn wagons. He kept a good ten feet behind them as the Negro put the girl's luggage into the back seat of his conveniently parked Mercedes and opened the streetside door for her to get in and then went round, opened his door, and climbed into the driver's seat. Chano buckled his white safety helmet made of steel. He straddled his Honda, which was powered by an engine he had souped up himself.

The Negro was off into the light, late-night traffic; up to 60th Street and then down Fifth Avenue to the forties and into the cluster of cheap, aging hotels between Sixth and Fifth Avenues—the Diamond, the Dixie, the Victoria, the Chesterfield, the Nash. They always took them to one of these. Chano kept twenty feet behind the Mercedes. It pulled up in front of the hotel called the Diamond. Chano stayed on his bike, giving them enough time to get into the lobby. Then he chained the bike and followed. He lounged by a dusty potted palm, watching and listening as the black registered.

Yes, Mr. Jackson, glad to see you again, said the ratty, sharp-eyed little night clerk.

That will be ten dollars, he said. And here is your key. Room three-oh-four.

No loitering, pally, said the night clerk, looking at Chano, who was lounging easily in the cracked leather easy chair. He took out the box of Tiparillos, flipped up, caught the tip between his lips. He lit up. He pocketed the box and his lighter in his black leather pocket.

I have an appointment, he said.

Well, just don't smell up the lobby with that seegar, said the night clerk.

Chano didn't blink, didn't smile anymore, as he stared at the man. The clerk opened his mouth to make some further remark when he got his gaze tangled in the look which Chano got in his eyes now and then. The clerk shut up, settled back in his chair at the switchboard and resumed leafing through an old magazine. Chano, watching the clock over the desk, gave them three minutes to get settled. He glided up out of the chair as if the chair itself had gently propelled him, and started up the dirty stairway.

Now looka here, pally, said the night clerk. You goin' a little too far this time. You can't just go up to a party's room without me callin' 'em first. Or else register here for a room of your own.

I'm not registering for a room, Chano said pleasantly. And you won't call. You'll sit there and keep your mouth shut.

I could call the police, said the clerk, unconvincingly.

Do that, Chano said. I got a pal who's a pal of the chief of the vice squad, Midtown Division. They got eyes on this fleabag. They're just waiting for a general bust. Because business has been falling off here on account of the shootings and the o.d.'s, you ain't paying the fuzz enough dues every week. I can testify that I just witnessed a well-dressed Negro and an underaged white girl register and go up to one of your boxes for a probable violation of the Harrison Act, the Sullivan Act, and probably an act of procurement. How does that taste to you, punk?

The night clerk dug his face deeper into the magazine.

I forgot I even seen youse, he said. Go right on up.

Chano went.

He stood a minute outside the door, listening to snatches of the black's spiel.

Club hostess. Start out as go-go girl in a club on Tenth Avenue. Within a year move crosstown to the nicer spots. Within a year and half earning three thousand a month. A pad on Sutton Place. Celebrities for dinner every week. Glory.

Chano knew the door was locked but he silently tried the knob. It was locked. A cheap lock. Cheap enough to rip out of the molding with a good kick of his boot toe. The door banged open and he stood on the threshold, hands in the pockets of his black leather jacket, his safety helmet flung over his arm by the straps. He smiled.

Hello, young lovers, whoever you are, he said.

Shit, man, what the hell you been smokin'? cried the Negro. Are you Heat? Is this a bust? You must be new in the midtown precinct. I pay my dues religiously every week! Religiously!

Religiously, chuckled Chano. And all along I had you pegged as a badly back-slid duck-water Baptist, Mr. Freddy.

The girl was down to her bra and Dacron panties and no shoes. She was sitting on a chair by a cracked writing desk next to a sagging bed.

Chano did not blink an eye when the Negro reached inside his jacket and produced a Smith and Wesson Police Special from his shoulder holster.

Chano chuckled. A little muscle was pulsating and twitching in the corner of his right jaw.

I am hip, he said. You can pull the trigger. People pull so many triggers in the hotels on this street that it sounds like Chinese New Year's down at Mott and Pell.

He paused; the muscle had stopped twitching.

Go ahead, he said. But something I picked up in Nam. Taking a pistol away from a man is like taking a toy from a baby. Now taking away a knife—that's a different matter. You got a knife? No? Stick with the gun. I'm foot-weary tonight. And I haven't taken a knife off a guy since one night on the Mekong. And gave it back to him, right in the left kidney.

Now the girl was on her feet, her little fists on her round hips, and seething mad.

Who the hell do you think you are?

Whom am I? asked Chano. Or who, as the case may be. Why, I'm the Stainless Steel Savior, sugar.

Well, now, git on out, cried the girl. Mr. Jackson and me—

we hain't doin' a damn thing wrong. We're tendin' to a business deal.

I'll just bet you are, Chano said.

She pointed with a furious, shaking finger to a freshly signed document on the little black writing desk.

I signed up already, she said. And I don't want nary person spoilin' hit.

I know what you signed for, too, Chano said. You'll start Mr. Freddy here hooking you with a big habit. Not too big—not yet. Then you do what he say—'cause that's his way. You start as a club hostess. Hustling for fifty dollars. Maybe a C. And maybe throwing a free benefit now and then for goodwill with the law. He's right. In a year and a half you'll be set up with a lush pad and makin' two or three thou a month. And there won't be a mark on your body except for a rapidly increasing little string of tracks inside your elbow, in the soft skin up from your wrist. And a two-C-a-day Jones on your back. You got to do a lot of hustlin' to support a habit that big. And you'll begin to show a little wear and tear after a year and a half. By the end of two and a half years you'll be hooking in the streets, hustling out on the bricks. And that don't pay so good. Because by then the Sutton Place apartment will cost too much. And you'll be livin' uptown— Amsterdam or Columbus. Some place like the Hotel Endicott. And that Jones gettin' heavier and heavier on your back. So you start pushin'. But that don't make it. You have no experience and no talent for that. Six months in the House of Detention till your trial comes up. Then maybe a ten-year suspended sentence on good behavior.

He studied her, from head to toe.

No, he said.

No what? she shouted.

No, you won't go the way my baby sister went, he said. You're together. Your mind will go first. Then Bellevue. Two months' observation and you—

Ignore this motherfucker, Dawn, the black said. Like he wasn't there.

Is that really your name? Dawn?

No, she shouted. It so happens I was christened Pearl Harbor Carter! Now jist how far d'yuh reckon I'd git with a stage name like that?

Better than Dawn, Chano said softly. Because soon it won't be Dawn anymore. It'll be Sundown. And Pearl Harbor on December the eighth will look better than you will.

Chano fixed his slitted gaze on the girl. And she could feel it. A little chill went down her back.

Dawn—Pearl Harbor? Chano asked. Whatcha figure Mr. Freddy's cooking up in that little Horn and Hardart coffee spoon over his little alcohol lamp?

He done showed me, she said. He done shot some in his own arm afore you come.

What is it, Dawn?

Hit ain't nary nothin' but a little Vitamin B Plus, she said. Plus a little added somethin' for stimulation.

Ever hear the word heroin? Chano asked.

Hell, yes, said the girl. What's that got to do with me?

Chano looked sad for the first time. But it went away.

You keep on buggin' us, honky, said Mr. Freddy, and I'm going to use this piece on you.

I told you to go ahead, Chano said. I am amply armed. What I got is equal to what you got when it comes to killing, and more.

What you got—a switchblade?

Something heavier than that, Chano said. I got these two hands. And they have bones of stainless steel.

Mr. Freddy put down the spoon in which he was cooking Dawn's fix and picked up the .38. He aimed it at Chano. Chano didn't have to see more than the knuckle begin to whiten as it squeezed on the trigger before he was gone. The shot clattered noisily in the room and a big chunk of plaster fell from the wall. It seemed to Mr. Freddy that Chano had not moved at all, that the chair had somehow folded and flung him face down near the edge of the bed. And he knew Chano was under that bed. And Mr. Freddy was scared for the first time that night. He began to dart around looking here, looking there, under the bed, and when he stood up Chano's forearm was around his neck, the shank of it like steel against his chin. With his free hand Chano threw the .38 across the room.

This is not bigotry, Chano said. I don't hate blacks. I'm color-blind—dig, Mr. Freddy. And I'm really sorry but you got to go.

And with seeming effortlessness he give a little twist to that stainless steel forearm and broke the Negro's neck.

Dawn stared at the dead body.

You dirty bastard! she shouted. Oh, you lousy sonofabitch! You jist done me plumb out of three thousand dollars a week! Damn you to hell and may you burn there!

Chano, ignoring her tirade and her little fists against his chest, reached in the hip pocket of his chinos and took out five C notes, folded them neatly, and handed them to her.

Don't get me wrong, he said. I'm not rich. But I'd rather be poor than have you look like this.

He flipped through the plastic sleeves in the billfold—Social Security, draft card, discharge, and finally came to the snapshot of his sister taken by the City of New York after her death. He held it out with the other hand for her to see. She gasped.

Who's that? Your grandma?

No.

Who is it? Lord, I could puke jist alookin'. Was she in a wreck or somethin'?

A wreck. Yes. The worst kind.

Well, said the girl soberly. At least, she never died young.

Twenty-one, he corrected her. My baby sister.

He took another C note out of the wallet.

Even if you clean me out, he pleaded, I can make more money. Money is shit. And shit is manure. And manure helps me make pretty things grow. Money don't signify where human life's at stake. I respect human life. But there are just some things I can't stand by and see happen to it. It's that simple.

He paused.

Now will you let me take you down to the bus terminal in a cab? he asked gently, pleading, not wanting to do what he knew he must do. You'll have six hundred dollars in your little pocket-book. And I'll pay for a one-way bus ticket back to your home-town.

Go fuck yourself! she cried, I come a bus-ridin' long enough. I got on at Morgan City, Lou'siana. Rode clean to Savannah. Changed to a nonstop Greyhound to here. And now you jist reckon I'm about to go back home now and have them laughin' and a pointin' and making smart cracks after all the braggin' I done afore I left?

Then I have another idea, he said.

There hain't nary other idea!

Yes, there is, he said gently. You could take this six hundred beans and I could get you a room at the YMCA uptown. And you could hunt till you found a good, decent job. Clerkin' at Bonwit's maybe. Or Sak's Fifth Avenue. Or even Mays down on Union Square.

Fuck you! she screamed. You done killed three thousand dol-lars a month for me tonight!

He drew closer to her and she spat in his face. He didn't bother to wipe it off.

Then nothing I say will change your mind? he murmured for-lornly, solemnly.

Nary nothin'! she shouted. Nothin', you meedlin', shit-eatin', gingham-toothed mother—

This makes me feel very sad. It always has. Always will, he said, and killed her with a sharp, painless stab in the space below her rib cage, destroying her solar plexus with the ax blade of his stiff straight fingers. He carried her body to the bed and laid it out. He put a Gideon Bible on the bed beside her. That would give the Heat something to chew over. Both deaths, he knew, would go into the dust-gathering Unsolved Homicide files. Even Coroner Halpern's squad—the best, he knew, in the land— would be unable to unsnarl this one. And Chano knew that he'd be back on duty on the hard bench at the bus terminal the next night. Sundown. Though he knew it couldn't last, that sooner or later the law would begin to see pieces fitting into a pattern.

He went now to the big easy chair and slumped into it. He sat

there for a good while, thinking about Esta Mae. Then he was up
on those swift elastic legs.

He hurried down the hall and down the stairway so swiftly and
so lightly that the night clerk didn't look up from his magazine
till he heard the vrooming thunder of Chano gunning his
Honda.

AND PRESENTLY HE DIED

Dreams of aborted poets, poems never written by people
who died too young, the massive dramas of the inexpressive
geniuses who never made it—these are the nightly
entertainments in Paradise.

> —Davis Grubb, notebooks

Have you heard about Cora Trimble? She's writing a novel! Imagine! And a murder mystery, too! Yes, I said Cora Trimble! Of all people! Prim, spinsterish, little Cora!

That's what her friends would say if they knew. But, of course, none of them did. Cora stood smiling to herself in the hallway outside her brother's study and watched through the etched pattern of the front-door glass as a scarlet leaf drifted slowly through the clear light of the late October afternoon.

Where is my tea, Cora?

In a moment, Charles. The kettle's boiling.

It's a small thing to ask—to have my tea ready when I come home.

Forgive me, Charles.

And she was gone off to the kitchen like a scolded schoolgirl. There was no sound there but the clock's sullen ticking. Cora rested her hands on the sink and leaned forward, suddenly a little faint. Her hands. She opened her eyes and looked at them. Old.

Fingers old. Flesh taut with the blue veins showing through. And the wrists that for thirty years she had kept sweet for someone—for whom she never knew—with the faintest ghost of perfume. Old. The kettle thumped loudly and she hurried to the stove. It was really no trouble at all—Charles's pot of tea. Nor, in fact, was any of the rest of it—Charles's meals, Charles's medicines, Charles's clean linen, fetching Charles's shoes to and from the bootblack's shop. Cora had done these things for thirty years with a wooden, cadenced ritual as patterned as the ticking of the kitchen clock.

Your tea, Charles.

Put it down on the table. Where is the brief I left on my desk this morning? The Lindsay case?

I never touch your papers, Charles. I dusted your globe and the bookcase.

I left it here. Confound it, Cora, I've told you never to touch my papers!

She lowered her blue-eyes to the lush Persian forest in the rug at her feet and imagined desperately that she was there—wandering among the gold, enchanted greenness with a far-off music in her ears.

Never mind. I remember now. I took it to the courthouse this morning. That will be all, Cora.

She hurried up the dark stairs to her room and leaned for a moment against the closed door, within the cool sanctuary of the breathless, faintly scented stillness—the vertigo still catching a little at her heart. She saw her still pretty face in the mirror but then the word whispered again in her ears. Old. Like a sorrowful counterpoint to some lost lovers' tune, the smell of oldness rose and mingled among the unmoving perfume in the air. Cora shook her head as she opened the lid of her desk and stared at the stack of manuscript that was neatly piled there. She smiled silently at her face in the mirror and pressed her tiny lawn hand-kerchief to her lips. She could imagine their voices again—the women at Gandy's Ice Cream Parlor where she went every Saturday afternoon for her solitary week's treat—a dipper of French vanilla. Or at Mr. Hannah's choir practice.

Have you heard about Cora Trimble? A murder mystery! Yes, Cora! She's writing one! Imagine! Cora that's never been outside of Moundsville since the day she was born!

It was not often that Cora saw herself as the rest of the town did, but there were moments when she leaned forward and glimpsed a figure in some dark mirror of the heart that could be none other than herself. The tan, high-buttoned shoes that she had stubbornly worn for a quarter of a century. Those and the plain, black taffeta gown that had not varied since the day of her father's funeral; the costume that had grown as much a part of Cora Trimble's very flesh and substance as the unflinching Presbyterian goodness of her smile and the faint, clear soprano of her voice in Mr. Hannah's choir.

She's so devoted to Charles! I swear, for all his fancy Harvard law school learning, he owes most of his success to Cora! She's his slave! I always say there's a woman behind every successful man you can name! Although I must say it's a pity Cora never married! She was a charmer, they say, when she was young—before the father died!

And she had never let them think differently; not once let slip so much as a hint of his cold tyranny of her that had more than once exploded into actual, physical cruelty.

Why, Cora dear! How did you get that nasty black-and-blue mark on your wrist?

Oh that! It's nothing, Ella! I dropped a frying pan on it last night when I was doing the supper dishes!

Great men were temperamental. Great lawyers like Charles. Men with cold, steellike cogs of logic in their heads. Sometimes they must let off a little steam. And with a woman like Cora in the house—meek, self-sacrificing Cora—a creature who almost asked to be struck or grabbed by the wrist in a furious, iron grip and thrust into the dark hall—to do so seemed as much a matter of course as letting her darn one's hose or fix the tea at five. And through the years Cora had ceased taking much note of it herself—at least, until the morning when the mailman brought the travel folder. It was the most trivial thing in the world—a gaudy leaflet from a steamship line. And yet, after staring at the pictures of beautiful Guatemala for a full hour that morning, Cora burst suddenly into tears and was gripped at last by the sudden, choking sense of all the lost years. Why, there *was* a world beyond the iron grille fence! There were lovely green forests that were real, after all—and not dusty, pastel dreams like the pattern in the Persian carpet!

That, of course, was the day that Cora began writing her murder mystery. At first it seemed quite impossible. But once it was begun it quite obsessed her until she spent every spare, precious moment at her writing, at her desk, in her room, with no sound there but her own pleased, excited breathing and the delicate, steady scratch of the pen. It went on for months, absorbing her so completely that she could scarcely wait for Charles to be out of the house in the morning so that she could be back at her desk again.

Cora!

Yes, Charles!

She hurried into the hallway and stood at the top of the stairway, her fingers gripping the newel post.

Cora, did it occur to you that for thirty years I have taken lemon with my tea? And that my habits have not changed in recent weeks?

Cora padded silently down the softly carpeted steps.

Forgive me, Charles! she called breathlessly and hurried to the pantry. Presently she stole soundlessly into the study and placed the saucer with the neat, golden slices by the Sèvres pot. And then she was back in her room again—back at the desk—and with a sigh she wrote the last line to the next to the final chapter.

—*And presently he died,* whispered Cora, rereading the phrase with satisfaction and placing the sheet neatly with the others in the stack of manuscript. She lowered the lid of her desk and hurried down the back stairway to the pantry to start her brother's supper. She fetched the lamb chops from the icebox and smiled gently to herself. She felt light and warmly exhilarated.

—*And presently he died,* she whispered aloud again and lighted the oven. Cora hummed lightly to herself. Tomorrow was Saturday—her ice-cream day. She decided with a little quickening of her heart that instead of the single dipper of French vanilla she would splurge beyond all reason and have herself a double raspberry soda. And so she did.

Cora!

Yes, Charles.

Where have you been?

You know where I've been, Charles. Every Saturday afternoon I go down to Gandy's with the girls from Mr. Hannah's choir.

You've been gone the greater part of the afternoon, Cora. You know I like an early supper Saturday evening!

Forgive me, Charles!

And then she lowered her eyes to his desk—to the stack of paper. And she caught her breath. This was not one of Charles's law briefs. It was too thick. Then she recognized the thin, spidery, seminary writing of her own hand. It was the manuscript of her book. So he had found it. And how could he not have? She had left it where he could not fail to see it on the hall table before she had left the house that afternoon.

Charles chuckled and lighted a black stogie. Cora breathed as lightly as she could, loathing the coarse, choking, male odor of it.

As you see, Cora, I've been amusing myself this afternoon!

So I observe, Charles.

I must confess, I've underestimated you, Cora!

I'm glad you like my novel, Charles.

I didn't say that. I find the whole thing completely naïve and implausible, as a matter of fact! Really, Cora, you've seen much too little of Life to attempt this sort of melodramatic claptrap! I should rather imagine you doing something a little more in the manner of Elsie Dinsmore!

Boldly, Cora sat down in the straight-backed chair by Charles's desk, never taking her eyes from his face.

I would welcome your criticism, Charles. More than anyone I know.

Very well. In the first place, your characters are all absurdly overdrawn. Your heroine is far, far too romantic to be believed in. Your villain—well, come now, Cora!—no one is quite that diabolical!

—*And presently he died.*

Cora listened to the faint, persistent bell of the tutti-frutti wagon far off down the golden October street.

I suppose you're quite right, Charles, she said. If anyone in town should know about these things it would be you.

This couple, for example! Husband and wife! They are utterly unbelievable as such! They seem more like brother and sister!

He blew a puff of smoke at her and smiled derisively, shaking his head and riffling the pages with his thumb.

Then, Cora said gently, How would you have it, Charles? You cannot believe that my heroine Clarissa would ever do away with her—her husband Jonathan?

Never in a thousand years! Charles chuckled. If it were a case of mine—I'd call it suicide.

Cora cleared her throat and nodded as she moved closer to her brother's desk. For a moment her eyes were lost in the forests of the carpet at her feet; the beckoning golden light quivered in its Guatemalan wilderness and, far off, the singing of the sun gods drifted sweetly on the air.

Charles smiled. But still, what about the last chapter—the one you haven't written? It's all a silly piece of rubbish but I'll admit I'm curious to know what childish denouement you've contrived.

In a moment, Charles, she said, for although her hand was as steady as a stone, she was having an instant's delay fetching the heavy pistol from the drawer of the desk.

THE NIGHT WATCHMAN'S DAUGHTER

Hearts and eggs never nourish us until they're broken.
—Davis Grubb, notebooks

Reba Zavronsky was the beautiful, blond daughter of the night watchman at Freiburg's livery stable back home in the town where I was born. Reba worked in the Empire Restaurant slinging hash and waiting on counter. The Empire Restaurant was run by an old ball player who claimed he was a full-blooded Sioux Indian. Man name of Charley Sycamore.

The trouble started on my sixteenth birthday. I went in the Empire Restaurant for a glass of lemonade about four o'clock in the afternoon. My old man had gave me a five-dollar bill and I felt just like hauling off and buying up half the town. When I sat down at the counter Reba Zavronsky come over to wait on me.

Hello, said Reba.

Hello, I said.

Reba stood there smiling at me, waiting for me to order. The more I looked at her the worse it got. Lordy, I never had seen such a good-looking girl. She was prettier than them ones in the movies. Any of them ones in the movies would have a hard time making a living with a girl like Reba Zavronsky in town.

Want something? she said in her low, sweet voice like the soft running of the river at night.

Yes, I said, clearing my throat loudly. I'll have a lemonade. I wanted to say beer only I knowed I couldn't get none. All the time I was drinking my lemonade me and Reba was talking and the worse I got to feeling about her.

From that day on it was the same. From that day on nothing Pap or the old lady could ever say would change me about me and Reba Zavronsky. I guess if things hadn't turned out like they done we'd have gotten married and settled on a piece of black land somewhere up in Prospect Valley where the ground is so rich even a broom handle will sprout if it's planted right.

Me and Reba went to the movies at the Orpheum that night. Pap didn't know nothing about it. Me and Reba sat through the double feature and then we went out and got ourselves some popcorn and a double chocolate malted. After that I walked Reba home to where she lived with her old man in the one-room flat over Freiburg's livery stable. I had on my new suit and my best white shirt and my brother Ike's patent leather shoes. I can't tell you how Reba looked and make it sound right. They tell about them girls in the books so much that the words is all wore out. For a girl like Reba Zavronsky it takes words that hasn't never been used before. Maybe there's words to tell but I don't know what they are.

I couldn't hardly believe it was really me. I wished some of them silly Martin girls was to come down Main Street and see me and Reba Zavronsky walking along arm in arm. Pap's always hinting around for me to date them Martin girls. Chiefly on account of their old man is head of the electric company where Pap works and worth a lot of dough. I can't see it. I can't see no future in sitting around with them dumb, ugly Martin girls with their buck teeth and skinny legs. I can't see the sense in sitting around the parlor with them Martin girls and listening to their old lady blab her mouth when there's a girl in town like Reba Zavronsky. Even if she is a Polack. Even if she is the night watchman's daughter. Them things don't matter—not when a girl's as pretty a blonde as Reba Zavronsky. At least they don't with me.

It was the summer the Polacks come to town. I'll never forget till the day I die. It was a funny thing about them Polacks that summer. Nobody knowed for certain where they come from. Reba wouldn't never tell me. Neither would Mike, her old man. Uncle Fred said they laid them Polacks all off when they got done strip mining up back of Shinnston that spring. But nobody knowed for certain.

Just about that time Fred Woodruff was getting ready to break ground for the new courthouse and Fred was looking for day workers and then them Polacks come breezing into town. Fred was tickled to death. He needed day workers and them Polacks needed jobs. So Fred put them all to work.

They come into town at sunup. They come into town from every which way. They come riding in Model T's with the fenders all bashed out of shape and the steam whooshing out over the radiators and the tires flat and the dust beating up behind them thick as chicken gravy. The mud was so thick on them flivvers a man could have raised corn in it. Them Polacks come riding in old busted down Chevys, too. In Buicks and old rattle-trap Diamond T trucks. Some of them even was riding bicycles. Pretty soon the whole town was packed full of Polacks—big laughing ones and fat women Polacks with little fat Polack babies climbing all over them. In the stores and in the restaurants—drinking beer in the Empire and standing around in the sun smoking cigarettes, laughing, cracking jokes, and winking at the pretty women.

When Fred Woodruff said he'd put them to work they all reported next day at sunup and started in digging. Even the fat women and the little kids was digging till Fred come around and said he thought the women and kids would be better off at home. But the kids and women still hung around—carrying water and lunches or else sitting around on the grass cracking jokes with the men folks while they worked. When the noon whistle blowed they all sat down under the big oak tree on the library lawn and dragged out their lunch. They had hard-boiled eggs and big thick jam sandwiches with the blue juice soaking through the newspapers they was wrapped in. They had coffee cake and baloney. Lordy, to hear them Polacks eating that food you'd have thought it was the greatest feed that ever was. The people in the town thought it was pretty disgusting the way they carried on. Common, my old man said.

The whole bunch of them had pitched camp out on the old Lewis property at the edge of town where the carnivals come. They pitched up tents and them that didn't have no tents slept in their flivvers or under the trucks. Some slept out under the stars along the grassy riverbank. Every night when they got done work and et their supper you could hear them Polacks singing and playing their mouth harps and raising a happy rumpus. It seemed like they figured they'd really struck it rich at last. You never heard such a rumpus when them Polacks started in to singing and drinking beer whenever the sun went down.

Pap was councilman then and he didn't like the way them Polacks was carrying on any more than most of the other people in town did. Pap said they wasn't no more Polacks than you or me but Gyptians and they'd steal the gold out of your back teeth if you didn't keep an eye on them. Pap said Gyptians would as soon stick a dagger in your back as sneeze. He said it was a known fact that Gyptians carried off girl babies and raised them up to be fortune-tellers and hootchy-kootchy dancers in them carnival sideshows. Fred Woodruff talked Pap out of getting the city council to drive them all out of town. Fred said it was a matter of putting up with the Polacks till the courthouse was built. It wouldn't be no sense in throwing the Polacks out till the job was done. I was glad. It was good having the Polacks in town. Things got awful quiet in the summer and the Polacks was good to see and good to hear. You couldn't get me to swallow that junk about Polacks being stealers. Reba Zavronsky was a Polack and so was her old man Mike and they never carried daggers or stoled nothing in their whole lives.

Pap swears to this day that Reba Zavronsky and her old man was back of it. Pap swears they got word to them Polacks when

the mines shut down that there was work coming up in the
hometown. I don't know. It don't matter to me if they did or
didn't. You can't blame people for sticking together in this big
land. I figure the Polacks would have found out anyhow. They
can smell work. A Polack can smell work a thousand miles away.

Pap didn't know up till then I was taking Reba Zavronsky out
to the movies twice a week. Or if he did he never let on. I
carried papers for the Moundsville *Daily Echo* and Pap never
asked me what I done with my money. And he seldom asked me
where I was going when I went out nights. But I reckon if he had
I'd have lied to my old man for the first time in my life. I'd have
done a lot more than lie to be with a blonde like Reba
Zavronsky.

One night after the movies me and Reba didn't stop in the
drugstore and we didn't go straight home. We walked down
along the river beyond the tannery where Dick Madden's orchard
starts. We walked along down the riverbank under the willows
where the frogs croak and you can hear the fast, warm river running under the muddy roots along the bank. The night was warm
as the inside of your hand and the fog was beautiful; all soft and
gray and you could smell the river smell in it and you could hear
the crickets and tree toads up in Dick Madden's orchard blowing
their little silver whistles in the soft, warm dark. Out on the
river the lanterns burned like little yellow fires where some of the
boys was laying in their john boats waiting for the old catfish to
take a notion to bite. You could hear their voices low and sleepy
coming at you across the dark water; cracking quiet jokes and
chuckling about their girlfriends. Reba Zavronsky sat down beside me in the short grass and leaned up against a young apple
tree. I couldn't see her good in the dark. Only the outline of her
round face glowed through the wispy fog and the faint bright
shine of her whisky-yellow hair. Her breathing was as soft and
slow as the flowing of the dark, warm river in the night.

Reba, I said suddenly, putting my arm around her shoulder
and shaking all over. Reba, do you reckon you and me could get
married?

She laughed a warm chuckle and laid her warm hand over my

trembling fingers; it was a soft hand that hard work and dirty
dishes hadn't never seemed to touch. I felt her golden hair brush
my cheek and her warm lips against my forehead.

You haven't answered me, Reba, I said, sadly.

I'm twenty-two years old, she said softly. I'm much older than
you, Harry. You're still just a child. Why, when you grow up I'll
be an old woman.

Reba's voice was sad. You could tell she wasn't making fun of
me. You could tell she knowed we was both up against something
pretty big and wonderful and terrible, too. There was big tears in
her pretty blue eyes.

It don't matter, Reba, I said. You couldn't never be an old
woman. I don't care if you're forty-two years old. I'm in love
with you. I want you to marry me someday. I thought about it all
night last night. Uncle Fred told me on my birthday he was
going to leave me a nice piece of bottom farmland in Prospect
Valley. It's got an orchard and a house and a barn. Pap's going to
send me to the state university to study farming. You and me
could—

I know, she whispered in a low, mournful tone. It would be
wonderful for us to do that, Harry.

Reba, I said, feeling wildly that maybe I could win her but
knowing deep inside that I never in a million years could ever
get me a girl like Reba Zavronsky. Reba, say you will. I'll be
through high school in three years and then I'll be free to do
what I please. I don't have to go to college to be a farmer. As
soon as I'm through high school we can get married. Then we
can settle down on my piece of bottom land in Prospect Valley.

While I talked I was fishing in my coat pocket for the present
I'd bought Reba that afternoon in Armph Booher's jewelry store.
It was a five-dollar-and-fifty-nine-cent wristwatch. I'd saved four
dollars out of my birthday money and earned the rest on the
paper route. At last I found it and handed it to her. Reba took
the little package with a low cry of surprise and joy and undid
the string. She couldn't see it in the dark but she could feel it
with her hands. And at last when she got it open she sat holding
it; hearing its small ticking in the warm, unbroken quiet of the

night. I stared hard through the dark at Reba's faint white face;
thinking and praying that I would see her mouth fixing to say the
words I wanted her to say. Reba was quiet for a long time before
she said anything.

It's wonderful, Harry, she said. It's the only watch anyone ever
gave me. Then she sat quiet and I could tell there was a smile on
her face as she felt the new wristwatch with her hands. I got the
wild idea that maybe it was all set now. Maybe it would really
work out so me and Reba could get married someday. I was so
excited I had to stand up. Then I helped Reba to her feet. We
walked back into town together. Under the streetlamps I could
see her face now. Reba glanced shyly now and then at the wristwatch on her slim wrist to make sure it was really there. A soft
smile curved her mouth and her eyes were warm when she
looked at me.

I could feel the leaves brush my head as we passed under the
trees along the street and I thought, You ain't such a baby.
You're big enough to feel the leaves brush your head. You're prac-
tically a man. Maybe it was all settled now. Maybe me and Reba
Zavronsky could get married someday and settle down on the
good, rich black farmland my Uncle Fred had promised me. I
made up my mind to one thing right then and there. I made up
my mind if I didn't get to marry Reba I wouldn't never marry
nobody. I swore a solemn oath right then under the trees of
Main Street that if Reba didn't marry me I'd be a bachelor like
Uncle Dick Madden and chase kids out of my apple orchard
every summer with a baseball bat. Reba scarcely looked at me all
the way home. But whenever I glanced over at her, walking
slowly along with her warm hand in my big hand, I could see her
round, lovely face and the faint smile on her red mouth. Her
eyes was bright whenever she glanced at the wristwatch on her
arm. She'd said nobody had ever given her a wristwatch before.
But I knew more than that. Reba never said much about it but I
knew. When Reba's old lady died she was just a kid. Since then
her old man had been the only one in the world that ever cared
anything about her. He darned her socks and sat up nights sew-
ing up the tears in her little faded dresses. Reba said nobody

hadn't ever given her a wristwatch before. What she meant was
nobody had ever given her any present in all of her life until
tonight. Nobody except her old man. I could tell this was what
she meant. I could tell by the look on her face and the way her
warm, excited fingers closed around mine.

Reba, I said, swallowing like my throat was swelled shut.
Reba, say you'll marry me when I graduate from high school.

She looked at me quickly and bit her lip.

Maybe, Harry, she said. Let me think about it a little longer.

My heart started beating like a jackhammer and my chest
stuck out a mile. I couldn't think it was true. I couldn't believe it
had really happened. It couldn't really be me. Something would
happen—

Harry!

Pap's voice boomed out in the quiet street like a shotgun going
off indoors. Me and Reba was just passing the public library and
we stopped dead in our tracks and stared across the lawn at Pap,
sitting on the wood bench about ten feet away. I couldn't see
him very well but I knowed it was my old man. I could see his
cigar glowing in the shadow under the tree and I could smell it
and I knowed Pap's voice when I heard it. Pap walked slowly
over to where me and Reba was standing. Reba's hand got cold
but she never moved a muscle. She never let on like Pap was
scaring her none.

Harry, said Pap and his voice had that awful, cold quiet in it. I
want you to go home. Your mother and I have been trying to
find you for two hours.

It's funny the things you remember about times like that. I
remember hearing the beer sign over the Empire Restaurant
squeaking as the spring wind blowed it back and forth. I'll remember that sound till the day I die. I reckon if ever I hear that
sound again I'll feel just like I felt then. I'll hear it and remember
what it was like to know that the whole world had gone and
busted like a red balloon.

Harry, said my old man. I hope you heard me.

Then he cleared his thoat and snuffed his nose the way he
always done when he started to get real mad. As a rule when Pap

cleared his throat and snuffed his nose like that he'd just about run out of things to say. Pap looked at Reba. Reba stared back at him sadly. Seeing it now in my head I can remember the way her face was. I can still see the ache in it and yet something behind her mouth ready to bust out laughing. Tears and laughter side by side. Maybe she could be like that—crying and laughing all at once. Some folks have to. I couldn't understand it then.

Pap took his cigar out of his mouth. I didn't think he could do anything to make things worse but he did. Pap looked down at the wristwatch on Reba's arm and then he looked at me.

Harry, he said. I've known for some time that this was going on. When Armph Booher told me today you'd bought a five-dollar wristwatch in his store I figured things had just about gone far enough.

I wondered if I'd be big enough to lick my old man if he started to take that wristwatch away from Reba. But Pap didn't have to. With a smile I guess he'll remember till the day he dies Reba took the wristwatch off and handed it to me.

Reba—I—I— I stammered.

Pap looked at me.

Harry, I've spoken to you for the last time.

A look at Reba's face told me there wasn't no use in hanging around no more. What ever was there was gone now. Pap had come along and blowed it all away with a puff of his cigar. Reba's sad, mournful eyes was telling me to do like Pap said. There wasn't no use in hanging around no more. There wasn't nothing to do but go home now and go to bed.

I never said nothing to Pap as we walked down the street not hearing anything but our own footsteps. Pap cleared his throat like he had something he felt he ought to explain to me. I never looked at him. And I never turned my head to look if Reba was standing there under the tree watching us go. I knew she was gone. I felt sick clean through. I felt like I'd just seen someone kick a baby to death.

When the courthouse ground was broken and the excavation was all done Fred Booher wanted to keep the Polacks working for him till the courthouse was built. They was great workers. They could do anything from carpentering to painting. Fred said you could say what you wanted to about them Polacks they worked better than most Americans. Pap got the city councilmen together and talked to Fred about it. The councilmen all said the people was tired of them hell-raising Polacks out on the edge of town. The council told Fred the people was tired of having them Polacks singing and drinking beer as soon as the sun went down. So the next morning Fred told the Polacks they was all fired and he was hiring a crew of men from Charlestown to come finish the job.

I'll never forget till the day I die the night before the Polacks left. They come into town about four o'clock that afternoon and bought five kegs of beer and a hundred pounds of beefsteak. They hauled it out to the camp and built a big fire to cook the steak over. After they'd got done eating they started drinking beer and playing their accordions and mouth organs and singing. You could hear them for miles around.

Reba Zavronsky quit her job at the Empire Restaurant that day. And her old man Mike told Jim Freiburg to start looking for a new night watchman for his livery stable. At sundown the two walked down Main Street together, lugging their little belongings in two banged-up cardboard suitcases, walking out of the town where they had spent most of their lives. When they got out to where the other Polacks was they was all glad to see Reba and her old man and hear them say they was coming along with the rest of them when they left town next morning. Then they all started in to singing and dancing and raising a rumpus. Lordy, to hear them Polacks singing and blowing their mouth organs you wouldn't never think they'd just got fired. You wouldn't think they had a worry on their minds. I guess they didn't. I guess they were just waiting for word to come flying over the hills and prairies from some other lonesome Polack somewhere in America; from the place where there was new jobs and new land to break. I guess them Polacks figured maybe there wasn't no use in worrying about tomorrow till tomorrow was here. And, come to think of it, there wasn't much could happen to them the way they all stuck together.

Pap didn't know about it till I was gone. Pap didn't see me slip out of the back door and down the street toward the river. I crept down among the willow trees till I could see the Polacks sitting around the big fire singing and laughing and carrying on. Then I saw Reba. She was standing with her arm around a tall, dark-haired fellow with a big Stetson hat on his head. He had his arm around her. Reba's face was warm and happy as she lifted her face and kissed him on the mouth. I stood there beside the tree, hearing the warm river slip by me in the shadows and listening to the tree frogs up in the orchard. In the morning the Polacks would be gone. Reba and her old man were going with them. And when they drove over the cool mountains in the morning Reba and her tall, dark boyfriend would sit up in the front seat of his old Model T and he'd hug her and feel her hair rub against his cheek. In the morning they would all go. They'd get on their bicycles and jump in these rattletrap old flivvers and hit out for somewhere up U.S. 50 where there was work and new land to break. I knew as I stood there hearing the soft river that I was looking at Reba Zavronsky for the last time. I stared at her as she sat smiling in the firelight up in the meadow with her head against the tall fellow's shoulder. I tried to think it was the same kind of smile she had that night on the riverbank when I give her that wristwatch. I tried to think watching her smile up into the face of the big Polack miner that there was sadness in her eyes that he couldn't understand and that the sadness was me.

I saw the distant fire smear as the tears flooded my eyes.

Good-bye, Reba, I said softly to myself.

I walked all the way home with the tears streaming down my face but I didn't make no sound. When I got in the house Pap was sitting in the living room reading the Moundsville *Daily Echo*. My old lady had gone to prayer meeting. I could smell Pap's cigar and I could hear him turning the pages of the newspaper. I tiptoed through the dark house and went out on the back porch and sat down on the steps. It was quiet and dark and the honeysuckle smelled as sweet as candy and everything looked sad and white out in the backyard in the moonlight—like stones in a graveyard.

Next day I knowed Pap'd ask me why I didn't plan to take one of them dumb Martin girls to the carnival when it come to town at the end of summer. I wouldn't tell my old man why but I knew I wouldn't ask either of them. I wouldn't tell Pap why but I knew that I wouldn't ever so much as look sideways at another girl. Never as long as I lived.

LONG PANTS

> I think the opposite of good is not evil but ambiguity. I
> heard this in my head.
>
> —Davis Grubb, notebooks

For several weeks there my big brother Melvin and I were not on speaking terms. Even his best friends were able to notice changes in Melvin after he started playing the piccolo in the high school band. First he began slicking his hair down with lilac oil and then he took to smoking ten-cent stogies. It was hard to tell which smelled worse, the stogies or the lilac oil, but between the two of them they made a smell that was different from anything in the world. Sometimes I would be walking down Pike Street and I'd smell this lilac oil and stogie smell and my heart would grow sad at the thought of how my brother Melvin had changed. I would remember the happy Saturday afternoons the winter before when he used to take me to the Orpheum Theater and afterward play cowboy with me in the backyard. It was not so long after Melvin started playing the piccolo in the high school band that he also started calling me Peewee. Now this was a hard pill to swallow. However, I would say to myself comfortingly: Melvin is seventeen and you are only twelve but it was only last winter that Melvin was wearing his cowboy suit out in the backyard. And it was not so long ago that Melvin would fall

63

dead when you shot him with his rubber revolver. My old lady
never knew that Melvin smoked ten-cent stogies. I didn't betray
him. Even if I was only twelve—I had my honor.

The trouble really started the night my old lady said no to the
long pants. For some time I had realized that in a few weeks I
would be thirteen years old and it would be humiliating to be
seen any longer in knickers and stockings. At last one evening
my old lady said yes. It was a happy moment. She promised me
that next Saturday afternoon she would give me the money and I
could go down to the One Price Only Clothing Store and buy
myself a pair of long pants. And then Melvin came galloping
into the room. He was getting ready to go over and see his
girlfriend, Wilma Snodgrass. Wilma played the oboe in the high
school band which I guess is why she and Melvin appealed to
each other. They had been going steady now for nearly three
months and it was plain that they would have children and get
married someday. Melvin's hair was all slicked down and shining
brightly with lilac oil and he had on his new suit. You could tell
he could hardly wait to get out the front door so he could light
up a ten-cent stogie. This was during the summer when Melvin
believed he was George Raft, so that much of the time it was
hard to understand what he was saying. It wasn't hard to understand him this time though.

What! screamed Melvin. Peewee in long pants! Ma, you must
be crazy!

My old lady looked sad and thoughtful. It would not take
much persuading to get her out of the long pants frame of mind.
She patted me on top of the head as I stood glaring at Melvin.

I know, she said, looking as if she was about to bust out crying. It does seem a little soon.

A little soon! hollers Melvin. Ma! Peewee is still a mere infant!

I could now clearly see another winter of knickers and stockings before me. My old lady wiped a tear from her eye with the
back of her hand.

Yes, she said. Yes, you're right, Melvin. I'll just keep my little
boy another year.

I did not curse my brother Melvin. I am a gentleman at all times whatever the thoughts that are in my mind. I just walked quietly from the room, whistling. Presently I heard Melvin clattering down the front steps on his way to Wilma's house. My old lady kissed me on top of the head.

You'll be grown up soon enough, she said.

But I just whistled much louder to keep from crying.

For a long time I sat on the front porch steps sadly smelling the lilac oil and stogie smell that my big brother Melvin had left behind him. I sat there thinking for a long time. At least I knew that, for his own good, my brother had to be taught a lesson. It would hurt me to do it but I had no choice. I would steal my brother's girlfriend, Wilma Snodgrass. After I had shown him my power, however, I would generously give her back to him. After all, Melvin and Wilma were going to get married someday. And besides I had no desire to keep her permanently.

The next day I took all the dimes out of my iron Statue of Liberty bank and counted them up. I had twenty-four dimes. Enough for a box of candy at least. And then I waited.

Two weeks later my brother Melvin left town for a weekend to help my Uncle Chad on his farm. It was the apple season and Uncle Chad couldn't afford a hired man to help him harvest his apples. I saw that my chance had come. That night I went upstairs and walked boldly into Melvin's room. I stared moodily at his old cowboy suit in the corner of the clothes closet. I gazed at the old rubber revolver that Melvin had shot me with so many times. I saw his old fingerprint set and his artificial detective's mustache lying dusty and forgotten on his table. I thought bitterly of the happy times we had spent only the winter before. It made me think of how Melvin had changed. And then I grabbed Melvin's bottle of lilac oil and poured some out in the palm of my hand. Wilma is the type of girl to whom this sort of thing appeals, I thought, comforting myself as I stood before Melvin's mirror rubbing the awful stuff into my shaggy hair. Otherwise you would not be doing this. But it was the hardest part of all: seeing myself at last in the mirror, fragrant and foolish, with my hair all plastered down like the head on a store-window dummy.

I grinned foolishly at myself, practicing the charm that I was going to use on Wilma. Then I put on my good knickers and my brown coat and my model aviation club badge and walked calmly out of the house.

Where are you going, dear? hollered my old lady.

Oh, nowhere much, I answered coolly, wondering if I had bitten off more than I could chew. Just downtown!

Well, don't be too late! she hollered back.

I walked quickly down the yard, kicking the fall leaves. There was a big yellow moon hanging high in the cool night and the air was sharp where the lilac oil had dripped down the back of my neck.

Well, I said to myself. At least you are not making a fool of yourself by smoking any ten-cent stogies. Except for a little lilac oil you are your natural self. You may be a mere boy of twelve but your personality is at least eighteen.

But just the same I was anxiously wondering what in the world I was going to say when Wilma Snodgrass opened her front door. After I had bought the dollar box of candy at the drugstore I walked slowly down the street toward Wilma's house. There was just one light burning in the front parlor and the leaves in the vines on the front porch whispered softly in the fall breeze. I sat down in the shadow of the big chestnut tree by the curb in front of Wilma's house, thinking. Did you grab a girl and kiss her the minute she opened the door? Or did you sit around and talk to her about it for a while? These things are not in books. No one tells you.

Well, I hissed, gritting my teeth loudly. Are you yellow?

Then I jumped to my feet and tiptoed quickly up the lawn toward the house. I will not deny that I hated the idea of wasting a whole good evening in the company of Wilma Snodgrass. I could never see why my brother Melvin wanted to marry her. I can think of more romantic things than a girl who plays the oboe. And besides she was always giggling in study hall with a bunch of other silly girls or reciting poems in chapel and stuff like that. Personally this kind of a girl would never appeal to me for marriage. But just the same I had come to steal her from my big brother and I had to see it through.

It was at that moment that I heard the music. At first I thought it was coming from the parlor and then I realized it was coming from Wilma's porch. It was unmistakable. I had heard it too many times before not to recognize it. It was my big brother Melvin's favorite record. Quietly I crept over to the edge of the porch and peered through the leaves of the honeysuckle vine. For a moment I was sure that my big brother Melvin had come home suddenly from Uncle Chad's farm and was having a date with Wilma. It could be nothing else. This was their song. And then I saw that it was Wilma all right but it wasn't Melvin that was sitting beside her on the porch swing. It was Charlie Bozo, the captain of the high school football team. Wilma's record player was playing Melvin's and her record and she and Charlie Bozo were sitting close together on the porch swing drinking root beer. I couldn't believe my eyes. In a few moments the record finished and Wilma went over and turned it off.

I'm tired of that silly old piece, she said, her red mouth pouting.

Don't it remind you of ol' Sweety Pie Melvin, says Charlie Bozo.

Oh, *him*! squeals Wilma, making a face. That's all over. He isn't even going to be in the band anymore!

How come? says Charlie, finishing his glass of root beer.

Oh! Haven't you heard? whispers Wilma, real excited. Professor Ricardo says we all have to make five dollars' deposit on our musical instruments or we can't play in the band. Well, of course, Daddy gave me *my* five right away! But Melvin's mother is *too poor* to give *him* five dollars—she takes in washings, you know—so Melvin has to drop out of the band!

Wilma snuggled up a little closer to Charlie and giggled.

I don't care though, she whispered. I'm tired of Melvin anyway.

The root beer glasses were empty.

Wilma and Charlie put their arms around each other and kissed for a long time.

I walked home down the quiet street with the big harvest moon throwing crazy shadows on the sidewalk under the trees. I thought to myself of Melvin in my Uncle Chad's apple orchard picking apples. When I went in the house I handed my old lady the box of candy.

Chocolate-covered peppermints! she exclaimed, throwing up her hands. Why thank you, dear! What makes my little boy so thoughtful tonight?

She kissed me on top of the head.

What are you doing, dear? she hollered upstairs at me a few moments later.

Washing my hair, Ma! I yelled back, staring at the lilac oil and soap suds swirling greasily down the washbowl beneath my nose.

Well, Melvin never said anything. I guess he was too proud. He never said a word to anybody about having to stop playing the piccolo in the high school band or about Wilma Snodgrass or Charlie Bozo or anything else. On the night of my thirteenth birthday, however, he came home from school with a big black eye. He sat there without saying a word all during supper, sighing loudly. His hair had no lilac oil on it anymore. You could tell it had been days since he had smoked himself a ten-cent stogie. He just sat there picking at his slice of my birthday cake and staring at his water glass.

Well, dear, said my old lady, looking across the table at me and smiling. Happy birthday! At least *you* have something to be happy about!

And she reached across the table and handed me a little birthday card. There was a five-dollar bill folded up inside of it.

There! said my old lady. Now you can go down to the One Price Only Clothing Store and buy yourself that pair of long pants you wanted!

I could hardly believe my eyes. At last the great moment had come. Now I would no longer have anything to be ashamed about.

Thank you, Ma, I said quietly, folding my napkin and tucking it through the little silver ring beside my plate. I hurried out into the hall.

Melvin's schoolbooks were on the little table by the umbrella stand and I could hear him out in the front yard walking around loudly in the dry leaves as I folded up the five-dollar bill and slipped it between the pages of his algebra book.

EVERY ROAD I WALKED ALONG

Time does not travel from here to there. It *is* from here to here.

—Davis Grubb, notebooks

He had seen her but twice in thirty years. The first time was on the stand singing with Tommy's orchestra at the Peach Blossom Festival Dance. The second time was six hours later at Cuba's, the campus diner, having breakfast with a town cop and six members of the football team. When he had gone over and asked for her autograph and nobody could come up with anything she could write with, she had just sat there giving him fifteen seconds of that brown-eyed look that was soon to be so famous. Then she had taken the wilted spray of peach blossoms out of her hair and handed him that. It was to be thirty years before he would see her again. And yet when he left the university and came back to Lowndesville, he had built a whole business around her voice and her small blond beauty and her then virtually unknown name.

She was called Francie Mason, born Magda Franceska in a mine-patch in the coalfields of Pennsylvania, north of Altoona.

She made it fairly big with Tommy that year, and then he fired her and for the year after that she made herself an even more prestigious name singing with various small groups around New York. By 1940 she had built a nice book of standards and originals by people like Phil Moore and Alec Wilder; the next year she joined Artie and won both the *Downbeat* and *Metronome* polls. Then again she seemed to drop from the news and for a frantic winter he lost sight of her career altogether. That spring he read in *Downbeat* that she was singing with Billy Husted's Cornhuskers, a territorial band out in Davenport, Iowa. The following fall she was back with Tommy and her real success began.

It was a roundabout way he built his restaurant around her. It was as if he meant the enterprise to remain his secret; as though, indeed, it was nobody's business but his own. He was that way about most things. He had never known his parents. He had been raised by two maiden aunts. He never married. He had never had a girl at college. Even at the Peach Blossom Festival Dance the brunette he escorted was, like the tux he wore, borrowed. He was an idealist about women in a way which radiated its warning to them. For if every woman likes sometimes to be thought a goddess, no woman with a mind wants to live up to the image of one already made. He was equally ethereal about other matters in life. For example, he had taken painting at the university with the plan of becoming a poet. It was his unearthly belief that he would support himself as an artist until he could make a living at poetry. When the two aunts died within a month of each other, he found himself the sole heir to fifteen thousand dollars and a lot in the Lowndesville business district. Inasmuch as college had at least taught him that he was both color-blind and without literary talent, he decided, with unprecedented worldliness, to open a restaurant.

Lowndesville in the late thirties was a prosperous industrial town of thirty thousand in the central plateau of West Virginia. It already had two rather good restaurants and nobody was especially impressed when word went round that the late Kemple sisters' nephew, Dale Martin, was opening a new one. Those who did not think him downright eccentric considered him, at

least, unrealistic and it was widely prophesied that the venture
would quickly fold. He called it simply the New Moon. This
surprised a few perceptive people who imagined that he might
have given it a truly bizarre name. It was, however, original and
appropriate in the extreme when you consider how Martin arrived at it. Francie Mason's big hit with Tommy's band in 1939
was "Lover, Come Back to Me." The song was by Sigmund
Romberg from a show of the twenties called, of course, *The New
Moon.* Martin never bothered explaining this to anyone unless
asked. And to most of them, it seemed too obscurely roundabout
to be worth remembering. Which was all right with Martin. It
kept the thing the way he really hoped it would be from the first;
his own secret, his own love affair. If he had called it Francie's
Place people would have asked him: Francie Who? And he
didn't really like passing his love affair around that way to be
handled by strangers. Still he did get questions now and then.
Because there were thirty different framed sixteen-by-twenty
glossies of Francie Mason hanging along the white walls above
the neat, linen-draped tables. And the jukebox was carefully
stocked with either Francie Mason records or tunes by the bands
with which her name, in those forgotten times, was linked.

As things turned out Dale Martin discovered that his talent in
life was food. The meals at the New Moon were modestly famous. The food got better through the war years while the
town's first restaurant almost went under and became, at last,
little more than another beer joint. After a while nobody paid
any attention to anything in the New Moon but the food. Who
cared if nobody knew any of the tunes that Dale Martin still had
in his jukebox? And who minded if they couldn't remember the
dark-eyed, pretty blonde who smiled down at them from every
wall? As for Martin he was utterly faithful. Still as dreams have a
way of doing she became to him a reflex. It was almost as though
he had married her and they were growing old together. Perhaps
the feeling that she never changed gave him the feeling that he
hadn't either. She was always that same pretty nineteen-thirties
princess in the pale chiffon formal smiling on through Depression
and Spanish War and Munich with the sweet, uncommitted in-

nocence of her time. Yet there was enough guilt in her look to
give it sex appeal. You imagined that under the vestal drape of
her evening gown's full lines grew legs by Petty. Her voice had
that petulant emphasis and breathless, pouting whine which pre-
cedes all really pure submission. She stood behind the black rod
of the microphone holding her left arm in the gesture of those
singers in those times, as if the arm were broken at the wrist. In
her bland school-girl fingers dangled a pale pink lawn kerchief
with which she kept faint, aloof time as she leaned back into the
breathing brass of Buddy's cymbal behind her. She bore no
resemblance to the girl-next-door. She suggested rather the
nameless college roommate of the girl-next-door: a dazzling, oth-
erworldly nymph who had visited once in the summer before the
war and left the male town in hubbub in her wake.

Meanwhile, she had appeared briefly in three feature-length
movies and a couple of band shorts for Republic. Twice she had
made personal appearances in the tri-state area: once with a
pick-up band at the Nixon Theater in Pittsburgh and again with
a hotel trio at a dance given by a glass-worker's local at Wheeling. He kept a scrapbook of her career. When her name appeared less frequently in the music magazines he combed
Chicago and New York and Los Angeles newspapers for rare,
stray items. Yet he never wrote her a fan letter. He had gotten
her photos from a local record distributor. He never wrote the
New York talent agencies who variously had represented her. It
had really never seemed important to him to *see* her again. What
could he have said to her? What could he have offered? Martin
was realist enough to know, at least, what things could never be.
It seemed as if he had all of her there in his New Moon. It was
his life, his livelihood, his place of nourishment, physical and
spiritual. And she was it. He listened to her voice in the supper
evenings as a kind of murmurous reassurance against his own
encroaching age. Music in general meant literally nothing to
Martin. Yet he listened to Francie's songs with a rare and practiced connoisseurship. The words said what they said to him and
he heard each as a kind of personal message. The fact that the
songs repeated endlessly the same sentimental statements both-

ered him no more than a man is annoyed by the familiar, pleasant clichés of his wife. They became the platitudes of a belovedness. When the records wore out, Martin replaced them—often at considerable expense. And it was all so harmless. Nobody minded Dale Martin's caprice. Nobody minded the old-fashioned music and the nineteen-thirties decor. Indeed, in the mid-sixties, first tourists and then Lowndesville people themselves found Dale Martin's New Moon rather camp. Though once in a while the face in one of the dusty golden frames struck a flash of memory in some traveler's mind. Who is she? Is it Toby Wing? Elissa Landi? Thelma Dodd? Didn't we know her once when we were young?

He was naturally troubled about her when she began to disappear. In the late fifties he had found that annoying little piece about her in the *New York Mirror*. It concerned her arrest with two men for drunk-and-disorderly in a San Francisco hotel lobby. Poor baby, he thought, Poor baby, still trying to teach those college linebacks how to hold their liquor. And then nothing more for about six years. Not a word until that morning when he opened the Lowndesville *Telegram* and saw her name in the ad announcing the country rock group that was making a one-night appearance that evening at Carmichael Auditorium.

He immediately decided, of course, that he should not go to see her. It was not that he objected to the thought of hearing her sing hillbilly and rock. This was merely added proof of her eternal youth, her golden humor, her inexhaustible versatility. If she had been appearing that night with Tommy and Jack and all the lads, it would have been the same. Some unspoken hunch within him, doubtless, warned that thirty years might not have really left her youth untouched. Yet here in the New Moon it was that: unscathed by scathing time. Yet there were times when he stood alone before one of her portraits in the dim light after closing when he would wish he had become an artist. Because he imagined how he would now, with some tasteful crayon, appropriately touch in the lines of love and laughter which time had surely by now given her face. And he would listen to the B&O National Limited blowing for a crossing behind the piedmont and imagine how her voice, in three decades, would have taken upon it the sensuous luster of full nubility. Still he knew he would have no business going to see her at the auditorium that night. When a man's dream has become reflex he does well not to tamper with it, the reflexes of the middle-aged being, at best, what they are. Besides it was a dance. He would have no one to take.

Still that night filled Martin with enormous excitement. Almost terror. He had a momentary thought of closing the restaurant and taking the bus to Fairmont for the night. Because he knew somewhere in the marrow of him that he was going to see her. After thirty years. Thirty years of seeing her every day. Yet now, again, he would really *see* her. Something in the marrow of him said it could not be otherwise. Him in this small West Virginia town and her in the same small town; it had to be. Chance would create it. And yet he could not imagine it. He could not conceive of the circumstances, of what he would say to her, how he would hand her a menu, how he would face her eyes. She might be angry at all of this. It might spoil everything. She might not even remember him. Or, if she did, she would see how he had changed. She would notice perhaps how much he had aged in all that time.

He stayed close to his kitchen that night. He kept the jukebox playing continuously and the water pitchers full of ice and the five waitresses constantly on their toes. He kept the marquee lights lit in front of the restaurant long past midnight. They shone brightly in all the somber stillness of the darkened small town street. Beneath the winter night only the light in the jeweler's window twinkled far up Pike Street. And the faint glow at the corner from the lights, half a block off, from the hotel where she would be staying. By two-thirty the thought that the dance would be out in another half hour filled Martin with excitement almost beyond endurance. It would not let him be still. Instead of trembling it made him want to walk, to pace endlessly through the cold night, working off a little of that stoppered, furious energy. It was too late for any customers but he kept the place still open. He left Helen, his oldest waitress, in charge of the cash register and began walking. He felt like a man who does not know if he is about to be freed of something or imprisoned by it forever. He went nowhere near the place where she sang that night. Still on the wind, in the rustle of bare trees above him, he could fancy that her voice blew there, husky with youth, a little drunk with the lost wine of that lost time. He could imagine her singing his old favorite from the thirties: from *The New Moon*. He heard the song, of course, without much melody, being quite without any ear for music, but rather as a kind of recitation. Rather like the chant of a priestess. And to the rhythm of her words he walked and the wind, quickening to bright edgedness with hints of gathering snow, blew the tuneless air about his ears:

Every road I walked along, I walked along with you—

To Martin's excited fancy it seemed a quite solid and dependable assurance, uttered thirty years ago, that he would, upon this night and for the third and perhaps most important time, see her again.

Of course, she had heard about the New Moon almost the first thing after she had gotten settled in her small, plain two-room suite at the Goff Hotel. It was too late for supper and she and the five-man group of musicians had walked to the auditorium about ten o'clock. When the dance let out at three-thirty, one of the musicians had offered to take her to the place. She refused and went alone to her bathroom and had another drink. She stared at the woman in the mirror for a while before deciding not to put on fresh makeup. She was farsighted and when she was not performing she wore spectacles with thick amber frames. She felt they lent her street face an air of settled dignity. She put them on and pulled on her gloves and mink coat and went to the window to stare out into the cold stillness of the stars. It was icy, bitter, and she looked down into the alley through the iron of the narrow fire escape landing. She hesitated a moment before turning out the light, then fetching a small bottle of red capsules from her dresser, she took two with the half inch of whiskey left in the hotel drinking glass. She had made up her mind to go see it for herself. Her mouth was tight with suspicion. Even in the cold street when she could see the name of the place on the marquee up the sidewalk she still believed it was another joke

one of the musicians was trying to play on her. They were an
older country rock group who thought it would be camp having a
once well-known older pop singer doing the younger songs. The
musician who particularly disliked her was a forty-year-old
rhyth_a guitarist named Cutey Blake. He had told her about this
place where he had had a sandwich and a beer and that there
had been her old songs in the air there. And her old pictures on
all the three, long, clean walls. Francie Mason stood so long in
the doorway that the waitress thought for a moment she was
sick.

Can I get you a table, ma'am?

What? Yes. Please. Do that, please, dear.

Is this all right?

What? No. Further in the back, honey.

She paused, smiling a moment hopefully, watching the waitress and all the while keeping her face lined up with the large
framed photo behind her.

Don't you know me? her smile seemed to ask. But all she said
was: Thank you. Yes, this will be fine.

She watched the waitress go over and put some coins in the
machine the way Martin had told her to keep doing all night and
pretty soon she was hearing Buddy's drum breaks again and
Georgie's tenor and Ziggy's trumpet and a whole lot of things
came blowing back along the winters of a moment, and all the
sweet, brief nights between the time when Artie added strings
and Glenn went down in the Channel.

Yes, I think I *would* like a drink, she said, wanting to make it
sound like her first that night; and she made it a double and sat
there numb and dumb as if struck hard across the mind, unable
to cry, unable to move a muscle of her face as the music
thrummed and cried all so far away and long ago. And all the
eyes of all the framed faces watched her and in her mind suddenly she could smell things as different as the powder room at
the Onyx and the chestnut man's steaming wagon at the corner
of Fifty-second near Ryan's, and the hot syrup on the waffles at
Whammy's and the cheap, balding A&R men who smelled like
hard money and London Docks pipe tobacco. In this strange

place so many things and people became so suddenly alive and in
the future, things she knew were really in the past and out of the
way of progress, where they belonged. She went into the ladies'
room to be sick and to cry and when she got there she could do
neither; nothing would come out of her, and she stood there
staring into her own forlorn eyes thinking snatches of Benny's
head arrangements and Sy's great intros and phone numbers of
which even the exchanges had vanished. When she went back
and had another double Old Forester she suddenly began to feel
calm, if not sober, and even a little swaggery about it all. Thirty
pairs of her lost youth's eyes stared at her and it seemed, in the
glow of that moment, that they were, for a young girl, extraordi-
narily understanding. She felt curiously grateful to them as
though they weren't going to be too hard on her. Still she was a
little unsteady on her way to the counter where the waitress was
busy with a *Sun Telegraph* crossword puzzle. She leaned across the
glass, studying the girl closely through her lenses.

Who is he? she murmured.

What, ma'am?

Who—who *is* he?

Who is who, ma'am?

The man who did—all *this?*

Mr. Martin is the proprietor, ma'am, said the girl. He should
be back in an hour, he said. He went for a walk, he said. We
usually close early. He said he'd be back in an hour.

I see. Thank you.

Did you wish to see him, ma'am? Was anything wrong?

Oh, no, she said, in that husky way that made the waitress
think of cities. Everything was fine, thank you, dear.

She paid her check and gave the girl a five-dollar tip and
started a little shakily toward the door.

Are you sure you're all right, ma'am?

She turned and smiled her best.

Yes, I'm fine, she said.

She pushed open the door, still smiling, feeling the cold slap
against her flushed cheek and flow chill against her eyes, under

her glasses. She winked at the waitress, smiled and tapped her
foot on an upbeat.

Livin' in a great big way, she said and went out.

She had decided to stand across the street where she could
look at the place from a distance and try to believe in it. She
wanted to stand for a while at a new perspective so she could
make herself believe it was not all just something the pills and
the drink had made up against her. It made her remember the
night Mildred and Red had saved her from an overdose of Early
Times and nembutols and the things she had seen that night.
But she felt sober even if her legs did feel drunk and she breathed
deep, tasting again the cold in the marrow of her, the snow coming, the snow already gathering behind the wind, and in that
invisible, snow-drenched air the walk steadied her as she made
her way back to the hotel. Because she hadn't been able to see
the New Moon across the street for the tears and the steam on
her lenses. And yet she couldn't cry either. The tears were just
there suddenly with no sobs to push them and hardly any feeling.
They ran down her cheeks and dropped off on her mink sleeves.
It was all like a knot in her hips; it was tied up by the thing that
made it hard to breathe, made it impossible to cry. She couldn't
cry at all, like sometimes you couldn't get the beat of a song. Just
the damned dumb tears in her eyes and she knew how that must
make her look; like a child's drawing coming apart in a cold
puddle.

When she saw him on the edge of the black leather settee by
the shuttered-up cigar stand, she knew right away who it was.
There was nobody else around but the night clerk and an aging
bellboy in the little back room behind the key-and-letter boxes,
but she knew that if there had been sixty people in the dim hotel
lobby she would have picked him from among them. It scared
her that she knew him. Because she felt now that thing that he
had felt. That she had to see him tonight. Because she wanted
to. Or because Chance wanted her to. And, like him, she was
not sure which was which.

You're Mr. Martin, she said lightly.

She had stopped a dozen feet away and stood in that poor
light, with some suggestion of an old bandstand pose, one foot
placed before the other. She made the eyes behind her glasses
warm.

Why, yes.

You—you came here to see Francie Mason, she murmured,
low, richly.

He stared a long moment blinking in the bad light, sleepy,
still cold from the night's long walk, the coming snow. He
blinked again. And she thought with a sudden panic that she
had been wrong. Because he looked quite through her.

You must be her mother, he said suddenly, with a kind of
polite reverence.

Her body shuddered as if struck by bullets. Her eyelids shivered and her face snapped up as if invisibly he had slapped her.
She leaned slowly into the marble pillar, knuckling her teeth
with a kid-gloved hand. He started toward her, murmuring a
bewildered unintelligible sound of concern.

Oh, you son of a bitch, she whimpered into her fingers. Oh,
you square, cruel son of a bitch.

She seemed to be shaking with a hard and soundless laughter,
her body bowed forward against the pillar, her back arched like a
drawn bow.

Get out, she whispered. Get out!

He fell back from the savagery of her voice and stared at her,
smiling in sorrowful understanding.

There now, he said. I know how it must be. All of them.
They must be after her everywhere you go. Smart young college
kids. The swinging 'gators. The wolves. I can just guess what a
mother is up against.

He smiled on; he shook his head with that infinitely kind understanding.

But you're wrong about me, he said. I'm not like them. I don't
want that from her.

She flung back her face till the heavy spectacle frames leaped
on her pinched, fine nose and her eyes fixed in hard passion on

the tawdry gilt of the moulded ceiling. She made the laughing breath again. It shook her body but there was no voice to it.

With me it's adoration, he said. And that's not like them. It's not even like love. It's just wanting to look and not touch. It's just wanting to hear and only *feel*.

Get out, get out, she sang, over and over, tonguing the words in a measured, contralto monotone, like some stuttering nonsense song of her heyday. Get out, get out, get out.

She sucked in breath hard through pursed lips and bowed her forehead hard into the cold marble to which she clung.

Get away, get away, get away, she chanted and struck her forehead in time to the words against the small, gloved hand she held fisted against the veined, polished stone.

Outside he felt the first flake of the snowfall. It lighted on his lip. It felt cold but, melting, left a warmness. He stood listening to the unleashed weeping which now rushed from her in the night-deserted lobby. He watched the snow gather in the dark air beyond the marquee light. The flakes seemed suddenly to materialize upon the dark and pause before hurrying to the street where they lay or swirled in small, glittering galaxies upon the asphalt surface. He hurried quickly away. His pace was livelier now. He was pleased to have come this close to her. He was glad to know, at least, of this older woman who had been custodian through all the years and cities of that fair child's unbanishable youth. And yet he wished he could have found the words, the wit, the way to have made her know that he was not like that sprawled continent of the others: the college boys and wolves, the corny hepcats, the hungry alligators, the squares from Delaware.

He sent the cashier home. Then he turned out all the lights except those in the juke box. He had a drink of straight whiskey, which was rare for him, and sat alone, listening to her small, ghostly voice against the padded, throbbing beat of Artie's band. And settling then within the glove of a melancholy but comforted reverie he watched the small, frail snow lay siege upon the empty street beyond.

It was nearly an hour before she appeared. Against the delicate, gathering white lace upon the pavements her shape was
clear. She looked a little older now, a little more stooped beneath the thick fall and high-turned collar of a trench coat she
had fetched from her room. The dumpy drape of a rainhat
framed the heart-shaped face which seemed even now, behind
the decade-old chic of the harlequin frames, grown somehow
more vividly hopeless. She did not see him. She stood on the
edge of the pavement across the street, as she had the first time,
to stare over in wonder and disbelief. But unlike then, she was
able to weep now. The crystal wind whipped round the steel
light pole in flagging gusts. It may be that she caught, now and
again, a blown fragment of the tune which wove itself in his air
behind the unlighted window. She had had more to drink and
then had grown afraid to drink anymore but not for fear of
drunkenness. It seemed to her instead that another drink might
shove her across the edge into a state of leaden soberness. And
this drunkenness was dear to her. Because the image and thought
of the New Moon was part of this drunkenness and she was in
sudden terror of losing it. Here was the shrine of her youth and,
at the same time, the sepulchre of her future. Nothing could
have stayed her feet from bringing her back to that place. She
thought of all her life's high moments: husbands and lovers and
the bond-drive letter from the president and the awards and the
song that Julie and Sammy wrote just for her; they were nothing
compared to this. And though drink, like all her friends, was no
friend anymore, tonight he was kind and told her she was home.
She knew that through the inexplicable whim of this strange
man all the treasures of her life had been scooped from a thousand gutters and set shining in one, clean place. One place in
the whole dingy, homeless land where all of her that was pretty
and healthy and talented was being kept alive, despite herself.
And this stranger, lonely as she, had done this. And there was
no sense reasoning upon it or wondering why. She felt very
afraid. She had the terrifying certainty that this was really all
that was left of her on earth. And so he must never see who she

was. He must never know what she was and know thereby that
she was no longer anything at all.

Mrs. Mason, you'll catch your death out there.

That was when she saw him in the doorway. When she
shrugged and straightened her slumped shoulders, it made her
look even older as she went slowly across the muffled street. She
settled her glasses more firmly upon the fine nose of her time-
ruined face. She licked her unpainted lips and smiled. And she
made the liquor embolden her to act it out for him; to be what
he thought she was, so that Francie Mason could go on being at
all. Because she owed him this much. And because she thought
she would die if the New Moon were ever to be changed and this
man's whimsy shouldered aside for fresh schemes. She crossed
the pavement to him. And she hoped her voice would sound a
little older for both their sakes. She looked at him, her face
tilted a little, his dark, shy shape against the uneven light.

Oh, you dear man, she said, huskily. How could I ever have
cursed you!

Come on in, he said. Don't mind that. I'll fix you a drink.
Listen. I understand. Do you think I haven't got any imagination? A daughter like that. And the sort of guys always hanging
around. Listen. She's lucky she's got you is all I can say. I'm just
sorry you got the wrong impression. My God, I wouldn't—I
wouldn't—

I know you wouldn't.

My God, I *couldn't*, he said. But I understand. I mean some
fellows think any girl in show business. Don't think I don't
know.

He waved his hand to encompass the pale walls from which
her faces stared. He smiled modestly, after so much talk.

What's your name? he said.

Magda.

That's a good name. You look tired. I'll bet it's not easy being
all the things you have to be twenty-four hours a day. Mother,
manager, plus a shoulder to cry on, I'll bet.

He frowned, groping for words to shape the thought that bothered him.

I hope you won't mind my asking. But you look so—so tired. Is she good to you?

Better than I am to her, my friend.

She sat at his table with the fresh drink in the gloved ring of her fingers. She felt the snow beyond and the cold wind beyond and all the winters past and future out there, and suddenly the walls seemed so fragile around them both. She studied his face, probing him, measuring his strengths and probabilities. She searched for a way to make them both believe in the girl up there in the hotel room.

Do you want to see her tonight? she said recklessly and took out cigarettes.

He laughed nervously and lit her smoke with a steady hand.

You mean wake her up at this ungodly hour?

She's used to this ungodly hour, my friend.

But if she's in bed.

She gets enough bed.

Still she might be asleep.

She doesn't sleep.

Well, I don't know, he said softly, watching the snow with her. I just don't know.

He shook his head gravely against the image of it.

She may not be asleep, he said. But still sometimes it's better not to wake things.

You mean you think she may have changed, she said suddenly, a little harshly. Gotten older. Maybe hard. That's it, isn't it?

No, he said thoughtfully. I know she's changed. Nobody doesn't change in thirty years. But that doesn't matter. Beauty—real beauty—it has so many different lives.

That's the trouble, she said. Francie has had so many lives.

Why do you say it that way?

Lives are like agents. Each one has his fifteen percent. Would you mind turning on the lights?

The lights?

Yes, please. I want to look at all the pictures.

He sprang to the switches. The light fell flooding across the photographs along the clean walls above the fresh, napkin-peaked tables set and ready for the breakfasts of mine-supply salesmen and early risen merchants. She got up quite steadily. She stood a moment, drawing her high gabardine collar closer about her ears. She shivered as if even there, behind that strong wall she could feel the cold of the fast streaking snow, its bright lines swift as time. She began moving among the tables, along the walls, moving chairs aside, standing to stare up at each. Panther Room and Meadowbrook and Palm Beach Alibi Club. Rhumboogie and Billingsley's Bocago and Johnny Bennett's Haig and Billy Berg's and Jack Lynch's Walton Roof. He watched her, letting her be. He knew it was a night he had long been moving toward. It was going to be a night he would not soon forget.

My, my, she said in a small voice. It certainly does. Time certainly does.

While he studied her, noting the good line of cheek and brow and lip, the well-cut ankle. He couldn't see her hair. It was tucked up inside that smart little hat. But he was sure it would be the fine same gold he knew so well. The fine family resemblances.

The world, he cried suddenly in an awkward burst of eloquence. The world must really be her oyster.

She looked at him from the back of the room.

Yes, she said thoughtfully. Yes, it was. But she was born Leo. And there is no R in August. Could I have another?

Drink or smoke?

Oh, drink, she said, coming back to him. Don't you read what it says on cigarette packs these days? It never says that on liquor bottles.

Did you take water? I didn't notice.

Thanks. But not too much water. Never too much water.

She thought the fresh drink would drive away the dangerous, new feeling she had that if he didn't soon recognize her she could not stand it. She wanted suddenly to go. But instead she turned and watched the swift snow flit etching past the window. She

smiled then and her great, broken eyes ranged the room and
then she looked at him almost cruelly.

She hasn't changed really, she said. You'd be amazed. You
might not even believe it. Time has hardly noticed her. She's
just like she is in this room. And all the years are just like that
snow out there. They haven't touched her.

He smiled at her, nodding.

Well, don't you believe me? she said with a husky edge of
savageness.

You don't have to tell me that, he said, softly. I know that. In
some ways I know Francie better than you do, Magda.

No, you don't, she laughed into her glass. It's nice of you to
say—but you really don't. But she still *is* beautiful.

And the thought of it spread like candleshine in her eyes and
warmed her face to a wreath of smiles.

Beautiful! Beautiful! she chanted, dancing in a small circle
before his table, her gloved hands uplifted and the ice chinking
in her glass. Oh, beautiful, beautiful, beautiful, she sang in de-
light. More beautiful than she was at any prom dance in those
springs before the war.

She stopped turning suddenly and stood with the glass uplifted
yet to the light. She looked down at him like an aging goddess
who has slipped through no fault of her own but because of a
widespread decline in belief. The smile faded slowly from her
lips.

I'll take you there. But I warn you— she whispered suddenly
in a slow, guarded, almost choking voice, and she shook her
head again and motioned to all the pictures with a compassing
swing of her glass. I warn you no one on earth is as beautiful as
this.

He hesitated, leaning toward her. And for a moment she was
afraid she had gone too far and that he would want her to take
him up to that emptiness. Then he bit his lip. He shook his
head. He smiled and suddenly looked as old as she.

She rocked upon her heels with the teetering, steady grace of
practiced drunkenness.

And so, she said. You're going to let old Magda go back to the hotel. Alone. Back to her lonely baby.

She saw his nod and shook the ice, staring deep into her empty glass. She shrugged and stretched.

Anyhow, that's where all good fairy stories should end, isn't it? she said. With lonely babies in their mothers' arms?

What will you tell her? he smiled.

I'll try to tell her about the New Moon, she said. If such a thing could ever be told.

Maybe you shouldn't, he said, solemnly, frowning a little.

Oh, yes, yes. Oh, my God, yes.

Why, Magda?

Oh, because she so much needs to hear it!

Doesn't she know how wonderful she is?

Yes, but women always need to be told. And once she's sure of it—

She laughed.

—then maybe she'll stop asking me. Maybe she'll let me alone. And let me get some very hard-earned sleep.

Before she went she stood looking up strangely, timidly, boldly into his face. She stood there between his diffident hands on her shoulders. She stood waiting, terribly. She stood hoping, searching, letting herself be searched, opening her face suddenly to the greatest intimacy of his eyes. Because for a moment she prayed that he would know her. He wanted to see her back across the street to the hotel because it was snowing so hard by now but she wouldn't let him. She searched his kind face a spell longer, then gave her crooked, little smile and pulled his face down and carefully kissed him on both eyes. Then she sobbed a word that he did not hear and would always wonder about after and was gone into the snow.

He sat alone a long time afterward. When he heard five o'clock striking in the kitchen he felt a sudden, savage hunger. The jukebox had stopped playing. He had not bothered to fetch another coin from the register. He fixed himself a big breakfast in the kitchen. He took it out front to the table nearest the window

to watch day rise behind the snow. The wild storm had seemed
to quicken. It whirled faster and faster beyond the glass. All of
the street lay like the painted village in a toy snowstorm ball. It
seemed certain to Martin as he stared at the snowfall's white
disguises that when the sun of noon came to banish them he
would find a different town beneath. Perhaps he would be
changed some way himself. It frightened him. He did not want
to change. And yet it seemed even now that behind the icy
whine of the wind, beyond the fragile walls of that night he
could already hear new songs. Yes, it seemed to him certain that
other songs would come. Perhaps the way the wind blew now
that was like the wailing rise of a trumpet. . . . Then he knew it
was not the wind and he knew it was not his fancy. Martin
grabbed his hat and shouldered out into the street. He felt the
lash of silver flakes against his eyes as he ran. Through the
muffled town he saw the red lamp of the car groping for the lip of
the alley behind the heaped snows at the hotel corner.

Daylight shone in a rim of icy fire beneath the cuff of black-
ness. Sloan, the hotel manager, was there with the scared-faced
bellhop and the two night clerks. They stood by the
Lowndesville police car. The light from its circling red lamp
dusted their staring faces. He moved between them toward the
place.

She must have been on that icy fire escape, Sloan said.

Who is she? someone else asked.

She was that singer. She was here last night with that bunch
at the Auditorium.

But they checked out at three A.M., the night clerk said.

Well, wasn't she one of them?

I don't know.

I guess they just left without her.

Martin shouldered past them with such physical authority that
each of them seemed to know instantly that he belonged there,
that he must go there. It was as though he had been coming that
way for years. It was as if this place in the snow were the end of
some long and difficult Arctic trek, a journey of considerable
peril and unrecorded loneliness. He saw her then. He recognized

her at once. He had not seen her in thirty years. But he knew her immediately. Because she had not changed. She did not lie as though she had fallen seven stories onto the snowy bricks of an alley. She lay with a curious premeditation of arrangement, as if she might have been carefully posed there upon an extravagant expanse of ermine by some early *Esquire* photographer. The snow had already begun to powder her face with its frivolous, bright patina. But he could see that she wore the same pink chiffon dress. He knew her; she had not changed. She lay almost in the gesture of a ballet. In her left hand she held the graceful pink lawn handkerchief with which she kept time to the orchestra's bright brass bidding. Her fingers pinched it tightly so that it did not blow away in the kicking puffs of snow that gusted across her. Her waved gold hair lay spilled about her on the mantled cobbles. She looked asleep and it looked like a good sleep, hard-earned.

He hardly thought about her the rest of that winter. By spring he seldom played her records on the jukebox. That summer he replaced her photographs with tasteful reproductions of modern French lithographs and op-art posters. He changed the name of the New Moon to Dale's Burger Pit. The place was altered almost overnight. The younger set never came there but the older married couples who fancied themselves of the Hip Generation found a certain mod quality about the place. Soon he opened a branch in the nearby town where he had gone to college. He made a small fortune.

He seldom thought of her again. But he thought a good deal about Magda. He fancied afterward that she had stayed around Lowndesville. He kept hoping that perhaps some night she would come in on the bus from Pittsburgh or on the midnight National Limited from New York. She seemed like a woman he would have liked to learn to know. He kept hoping he would see her. But he never did.

On summer nights when couples were all through ordering and just wanted to sit there till closing time, Martin would go stand in the screen door. He would watch the faint glow of light from the hotel round the corner. In the early hours when the fog came up from the river and paled the dark town in its clasp like the cheap ghosts of winter snow he would prowl the empty streets. Now and then in his tone-deaf way he would whistle the unrecognizable fragment of a tune. Often he would stop and seem to tilt his head and listen. And then walk on.

THE LAST OF THE CHIEFS

By morning light I saw moonstains on the Persian rug.
—Davis Grubb, notebooks

Nobody remembers them now in the hometown. The old ones are all gone who knew those two—Sam and his brother Luke. And who really knew them? you might well ask. For a stranger pair there never was—Sam with his quiet, gentle-born ways and Luke, loud and drunk and more brother to the Devil than to Sam. You'd never really have taken them for brothers at all if you had seen them together there in the little shop. Like as not you wouldn't have seen Luke at all but you'd have seen Sam— squatting with his plane and chisel and mallet in a great clean heap of shavings as white as his own fear-stricken face. Then you might wonder what the boy was afraid of until you heard his older brother high in the garret of the old blue building, smashing a bottle into the rafters or putting his fist through a pane at the sight of his own fierce face in the glass.

It was Sam who did all the work. The business would have gone to vinegar if it hadn't been for Sam. Though you might say Luke had been the brains at the first. And you might thank him for that, if for nothing else, since the business did put the hometown on the map in a manner of speaking. Old Judge Bruce remembered the brothers' coming—just before the war with

Spain—and of his lending Luke five hundred dollars to make a
start. The judge used to say Luke wasn't a bad sort then and Sam
was just a boy of four or so. Still the portents were there—the
hint of early darkness in the eyes of Luke, the first wild curve of
genius in the boy's hands.

People would ask you, on the packet to Wheeling or in the
lobby of the Brass Hotel after dinner, Where are you from? And
when you had told them, you were proud somehow when they'd
say, Oh yes! That's the town where they make the cigar store
Indians. Sometimes—if they were high-and-mighty-turned—
they would snicker a little. But just the same you were proud
because, before the coming of the brothers, the hometown was
no different from a hundred others along the Ohio as far north as
Pittsburgh and on down to Louisville. A little prettier than most,
perhaps—with its sleepy, tree-covered streets and the fine brass
cannon on the courtyard lawn. But no different.

It was after the war—the Spanish war—that Luke took to
drinking. Judge Bruce said Luke put down his chisel one day and
never picked it up again and with the same hand picked up a red
bottle and never put that down. From that time on it was young
Sam who did all the work and it was really then that the town
began to grow famous, for the chisel went magic in the hands of
the boy and the Indian chiefs stood in more than mere wooden
majesty about the walls of the little workshop of the blue frame
house. And the big wooden crates went out into the land by the
score, by packet and by rail—to parts of the Union as far north
as the Nutmeg State and as far downriver as the Sugar Coast
towns. It seemed to us that every village in the world had a
tobacco shop with a cigar store Indian chief from the brothers'
little shop. Arley Francis bought the last of them to stand in
front of his place and it was the only one in town, really—the
only one we could call our own—and there it stood—the last
and the greatest of the chiefs—before the window of Arley's tobacco store (heaped high with fragrant Kentucky twist and spicy
bright Burley and Maryland kite-foot) for the daily worship and
wonderment of boys both old and young. It was better than life
size (or so it seemed)—lithe and hard-boned and broad-shoul-

dered as all Americans know an Indian should be; its face richly
glorious with tough-grained mahogany dignity and long-suffering
pride; its wooden feathers as glinting and iridescent as if they had
been plucked that very morning from a turkey's tail. Indeed it
almost seemed to be trying to speak and this was something else
in the face—something about this last of the chiefs that was not
to be found in any of the others. Something strange and dark.
But that's Ev Limber's story—not mine, really. Ev lived in the
slatternly boardinghouse that leaned out over the trash-deep alley behind the brothers' blue frame house. Poor soul. Nobody
ever leant an honest ear to anything Ev ever said—not without
making some mean joke that sent the poor old fool mumbling
angrily off down the street. But Ev had eyes and he had ears.
And what Ev saw and heard that spring and summer when Luke
disappeared forever and the young boy and the dark girl went
down the river never to return seems to me to have the ring of
truth—if not of fact. Who would believe that old simpleton?
people would say, like as not. And I would answer, I would. And
so might you.

Luke, lying in his tangle of dirty bedclothes with two weeks'
growth of beard on his face, eyed the musty rafters of his attic
room one spring morning and decided he would take unto himself a wife. He got up and went over to stare at himself in the
cracked brown mirror over the washstand. Downstairs the rap of
Sam's mallet on the chisel head made the only sound in the
house. Luke fetched his razor and lathered up and shaved. Then
he went to the trunk under the window and got out his meeting
suit, brushed it carefully, and laid it on the cot. After he had
bathed and dressed he stared at himself again in the glass. His
square, brutish face mugged and grimaced with pleasure. Then
he went down the stairs, whistling an evil tune and pondering in
his head which father in the town he would honor by making his
daughter the wife of one of the world's great men. Judge Bruce
should be the first—the gentle, sad Matilda should be the bride
of Luke.

The boy Sam was busy at the workbench.

How long will you take with that figure? asked Luke in a voice quiet with cruelty.

I don't reckon, said Sam, that it should take me more than an hour past suppertime, Luke.

You've been on it a week! shouted Luke. It will be done by four o'clock or else I'll fetch you such a wharping as will shake the back teeth from your head.

And with that he struck his brother a blow on the shoulder that knocked the mallet from his fingers and sent him bumping among the wooden horses.

Then Luke straightened his shoestring tie and went out the door, headed for Judge Bruce's office on Court Street. This part of it is gospel fact, for the Judge told of that morning long years after. I can remember his fine black Virginia eyes crackling with anger when he would tell of Luke striding into the little office, done up like a Natchez gambler and flicking ashes insolently among the Judge's papers.

I have decided to make your daughter my wife, Luke had said. Just like that. There was no humility in that dark heart.

Yes, Luke was a big man, and likely could have broken the Judge in the fingers of his left hand, but that morning he fled like a whipped feisty dog when the old man snatched a riding crop from the glass umbrella stand and hided him into the street. But this was not to be the end of the business. All that morning Luke visited the town's fathers, each time a little less arrogance showing in his cruel blue eyes, but each time a little more bitterness and helpless rage. By eleven o'clock that morning he had been chased out of every office and store in town—twice with a buggy whip laying stoutly about his ears and three times with the cold tip of a pistol under his coattails. At high noon he was drunk, his fancy Louisville duds all disheveled and filthy, his hair stringing miserably down over his hard, raging eyes. Up the middle of Pike Street he came, a red bottle in his hand and curses against the townspeople echoing in the street against the storefronts. When he staggered at last into the workshop Sam put down the linen cloth and the jar of wax and met Luke's wild eyes bravely. The chief was finished—two hours before the four o'clock deadline—but the boy knew just the same what he was in for. And the grand wooden figure of Cornstalk stood up as hard and unflinching as Sam's own courage and watched as Luke belabored Sam for ten minutes with a stick of maple.

At nine that night Luke woke up, opened his bloodshot eyes and rolled on his back to stare into the dim garret timbers of his room. The empty red bottle fell and broke tinkling on the floor beside him. Shadows swelled, took form, and broke again into cobwebs of nothing before Luke's swollen eyes. The incredible faces of the morning sprang into his vision—the faces of the townsfolk who unbelievably had turned down this magnanimous gift he had tendered them. Luke got up, stumbled, crashed into the rickety, peeling washstand and stared at himself in the mirror. Slowly his huge fist knotted, rose, and shattered through the looking glass.

Damn them! he roared, snatching the frame from the wall and hurling it into the shadows. Damn them all! I'll have me a wife—the prettiest wife in all the river lands! I'll have me a wife even if—even if—

Then the scowl went from Luke's face and gently there were the beginnings of a smile. He groped his way back to the cot and sat on the edge.

Why yes! he whispered. Why yes—that's it! Yes!

And he chuckled to himself. The idea tickled him almost beyond endurance. It delighted him—growing first from a small delicious fancy to a roaring, riotous certainty. Luke lay back on the cot, rolling from side to side and bawling with laughter. Then after a bit he stopped, listening. The old house, but for the distant ticking of a deathwatch beetle somewhere deep in the wood, was silent. Sam slept downstairs on his raggedy straw tick amid the wood shavings of the toolroom. Rising, Luke lighted his lamp. He went stumbling cautiously down the narrow stairs, his huge shadow throwing long Indian shapes along the damp yellow plaster of the walls. Then, holding the guttering lamp high above his head, Luke strode heavily into the room where Sam was sleeping.

Get up! he roared.

Sam, frightened out of his wits, sat up under the dirty patch-work quilt and rubbed his eyes.

Get up, I said! bawled Luke again, fetching Sam's shoulder a shove with the toe of his boot.

Sam stood up in his nightshirt, shaking more from the thin cold of the damp river night than from that fear of Luke that he had long since learned to swallow with his daily bread.

What is it, Luke? said Sam quietly, trying to steady his chattering teeth.

Tomorrow, said Luke, putting the lamp on the workbench and fetching out tobacco and paper to make him a smoke. Tomorrow I'm having Frank Tomlinson to fetch over here the finest maple log in West Virginia. Tomorrow you'll start to work.

Is it to be Tecumsah or Cornstalk? asked Sam.

Neither, damn you! roared Luke. It's not a damned cigar store chief you'll be starting on tomorrow!

He crouched over the lamp, his huge hands cupped round the smoky chimney to catch a light for his cigarette.

This is for me, he chuckled. This, Sammy boy, is for me! You're going to make me—a wife!

A . . . a . . . wife, whispered Sam, staring into the madness that raged and stormed there behind Luke's blue eyes.

A wife! roared Luke. A woman ten thousand times more beautiful than any of these simpering calico trollops with their fancy cotillions and their high and mighty ways! A beauty, Sammy! A real beauty—five foot seven and not an inch more nor less! Black hair and black eyes and the fight and lust of Cherokee royalty in her veins! I'll show these wharfboat lords a man's woman!

And with a storm of wild, terrible laughter he snatched up the lamp and left the room in a darkness that fairly rose to clutch Sam's throat.

A wife, thought Sam, sinking back down in the dry straw pallet. A wife for Luke. A woman—

And drawing the quilt tight against his quaking lips Sam lay long into the night, listening to the creaking house and the blowing of a boat beyond the Devil's Elbow. Then as gray daylight crept over the windowsills like the fingers of Dread it-self, Sam pressed his face into the fragrant straw of his pallet, crying for the first time in years.

At seven o'clock that morning when Luke appeared at the bottom of the steps Sam looked up from the workbench in sur-prise. Luke was dressed in his best checked suit and his Stetson hat and his hair was combed and reeking with pomade. Under his arm was his fat trunk.

Where are you going, Luke? said Sam.

First, said Luke, putting the trunk by the doorway, I'm going to see Frank Tomlinson about that maple log. Then I'm catching the morning packet to Louisville to fetch a trousseau for my bride. The night I get back we'll be married.

Sam clutched the edge of the workbench till his knuckles grew white as ice.

Married, he whispered. Married—to a—wooden figure!

Married! roared Luke. Not to a wooden figure but to the prin-cess of the Cherokee Nation, Sammy my boy! So sharpen your chisel! Mix your colors gently! Fetch down a jar of rarest wax and a pack of finest sandpaper! For if I come back on the Pitts-burgh packet three weeks from tonight and you haven't fash-ioned me a wife fit for the love of the Grand Mogul himself—I'll pick you apart with these two bare hands of mine!

Judge Bruce used to tell of the morning of Luke's leaving. Re-membered seeing him through the dusty window of his law of-fice, lugging his trunk on his big shoulder, his mad face set toward the chimneys of the morning packet standing at the wharf. He remembered, too, just before noon, seeing Frank Tomlinson's mares pull the sagging old wagon up to the brothers' shop and Frank unload a beautiful log of purest maple. Was Luke gone forever? everyone asked. And the men of the hometown, however much they hated him, were still guardful of the fame and business the brothers had brought and the town mothers worried, too, but about poor Sam—seventeen now and lonely and scarred from his long, bitter apprenticeship.

For a whole week after Luke's departure nobody saw Sam. By day, passersby would peer through the flyspecked windows of the shop but caught no sight of the boy and by night no lamps were lighted. Some thought Sam had run away, but none of them knew the fear he held toward Luke or they'd have known how unlikely he was ever to try to escape it. Ev Limbers said—and this was a wild guess for no one ever knew for sure—that Sam had gone down into the woods along the river that week in search of tints and dyes subtle enough for his masterpiece. Colors more perfect and exquisite than the store-bought stains he used on the chiefs; wild, wilderness colors, perhaps—the black juice of the pokeberry for eyes and hair—the blood of a she-fox for the red of lips more red than lips have ever been—and rare, red earth for the dusky, wild flesh. And questing, too, perhaps, after some new woodland cunning he would need.

Then one morning the people heard the familiar sound of mallet and chisel in the old workshop—heard the steel bite into the close-grained wood and the sound of the plane being honed cut through the mist of eight o'clock. Those who came to peer through the windows saw nothing, for the blinds were pulled to the sills, and all the curious ones had to chew on was the sound of the patient bite and cut of the tools in Sam's skilled hands and the rasp of sandpaper and now—strangest sound of all from that troubled, tragic house—the whistling of a boy.

On Friday evening of the second week Judge Bruce's kindly wife, Grace, who had baked a whole heaping kitchen table full of green apple pies, caught up one of them in a clean tea towel and headed for the blue frame house with the pie wrapped still steaming in the starchy cloth. It was dusk and behind the cracked blinds of the workshop she could see that Sam had lighted a lamp and was working on into the evening. Grace knocked three times on the old door and waited. It was a long time before Sam came, though she could hear his hurried footsteps among the dry chips inside. Then he was there—the door opened to just a thin bar of yellow light.

I brought you a pie, Sam, Grace said, trying to get a peek inside. I thought you might be hungry.

Thank you, Mrs. Bruce, said Sam softly, opening the door a foot or so to reach out and take it. And in that moment Grace caught a glimpse of the room within and gasped. Indeed, she blushed hotly—a talent which came easily to women of her time.

Thank you, Sam said again, and hastily shut the door.

Judge Bruce never believed her—what she said she had seen. Nor did any of the women of her Flinch Club. And that was just as well, for the people of the hometown, for all their goodness, were not what you might call a band of freethinkers. Even Grace herself was never sure that her rheumy eyes had not been mistaken—betrayed by a trick of dusk and lamplight and old age. Still it seemed, most certainly at the time, that standing behind Sam by the workbench in the brothers' shop had been the wooden figure of a beautiful young girl—her naked flesh the color of rarest Pocahontas County maple, eyes and hair the rich black of the pokeberry, and lips like the flame of autumn leaves. In the end Grace told herself that she hadn't really seen it. Luke was the evil one of the family. Not poor Sam.

Well, the story from there was mostly Ev Limber's and not really mine—any of it—belonging as it does to Ev and the Bruces and the people of the hometown. But it was Ev's part of the story that, more than anything, brought an ending and some sense to the thing. For it was Ev who saw it all, he swore, with his own eyes that strange night that Luke returned from Louisville to claim his Indian bride.

Sam had worked those three weeks until his eyes at night burned in his head, burned after he had closed them with the red shine of the maple grain and his hands were blistered and cracked from the tireless shaping and cutting and rubbing of the long, devoted work. For the first ten days he had worked with the desperation of fear. Then in the days of the last week, he found himself, oddly, discovering a lightness and joy in his work so that, when he was not thinking, he would find himself whistling or humming softly to himself. As he worked, the figure grew more perfect and smooth and finished—the mouth at last seemed almost as if it would speak and Sam knew some way how the voice would be—husky and thrilling as free winds through red leaves at the end of summer; sad, too, with a sadness that he had sometimes seen in the eyes of the chiefs. Sam worked patiently and tirelessly and at night his sleep was broken with the vision of his labor and, almost imperceptibly as the days passed, the labor of fear became a labor of love.

On the night of Luke's return, Sam gave the figure one last brisk rub with hot linseed oil and stepped back, his heart pounding in his throat, to survey his creation. A spring storm stirred and muttered in the hills down the river and the air of the room seemed fresh and living from the cool wind that blew from the open back door to the alley. And it seemed to Sam almost as if the bosom of the girl rose and fell above her wild wilderness heart that night and he laid his fingers on one tawny shoulder half expecting it to shiver under his touch. Then—scarcely knowing he was doing so—Sam stepped up to the figure and kissed its wooden lips. In the instant that followed Sam was sure he had lost his mind. The spring thunder spoke once downriver and a gust of wind blew through the house from the open door and sent the flame in the lamp chimney dim and guttering on its wick. Sam's ears couldn't believe themselves. Yet he had heard it.

I'm cold, she said.

Yes, Ev Limbers, who was watching from the open door far back in the dark kitchen, swears to that.

I'm cold, she had said. And her voice had been exactly as Sam had heard it in all those troubled dreams. And looking up, the poor, fear-crazed, blushing Sam had seen the Cherokee princess standing there, hugging her arms about her small breasts and shivering in a mighty mortal way.

Sam ran in terror from the room and hid himself in the pantry for many minutes, trying to get his mind in order and hearing nothing but his own roaring thoughts and the tea thumping under the kettle lid on the stove. Fearfully he fingered the thing over in his rioting mind—half-knowing it was true, half-wondering if he had really lost his wits. Then Sam sat up straight in the split-bottom chair and straightened his shoulders.

She's cold, poor dear! he cried to himself reproachfully. You heard her say that! Go fetch her some clothes!

They were old and faded and musty in the trunk by the cellar door—clothes that some long-dead female in the family had left behind: a pair of patent leather slippers with green brass buckles, a calico dress, and a yellowed linen petticoat. Trembling, Sam gathered them up and ran to the door. He reached them around the doorsill for her to take. It seemed unreal again when the little hand reached out and took them—a hand that was warm with life. And yet strangely Sam was past the panic of it, and he found himself thinking pleasedly, She *is* nice. Modest as a young girl should be. Indian through and through but not a heathen like the pictures in the books. A real Cherokee princess with breeding and good blood in her heart. He stood for a long while by the door, listening to the sounds that came from the room— the rustle of the ancient linen and the pleased birdlike cries of a girl's voice at the still-gay colors of the calico print. Sam knocked softly. Then he peeked round the corner. There she stood in the middle of the room in the pile of maple chips, smiling shyly at him, her black eyes warm with something that frightened and pleased Sam at the same time.

Am I pretty? she cried, in that enchanting voice.

Beautiful, sighed Sam. Simply beautiful.

He felt behind him for a chair and sat down somewhat shakily, his legs crossed, his fingers folded over his knee.

My brother, Sam said, clearing his throat uneasily. He'll be home tonight. I reckon he'll fall in love with you first time he sees you! I reckon any man who didn't—

At this she gave a little laugh like a handful of tossed gold coins—a laugh that somehow surprised and bothered Sam—then away she went, bustling about the room, as women will, trying to set things in order.

Luke . . . continued Sam uneasily, trying to keep his eyes off her; staring high into the cobwebs on the ceiling. He cleared his throat again. You're going to be married to him, you know. Tonight.

At the sound of her voice—that same impudent little laugh— Sam looked down at her quickly and grew instantly pale and sick. She was smiling wickedly and shaking her head. Sam jumped to his feet.

But you've got to! he cried. Don't you see? That's the whole thing! You've got to marry Luke! If you didn't—I don't know what he'd do!

But still she smiled that stubborn little smile and still she shook her head till the black tresses swung. And fetching a broom she began to hum a little tune to herself and to sweep up the long years' accumulation of sawdust and shavings on the floor.

Oh, no. Oh, no! she chanted, with the gay little tune to her words. I will not marry Luke!

And dancing past Sam she reached up and pinched him pertly on the nose.

Lord God! cried poor Sam, confronted for the first time in his life with feminine perversity. You don't know him! You don't seem to realize that he figures to marry you first thing he gets off the boat tonight! He's gone clean to Louisville to fetch back a big trunkful of pretties for your honeymoon! Dresses and gowns and camisoles and dancing pumps! Sam, he says to me the morning he left, Sam, make me a wife!

I will take care of him! sang the girl and danced around the middle of the room like a golden toy, the old calico skirts whirling and twisting about her slim, dark legs.

The packet docks at midnight! cried Sam. That's only a half hour away! You don't know him! He'll kill us both!

I will take care of him! sang the girl, like some wild, free bird of the woods.

I know what! cried Sam. We can run off—now! We can run off and Luke need never know—!

Oh, no. Oh, no! she chanted, her white teeth flashing in her dark lovely mouth. We'll not run away. I will take care of Luke!

And all poor Sam could do was to stand and watch her dancing round the room and wonder what to do and try to think what she could mean—that she would take care of Luke. But she would not say what it would be and all the answer Sam got for all his querying was that strange, secret smile on her singing lips and the mystery in her eyes that were deep as the pools along the shore under the willow trees.

When the boat blew for the landing Sam made up his mind that he would fight Luke for the girl if it came to that; knew now that he loved her and that he could never let Luke take her for his bride. The two of them sat waiting in the workshop: Sam, uneasy but hard and ready as he had never been before—a man now—and the Cherokee princess, calm and smiling on a split-bottom chair before the door. Then they could hear him coming up the street, loud and drunk and full of the old cursedness that the town had always known him for.

Sam ran to the window and peered from behind the drawn shade into the dim yellow gaslight of the street.

Lord God! he cried. If you could ever see him. He's all done up like an Indian chief. With feathers hanging clean to his heels!

But she didn't have to see. She could hear him.

It's me! Luke roared. The chief of the Cherokee Nation hisself! Come to claim his little dark-skinned bride!

And striding up to the door he kicked it open and stood teetering on his heels, staring drunkenly in at the girl smiling at him there.

O, ho! roared Luke, throwing down his trunk. You've done well, Sammy! It's my princess for sure!

Sam felt the surge of anger pound in his head and reached behind him for the wooden mallet. But then—Sam thought his heart would burst. He would not believe his eyes. Luke was walking toward the Cherokee princess with outstretched arms. And she unbelievably, was stepping between those arms with her dark, lovely face uplifted for a kiss. And then as suddenly as she had kissed him she stepped back and smiled at Sam. Sam moved cautiously forward with the mallet clutched in his fist. But Luke did not move. Luke did not breathe. He stood taller somehow than he had been—immovable, mute and darker than before—his hands outstretched for all the world like the wooden chiefs that had made his fame. Still unbelieving, Sam stepped forward and ran his fingers across the wooden face, the wooden feathers,

the wooden clothes, the dark immovable woodenness that was
all of Luke now.

Judge Bruce remembered the day that Sam sold the last of the
Indian chiefs—and the most magnificent—to Arley Francis and
left next day with his strange dark bride on the packet for New
Orleans. Nobody ever saw them again and nobody ever saw Luke
again—though Ev Limbers says that's not so. Ev says you could
see Luke for years after—any day you pleased, rain or shine—in
front of Arley Francis's tobacco store. Ev says—but then everyone in the hometown knew he was mad—that the kiss that gave
the Cherokee princess life was the kiss that turned Luke to wood.
And I for one would never say he was wrong. For nights sometimes when the river fog made things seem not quite as they are
or when torrents of March rain would flood over the gutters of
the little tobacco shop and stream down the wooden face of the
last of the chiefs, it seemed to some that far beneath the polished, painted face there raged a dark and secret struggling.

RETURN OF VERGE LIKENS

There would be some dignity to acts of revenge if they were not usually symbolic.

If a man avenged himself for a wrong against the men who did the wrong, it would be fair.

Yet, most people are wronged by a parent and take it out on a lover forty years later and ten times removed from any conceivable guilt.

Or a ruler who had an evil nurse may topple kingdoms as her surrogate and because of his hatred of her.

—Davis Grubb, notebooks

And the funny part was that not even Riley McGrath's own friends blamed Saturday Likens for killing him. Some even found a kind of wry, burlesque justice in it; as much in the humiliating posture of Riley's actual death as in the ponderous and infallible method that Saturday went about bringing it to him. Because whatever fear or awe or envy the people of Tygarts County held toward Riley McGrath, self-elected emperor of our state, they knew that he'd had no right to shoot down Saturday's old father Stoney Likens that night.

Some said there was a woman mixed in it somewhere—a seventeen-year-old hustler from Baltimore Street—and like as not this was the truth. Stoney Likens had worked at odd jobs for

Riley McGrath for nearly twenty years, off and on, so the probability of any business disaffection was slight. At any rate the two men came together that night in the Airport Café on Route 50 and nobody remembers exactly what happened from then until the moment when Riley McGrath snatched out his special deputy's revolver and shot Stoney McGrath once in the liver and through the lungs twice. The two boys Saturday and Monday came when Sheriff Reynolds sent for them and viewed the body of the old man with bleak, hill-born muteness.

It was Mr. McGrath that done it, explained Fred Starcher, who ran the juke joint. But Stoney taken and swung at him with a beer bottle. So it was self-defense.

Saturday looked at Fred and Sheriff Reynolds with the flat blue eyes that Riley McGrath was to see so close and with such finality on a day fifteen months hence.

Daddy didn't have no gun on him, Saturday said patiently. So I can't see no fair reason why Mr. McGrath had to shoot him. If Daddy had had a gun then it would have been different.

Fred opened his mouth to explain how it all was again and then he saw Saturday Likens's eyes, cold and flat as creek stones.

Well, it seemed to me like it was self-defense, he said, looking away.

Although it wouldn't have mattered anyway. Self-defense or premeditated murder or just plain target practice. Because there wasn't a man in the state of West Virginia who could stand up against Riley McGrath for very long without losing his job, his bank account, or some of his blood. And when word spread round the county that night that Riley McGrath had shot old Stoney Likens, everybody knew well and good that there would be a brief hearing at the spring session of criminal court and nobody would say very much about Law and nobody would look at anybody else very often and afterward Riley McGrath would have a little drink of apple brandy with Judge Beam back in the little, dusty records room of the county courthouse and they would tell a joke or two and that would be the end of it.

It isn't self-defense, Saturday reiterated to Fred Starcher there by the jukebox, when a man with a gun shoots down an old man that don't have none.

And the brother Monday had stood by dumbly heeding the exchange, slack-jawed with fascination, eyes darting from first one to the other in their turn, head cocked, the moon face bland with an almost blasphemous and idiot innocence. Then suddenly, like wraiths, he and Saturday were gone out of the place into the March dark, roaring up Route 50 in Stoney's old fruit truck to the farmhouse where they had lived with their father since the frail, eternally whimpering Clara Likens had died more than a decade before.

Bud, don't take it so hard, Monday said. Like as not Mr. McGrath was drunk.

The flat eyes turning from the highway to Monday shone with loathing in the dark.

He was your daddy, too, Saturday said. Your blood kin. You gutless son of a bitch.

Don't talk that way, Bud! whined Monday. If there was something to be done I'd be all for it. But there ain't. There just ain't!

There is, said Saturday, the flat eyes fixed to the traffic stripe. There is something to be done and I am fixing to do it.

What?

Monday exhaled the word like a breath of pipe smoke.

Kill Mr. McGrath, said Saturday.

Kill— Bud, you must be crazy! Monday cried out. Mr. McGrath's the biggest man in Tygarts County—maybe the whole state of West Virginia! He's got that big thirty-eight strapped to him everywhere he goes—even when he puts his nightshirt on! Why, Mr. McGrath owns every slot machine, punchboard, and two-dollar hustler on Baltimore Street. Don't Senator Marcheson hisself sit and drink whisky with Mr. McGrath in the lobby of the Stonewall Jackson every time he comes to town? Don't every policeman in town tip his cap when Mr. McGrath walks by?

That don't matter a bit, said Saturday. I'll find a way. It may take me a good long while but I'll find a way to do it.

And there was no arguing. Because that was all Saturday ate
or drank or breathed or dreamed about from that night on. Monday seldom mentioned it to his brother again and when the two
of them had finished the ten-hour shift at the box factory they
would drive home together in the old fruit truck, Monday mute
and troubled by his brother's side, knowing what his thoughts
were without ever asking or having to ask, feeling the raging
brain of Saturday weighing and sizing the several and various
countenances of assassination, discarding parts of the plot as he
might throw away bits of machinery that did not fit a motor he
was building.

One night after supper when they were alone and neither had
spoken for nearly an hour, Monday felt suddenly as if the im-
palpable violence of Saturday's obsession had secretly been
turned on him.

Then God damn it! he shrilled to the pale, quiet profile of his
brother there in the shadow of the porch eaves. Then God damn
it, why don't you just get it over with! Why don't you hide out
along the fence by the Airport Café some night and shoot him in
the back! He comes there every night with that black-haired
Mary from Clark Street! Every night— Why don't you—

No, said Saturday, thoughtfully, with neither surprise nor anger at Monday's outburst. I want Mr. McGrath to see my face
when I kill him. If I take and shoot him down that way, why, he
wouldn't never know it was me that done it to him. When I do
it I want Mr. McGrath to look at my face a good long while and
know who it is. And I want the killing to take a long, slow
while.

Monday stood up, shivering, and went on to bed, leaving Saturday on the porch amid the winking fireflies and the unnatural,
cloying sweetness of the honeysuckle that the long-dead Clara
had planted there.

Riley McGrath was getting a shave in Rush Sigafoose's
Number One chair when Monday found him the next morning.
Monday was shaking so badly that he was afraid he would not be
able to make his speech. He had lain awake all that long night
considering it in the dark: what he would say, how he would say

it. He sat down in one of the straight-backed chairs, under the little shelf with its rows of shaving mugs: the gilded and scarlet roster of the town's genteelly successful. When the morning ritual was finished, Riley McGrath stood up, sartorial and elegant in his tailor-made sharkskin suit, and stripped a bill from the expensive billfold. When he handed it to Rush Sigafoose, Monday stood up, quaking.

Mr. McGrath, said Monday, wringing his cotton cap.

Yes, son.

The quiet, gray eyes were strangely palliative; friendly and yet, at the same time, filmed, like the blue of a freshly polished gun barrel.

Mr. McGrath, Monday said, feeling a little courage coursing back. I sure wish I could talk to you for a little while.

Certainly, son, muttered the great man. Come along across the street to my office. I have an appointment in half an hour with Judge Beam but I can give you a moment of my time. It is my feeling that a man should never grow too important to keep in touch with the people of his hometown.

The office, like a country squire's—musty, small, untended; curiously humble for such a man as Riley McGrath—was deathly still as the two men seated themselves: Monday Likens in a stiff split-bottom chair by the window and Riley McGrath in the creaking swivel behind the old, scratched desk upon which he had parlayed the destiny of a state. Monday watched as Riley licked the tip of an expensive Havana and clipped it thoughtfully.

It's about my brother Saturday, said Monday, wetting his lips and staring at Riley McGrath's sober blue tie. Our daddy was Stoney Likens.

Riley McGrath cracked a kitchen match into flame with his thumbnail. He puffed silently for a moment, and though Monday could not see them he could sense the gray eyes appraising him, weighing the situation, seeing it simultaneously from every angle.

That matter was settled during the last term of Judge Beam's court, Riley McGrath said presently. Your father attacked me, son. I shot him in self-defense that night. Nobody regretted the incident more than I did.

It's my brother Saturday, Monday reiterated as if he had not been listening at all. I don't want nothing to happen to my brother, Mr. McGrath.

Nothing need happen to him, son, grunted Riley McGrath, leafing through some papers on the desk, already finished with the interview.

Something might, Monday said.

He cleared his throat and listened to the coaxing, idiot shrilling of a wren outside.

Saturday claims he is fixing to kill you, Mr. McGrath, Monday said.

Riley McGrath leaned back in his chair and blew a cloud of smoke toward the dusty yellow windowpanes.

That's a very foolish idea for your brother to entertain, he said. Very foolish, son.

I thought, gasped Monday, and then swallowed. If maybe you was to send for him, Mr. McGrath. Talk to him. If maybe you was to explain to him how it was that night—how it was self-defense after all. It might help, Mr. McGrath. 'Deed to God, I just don't want nothing to happen to Saturday. He's all I got left now.

Nothing will happen to your brother, son, said Riley McGrath. So long as he behaves himself in this town.

And Monday sighed and stared at the hands, twisting the cap in anguish on his knees.

I understand, however, said Riley McGrath (the eyes gone cold as death now), that the death of your father may have brought about certain inconveniences—and expenses. I've thought about it often. And now I'm going to do something about that. Something that—although I don't feel I'm actually obliged to do—I think may spread oil on troubled waters.

And Monday watched Riley McGrath open the shiny alligator billfold and count out the five one-hundred-dollar bills; watched as he slipped them into an envelope, sealed it and tossed it across the desk.

There now, he said, not smiling and, at the same time, not unsmiling. I trust you and your brother won't think too unkindly of me from now on.

Saturday didn't say anything right away when Monday finally got around to confessing what he had done that day in town. It was after supper and Saturday squatted on the porch steps cleaning his rifle and listening silently as Monday babbled on apologetically.

That sure was a damn fool trick, Monday, Saturday said after a bit. But it don't change nothing. There is nothing you can do about Mr. McGrath getting killed and there is nothing he can do about it neither. It will happen certain as sunrise or Doomsday and there is nothing ary mortal in this county or in the state of West Virginia can do about it.

And then Monday was quiet for a good while before he pulled out the manila envelope and hopefully told his brother about the five one-hundred-dollar bills. Saturday lay down the rifle and came up on the porch to the rocker where Monday sat and took the envelope out of his hands. He looked at it and then he looked at Monday, not laughing, not angry, not glad, not even seeming to think or feel anything at all.

This will make it a good deal easier, Saturday said. It will save a lot of time and fuss, I reckon. It will bring the day that much closer. I hope you thanked Mr. McGrath, Monday.

Bud, I . . . I don't . . . I don't recollect. Yes . . . I think . . .

I hope you thanked him, Saturday said again, folding the envelope and stuffing it into his shirt pocket. That was real nice of Mr. McGrath to do that.

All that night Monday listened to Saturday moving restlessly about the house and when dawn stood suddenly white against the windows he started from a brief, troubled slumber and saw his brother by the bed; dressed in the single cheap blue serge suit he possessed, his good white shirt a vivid, stubborn triangle in the shadow, the square, small face mute and impassive as ever. Then Monday saw the cardboard suitcase in Saturday's hand.

Where you goin' to, bud? gasped Monday, sitting up in bed. What—

I'm catching the morning bus for Charleston, said Saturday.
I'll be gone a good long while, I reckon. Good-bye, Monday.

Where?

To Charleston, said Saturday. I told you that once. I'm going
to school with that money.

School! whispered Monday, feeling a great wave of relief.
Why, that's real fine, bud! A body can't do with too much edu-
cation and that's for sure. What kind of school?

The kind of school, said Saturday (and even in the dark,
Monday could feel that the eyes were not looking at him or at
anything at all) where I can learn to kill Mr. McGrath the right
way. Slow. The way that he'll have to look at my face a good
long time and know it's coming and there'll not be any way for
him to get out that big blue pistol of his like he done the night
he taken and shot Daddy. I been figuring it out all night, Monday. I know where it will happen now and I know how long it
will take. I don't know when I'll be back. Take good care of the
place, Monday.

And that was all there was to it. Monday had crept naked and
shivering to the dusty window and watched the thin, unforgiving
shape fade into the early April mist on its way up to the bus stop
on Route 50; moving as inexorably as a juggernaut or the piston
of some machine that had neither volition nor personal motiva-
tion.

Monday worked on alone at the box factory during the next
lonely months, moving about uneasily, needing the compan-
ionship of Saturday and yet dreading the day when his brother
should return. Often he would start up, sweating in the dark, a-
crawl with panic; believing suddenly that he should run to Riley
McGrath and try again to warn him, to communicate to him
somehow the awful, inexorable purpose of which Riley McGrath
could not be aware, inasmuch as he neither knew, nor had ever
so much as laid eyes on, Saturday Likens's person. But then after
a space of time it seemed to Monday that Saturday had gone off
forever; become dissolved finally among the faceless peoples who
inhabit the anonymous world of bus station restaurants, cheap
hotel lobbies, and Pike Street pool rooms. And at last it even

seemed that neither Saturday, nor the murder, nor even Riley McGrath himself had ever existed at all. Yet sometimes on a morning when Monday strode down Beech Street on his way to work he would spy the great, gray body of Riley McGrath sprawled out in Rush Sigafoose's Number One chair with the towels heaped and fuming on his pink, imperturbable face and Monday would shiver at the sound of Saturday's words, returning like some unholy visitation.

This was nearly sixteen months later. And never so much as a letter. No—there had been a penny postcard in the first week. Only one. With no message on it at all. A postcard from a drugstore with a picture of the Kanawha County Courthouse; lithographed in bright, blasting colors depicting the greenness of some implausible spring burgeoning in the trees among the immemorial brass cannon in the yard: colors with the cheap, naïve innocence of flowers at a country funeral yet still somehow in themselves mutely obsessed with all the candid malevolence of Saturday Likens's scheme. No message at all. This would be Saturday's way of telling his brother that he had arrived.

Of course, Riley McGrath himself had dismissed the whole business from his mind months before. Because, naturally enough, he had never really been frightened in the beginning. And the five hundred dollars had been like a twenty-five-cent piece pressed into the hand of a pouting child. Yet, for some reason the whole affair came into his mind that last morning in Rush Sigafoose's barbershop as he watched Monday swing past, eyes on the pavement, the black lunch pail in his hand. He had noticed the boy often on his way to work in the mornings and almost always Monday had glanced up through the fly-specked plate glass with a furtive, guilty look, not meeting the eyes of Riley McGrath; not really ever rising above the candy-striped towel beneath the fat chins, so that the recognition was barely implicit. And now Riley McGrath lay back smothered and wallowing in Roman comfort under the steaming towels, chuckling and remembering the whole absurd fuss as Rush Sigafoose's new barber crisply stropped the razor and whistled to himself.

Rush! Riley had murmured from beneath the steaming cloths. How's Nevada and the kids?

Rush Sigafoose remembered that part of it well because those were the last words Riley McGrath ever said to him. Rush said afterward that it was a long while before he knew anything was wrong at all. He had gone back into the storeroom for some fresh towels and a bottle of bay rum and even then, after he had returned and had been puttering around the marble shelf under the mirrors for nearly five minutes, he wasn't up to what was going on. And then he looked up and saw them in the mirror, fixed and frozen like protagonists in some monstrous waxworks pantomime: Riley McGrath, his head strained back in the headrest as far as it would go, the face purple and livid by turns, eyes starting from his head, mouth shaping idiot words that Rush could not hear and didn't much want to. Rush Sigafoose dropped the comb he had been cleaning and started toward them.

Don't come a foot closer, Mr. Sigafoose, smiled Saturday Likens softly, with the bright hollow-ground razor light as a hair on Riley McGrath's pulsing throat. For if you do—I'll cut Mr. McGrath clean to the neckbone.

So Rush sat down shaking and sick to his stomach and watched them for nearly half an hour there, trying to make out what it was that Saturday Likens was saying to Riley McGrath. Rush said that was the part of it that made him sickest of all: Saturday taking the pains to shave Riley and then telling him who he was and talking to him all that terrible, patient time with the cold, honed razor pressed taut against the fat folds of his throat; taking all that time to kill him and all the while talking in that slow, crooning voice; the way a man talks to a woman when he is making love to her, or the way a stable groom talks to a scared horse.

Rush used to tell about that part of it next to last and then he would always wind up the story in the same way. About Saturday having gone to barber college down in the capital city for a year and a half on that five hundred dollars. Just to learn how to kill a man slow. Rush had hired him the morning before—not knowing him from Adam himself—and that's the holy irony of it. Rush Sigafoose said that Saturday was the damnedest natural-born barber he'd ever seen. He swore to that. Because when Doc Brake came down from the courthouse that afternoon and looked at Riley McGrath's body he said there wasn't so much as a mark on his throat. Not so much as a single scratch.

THE CREST OF '36

Her pretty feet and the dark tendrils of hair at the nape of a
woman's neck—these are her glories, too.

—Davis Grubb, notebooks

. . . at some point of our youth we all go through a love
affair with Her.

—Mark Twain

I don't know if she was black or white. Maybe some of both. Or
maybe Indian—there was some around Glory, West Virginia,
who said she was full Cherokee and descended from the wife of a
chief who had broken loose from the March of Tears in the
1840s. Some said not descended at all—that she was that very
original woman grown incredibly old. Colonel Bruce theorized
that she was the last of the Adena—that vanished civilization
that built our great mound here in Glory back a thousand years
before Jesus.

What does it matter?

Does a seventeen-year-old boy question the race or origin or
age of his first true love?

You might well ask, In the first place, what ever possessed the
Glory Town Council to hire on Darly Pogue as wharfmaster? A
man whose constant, nagging, gnawing fear—a phobia they call

it in the books—whose stuff of nightmare and the theme of at least two attacks of the heebie-jeebies or Whisky Horrors was the great Ohio River.

Darly feared that great stream like a wild animal fears the forest fire.

There were reasons. It is said that, as an infant, he had floated adrift in an old cherry-wood pie safe for six days and six nights of thundering, lightning river storms during the awful flood of 1900.

Now I read up a lot in those little five-cent Haldemann Julius Blue Books from out Kansas way, about reincarnation and the Soul.

There was one of those little nickel blue books that says man doesn't reincarnate from his body to another human body to another human and so on. It held that our existence as spiritual creatures is divided by God among air and water and land. And we take turns as fish or birds or animals. Or man. A lifetime as a dolphin might be reincarnated as a tiercel falcon to ply the fathomed heavens in splendor and, upon death, to become again a man. Well, somehow, some way, some thing whispery inside Darly Pogue told him that the good Lord now planned that Darly's next incarnation would, quite specifically, be as an Ohio River catfish.

You can imagine what that did to Darly, what with his fear of that river.

And where could such mischievous information have originated?

Maybe some gypsy fortune-teller—they were always singing and clamoring down the river road in the springtime in their sequined head scarves and candy-colored wagons—maybe one of them told Darly that. In my opinion it was Loll who told him herself: She could be that mean.

And it was, of course, a prediction to rattle a man up pretty sore. I mean, did you ever look eyeball to eyeball with an old flat-headed, rubber-lipped, garbage-eating, mud-covered catfish? I didn't say *eat* one—God knows that nothing out of God's waters is any tastier rolled in cornmeal batter and fried in country butter.

I said did you ever look a catfish square in the whiskers? Try it next time. It'll shake hell out of you. There's a big, sappy, two-hundred-million-year-old grin on that slippery, skewered mug that seems to ask: *Homo sapiens,* how long you been around? The critter almost winks as much as to remind you that you came from waters as ancient as his—and that you'll probably be going back some day. But, pray the Lord, you'll exclaim. Not as one of *your* ugly horned tribe!

What sense does any of this make?

To hire on as wharfmaster a man who fears the very river?

To position such a man twenty-four hours a day, seven days a week in a kind of floating coffin tied with a length of breakable, cuttable rope to the shore?

Not much rhyme nor reason to this, eh?

But wait.

What if that man has ready and unique access to the smallest and greatest of the great river's secrets. Suppose he can locate with unerring accuracy the body of a drowned person. Suppose he can predict with scary precision the place where a snag is hiding in the channel or the place where a new sandbar is going to form. Suppose he can prognosticate the arrival of steamboats—hours before their putting in. What if he can board one of those boats and at one sweeping glance tell to the ounce—troy or avoirdupois—the weight of its entire cargo?

There wasn't a secret of that old Ohio—that dark, mysterious Belle Rivière—that Darly Pogue didn't have instant access to. Except one. That one, of course, was the secret he was married to: Loll, river witch, goddess, woman, whatever—she was the one secret of the great flowing Mistress that Darly did not understand.

But she was, as well, the source of all the rest of the great river's secrets.

Loll.

Dark, strange Loll.

What could possess a man to live with such a woman and on the very breast of that river he feared like a very demon?

The business all began the morning the water first showed signs of rising in the spring of '36. Everybody around Glory came down to the wharfboat full of questions for Darly Pogue and asking him either to confirm or contradict the predictions now crackling in the radio loudspeakers.

You see, I have not told you the half of Loll—what kind of creature she really was.

Look at Loll for yourself.

Imagine that it is about ten o'clock in the morning. Wisps of fog still hover like memories above the polished, slow, dark water out in the government channel. Loll creeps mumbling about the little pantry fixing breakfast for me and Darly—cornbread and ramps with home fries and catfish. Mmmmmmm. But look at her. Her face is like an old dried apple. A little laurel-root pipe is stuck in her withered, toothless gums. Her eyes wink out of deep, leathery wrinkles like mice in an old shoebag. Look at the hump of her back and her clawlike hands and the long, shapeless dotted Swiss of her only dress. This is her—this is Darly Pogue's wife Loll.

So what keeps him with her?

Why does he stay with this old harridan on the river he so disdains?

You are on board the wharfboat, in the pantry, looking at this ancient creature. Glance there on the table at the Ingersoll dollar watch with the braided rawhide cord and the watch fob whittled out of a peach pit by a man on Death Row up in Glory prison.

I said about ten o'clock.

Actually, it's five after.

In the morning.

Now turn that nickle-plated watch's hands around to twelve twice—to midnight, that is. Instantly the scene changes, alters magically. The moon appears, imprisoned in the fringes of the vast violet willow tree up above the brick landings. The stars

foxtrot and dip in the glittering water. A sweet, faint wind stirs
from the sparkling river. Breathe in now.

What is that lovely odor?

Laburnum maybe.

Lilac mixed with spice-bush and azalea. With a pinch of cin-
namon and musk.

Who is that who stands behind the bedroom door in the
small, narrow companionway?

She moves out now into the light—silvered by ardent, panting moonshine—seeming almost like an origin of light rather
than someone lit by it.

You know you are looking at the same human being you saw at
ten—ten-oh-five, to be exact—and you know it cannot be but
that it is: that, with the coming of nightfall, this has become the
most beautiful woman you have ever seen or shall ever look upon
again.

Ever.

In your lifetime.

She is naked save for a little shimmery see-through skirt and
sandals and no brassiere, no chemise, no teddy bear nor anything
else.

And she comes slipping, like a little flamewoman, down the
companionway, seeming to catch and drag all the moonlight and
shadows along with her, and knocks shyly, lovingly, on the
stateroom door of Darly Pogue.

Darly has been drinking.

At the first rumor of a flood he panicked.

Loll knocks again.

Y-yes?

It's me, lovey. I have what you've been waiting for. Open up.

Can't you tell me through the door?

But, lovey! I want your arms around me! cries Loll, the star-
light seeming to catch and glitter in the lightly tinseled aureole
of her nipples. I want to make love! I want to make whoopee!

You know I cain't get it up whilst I'm skeert bad, sweety!

Oh, do let me in!

Aw, shucks, I got a headache, see?

All right, the beautiful girl pouted.

Well? squeaked poor Darly in a teeth-chattering voice.

Well, what, lovey?

The crest! The crest of thirty-six! cried Darly. What's it going to be? Not as bad as twenty-eight or nineteen and thirteen, surely, or back in awful eighteen and eighty-four. Is it? Oh, don't spare me. I can take it. Tell me it hain't going to rise that high!

What was the crest of nineteen-thirteen? asked Loll, her pretty face furrowed as she thumbed through her memory. Yes, the crest of nineteen-thirteen at Glory was sixty-two feet measured on the wall of the Mercantile Bank.

I think so, grunted poor Darly. Yes. That's right. And the crest of thirty-six—it can't be any higher than that.

The crest of thirty-six, Loll said quietly, lighting a reefer, will be exactly four hundred and fifteen feet.

Darly was quiet except for an asthmatic squeak.

What? I'm losing my hearing. It sounded exactly like you said four hundred and fifteen feet.

I did, said Loll, blowing fragrant smoke out of her slender, sensitive nostrils.

Whoooeee, screamed poor Darly, flailing out now through the open stateroom door and galloping toward the gangplank and wearing a gaudy pair of underwear for which he had sent away to *Ballyhoo* magazine. He disappeared under the trees somewhere up on Water Street.

That left me alone with her on the wharfboat, peering out through a crack in my own stateroom door at this vision of beauty and light and sweet-smelling womanhood. By damn, it was like standing downwind from an orchard, that woman's sweet smell!

I swear she didn't look more than eighteen—about a year older than I, who hadn't ever seen a naked lady except on the backs of well-thumbed and boy-sticky cards that used to get passed around with an occasional Tillie the Toiler or Maggie and Jiggs comic in high school homeroom.

She didn't look like anything on those cards or in those little comics.

Nothing at all.

There were lights on the river: boys out jigging for frogs or gathering fish in from trot lines. The lights of the lanterns flashed on the waters and seemed to stream up through the blowing curtains and glimmer darkling on that girl.

She was so pretty.

She sensed my stare.

She turned and—to my mingled ecstasy and terror—came down the threadbare carpet of the companionway toward my door.

She came in.

A second later we were into the bunk, with her wet-lipped and coughing with passion and me not much better.

Afterward she kindly sewed the tear in my shirt and the two ripped-off buttons from our getting me undressed.

Whew!

All the time we were making love I could hear her husband— poor, dear Darly Pogue—somewheres up on Water Street reciting the story of the Flood from Genesis, at the top of his voice.

And I hain't by God no Noah neither! he'd announce every few minutes, like a candidate declining to run for office. So I hain't not your wharfmaster as of this by God hereby date!

The moon fairly blushed to see the things we did.

And with her doing all the teaching.

All through it you could hear the crackle and whisper of static from the old battery Stromberg Carlson—that and the voice of poor Darly Pogue—high atop an old Water Street elm tree, announcing that the Bible Flood was about to come again.

Who are you? I asked the woman.

I am Loll.

I know that, I said. But I see you in the morning—while you're fixing me and him breakfast and—

I am a prisoner of the moon, she said. My beauty waxes and wanes with her phases.

I don't care, I said. I love you. Marry me. I'll borrow. I'll steal.

I pondered.

I won't kill for you—but I *will* steal. Will you?

No.

Do you love me at all? I asked then in a ten-year-old's voice.

I am fond of you, she said, giving me a peck of a kiss: her great fog-gray eyes misty from our loving. You are full of lovely aptitudes and make love marvelously.

She pouted a little and shrugged.

But I do not love you, she said.

I see.

I love him, she said. That ridiculous little man who refuses to go with me.

Go? Go where, Loll? You're not leaving Glory, are you?

I'm not leaving the river, if that's what you mean. As for Darly Pogue—I adored him in that Other. Before he went away. And now he won't go forward with me again.

Before when, Loll? Forward where?

I got no answer. Her gray eyes were fixed on a circle of streetlamp that illuminated the verdant foliage of the big river elm—and among it the bare legs of poor Darly Pogue.

And now, she said. He must be punished, of course. He has gone too far. He has resisted me long enough. This final insult— his desertion of us both.

Both? I looked at her questioningly but she didn't explain.

I was getting dressed and in a hurry. I could tell she was talking in other dimensions about Things and Powers that scared me about as bad as the river did Darly Pogue. Yet I could see what her hold on him was—how she kept him living in that floating casket on top of the moving, living surface of the waters: that great river of pools and shallows, that moving cluster of little lakes, that beloved Ohio.

I eased her out of the stateroom as slick and gentle as I could, for I didn't want her passing out one of her punishments onto me.

But I knew I would never be the same.

Not after Her.

She had her fishhook deep in me.

And I suddenly knew two new things: That I was going to spend my life on the river. And that I would never marry.

Because Loll had spoilt me for even the most skilled and loving of mortal caresses.

And, what's more, she sewed my buttons back on that morning. Though the hands that held my repaired garment out to me—they were gnarled and withered like the great roots of old river trees.

Well, you remember the flood of '36. It was a bad one all right. There's a river custom to take a drink of whisky for every foot the old lady rises and I tell you Glory was a tipsy town that spring.

It was weird—looking down Seventh Street to the streetlight atop the telephone pole by the confectioner's and seeing that streetlight shimmering and shivering just ten inches from the dark, pulsing stream—that streetlight like a dandelion atop a tall, shimmering stalk of light.

Beautiful.

But kind of deathly, too.

It was a bad, bad flood in the valleys. Crest of fifty-nine feet.

But then Loll had predicted more than four hundred.

Forecast it and scared poor Darly Pogue—who knew she was never wrong—into running for his life and ending up getting himself the corner room on the fifth floor of the Zadok Cramer Hotel. There was only one higher place in Glory and that was the widow's walk atop the old courthouse and this was taller even than the mound. But Darly settled for the fifth floor of the Zadok. It seemed somehow to be the place remotest from the subject of his phobia.

I was living in the hotel by now so I used to take him up his meals—all prepared by the hotel staff: Loll had gone on strike.

Darly didn't eat much.

He just sat on the edge of the painted brass bed toying with the little carved peach pit from Death Row and looking like he was the carver.

She wants me back. And by God I hain't going back.

Well, Darly, you could at least go down and see her. I'll lend you my johnboat.

And go back on that wharfboat?

Well, yes, Darly.

Like hell I will, he snaps, pacing the floor and walking to the window every few minutes to stare out at block after town block merging liquidly into the great polished expanse of river.

On the wharfboat be damned! he cried. It's further than that she wants me. She wants me to go forward with her into—

I felt a kind of shiver run over me as Darly seemed to shut his mouth against the unspeakable. I closed my eyes. All I could see in the dark was the tawny sweet space of skin between Loll's breasts and a tiny mole there, like an island in a golden river.

But I'm safe from her here! he cried out suddenly, sloshing some J. W. Dant into the tumbler from the small washbowl. He drank the half glass of whisky without winking. Again I shivered.

Ain't you even gonna chase it, Darly?

With what?

Well, hell—with water.

Ain't got any.

I pointed to the little sink with its twin ornamental brass spigots with the pinheaded cupids for handles.

That's for washing—not drinking. It's—

He shuddered.

—it's river water.

He looked miserably at the little spigots and the bowl, golden and browned with use like an old meerschaum.

I tried to get a room without running water, he said. I do hate this arrangement awfully. Think of it. Those pipes run directly down to—

Naturally, he could not finish.

The night of the actual crest of '36 I was alone in my own room at the hotel. Since business on the wharfboat had been discontinued during the flood there was no one aboard her but Loll. The crest—a mere fifty-nine feet—was registered on the wall of the Purina Feed warehouse at Seventh and Western. That was the crest of '36. And that was all.

You would think that Darly would have greeted this news with joy.

Or at least relief.

But it sent him into a veritable frenzy against Loll. She had deliberately lied to him. She had frightened him into making himself a laughingstock in Glory. Four hundred and fifteen feet, indeed! We shall see about such prevarications!

In the johnboat, he rowed his way drunkenly down the cobbled street to where the water lapped against the eaves of the old Traders Hotel and the wharfboat tied in to its staunch stone chimney top.

Loudly Darly began to read the story of the Flood from Genesis. He got through that and lit into Loll for fair—saying that she had mocked God with predictions of a Flood.

Loll stayed in her stateroom throughout most of these tirades and when she could stand it no more she came out and stood on the narrow little deck looking at him. She was an old crone, now, her rooty knuckles clutched round the moon-silver head of a stick of English furze. Somehow—even in this moon aspect—I felt desire for her again.

You lied, Loll. Damn you, you lied. And you mocked the holy Word!

I did not lie! she cried with a laugh that danced across the renegade water. Oh, I did not I did not I did not!

You did! screamed Darly and charged down the gangplank from the big johnboat and sprang onto the narrow deck. No one was near enough to intervene as he struck the old woman with the flat of his hand and sent her spinning back into the shadows of the companionway.

The look she cast him in that instant—I saw it.

I tell you I am glad I was never the recipient of such of a look.

Darly rowed back to his hotel and went in through the third-story windows of the ballroom and up to his room on the fifth.

He was never seen alive on earth again.

He went into that little room on the top of the Zadok Cramer with a hundred and twenty-six pounds of window glazer's putty and began slowly, thoroughly sealing up his room against whatever eventuality. It was a folly that made the townsfolk laugh the harder. Because if the water had risen high as that room—wouldn't it surely sweep the entire structure away and riding high for Cairo down the line?

Yet the flood stage continued to go down. It was plainly a hoax on Loll's part. Yes, the waters kept subsiding. Until by Easter Monday it was down so low that the wharfboat could tie onto the big old willow at the foot of Water Street again.

Everything was as usual.

Or was it?

There had been a savage electric storm on the last night of the flood of '36. The crest of '36 was a grim one but it was nothing near what Loll had warned.

And there was no way to question her about it.

Because during the storm—at some point—she disappeared, as Darly was to do, from off the land of earth.

It all came out the next week.

Toonerville Boso, the desk clerk, hadn't seen nor heard of Darly Pogue in three days and nights. An old lady in 407 reported a slight leak of brown water in the ceiling of her bedroom. Sigafoose approached the sealed room on the morning of the Sunday after Easter and he, too, noted a trickle of yellow, muddy water from under the door of Darly's room. There was also a tiny sunfish flipping helplessly about on the Oriental carpet.

You remember the rest of it.

How a wall of green water and spring mud and live catfish came vomiting out of that door, sweeping poor Sigafoose down the hall and down the winding stairs and out the hotel door and into the sidewalk.

That room had been invaded. From within. Yes, the spigots were wide open.

Everyone in Glory, every one in the river lands at least, knows that the ceiling of that hotel room was the real crest of '36. Colonel Bruce, he worked with transit and scale and plumb bobs for a month afterward—measuring it—the real crest of '36. It was exactly four hundred and fifteen feet.

I know. I know—there were catfish in the room and sunfish

and gars and a couple of hugh goldfish and they were all too big
to have squeezed up through the hotel plumbing let alone
through those little brass spigots. But they did. The pressure
must have been enormous. And it all must have come rushing
out and filling up in the space of a few seconds—before Darly
Pogue could know what was happening and could scream.

The pressure of love? I don't know. Some force unknown to us
and maybe it's all explained somewhere in one of those little
five-cent blue books from out Kansas way—I guess it was one I
missed. The pressure to get those fish and a few bottles and a lot
of mud and water up the pipes and into that room was, as I say,
considerable. But nothing compared to the pressure it must have
taken to get Darly's body back out into the river. Out of that
room. Into the green, polished, fathomless mother of waters.
Love? Maybe it's strong enough. At least, the love of someone
like her.

No trace of her was ever found. No trace of Darly either—
except for his toupee—it was the one part of him that didn't go
through the spigot and it was stuck, like a piece of dead seaweed,
against the nozzle.

Go there now.

To the river.

When the spring moon is high.

When the lights in the skiffs on the black river look like
campfires on stilts of light.

A catfish leaps—porpoising into moonshine and mist and then
dipping joyously back into the deeps. Another—smaller—appears by its side. They nuzzle their huge homely faces in the
starshine. Their great rubber lips brush in ecstasy.

And then they are gone in the spring dark—off for a bit of
luscious garbage—old lovers at their honeymoon breakfast.

Lucky Darly Pogue! O, lucky Darly!

THE LAST DAYS OF PONCHO PETE

Every quiet writer invents his own clichés. Every bad writer uses them. Every mediocre writer frantically avoids them and that's one reason so many mediocre writers today are considered great.

—Davis Grubb, notebooks

I don't know what would have happened that winter if it hadn't been for Tom Mix! I reckon our brains would just have busted under the strain. If it hadn't been for them Saturday afternoons at the Moore's Opera House there just wouldn't have been nothing to live for that year—not around the hometown anyways. Me and Eddie Sigafoose and Stanley Stump used to think the sixth-grade teacher was bad enough. But when it come to real fancy meanness, that seventh-grade teacher had her beat a hundred ways. And just as if it wasn't bad enough having Miss Langfitt to put up with, there was them three simple girls making things worse!

Peter! Miss Langfitt would holler, them black, beady eyes of hers biting at me like mean little horsegnats. Stand and recite the boundaries of the state of West Virginia!

Well, sir, do you know I wouldn't get no further than
Massachussetts till that derned woman would be crawling all over
me like a mule driver. And directly that prissy little pigtailed Jo
Ann Bruce would stick up her hand and directly she'd be rattling
it all off like she was reading from the book. And if it wasn't Jo
Ann it was Mary Jane Lowther or that daggone Betty Snow.
They all lived in the same block on Mulberry Street and they
always done their homework together. That's what made the
whole thing so downright sneaking unfair! What chance did me
or Stanley or Eddie have with them three girls and Miss Langfitt
all ganging up against us?

We talked about it a lot that winter—running away to Dodge
City and getting ourselves jobs as stage drivers on the Wells-
Fargo. And I reckon we'd have done it, too, if it hadn't been for
Tom Mix. We saved up from our paper routes and bought us
three genuine, pearl-handled six-shooters that was up in the window at Stilwell's Store. And every Saturday afternoon we'd set
there in the front row at the Moore's Opera House and eat our
Brown Cows and holler ourselves hoarse for good old Tom. Mister Shackleford that run the Moore's Opera House used to come
up and stand by the popcorn machine when he got done playing
the piano for the show and when me and the Texan and Black
Stanley, King of the Rustlers, would come swaggering up the
aisle don't you never think he wasn't scared of us! The Texan
would go walking out ahead of us all stiff and bowlegged and
there was that steady, hard light in Black Stanley's eyes as he
looked up and down Pike Street for some sign of that pesky sheriff's posse. Old Mister Shackleford's eyes would twinkle with fear
and sometimes he'd give us a nickel bag of hot buttered popcorn
for nothing. I reckon he figured it wouldn't hurt none to stay on
the right side of hombres like Poncho Pete and his lawless crew.

It was that derned pearl-handled six-shooter of mine that
started the whole thing. That spring Eddie figured out a way of
strapping his gun onto his leg with a rubber band and going to
school without nobody knowing it was there. So it wasn't long
till we all got rubber bands and was doing the same.

. Peter! hollers Miss Langfitt that awful afternoon in May. Stand and recite the names of the Middle Atlantic states!

Well, sir, do you know I didn't even get past New Mexico till that daggoned rubber band busted and I felt my six-shooter go sliding down through my long underwear all cold and ghastly and hit my shoe and go bouncing and clattering across the school-room floor. There wasn't a sound for a minute. And then them simple girls all went to giggling and Black Stanley and the Texan got kind of sick-looking and Miss Langfitt just stood there tapping the palm of her hand with a ruler like she was keeping time to music. I could have stood it, I reckon. I could have been shamed and humiliated by a woman and still been able to go and face Tom next Saturday if it hadn't been for that derned Jo Ann Bruce. That pearl-handled six-shooter of mine hadn't even quit sliding across the floor till Jo Ann bent over with a little simper, picked it up, and handed it back to me. Right then was when Miss Langfitt spoke up.

Thank you, Jo Ann! she says. What a perfect young lady you are to hand the little boy back his plaything!

Betty Snow and Mary Jane Lowther and all the other kids sat there tee-heeing and stuffing their hands over their mouths and Black Stanley and the Texan both looked like they'd been snake-bit and was a thousand miles from the Last Chance Saloon!

And, since the little boy has been foolish enough to bring his toy to school! Miss Langfitt says in that old, scratchy voice of hers that always sounded like she needed to clear her throat, and *you*, Jo Ann, have been *lady enough* to hand it back to him—

She blinked her little black eyes real fast and smiled like she'd just thought up the best old joke in the world.

—I'm going to assign the plaything to your safekeeping! And when Peter has become a *gentleman*—and I'll trust your judgment about that, Jo Ann—you may return it to him!

Me and the Texan and Black Stanley sat for a long while in the tall prairie grass over in Mister Newman's vacant lot that evening after school. Nobody said nothing for a long time. The golden Arizona sun sank into the West Virginia hills and the skulls of the buffaloes grinned at us in the dusk. Directly the Texan give out a little grunt and pointed off toward the school-house.

Look at 'em! he says. If that ain't a sickening sight!

Down the sidewalk, all prissy and smiling, walked Miss Lang-fitt with an arm full of test papers to grade that night. And chattering along beside her was them three darned girls—Jo Ann Bruce and Betty Snow and Mary Jane Lowther.

Shinny! says Stanley, spitting in the grass. Look at 'em, will yuh! You'd think there was somethin' wonderful about gettin' to walk home with that ol' buzzard every night!

It ain't hard to see? I says, why Tom don't never have no truck with 'em!

Who? says Stanley.

Wimmen! I says. You won't never catch ol' Tom gettin' mixed up with 'em! No siree! They don't mean nothin' but trouble and ol' Tom knows it!

The Texan's eyes narrowed to two slits of blue ice as he twirled his six-gun and stared off into the Black Hills of South Dakota.

Pardner! he says. Reckon she'll give you your pistol back?

Shinny! I said. I don't know! I just know one thing! I ain't goin' crawlin' to her for it!

Pardner, says the Texan directly. Ol' Tom wouldn't be takin' this lyin' down!

Shinny! I said, spitting up in the air.

He's right, Poncho Pete! says Black Stanley. We gotta do somethin'. Once them wimmen gits the upper hand—

What can we do! I hollered. You heard what Miss Langfitt said!

Nobody said nothing for a long while. If it hadn't been so close to suppertime there's no telling what would have happened. You could smell the ham steak and potatoes frying over in Mister Newman's kitchen. If it hadn't been for that I reckon we'd have just picked up and headed for Texas right then and there! All of a sudden Eddie Sigafoose give out a holler and jumped in the air.

I got it! he yells. I got it!

Me and Black Stanley both looked at him like he'd went crazy.

We'll kidnap Jo Ann! says the Texan.

Shinny! says Stanley, chewing on a blade of grass. What'sa matter with you, boy! You gone loco or somethin'! Shinny!

No! says Eddie. Don't you see! We won't kidnap her, exactly! We'll just get her and hold her long enough to throw a scare into her! Then maybe her and them other two dumbbells will leave us alone!

Shinny! says Stanley, getting up and walking away in disgust. You gone loco, boy?

Don't you see! hollers Eddie, jumping up and down in the grass. Pete here will call her up as soon as he gets home and ask her for a *date!*

I couldn't say nothing I was so mad.

Get it now? says Eddie, all excited. You get a date with her and then me and Black Stanley—

I pushed Eddie so hard he fell down backward in the grass. He just set there with the breath knocked out of him, swallering.

All right! he hollers directly. All right then! If you're so dag-gone smart maybe you know somethin' better!

Hold on here a minute, pardners! says Black Stanley, walking back over all bowlegged and serious. Maybe the Texan's got somethin' there, Poncho Pete.

That's disgusting! I hollered. That's downright *sickening!*

Hold on, pardner! says Stanley, hooking his finger around the pearl handle of his gun. You don't understand—

I ain't gettin' no date with no girl! I hollered, all hoarse and sore. That's all I understand! I ain't gettin' no date! What would Tom say about—

Tom's smart! hissed Stanley. Don't you see! Don't you 'member last Saturday when Tom made out like he was an Injun and sneaked right into Sittin' Bull's village big as life! That ain't sayin' Tom Mix likes Injuns, does it? Just like you gettin' a date with Jo Ann tonight! That don't mean you like girls! *You're a spy!*

Well, they had me there. I never said nothing for a while.

You know that big mud hole down back of McFadden's Livery Stable? whispered Stanley.

Yeah! says the Texan. You get a date with Jo Ann tonight and ask her if she'd like to take a little walk down Mulberry Street in the moonlight! You know how them girls all go for that lovey-dovey stuff! Well—she'll be all dressed up in one of them fancy dresses of hers and me and Black Stanley here is hidin' behind a cactus down by Dead Man's Pass and—

You fellers mean—mean push Jo Ann Bruce in the mud hole? I whispered.

Heck, yes! hissed the Texan. I reckon that'll learn her to leave us be!

I studied on it for a while but the more I thought about it the less I liked it.

Shinny! I says. They'd put us in jail!

Won't nobody know who done it! whispered the Texan. Don't you see! It'll be dark and we'll have masks on and you'll be there to help her out of the mud and act like you're chasin' us and directly you give up and get her back home! And then when her ol' lady asks you what happened you just say you was jumped by two mighty mean hombres down back of the livery stable! Jo Ann'll know we was back of it someway! But she won't be able to *prove* nothin'!

Shinny! I whispered. It's too derned risky! I'm scared for fear—

You reckon Tom'd be scared! whispered Black Stanley. Was Tom Mix ever scared by anything with skirts on! Answer me that, Poncho Pete!

The sweet smell of them fried potatoes and ham steak was drifting stronger out of Mister Newman's kitchen window and itching all round inside me worse than ever now.

Pardners, I says, my eyes narrow slits of fire as I stared off into the yellow dusk of Wyoming. I reckon if Tom wouldn't be afraid—I ain't neither! Now let's head for the chuck wagon!

I should have knowed better. It just goes to show you how women can drive a man to most any orneriness in this world and first thing he knows he's all mixed up worse than he was before.

Jo Ann sounded just tickled to death when I called her on the phone after supper that night. She said she'd just love to have me come calling on her that evening. Right then and there is when I should have backed out. Tom Mix is one thing and I'm another. Tom might have done all right with the women he knowed but I'll bet he never run up against none like Jo Ann Bruce or Betty Snow or Mary Jane Lowther.

Ma seen me after supper, all dressed up in my good blue Sunday suit. She like to fainted.

Peter! says Ma. Are you sick?

No'm, I says, grinning all sick and guilty looking like I'd just murdered somebody and there was a big sign around my neck telling all about it.

Where are you goin', Peter? hollered my old man from the front porch.

I swallered real hard and straightened my tie.

I got a date, Pap! I squeaked.

One night the summer before, me and Stanley had smoked up a whole pack of Kentucky Sweethearts and my voice had been acting up ever since.

A date! squawks my old lady. Heavenly days! A *date!*

She busted out crying and headed for the kitchen.

My little boy! Ma hollered. Grown up! My little boy goin' off on his first date!

Out on the front porch my old man kept on reading the paper as hard as he could. I walked out in the hallway with the red crawling up the back of my neck faster than a grass fire. Outside on the front porch I could smell the honeysuckle vine mixing in with the smell of my old man's cigar smoke. I just stood there gritting my teeth. Tonight Poncho Pete was riding to his most dangerous rendezvous and then my old lady has to go blubbering around the house talking about her little boy!

It must have been a quarter past eight when I walked up Mulberry Street to Jo Ann's house. Across the street I could hear Betty Snow and Mary Jane Lowther setting in the swing on Mary Jane's porch, whispering and giggling. I knowed then that Jo Ann had told them both as soon as I'd called her. I didn't give a

darn. Let them laugh! Them simple girls would be laughing out
of the other side of their faces before this night was past! Black
Stanley and the Texan was hiding down in the hydrangea bushes
by the porch when I come up the walk. I was nervous enough as
it was. They like to scared me to death just as I started up the
steps.

Pssssst! I heard the Texan whisper.

I jumped a good two feet and stared all wild and crazy down in
the shadows there by the porch.

It's the Texan! he hissed. And Black Stanley! Good luck,
pardner!

I seen the spring moonlight glint on their six-shooters and
when I looked closer I seen the red bandannas over their faces.

Good luck, Poncho Pete! whispered Black Stanley. Us
hombres'll be waitin' for you down by Dead Man's Pass!

Shinny! I whispered, waving my arms at them. You guys loco
or somethin! You want her ol' man to see you!

I was shaking so bad after they'd ducked back in the shrubbery
I could hardly get up them steps onto Jo Ann's front porch. And
when I heard her coming after I'd twisted the doorbell it was all I
could do to keep from turning tail and running like a yaller
coyote.

Good evening, Peter! says Jo Ann, in that sticky sweet voice
of hers.

I give her my hat and while she went to hang it up I just stood
there shaking and rubbing my cold, sweaty hands on my blue
suit. Directly here come her old lady down the hall. I looked out
the screen door into the warm spring dark and wished I was setting down there in the shrubbery with Eddie and Stanley. But
there wasn't no backing out now.

Good evening, Peter! says Jo Ann's old lady, grabbing my
hand and pumping on it real fast. It's so nice of you to come
calling on my daughter!

Yes'm, I says.

Then she just stood there grinning at me and me trying to grin
back and not making much of a show of it.

Well! she whoops out directly. I'll let you two young folks alone now and go back to my baking!

Directly here comes Jo Ann again, smiling and waving them big, simple brown eyelashes at me.

Shall we go sit in the porch swing, Peter? she coos. It's such a lovely May night!

I don't care! I says.

It was dark and warm out and we sat down together on the swing. I sat way over in the other corner so's there wasn't no chance of bumping into her.

My! sighed Jo Ann, taking a deep breath and letting it out again. Isn't the springtime nice, Peter?

Yes'm, I says. It sure is!

She had on one of them derned dresses that was all lacy and white and frothy like an ice-cream soda and she had a pink ribbon in her hair and some kind of sickening perfume splashed all over her. I just sat there on the swing thinking about Tom Mix and getting madder by the minute and feeling like busting somebody in the nose. I could hear Stanley and the Texan moving around down in the shrubbery trying to get comfortable.

What's that! whispers Jo Ann, moving over against me all of a sudden.

What? I squeaked, trying to get farther over on the porch swing so she wouldn't rub off none of that derned, sickening perfume on me.

I heard something! gasped Jo Ann, moving up against me all the harder. Down there in the shrubbery!

I stared off into the trees, just hating everything.

It ain't nothin' but them pesky long-horned cattle out on the range! I says, more to myself than her.

It's *wha-at*? says Jo Ann.

I mean—it's *dogs*! I says, real quick. Or cats! Or somethin'! It ain't nothin' to be scared of, Jo Ann!

Oh! sighed Jo Ann, real soft. I'm glad you said that, Peter! I was frightened terribly for a minute! Peter, I certainly am glad you're here!

Yes! I says. Ain't it just grand!

Peter! she says softly.

What? I says.

By that time I'd just plumb give up trying to move away from her. There wasn't no more swing left.

Peter, says Jo Ann. I'm *terribly* sorry about what happened in school today!

I waved my hand at her.

Shinny! I says. That ain't nothin'!

I was trying to pick it up before Miss Langfitt saw it! she says. I thought maybe I could hide it in my desk real quickly before she turned around and then give it to you after school was out! But then she saw me! And I had to hand it to you then!

It don't matter, Jo Ann! I sighed. I never cared much for the derned thing anyways.

Well, sir, it was a funny thing. I hadn't meant to say that no more than nothing! It just popped out before I even knowed it was coming. That's the way women do—twist a man's tongue all around till he don't know *what* he's saying. Tom knowed. That's why you'd never catch old Tom having any truck with them. Old Tony was enough for Tom. And yet here I sat—Poncho Pete— jabbering with a girl like it wasn't nothing to be ashamed of at all and then coming right out and saying I didn't mind her disgracing me in school and taking my pearl-handled six-gun away from me to boot!

I hope you're not angry! Jo Ann says. I like you, Peter! I'm glad you called me up tonight! You're not a bit like that Sigafoose boy or that awful Stanley Stump!

Yes, I says. Ain't they *vulgar!*

Well, sir, by that time I was sicker than a goat. I felt all mixed up and mad and wanting to bust somebody in the nose something terrible. And the way that derned Jo Ann Bruce was talking wasn't helping me none. And the way she was smelling— like cotton candy and baby powder and sweet cream all mixed up together. I peeked in the parlor window to see if her old lady was around and all of a sudden I seen it—my six-shooter lying there on the grand piano seat. And I couldn't do a derned thing about it when my eyes filled all up with mad tears and I realized all of a sudden that the derned gun wouldn't really shoot—that it wasn't nothing really but—

Peter, says Jo Ann. Mama says Miss Langfitt was very unfair to you today! Mama says I can give you back your cap pistol tonight! And what's more I'm going to!

Shinny! I said, waving my hand in the air. Shinny! That old thing! I'm . . . I'm . . .

Then Jo Ann's old lady was hollering at us from the hall.

Jo Ann! she says. If you and the young man will come inside I've got something for you!

So we went in the parlor and derned if Jo Ann's old lady hadn't fixed us up a big pitcherful of lemonade and a silver plate full of oatmeal cookies she'd just got done baking. Jo Ann poured me a big glassful and passed me the cookies just as I looked out the parlor window and seen them. I like to dropped my glass on the oriental rug.

Peter! says Jo Ann. Don't you care for lemonade?

Yes'm! I squeaked. Shinny, yes! I just love it!

I looked out the window again, just to be sure, and I seen them plainer this time—the Texan and Black Stanley glaring through the shrubbery at me and making faces and motioning for me to hurry up and get Jo Ann to take that walk down back of McFadden's Livery Stable. Jo Ann went and turned the radio on and sat down on the davenport and smiled at me. I sat down real quick in a straight-backed chair and drank my lemonade and stared at my pearl-handled six-shooter there on the grand piano bench. I tried to swallow the cookie and I tried to drink the lemonade and the music was coming out of the radio real soft and I could smell the way Jo Ann smelled and I didn't know which end of me was up. And when she went out in the kitchen to get some more cookies I run to the window and stared out like a crazy man. There they was. Black Stanley just couldn't take his eyes off that pitcher of cold lemonade but the Texan was glaring at me and motioning for me to hurry up. I don't know what come over me then. But I shook my head and waved my hand for them to go away and then I went and sat back down real quick in the chair.

More cookies, Peter? says Jo Ann, when she come back from the kitchen.

Yes'm! I said, watching out the window with the corner of my eye.

Jo Ann went over directly to tune the radio in better and I got a good look out the window. There they was—Black Stanley and the Texan—marching up and down outside the window and making faces at me and shaking their fists and letting on how they was really going to give it to me good once they laid hands on me. When all of a sudden it just come over me—I didn't care. Old Tom had faced a lot worse than that and come through. And when I got up to go home a half hour later I still didn't care. And then when Jo Ann brought me my hat she was real close to me there by the screen door and my face brushed against hers—well, you couldn't really say I kissed her! My mouth just brushed her lips and I could smell that cotton candy and baby powder and sweet cream smell again and Lord, I didn't care for nothing then! I'd have went out bare-handed and faced them all!—Black Stanley and the Texan and Sitting Bull and Jesse James to boot! I only knowed one thing! There wasn't nobody going to push Jo Ann Bruce in no mud hole back of McFadden's Livery Stable while Poncho Pete was in town!

Good night, Peter! Jo Ann said softly as she shut the screen door.

I walked down the steps into the warm spring night.

Good night, Jo Ann, I said.

It's a funny derned thing but I wasn't scared a bit. I knowed that somewhere down Mulberry Street the Texan and Black Stanley was waiting to punch me in the eye. And if anybody got pushed in the mud hole that night it would like as not be me. But I didn't care a bit! I walked down the brick sidewalk under the dark, quiet trees of the hometown and I was ready for anything. I couldn't see them nowheres. And then I heard Stanley's voice and there wasn't no mistaking it—and then I heard a giggle up on Betty Snow's porch and the tinkle of ice in a frosty pitcher and then I heard Eddie Sigafoose's voice and Mary Jane Lowther was asking him if maybe he'd like to have another glass of grape juice. The spring moon stood high in the trees over Mulberry Street. I felt mad and glad and sad all at once. I swear I could almost hear them—the ghost hooves of the wonder-horse Tony fading off into the night. The mountains of Nevada melted slowly in the dark and the bones of the buffaloes crumbled into the lawns without a sound. Then I heard Jo Ann's voice, calling me. I turned around and looked at her standing there, the porch light shining on her hair.

Peter! she called softly. You forgot something!

She had that daggone cap pistol in her hand!

I felt the red crawling up my neck and waved my hand at her. I walked on slowly toward home.

Dern that simple Jo Ann Bruce anyhow! I said out loud. What the shinny does she think I am—a kid?

MAGENTA BLUE

The voice of God is never loud enough to drown out, in
the ears of a father, the cries of a hungry child.
—Davis Grubb, notebooks

After more than a month of it, people began to notice Yancey
there. She never bothered anybody doing it; never blocked anybody's way along the wooden sidewalk. She just stood there staring through the plate glass window at something in the window
of Mister T.O.'s Swap and Shop store. But at what? There were
so many things in that long, dusty showcase behind the glass.
Well, whatever it was everybody knew she wasn't ever going inside to buy it, for she was a Wyatt and the Wyatt family lived
down on the creek bank beyond the town garbage dump and all
the families there in that place called Ruby Trees they lived off
welfare checks and food commodities from the DPA and not a
penny they could really call their own. Still, that didn't keep
Yancey Wyatt from staring through that fly-specked window at
whatever it was—sometimes staying there for as long as half an
hour at a time—shifting from one foot to the other, her thumbs
hooked in the belt loops of the boy's denim jeans she wore under
the tails of her floppy blue man's work shirt. Town folks were
always making guesses and bets on what it was she was staring at.

Wanting. Wanting till it hurt. There wasn't much else to guess
or bet on back in that hard year of 1934.

And then one afternoon Yancey surprised the whole town.
She took a deep breath and walked right into Mister T.O.'s store
bold as brass. She didn't come slinking in neither, for she was
proud as she was pretty, with long black shining silky hair the
color of sloeberries and eyes the shade of the wild iris that grew
in those West Virginia hills.

And what can I do for you this mornin', Yancey? Mister T.O.
asked.

In the window yonder, she said. You got a blue silk dress and
I'd admire to see it close and know how much it costs.

She paused, gathering in more breath.

Hit's on a coat hanger, she said. Back behind that ugly old
gasoline-powered Maytag washer where the daylight don't hit it
square. I'd admire to see it up close.

Yancey, Mister T.O. said softly, ever'body in town knows your
family. And they know that there ain't a livin soul down the
streetcar tracks at Ruby Trees could afford that dress anymore
than if it was a mink coat.

Still Yancey never changed expression.

I never come here this morning to buy that dress, she said. I
just come to see it up close. In a good light. And feel of it. And
find out how much you're askin for hit. And I figured maybe to
make a deposit so's you could hold it for me till—

Till what, Yancey? asked Mister T.O., gentle-voiced as ever.
You know as well as me that that dress would cost you half your
folks' monthly welfare check.

Mister T.O., would you please be so kindly turned as to fetch
that blue silk dress out in the light here over the counter so's I
can see it up close?

Mister T.O. saw she was set on it so he made his way toward
the show window, got the dress, came back with it, a little sadness in his eyes, and laid it out on the smooth wood of the
counter.

Yancey stood there a spell, staring at it, not moving, not coming close to it yet. Then she laid her long white fingers on the

surface of it, kept them there a second, and then commenced to move them back and forth, as though caressing the skin of a loved one.

Finally, like a wakening dreamer, she lifted her eyes and looked at Mister T.O.'s face again.

Now, she said, real businesslike, I done saved me up a pint mason jar of nickels and dimes and a few two-bit pieces, she said. Eleven ninety-five's worth.

How'd you get hold of all that money, child?

Yancey's face was still expressionless; she never batted an eyelash.

I'd be beholden, Mister T.O., if you wasn't to call me child, she said. I'm a woman now and this here town hit will know it before spring. As for the eleven ninety-five I earned it berry pickin' and peddlin' them from door to door for fifty cents a bucket. I done it till school opened and I had to quit. Now how much does this here blue silk dress cost, Mister T.O.?

Times is hard, Yancey, said Mister T.O. There's a Great Depression on.

For the first time Yancey smiled.

The Depression, she said. We never noticed much change. There was just more of us in it.

This dress is worth every penny of fifty dollars, said Mister T.O. But times bein' what they was I got it from a rich lady from Saint Albans for twenty-five. Now, I can't let go of it for a cent less than thirty-two fifty.

Yancey nodded.

Good, she said. I can run home right now and fetch back that pint mason jar of money and leave you have it for deposit. Ifn you agree to it.

But where'll you come by the balance, Yancey? asked Mister T.O.

Berry season's over, she said. But the black walnuts is just commencing to fall. And I been up in the woods pickin 'em. There's three hours of daylight after school lets out. And weekends. I got me nigh unto seven bushels picked already. And when my homework's done I'm up half the night hullin' and crackin' 'em and picking out the meats.

Mister T.O. lowered his gaze to the dress, touched it with his own fingers, smoothing it out.

In the first place, Yancey, he said. This here ain't no common plain ordinary silk dress. That rich lady from Saint Albans she told me that. This here blue silk it's what you call Magenta.

He shook his head in bafflement.

Now I don't know a bit more than you do what Magenta means, he said. I only know it makes it special and different.

He pondered a moment.

In my judgment, he said. Magenta must be the country it come from. That's why the price is so dear.

Up to now Yancey's face had been set and motionless. It still was—except there were tears in the long black lashes of her irish-blue eyes and a tremor on her small, pretty mouth.

I just plain got to buy me that dress, Mister T.O., she said evenly.

But why, Yancey? asked Mister T.O.

Don't ask me that, Yancey said quietly. For I'll not tell you. Just believe me when I tell you I just purely got to have that blue silk dress. There's eleven ninety-five in the fruit jar at home. And them black walnut meats—they'll fetch me another five. That comes to a nickel short of seventeen dollars. And common sense tells me that's a fair enough amount for you to hold it for me. Till I lay hands on the rest.

She stared a moment more, her face still a mask but one tear streaking down her cheek and into her mouth. She licked it impatiently away.

Please, Mister T.O., she said.

Mister T.O. couldn't take it any more.

Yancey, he said, I sing first tenor in the Baptist Church choir. And I swear to the Lord I'd not be able to get through the first verse of the Doxologer if I was to tell you no.

Yancey swallowed hard then, hooked her thumbs in her belt loops, getting set for the hardest part of all.

Mister T.O., she said, Part of what I just asked you was fibbin'.
I mean about your holdin that dress for me till it was all paid for.
What I meant was can I take it with me now. For it's now that I
need it. Later I won't. Now's the time I just purely have to have
it. So I'm askin' you to leave me have it now. And I'll bring the
money I got to you today. And will you trust me for the rest? I
tell you it's now I need it. And the Lord only knows I wisht I
could tell you the reason why. But I can't. Will you now?

Mister T.O. gave Yancey the dress. Even wrapped it up fancy
in a man's cardboard suit box.

When Yancey came racing in the house she didn't even stop
to say a word to Ma or Grandma Sweet Potato about what she
had in the box. And they were both full of wonderment. For it
was the first time anybody had ever carried a store-box through
the door of that old miner's shack. Yancey went to her room and
locked the door. She didn't open the box. She just laid it on the
floor under the windowsill where the autumn sunlight could fall
on it. Then she flung herself on the bed, hugging her full little
breasts tight in her arms and rocking from side to side on the
ragged old quilt. Before long she got the giggles at the way she
was taking on and laughed so hard she rolled off the bed and
onto the rag rug Grandma Sweet Potato had made for her room.
By chance then she looked under the bed, back against the base-
board, where she kept the little mason jar of coins. It wasn't
there. Yancey scrambled under the bed, looking everywhere. But
it was gone. That was when she heard Ma's hand trying the
doorknob. She got up and went to the door, unlocked it and
stood aside as Ma came in. Ma sat down slowly on the edge of
Yancey's bed, not looking at Yancey at all.

I never had no choice, Yancey, she said.

Yancey's face was a stolid, fixed, emotionless mask again.

It's all right, Ma, she said. There's things that's meant to be
and there's things that just ain't. That's no news to me nor you
neither one, Lord knows.

The man from Consolidated, he come this mornin right after
you had went to town, Ma said then. He claimed since this was
still company land this was a miner's house and they was raisin'

the rent two dollars a month. And he claimed we was five
months behind and ifn we didn't come up with that ten dollars
before sundown tonight he'd have Harley Steptoe and two deputies out here and put us and every pot and pan and stick of
furniture out on the cinders along the streetcar track.

But why, Ma? Yancey asked. Ever'body knows that seam's
plumb worked out. Consolidated shut down that mine bettern'n
four years ago.

That's so, Ma said. The seam under the hill—the very one in
which Dad and them two poor young Polacks got killed in—hit's
plumb worked out. But Consol got to diggin around and found
surface coal on the hilltop. And them and the WPA's going to
start strippin' early in the spring. Soon as the thaw sets in.

Yancey nodded. She didn't say a word. Her face showed no
emotion no shock, no sense of loss. She went to the window and
picked up the cardboard box. In a moment she was striding up
the streetcar tracks to town again. When she came in the front
door of Mister T.O.'s store she didn't say anything or show anything in her face either. And from his rolltop desk at the rear of
the store Mister T.O. watched as Yancey placed the box on the
counter as careful as if it had something in it like glass or
chinaware that might break. And without a word or a look she
paced swiftly out the door and was gone.

She went in her room again when she got home, locked the
door, stretched out on the quilt once more and, folding her fingers behind her head, lay staring at the rain-stained ceiling. Ma
had seen a thing in her face to know enough to leave her alone
just then. She didn't even call her when suppertime came. Before she undressed for bed and got into her flannel nightgown
from the welfare, Yancey unlocked the door because she knew,
sometime in the night, Ma would be coming. She didn't sleep
though. She laid there trying to figure out where Magenta was. It
was an island in the Pacific she decided at last—with a name as
pretty as that, it had to be—an island with white beaches and a
wind off the sea that blew droplets of spindrift against your face
and set the long leaves of the tall palm trees clashing like toy
sabers, and she could fairly hear the crash and drawl of the

breakers as they broke and withdrew upon the beach. She didn't
begin to cry till long past midnight and, as luck would have it,
that was when Ma knocked and Yancey told her to come in and
watched through her tears as the older woman set the coal oil
lamp on the cracked veneer top of the chest of drawers and sat in
the straight-backed rocking chair at the foot of Yancey's bed.

It ain't all bad, Yancey, Ma said, after a spell. I been through
it. Grandma Sweet Potato she's been through it. It ain't all that
bad.

I know, Yancey said, angrily scrubbing away the tears from her
face with the quilt and getting her face set in that mask again.
I'll get hold of the money somewhere else. Money is just money,
Ma.

I ain't talkin about the money, Yancey, Ma said. And you
know what it is I *am* talking about.

She paused, rocking slowly in the chair.

Yancey, you done missed three monthlies already.

That's right, Ma, Yancey said. I went and got myself knocked
up.

No, Ma said. I never use that word about a gal who's carryin' a
love-chile in her belly. Knocked up's a word for gals like Jewel
and Esta Mae.

It's all the same thing, Ma, Yancey said. Words don't change
it.

That's not so, Yancey, Ma said. I know hit's a love-chile by
your face. I seen them signs in another face oncet, Yancey—my
own face in a looking glass—seven months before I birthed you.

Yancey sat up suddenly in the bed, glaring out the window at
the silver of autumn moon.

Hit just don't seem fair somehow, she said. Jewel and Esta
Mae they done it for years and never once got knocked up. And
little old me—the first and one and only time I do it I git
caught. Knocked up. Call it what you please, Ma. I never done
it but that once.

I know that, Yancey, Ma said. For you ain't had but one date
in the past year. And that was with Smilin' Tommy Cotter.

That's right, Yancey said. I stayed clean away from boys for

years. Much as I wanted one. I was jist bound and determined
nothin' was ever goin to happen to me like it done happened
with Jewel and Esta Mae. I was bound and determined to be the
first Wyatt gal—the first gal in all of Ruby Trees, for that matter—to get through high school and get myself a position in
town. I mean position—not jist a job.

She paused.

Now that's all changed, she said. I'll commence to showin' in
a month or two. And have to quit school. And not git to graduate with the senior class. Nor git that position.

Now she smiled and gave a proud little toss of her chin.

But you know a crazy thing, Ma? she cried out. I don't care. I
want this baby more than I ever wanted no high school diploma
nor a good town position either one. Because when I clumb in
the backseat of Tommy's car that night it seemed the cleanest
thing in the world. Because I just pure adored him so much I
couldn't bear to deny him something he wanted so bad. And
when he done it it hurt. But it's a funny thing, Ma—that hurt
felt better than the goodest feeling I ever had. That hurt it pleasured me because it pleasured him so!

She paused, pondering, then glared hard at Ma.

And this baby inside me, Ma! she cried out. I mean to keep it!
And the Children's Worker from the DPA can come out here
with Harley Steptoe and all the deputies he can round up and
the chief of police and the FBI and they'll never lay hands on
this baby or me neither one! I'd throw me and the baby both in
front of the streetcar afore I'd let them! I'll not go to Salem
neither. And I'll not see Tommy's child farmed out to no foster
home. And you just better believe it, Ma!

I do, honey, I do, Ma said gently. I'm all on your side. If they
come—I'll even help you fight them off.

Yancey giggled then.

Ma, I swear I'm the craziest little thing ever walked this earth.

Why, honey?

Because when I went to town this mornin' I talked Mister
T.O. that runs the Swap and Shop store on Pike Street into
lettin me pay part on a fool thing I never needed nor wanted so

bad in all my born days. That's what the money in the mason jar was for. And all them nights of late when I been stayin' up to all hours gettin' the meats out of them fool black walnuts—I figgered to sell them and pay that on it too. And Mister T.O.— 'deed I'll never be able to look that man in the face again. Because he trusted me. And that was what I come a runnin' in with in that cardboard box this morning, Ma. And then had to take back when I found the money was gone.

What was it, Yancey?

It was a gen-uine Magenta blue silk dress, Yancey said. Oh, Ma, if you could jist have seen it! I mean in a good light! You can see it now if you go past Mister T.O.'s store. For I reckon it's back in the show window now. But it's back behind an ugly ol' gasoline Maytag washer where you can't really tell! Ma, hit was more than jist a silk dress. Hit was a Lady's dress. I spent the livelong summer lookin' at that dress in Mister T.O.'s window. And dreamin' of the Friday night I'd show them all up at the WCHS Radio County Jamboree when I come walkin' in a-wearin' hit. And for the whole livelong night they'd stop thinkin' of me as Yancey Wyatt from Ruby Trees. And know I was a Lady. And I was jist plumb certain that Smilin' Tommy, who'd be up there on the stage playin' his gui-tar and singing "Cheatin' Heart" or some sich tune, he'd take one look at me and never want to even look at another gal in all his life.

Ma smiled softly, and rocked a little faster.

But the first night Tommy set eyes on you, Ma said, you wasn't wearin' nothin' but your usual, Yancey. Blue denim jeans. And a floppy blue man's work shirt. No, Yancey, hit ain't clothes that catches a man by the heart. If he sees what he wants in a gal she can be dressed in a frock sewed out of flour sacks and burlap!

Yancey shook her head.

Hit warn't jist to hook Tommy I wanted that dress, Ma, she said. Maybe hit was in the beginning. But after a while that dress commenced to mean something else to me. Like it jist purely hypnotized me. Even without ever layin' eyes on Tommy I'd still want that dress, Ma. Maybe because it would have been the only

real nice thing I ever owned. Maybe it's because I knowed all
along it was from some faraway wondrous place like Magenta.

She got to thinking then and sometimes thinking instead of
feeling is the worst thing a female can do. She knotted up her
little white fists and beat the quilt.

I love Tommy, she said. And I'll fight to keep his child. I'd die
to keep his child. Because like as not that's all I'll ever git out of
him. But love him like I do I hate him just as much.

Ma smiled.

I know that feelin', too, Yancey, she said. And I know, too,
that Tommy Cotter ain't a bad boy. He's jist a little late a-stop-
pin' of sowing his wild oats, that's all. He had hisself a good job
at Dupont till the big layoff last spring. Still he'd earned enough
there to buy that little piece of land up the streetcar tracks
beyond Ruby Trees. And he built hisself a little house on it with
his own hands.

I know, Yancey said. And now he jist lives off what they pay
him a-playin' and a-singing ever' Friday night at the WCHS Radio Country Jamboree.

He makes a little money another way, too, Ma said.

How?

Ma shook her head.

Never you mind, Ma said. Ifn I was to tell you hit would jist
trouble your mind. And trouble-mindedness can mark an unborn
baby, Yancey. Jist leave me say that what he's doin is not his
fault.

And she was gone, closing the door easy behind her, like closing it hard might waken the sleeping child in Yancey's flesh.

Yancey didn't wait till she began to show to quit high school.
She quit the week before Christmas and took a job washing
dishes and waiting on tables part time at the Greek's restaurant
on Main Street. Doing that, she was able to make up the extra
two dollars to pay the raise in the mine company's rent. She
never went near Mister T.O.'s store on her way home from
work—to stop and stare for a spell. Even when it was a freezing
night and snow a-falling.

Meanwhile, up to the very end, Ma went around the house with a perpetual secret smile on her face that like to drove Yancey mad with outrage. Like she knowed a secret that Yancey didn't. One night she just couldn't stand it any more and stomped over to the coal stove where Ma was fixing dinner and snatched the saucepan of mustard greens out of Ma's hand and slammed it down on the stove.

Ma, I swear I can't make you out! Yancey cried. Knowing what I'm going through and you just fanning around the house humming to yourself with that daggone smile on your face.

Ma looked at Yancey gently, her face full of little lines like the marks on the map of an ancient and troubled country that seen many wars, many hard times.

You reckon what you're goin' through is bad, Yancey, she said softly. But hit ain't but a drop in the bucket to what Tommy Cotter's goin' through.

And she picked the saucepan up again and put it back over the hot place where it could simmer. And never said another mumbling word.

It was a cool afternoon in late April when the first pain hit Yancey. She was so stunned by it that she could barely hang on to the edge of the sink to keep from falling in the sudsy sink full of dishes. The Greek saw her. He came hurrying over.

You go home now, he said. Your time has come. You better go home. Fast.

The pains kept coming faster now as she hurried down the streetcar tracks. Twice she fell to her knees, biting down hard on her fist to keep from screaming. But she got up both times and kept staggering on. But when she got through the screen door everything went black. And then, like a swimmer surfacing and shaking water from her eyes, she was awake and filled with a peace she had never conceived could be. Because she could feel it in her arms, part of her, part of him! yet itself now and free of her flesh and his seed—the baby crying its fat, quacking cry till it found her breast and fixed its tiny toothless mouth upon her rose-ate nipple and fed upon her substance. And the harder it suckled the stronger she felt. She saw Ma and she saw Grandma Sweet

Potato in the rocking chair: the sleeves of the old woman's welfare sweater rolled to her wrinkled elbows and the skin still pink
from the hot water in which she'd had them whilst midwifing for
Yancey.

It's a boy, Ma said. Every bit of eight pounds. And not a mark
on him in spite of all your trouble in mind these past nine
months.

Did I have a hard time a-birthin' him? Yancey asked, feeling
strength flowing back into her with every drop of milk that
flowed out into that greedy little mouth. I mean did it tear me all
up down there?

Wasn't nothin to it, she said. Just like pullin' off your bobby
socks. It's always that way with us Lowther women.

Ma wore a Mickey Mouse wristwatch that had come in last
year's welfare Christmas basket. She stared at it now.

It ain't but three in the afternoon, she said. Just time enough.
For the County Courthouse hit don't close till five.

At the mention of that place of terror Yancey clutched the
baby so hard against her that two strong men couldn't have pried
it loose from her embrace.

I won't go! she shouted. You're on *their* side, Ma! I can't
hardly believe it but you are! Well, they'll not have him. You'll
all have to kill me dead afore he leaves my arms. I ain't got me
no gun! But there's that good sharp meat cleaver over the stove!
And I'll use it, too, when they come for him.

She stopped for breath, clutching the suckling child so close
Ma was half afraid she'd smother it in the softness of her full
young breast. And the thick dark lashes round her iris-colored
eyes were aglitter with tears of outrage and defiance.

She glared at Ma, who had sad wisdom and pride in her face.
She glared at Grandma Sweet Potato, who was rocking fast in
the chair and laughing till her toothless gums showed pink.

You all think I'm jist a-whistlin' Dixie, don't you? Yancey hollered. You think I ain't strong enough to make it out of here
before they come to take the baby! Well, you just watch this
then!

And she pulled the baby gently loose from her breast, laid it

on the quilt where it would not fall off, and with that turned a
cartwheel like she'd learned in high school gym class. Then she
ran to the old chest of drawers and commenced pulling drawers
open and flinging out the few clothes she had. Then she pulled
on her Levis and the man's blue work shirt and her socks and
sneakers and commenced packing her duds in dad's old World
War I kit bag, slung it over her shoulder with one arm and
fetched up the baby, wrapped in her old quilt, and held it against
her with the other. And stood glaring at them both.

She moved toward the door, paused, stared at them.

And if whenst I'm gone, she said. That no account, heart-
cheatin', girl-triflin' Tommy Cotter should come askin after
me—you tell him that ifn he was the last man on earth I'd not
never—

But I ain't the last man on earth, Yancey, Tommy said, and he
was blocking her way through the door. Even if I was the first.

Ma and Grandma Sweet Potato hurried out of the bedroom,
shutting the door softly behind them. Yancey's eyes flashed fire as
she stared up at Tommy Cotter.

I don't know what brings you here today, she said. To gloat—I
reckon. Well, go on then. Have your fun against I leave!

Then her face fell all apart and she commenced to crying.

I never meant to say that, Tommy, she sobbed. Because you're
right—it was the first. For me anyways. And it's a funny thing to
say but you acted that night like it was the first time for you, too,
though I knowed then as I know there's been a hundred girls
afore me.

It was the first time, he said. How'd you ever know that? The
first time for me ever' bit as much as it was for you, Yancey. And
I can't explain it to save my life.

He paused, his face coloring up: the stain of pink creeping up
from his neat blue collar to his hairline.

Yancey, he said. Take the baby and go set on the bed. And
then I'll come and kneel at your feet. For what I got to say ain't
fit for me to say standing up.

And she did as he told her. And she sat there staring down at him there, looking up into her face with those same eyes the baby had.

Yancey, he said. When your ma said that about you going to the courthouse she meant with me. To get our blood tests and the license and be wedded today. E'er the sun goes down. E'er the rising of the moon.

Yancey did not speak; could not speak, and the chuckling baby was sucking against the breast laid bare from her open shirt.

Yancey, Tommy said. You don't never know what this past winter's been for me. A-runnin' to hell headlong with Jobelle. A-figuring she'd make me fergit you. And known deep inside I didn't want her to.

He swallowed with difficulty.

Yancey, I been a trifler and a scoundler since the age of twelve, he said. You mind that tune that was playin' on the car radio that night you and me clumb in the backseat?

I sure do, she said. I couldn't never fergit it.

And she sang the first two lines in a clear, bold young voice; unabashed and marveling at the things that make men ashamed to speak of.

Cherry, Cherry—you're hard to get!
Cherry, Cherry—I'll get you yet.

That's it, Yancey, he said. That night wasn't only the first time for you. It was the first time for me, too. And after that first time I wasn't never the same. Though I tried to fergit. By runnin' around the county with Jobelle Stathers. I figgered she was so different from you that she'd drive that memory from my heart. But it just wouldn't cut.

Yancey waited, silent, not making a sound: listening to the suckling child and feeling stronger than in all her life.

There's more to my tale, Tommy said. More sinnin', too. Yancey, I been runnin' a still up in that high stand of timber and rhododendron thicket at the head of the dry creek bed below my house. There wasn't no other way I could make money enough to keep Jobelle. And yesterday afternoon I busted up with her. For keeps. Knowin' well and good her cheatin' heart would have its revenge on me. That she'd go to the State Police or the Internal Revenue men and snitch on me. So I made up my mind to go up there and take along my ax and my twelve-pound maul and smash it to pieces. And I taken a can of coal oil to burn that still-house down. And all the time I knowed ever' minute counted. But there was somethin' else—somethin' more important I had to do first, Yancey.

What thing, Tommy? she murmured gently.

All last summer, he said. And all last fall. And all winter long—I'd see you ever' day standing out on the boardwalk in front of Mister T.O.'s store staring in the show window at somethin' you wanted so bad you could taste it. And hits down at my house this very minute. Waitin' for you.

He hesitated, not looking at her now, looking instead at the baby. I ask you to come to the County Court House this very afternoon and be my bride.

Afore I answer yes or no, Yancey said, I'd admire if you was to get up off'n your knees and ask me standin'. I just don't admire to see no grown-up, strong, tall, handsome man on his knees to no woman. For if we're to have a roost together, Tommy, I don't aim to rule it. For I warn't raised up thataway.

Tommy stood up.

Will you, Yancey?

She didn't answer yes because the word wasn't big enough for all the yes she felt. But he could read the answer there all right. It was in her smile.

They got the baby and wrapped him up good in the quilt, for it was late in the afternoon and commencing to cool, and drove him to the Presbyterian chapel in town where he was christened Delano Llewelyn Wyatt Cotter—the first two surnames being those middle names of the President and John L. Lewis. And then they drove back down the creek road toward Tommy's one-room house below Ruby Trees a mile or two along the streetcar tracks.

I can't hardly wait till we get to your house, Tommy, Yancey said. My heart's just fairly in my throat a-thinkin' about it. Havin' it at last—the thing I've been wantin' all these months. And now it's twicet as precious to me since it was you who bought it for me.

When they got to his little shack he made Yancey hold her hands over her eyes as he led her up the steps of his small back porch, through the doorway and into the room.

I can't abide waitin' a minute more, Yancey cried out then. Besides—I already know what it is. Lord only knows I've stood there a-starin' at it through the window enough times. Can I take my fingers away and look at it now, Tommy?

Now, he said proudly, and she snatched her hands away and opened her eyes and saw it. The Maytag washing machine. She gasped, and then she threw back her pretty head and laughed a little and then cried a little and then did both at once. But when, at last, her gaze fixed upon it, her cheeks were rosy with joy and her big iris-colored eyes were gleaming with happiness.

It's beautiful! she murmured in his ear. Oh, so beautiful. 'Deed, it's the beautifullest thing I ever laid eyes on!

PICAYUNE PETE AND THE NINETY-PROOF COW

I used to be sad as a child when the movie was almost over.
I used to be sad, later, as a man, when life was almost over.
Forgetting in both cases the marvelous "coming
attractions."

—Davis Grubb, notebooks

To begin with French Marsh had it coming to him. There ain't a one of the boys that won't tell you that. It just wasn't natural nor fair for French to be getting the best of poor Picayune Pete that way, year after year. Down home on the courthouse steps when the boys ain't busy swapping watches or jackknives or double-barreled wedding-makers they're telling the story of Picayune Pete and the wonderful Ninety-Proof Cow and how Pete finally got the best of French Marsh in a swap.

Now swapping in Harrison County is what horses is to bluegrass men. It's like three-card monte to a Cincinnati gambler or gossip to a homely oldest daughter. It's a sport that just naturally gets into a man's hide tighter than a chigger in August till he'll swap the laces out'n his boots or the buttons off his pants if he thinks there's a chance to skin somebody. And poor Picayune

Pete just naturally couldn't never seem to get the hang of it. For no matter how hard he tried he always come out on the short end of the stick when it come to swapping with that ornery French Marsh.

French run a barbershop across from the Waldo Hotel and had a nice twenty-acre farm up on Buckhannon and poor Picayune Pete lived on a half acre of creek bank that was just naturally too poor to pick a fuss on. French lived in a good waterproof farmhouse and had fifteen head of cattle while Picayune Pete lived in a tin-roof shanty with no other company but the songbirds in the trees and a pet coon in an orange crate. The boys all knowed it was a pity—French always getting the best of Picayune Pete that way. But there wasn't a one that could keep from laughing the time Pete swapped French a brand-new hayfork for a Mickey Mouse wristwatch that had been saying eight o'clock for five years. Or the time French got Pete's flashlight for an old set of mail-order false teeth that couldn't make a soggy doughnut yell. The only thing in the world that Picayune Pete ever did manage to hold onto was that squirrel rifle of his and the boys all knowed it was just a matter of time till French Marsh had that. The gun was a dandy and the Lord knows Picayune Pete needed it bad enough for he was most always dead broke and half the food on his table was game he'd shot up Jackson's Run. That squirrel rifle was French Marsh's big mistake in a way. He might have knowed as soon as he'd swapped that off Picayune Pete the derned fool's luck would change.

It was a hot August morning when French come to town and led that poor old dried up muley cow into the courthouse yard. The boys all stopped swapping and come over and looked at the old critter, chuckling and joking and jabbing each other in the ribs and keeping their eyes peeled for Picayune Pete.

That cow ain't one of your herd, is she, French? says Bill Carruthers, the retired bootlegger.

Hell no! laughed French, winking at the boys. I got her off an old Indian woman down at Volga last week for four dollars. From the looks of her she ain't give no milk for ten years and I'll be damned if I know what make she is! I only bought the derned critter to swap off on Picayune Pete for that squirrel rifle of his!

Just then they seen Pete shuffling down Pike Street with a yellow basket in his hand and they all stood around in a circle to see the fun. French Marsh was a shrewd one. He never even looked up when Picayune Pete come over to him and set the basket down. The old cow was tied up to a little sycamore over behind the statue of Stonewall Jackson's horse and Picayune Pete didn't see her. He bent down and pulled back the piece of burlap from the basket so's French and the boys could see what he'd brought to swap.

What's he worth? says Picayune Pete, squinting his eyes and trying to look real tricky and clever. Down in the basket blinking his eyes was the gayest little Bantam rooster you'd ever want to see. French Marsh reached in and held the critter up by his feet. Directly he sort of grunted and put him back.

Ain't worth much, says French, spitting a big brown splash on the sidewalk and thinking about that fine squirrel gun. Don't lay no eggs! Just a play-toy for the kids! Ain't fit to eat!

Well now, what'll you swap, French? says Picayune Pete and you could just see the swap fever starting to crawl all over him.

Well, says French, taking out his jackknife and starting to pare his thumbnail with it. If you was to throw in that squirrel gun of yours—I might just swap you that fine little cow over there.

Picayune Pete looked up and shaded his eyes with his big, bony hand. Then he walked slowly over to where the old critter was tied to the little sycamore tree. The boys all started poking each other in the ribs and giggling. Picayune Pete studied the cow for a spell—feeling of her ribs and getting down and staring first in one eye and then in the other and then looking her in the teeth.

You'll never get a better cow! says French, and that was gospel truth, though French never knowed it then. She's a little old, I'll grant ye. But with the right kind of feed and a little lovin' kindness—

But Picayune Pete wasn't listening. Directly he come back over to French Marsh and took him by the hand.

Well now, he whispered, his eyes all wild and his face kind of pale. I just naturally can't believe it! I just can't remember what I've ever done to rate such a mess of good luck all in one day!

Then it's a swap? says French Marsh, snapping his jackknife closed.

Is it a swap? says Picayune Pete. Well you can just bet your Aunt Fanny it's a swap, French Marsh, and no backin' out neither! But there's just one thing I can't understand! You're supposed to be a cattleman, French! I give you credit for having better sense!

What do you mean? says French, getting suspicious. You ain't went and busted the stock on that squirrel gun, have you, Picayune Pete!

No, says Picayune Pete in a dreamy, long-gone kind of voice. That rifle's as sound as the morning she come from Frank Stout's hardware store! It's just that I can't understand a smart cattleman like you, French Marsh—*not knowing!*

Not knowing what! hollered French Marsh, getting a little riled. That there's a fine little cow, I'll grant! I wouldn't swap her off on you if she wasn't!

Picayune Pete sat down on the courthouse steps like he just didn't have no more strength to stand. He shook his shaggy, sandy head slowly like he just couldn't believe it.

My granny told me once, says Picayune Pete, in a voice that seemed meant for him alone to hear. That she seen one once at the Nicholas County Fair and that was nigh a hundred year ago! She said it cost her a perfectly good greenback dollar bill *just to take a look!* And my pappy said he'd heard tell of 'em but he'd never seen one and to think that now— Well I just naturally can't get it through my head it's me a-settin' here!

The boys had all quit laughing now and had all went over to look at the cow and see if maybe they hadn't missed something.

Cows is cows! said French Marsh, hitching up his pants.

Well no, says Picayune Pete, going over like he was in a trance and untying the rope from the little sycamore tree. That's just where you're wrong, French Marsh. There's plain, ordinary cows and then there's the other kind.

What other kind, you derned fool! hollered French Marsh, stuffing a big chew in his cheek. Listen here now! I was as good as raised up in a cow barn and there ain't a thing you can tell me about cows that I don't already know!

You was raised in the bottomlands, French, says Picayune Pete. You wasn't raised in the mountains. There's a few things a mountain man could tell you about cows that you don't already know. You got her off of an Indian, didn't ye?

Well, yes, says French. How'd you know that? What's that got to do with it anyhow? Cows is cows!

Well no, French, says Picayune Pete, his eyes all lit up like a Holiness preacher. He walked away, leading his cow down toward the street. No, says Picayune Pete. That's there's just where you're wrong. There's plain cows and there's the other kind. I'll bring you that squirrel gun this afternoon. And just so's you won't feel I'm cheatin' you so bad I'll throw in a box of ca'tridges.

Well, when you thought about it a while, a cow—most any cow—would seem like a wonderful thing to a man like Picayune Pete that never had nothing in his breakfast tin cup but cold well-water. And French Marsh knowed his cattle—there was no two ways about that. That poor, old, hornless muley cow certainly looked like she'd seen her best days and left them far behind. Still it was plain that French was uneasy and suspicious and sort of half afraid that maybe Picayune Pete knowed more about that cow than he'd said. It was true that French Marsh was a country boy and knowed the ways of the bottomlands well enough. But Picayune Pete was a mountain man and as full of lorn, lonely secrets as the waters of the wild Cheat River. He brought French the squirrel gun just as he said he would and then for a week nobody seen hide nor hair of him. French and the rest of the boys was setting on the courthouse steps that Saturday afternoon when Picayune Pete come back to town.

Hell, French was just saying. No wonder he ain't showed his face around the courthouse for the past week! He knows well and good he ain't got nothin' more to put up!

It was Bill Carruthers that seen Pete first and then French seen him and like to fell over backward in the grass. For Picayune Pete was dressed to kill, in a fancy green-check mail-order suit and a yellow straw hat and fancy brown-and-white shoes.

Bill, says French Marsh. Remind me to go over to Doc Blankensop's Monday and git these glasses changed. When I first seen that dude over there I could have swore for a minute it was Picayune Pete.

Well it is! whispered Bill, his eyes sticking out like pool balls. Unless my peepers has failed me, too! It's Picayune Pete and he's all decked out brighter than Cap'n Billy Bryant's showboat!

French snatched out his tobacco plug and tore off a chunk.

Good day, says Picayune Pete, sauntering across the courthouse lawn. Would any of you gentlemen care to join me in a glass of beer this warm August day?

Well, to see the look on French Marsh's face was worth the quarter you'd pay to see a moving-picture show. He sat there with his chew between his teeth like he didn't have the strength left to bite it. And directly Picayune Pete is leading the boys across Pike Street to the Recreation Pool Room, leaving poor old French Marsh setting there like he didn't have no more sense that a toad in the mud.

Charlie! says Picayune Pete, flapping a greenback on the big, shiny bar. Beers for these gentlemen, Charlie!

Old Charlie Polk, the bartender, put down his love-story magazine and come over and put his spectacles on and stared at Picayune Pete and then he picked up the greenback and stared at it and then he took it over in the light and studied it some more. Then he drawed the beers. For thirty years Charlie Polk had tended bar in the Recreation Pool Room and hadn't never seen Picayune Pete drink a beer unless somebody else was buying.

French! says Picayune Pete, when French come shuffling in directly all dazed and goofy-looking. Don't miss out on this free beer now! If it wasn't for you I wouldn't be buyin' today!

Picayune Pete! says French Marsh in a hoarse whisper. Who are you tryin' to kid! Where'd you steal that dollar?

I never stole it! laughed Picayune Pete, smacking his lips all white with lager foam.

Then where in time did you lay your hands on money for them beers! hollers French, slapping his hand on the bar. And all them fancy duds!

Well, sir, says Picayune Pete. I owe it all to Nellie, French! Ever' damn bit of it! She's the most wonderful little cow that ever chawed a cud!

What! hollered French, slapping the bar again. You ain't standin' there tryin' to tell me that you went and sold that derned muley cow for *money!*

Nope! says Picayune Pete, helping hisself to a pretzel and a sausage from the free lunch.

Well, you ain't gettin' no milk from her, are ye? hollered French Marsh.

Nope! says Picayune Pete, with his mouth full of pretzel and free-lunch sausage.

Then where'd you git the money at! hollered French Marsh.

Picayune Pete held up his hand for silence.

Gentlemen, he says, his voice like a man getting ready to come out for sheriff for the third time. I got no more time to stand around here jawin'! Nellie ain't been fed yit! It's time I was gittin' on home!

And with that he walked out and left French and the boys scratching their heads and trying to figure it all out.

It was a good half hour past sundown when French and Fred Burke, the Constable, walked up the tracks to Picayune Pete's and hid up in a laurel thicket above the streetcar tracks so's they could watch.

You just wait, Fred! French Marsh was whispering. That devil is up to something illegal and ornery or I miss my guess! He showed up in town today dressed like a drunken pallbearer and throwin' money around like it was feed for the hogs!

Down in Picayune Pete's shack they could see a little oil lamp burning in the window and a curl of blue smoke drifting up through the trees from the stovepipe on the roof. But the thing that French Marsh couldn't take his eyes off of was that little new building down on the creek bank. It wasn't fancy and it wasn't much and it was mostly old tin and cardboard and secondhand joists but there was one thing plain to see. It was a cow shed.

I'll be damned! says French Marsh, scratching his head. That derned muley cow ain't died yit!

Which? says the Constable.

Never mind! whispers French. Looky there! He's a-comin' out of his shanty! He's got a milk pail in his hand! He's walkin' down to the cow shed. He's a-goin' to milk her! Well I'll be blamed! If I'd ever have thought that dried-up critter would ever—

Hssst! says the Constable. He's gone inside. Now let's you and me just sneak down there and spy around Picayune Pete's shack a little while he ain't there!

Then went down through the laurels easy so's not to make any noise and they tiptoed down through the yard, trying hard not to trip on the tin cans that was everywhere, and directly they slipped inside the door.

There now! whispered French Marsh, all hoarse and excited. What'd I tell you, Fred! Just looky there! He's been *stillin'*!

Well, if there was one jug of corn whisky in that little shanty there was fifty. There was glass jugs of it and stone jugs and coal-oil cans. There was booze in the tin cups and booze in the wash-tub and booze in the well bucket. There was mason jars full of it and jelly glasses and lard cans full to brimming. And the sweet-ness that filled the air was enough to make a preacher thirsty. The Constable picked up a jug, crooked his elbow and took a good snort.

Hot damn! hollered the Constable. Now that there'd make a rabbit go up and spit in a hound-dog's eye! Lord, ain't it a shame—having to run a talented man like Picayune Pete into the jailhouse at Moundsville for a year. I say that any man who can make—

Hssst! whispered French Marsh. It's him a-comin'!

Howdy, Constable! says Picayune Pete, coming in the door and setting his pail by the window. Howdy, French. Don't stand on ceremony. Pull up some chairs and set!

No, says the Constable, looking sadly around at all that fine booze and sniffing the sweetness of it into his head. I'll not do that. The people of the county elected me to keep the laws of West Virginia, Picayune Pete. And you know just as well as me that stillin' is agin' the law!

Stillin'! hollered Picayune Pete, sinking down in a chair, looking all ghastly and mortified. Why, Constable, what's got into you! What ever made you to think I was stillin'!

Them jugs! That's what! hollered French Marsh, slamming his fist on the table. That washtub there and them mason jars full of moonshine! You'll not worm your way out of this one, Picayune Pete! You been awful damn smart here of late but you outsmarted your own self this time!

French! gasps Picayune Pete, throwing up his hands. What's got into you! Why if I'd a-figured you never knowed what kind of a cow that was you swapped me 'deed I wouldn't never have shook on it!

What's the blamed cow got to do with it? hollered the Constable. Say what's a-goin' on here! Is this some kind of a joke, French?

Hell yes, it's a joke! hollered French. This derned bootlegger here keeps a-talkin' about that dried-up old muley cow I swapped him last week like she was something wonderful!

Well now, says Picayune Pete, holding up the brimful dairy pail for French and the Constable to see. She *is* wonderful! Today she wasn't lettin' down so good and only give me two gallon. But I never scolded her for I knowed she tried. Yesterday she had a three-gallon day and Monday she had close to a four. That don't sound to me like she's dried up, does it to you, Constable?

Picayune Pete! hollered the Constable. What are you tryin' to say!

Why just this, Constable, says Picayune Pete. I just can't see no cause for me gittin' the blame for French Marsh not knowing his cattle! If French Marsh ain't got no more sense than to go and swap away one of the finest Ninety-Proof Cows that ever—

One of the which? screamed French Marsh, like he was getting ready to have a stroke.

Ninety-Proof Cows, says Picayune Pete. My granny used to tell me about them when I was still a boy in knee britches. She said she seen one down at the County Fair at Summersville and it cost her good hard money just to *look!* My own pappy said he'd never even seen one and the Lord only knows I never figgered to neither—let alone *own* one!

Ninety-Proof Cows, says the Constable, setting down and pouring hissels a good brimming tin cup full. Well now I never heard tell of them kind of cows. Did you, French?

But French was too burned up to answer. All he could do was just set there and grind up his chewing tobacco.

Well, sir, says Picayune Pete. The Indians down in Pocahontas County, the Lord knows how long ago, bred and raised them critters on corn and rye and ground-up sassafras and buckeyes and a little turpentine throwed in and just a smidgin' of lye and a few draps of copperhead p'izin—

You mean to stand there, Picayune Pete! screamed French Marsh. With your bare face hangin' out and try to tell me you've got a cow down there in that shed that gives whisky instead of milk!

Well now, says Picayune Pete, holding up the pail for French Marsh to see. That there ain't nothin' I'd ever put in a little baby's bottle unless I was big enough to whup him!

I don't believe it! French hollered. I'll have to see it and then I won't believe it!

Well then, come on down to the shed! hollered Picayune Pete. Nellie ain't shy!

So down to the cow shed they went and there stood Nellie, happy and dreamy looking as could be, with a good big mouthful of the Indian feed. And Picayune Pete went over to her and mumbled some little foolishness in her ear and scratched her back and then he fetched a pail and set down on the milking stool and went to milking her and singing a lorn, lonely little mountain tune as he worked. French and the Constable bent over his shoulder and watched and seen there wasn't no trick to it and heard the sharp little jets in the pail and seen the likker and their mouths was hanging open a foot.

I don't believe it! whispered French Marsh, all hoarse and

shaky, when Picayune Pete stopped directly and held up the pail for them to see.

Well, says the Constable. I don't neither but I seen it. And I'll be damned if that there ain't the finest mountain dew that ever broke up a tent meetin'!

When they heard the crash, both Picayune Pete and the Constable turned around and there was old French Marsh stretched out cold like a pole-axed steer on the cow shed floor. The Constable eased him up and Picayune Pete fanned him with his hat and give him a drink from the pail and directly French opened one eye and sighed like a horse with the bullheaves.

Well, says the Constable. I'll be damned if I'm a-goin' back to the Sher'f with a story like this, Picayune Pete! You sure as hell can't put a cow in the jailhouse and as far as I can read the Law from here there hain't a thing we can pin on you! In my judgment the case is closed shut for lack of evidence! Come on, French! Git up on your feet! My missus is keeping supper warm fer me!

Picayune Pete stood there listening to the two of them going up the tracks toward town—French Marsh hollering and swearing and the Constable just shaking his head and saying he wouldn't have nothing more to do with it.

How the word ever got back to the boys at the courthouse was never known. French Marsh surely was the last one in the world to want it told and the Constable said he'd keep it under his hat for fear the Sheriff would fire him for drinking on the job. But somehow the fellers got wind of it. And for months all French Marsh did was to put up with ornery jokes and jibes and when he wasn't doing that he was trying to think up some way to get Picayune Pete in the swapping mood again.

Picayune Pete, French would say, every time he got the chance. I've got a mighty fine Hereford stud over at my place and I thought maybe you might—

Swap Nellie back? Picayune Pete would say. Hell no, French Marsh. I just couldn't do that. Nellie and me is like brother and sister. Them Ninety-Proof Cows is sentimental critters, French! I just naturally don't think she'd be happy with nobody else!

And that would be all there was to it and French would go off by hisself and brood on it and not understand that it warn't so much the three dollars a gallon that Picayune Pete was getting up in the Monongalia mine towns or down in the lumber camps on the Cheat that made him so fond of the Ninety-Proof Cow. A man like French Marsh—born and raised in bottomlands—wouldn't never understand the heart of a mountain man like Picayune Pete that was as deep and lorn-lonely as a night wind moaning in a high holler tree. As for Picayune Pete, there was no denying he was prospering something scandalous. After a while he'd saved up enough to buy hisself a Model-T for his deliveries and the next thing folks knew, he'd built a new cow shed for Nellie—a good one this time—out of brand-new pine two-by-fours with a pretty little tile trough for Nellie's feed and nice feed-sack curtains in the windows. Blakey Snyder had a ten-acre farm down the streetcar line a piece and Blakey used to let Picayune Pete put the Ninety-Proof Cow out to pasture with his herd in exchange for a gallon or so of the wonderful mountain dew. And Blakey's critters seemed to know that Nellie was something extry special for they treated her with a gentle and critterlike respect. Sometimes on Saturday afternoons Picayune Pete would bring Nellie to town in the back seat of his Model-T—all brushed and sweet-smelling with lilac hair tonic on her back and a little blue ribbon on one ear. And whenever he'd come driving her down past the courthouse where French and the boys was setting in the shade of Stonewall Jackson's horse it was enough to drive poor French Marsh out of his mind just to think what he'd swapped away. And the boys that used to mock old Picayune Pete were fiddling another tune when they heard the story of the Ninety-Proof Cow. For in a way it was a miracle—that a feller who'd been so dumb all them years could have sprouted brains so quick. Then come that awful Saturday when Picayune Pete brought the Ninety-Proof Cow to town for the last time and it seemed as though whatever brains he'd growed was surely gone to seed. Down Pike Street come Picayune Pete in his Model-T with Nellie rared up in the back seat chawing on a popcorn ball Picayune Pete had bought for her at Mr. Garvin's Candy Store.

Howdy, French! hollers Picayune Pete, pulling over to the curb and climbing out.

Hullo, Pete, says French Marsh, as beat-down looking as a sheep-killing dog.

French, says Picayune Pete. You and me hain't swapped now in close to a year. I woke up this mornin' and just got to itchin' all over. It was the swap fever, French, and it was just a-crawlin' all over me so bad I couldn't hold still in the bed.

Well, you can just bet old French Marsh's ears pricked up at that. He bit off a chew of tobacco real slow and thoughtful and tried to look like he wasn't much interested.

I don't know, says Picayune Pete. There for a while durin' breakfast I got to thinkin' maybe I might swap you back Nellie—

Well, the boys all gathered round and looked at Picayune Pete like they just couldn't believe their ears. And from the looks of French Marsh he was having a little trouble getting the idea straight in his head, too.

Well, gulps French, trying to keep from swallowing his chew. I might maybe give that a little thought—

On the other hand, says Picayune Pete, with a sad, dreamy look in his eyes. It just naturally busts me all up to think of partin' with my Nellie! Her and me has growed closer than paint to a barn wall. But you know somethin', French! It's been a-worryin' me! It's got so I can't sleep good of a night thinkin' about the way I skinned you in that swap!

Well, the boys looked at one another with their mouths hanging open and then they looked at Picayune Pete and then they just shook their heads. Poor Picayune Pete! Wouldn't never learn if he lived to be a thousand! It was plain to see that French Marsh was having a hard time holding hisself back. He strolled slowly off under the sycamore tree where he'd tied the Ninety-Proof Cow that day and sat down in the grass and shut his eyes.

Well, says French, shutting his eyes and dreaming of a mountain of sparkling moonshine jugs and greenback dollar bills. I just want you to know one thing, Picayune Pete! If I was to swap the little critter back it's just because I've growed so fond of her lovin' disposition myself! I don't never touch likker 'cept for medicine and my missus don't neither and seein' as how we're both church members I sure couldn't go 'round *sellin'* the stuff! No indeedy!

Well, I'm right glad to hear you say that, French, says Picayune Pete, with a tear gleaming in his eye. 'Deed it just busts my heart to think of losin' Nellie! But it's worth my peace of mind! A man's got no right to go through life skinnin' his neighbors the way I done you, French! I'll be damned if he does!

In that case, says French Marsh. I'll tell you what I'll do, Picayune Pete. I'll swap you fifty dollars' cash on the bar'l head, your squirrel gun back and my genu-ine gold watch!

Well no, says Picayune Pete, frowning and scratching his sandy head. No, that don't seem quite fair to me, French! I'll be damned if it does!

Lord a'mighty! says French. All right then. I'll throw in that brand-new jackknife I swapped off you two years ago!

Picayune Pete wiped a tear off his leathery cheek and shook his head.

Well no, says Picayune Pete. You're a-goin' the wrong way, French Marsh! I don't want nothin' more than what I give! I ain't askin' nothin' more for Nellie but four bits for the banty rooster and my squirrel gun back!

Well, the boys all hitched their pants up and spit and wandered off disgusted-looking. There just wasn't no sense to a man like Picayune Pete. He was just dumber than Ned in the first reader and no two ways.

It's a swap! roared French Marsh, jumping to his feet and grabbing the hand of Picayune Pete. Then he lit out across the courthouse yard for his barbershop and directly he come tearing back with the squirrel gun in one hand and a four-bit piece in the other.

Now! hollered French Marsh, running over to the Model-T and leading Nellie down out of the backseat. Now you derned halfwit, Picayune Pete! The critter's mine agin'!

Yes, said Picayune Pete softly, wandering out and climbing up under the steering wheel with the tears gleaming in his eyes as he took his last look at the Ninety-Proof Cow. She's yours, French.

And it tears my heart to see her go. 'Deed I reckon I'd go down to Summersville and stay drunk for a year if it wasn't for the *calf*!

The which! says French Marsh, stroking the ears of that wonderful four-legged moonshine still.

The calf! sobs Picayune Pete, starting up his motor with an awful roar. Nellie's calf! 'Deed if she ain't the prettiest little tan-and-white darlin' you ever did see! Looks like she'll be even sweeter than Nellie there! Nellie thinks so, too! It's just naturally made a new cow out of her!

What do you mean! screamed French Marsh, over the thundering backfires of the Model-T.

Look in her eyes, French! Look in her eyes! sobbed Picayune Pete, just before he took off down Pike Street. It's mighty plain to see that you got a lot to learn about Ninety-Proof Cows! You wouldn't think much of a mother that'd give her youngin' hard likker, would ye? Well, Nellie ain't no different—

What are you talkin' about! bellered French Marsh, with the sweat breaking out all over his face.

Why just this, French! hollered Picayune Pete. I was glad to hear that you and your old woman is both Temperance folks! Because you won't have to worry none about Nellie! Just look at that light in her eyes, French Marsh! It just as much as says she don't never intend to give nothin' but milk agin' to her dyin' day!

GREEN THUMB

Lamed irreparably by the wind, the rain came *limping* down
the light—on the cold steep crutch of the moon.
                                    —Davis Grubb, notebooks

Nobody in Glory ever blamed Uncle Hildreth for killing his
wife, Old Jo. Folks even wondered how he had held back from
doing it as long as he had. Doctor Bruce once referred to her as
"a virago and a harridan" and the dictionary in the Glory Public
Library wasn't big enough to have those words so we let it go.
We knew what they meant. For somehow the very sound of them
fit her. Bitter. Ornery. Foul-tempered. A tongue like a water
moccasin. Mean as gar broth. Yes, as some maintained, downright possessed of devils. And at last, after twenty years of marriage to Uncle Hildreth she just went one step too far that day.
Despite his long-suffering Christianity.

In the morning he had gone up the river along the road to
Glory from his little farm, down below the bend in the Ohio
pilots call the Devil's Elbow. He made a few purchases—includ-
ing a hatchet—at Mr. List's General Store, spent the afternoon
getting drunk up in McFadden's orchard, had at last gone home,
was met most likely with one of Old Jo's screaming tantrums,
and the straw done broke the camel's back. He killed her. With
the new hatchet. It was there on the floor—all bloodied up with

173

a few strands of her iron-gray hair on it. But not a sign of her body. After he had finished killing her and left the kitchen splattered with blood and gore from ceiling to floor he had somewhere, somehow disposed of her body, hitched his roan mare to his rockaway buggy and headed off down river southwards.

It was in April of the year 1901. I mind it because it was the same year the old English queen died. I was an orphan of ten, living with my Aunt Jane Lockwood who was Uncle Hildy's sister and lived on the hill just above the little orchard behind Hildy's house. It's a marvel to me I didn't hear the screaming ruckus of her killing that afternoon. As it was, I was the first one to discover the scene of the crime. Aunt Jane had sent me down the hill to borrow a cup of sugar for a peach cobbler and when I walked into that kitchen it was a sight to behold. Not that I was the least bit scared, nor shocked, nor surprised. If you want the truth of it I was secretly glad. For it don't help a boy of ten grow up when he daily witnesses a fifty-year-old kin of his take the abuse old Jo handed out to Uncle Hildy.

I sat on a split-bottom chair in that kitchen for a good ten minutes taking it all in. Looking. Smelling. For blood has a smell—scary to some, but not to me. I saw it as a Justice. One a long time in coming. A Justice. After a spell I left and went walking up the road to Glory, taking my time, too, and whistling carefree as a meadowlark and rolling a hoop ahead of me with a stick. A grown-up would have gone straight to the sheriff but I know ours had about as much common sense as would fill Aunt Jane's solid-gold thimble. Instead I went to the house of old Dr. Bruce—the wisest, best learned man in all our bottomland country—and who had birthed more than a thousand babies since he came to Glory from Tidewater, Virginia, long before the War, and lived to see some of those babies grow up and die natural deaths. That day he was in his little office—a small octagonal building on the corner of his lot, away from his house, and was examining the foot of an old Swiss farmer with the gout. But when he taken one quick look at my face he read something in it plain as newsprint and sent that old farmer packing. Then he told me to take a chair while he kept on studying me on the other side of his desk in his black leather rocking chair.

Something has happened to Miss Lockwood, boy? he asked.

No, sir, I answered. Aunt Jane's just fine, Dr. Bruce. It's about Hildy. My uncle. He's went and killed old Jo his wife with a hatchet.

And?

Her body must be in the river, I said. For it's not there. Neither is Uncle Hildy. I reckon after he done it, sir, he hitched our roan to the rockaway and took off south.

Dr. Bruce had a way of calming you down, no matter what. He was used to Death. But then he was used to Birth, too. Now he stroked his elegant white mustache.

Are you surprised or upset, boy?

No, sir.

I paused.

I not only ain't surprised nor upset, I went on. I'm proud.

He nodded.

I can appreciate that, he said. You're a Cresap. He was a Cresap. It was hard for you to see one of your kin take such abuse without lifting a hand to strike back. Till now.

I swallowed hard.

Will they hang him, sir? I asked. On the gallows up at Glory State Prison—when they catch him?

Maybe they won't catch him, Dr. Bruce said, a gleam in his eye. Your uncle probably put her body aboard his skiff, rowed out into the middle of the river and dumped her in. So it's not likely she'll ever be found what with the high stage the river's at this spring and the fast current in the channel. She's probably halfway to Louisville by now.

He paused, smiling gently.

You love your uncle, don't you, boy?

I do, sir. He taught me to hunt groundhogs. How to lay trot lines. How to gig for frogs in the shoals with a lantern at night.

And you'd not want to see him hanged, said the doctor. Nor

would most people here in Mound County who will look upon
your aunt's murder as a Justice.

Again he paused.

Yes, he said. A Justice. So that even should Hildreth Cresap
be apprehended somewheres down river, boy. I doubt if they
would even try him for murder. In the first place there is no
corpus delecti—no body of the victim, that is—and I think even
if there were, that any grand jury would call it a clear-cut case of
justifiable homicide. Or even self-defense. For many's the time
I've had to put a leech to a black eye of your uncle where that
harridan and virago of a wife had struck him.

He leaned back in his rocker behind the polished black walnut
desk.

He will be a sad loss to this community, he said. Now that
he's run off. For he was a remarkable man, boy.

You mean with that green thumb of his.

Yes, said Dr. Bruce. But that's not all. He had qualities of
thrift, honesty, hard work. And living with Old Jo for twenty
years should in itself earn him wings to sit at the feet of the Lord.
But, as you say—that green thumb of his—it was astonishing.
He could make anything grow. Now I take into consideration
that this black river bottomland soil is more than commonly arable—

What does arable mean, Dr. Bruce, sir?

I apologize, he said. Sometimes I forget you're only a boy. It
means land well suited for the growing of crops. And this soil
along the Ohio has been famed for its fertility since long before
the Revolution. Still some things will simply not grow there.
Although—

He rocked to and fro behind the desk, the tips of his fingers
pressed together thoughtfully.

I'll wager, he said. That if Hildreth Cresap had planted lemon
seeds in that land of his we'd be sipping ice-cold lemonade from
one of his trees come some long, hot summer day.

He swung round now and faced me again.

But back to the murder of his wife, he said. There is no corpus
delecti. There is a murder weapon?

Yes, I said. A hatchet. With blood and a few of her old gray hairs stuck in the blood on the blade.

Dr. Bruce shook his head.

I'd not fret and fume a moment over your Uncle Hildreth's future if I were you, young man, he said. He will like as not drift westering—like so many since the War—and start a new life in Texas or California.

You reckon he'll get married again, sir?

He's only fifty-odd years old, said the doctor. Yes, I wager he will.

I cried out in an irrepressible cry of joy.

Golly, Doctor! I cried. Then maybe you and me and Aunt Jane can take a sleeping car west and visit him and his new missus. And it will be grand. Because this time he'll surely pick a wife as decent and Christian as old Jo was evil and possessed of devils.

No, said the doctor. He will not marry a different sort of wife.

But, sir—surely he's had his fill of her breed.

Boy, said the old doctor gently. Some men have the irresistible urge to marry the wrong kind of women. One who'll make life miserable. And if Hildreth marries again—I'll wager he'll pick a mate even meaner and more contentious than his late wife Josephine Lindsay. And don't ask me the reason why for I don't know the answer. I know only that I've seen it time and again—all my life.

This purely baffled me. But not I—nor anyone else in Glory—was ever one to question the judgment of Dr. Bruce. Not even on that terrible night—later in the summer—when things came to their fearful culmination. After the sheriff had visited the scene of the crime, gone back to the courthouse and reported the disappearance and probable murder of Josephine Lindsay Cresap by person or persons unknown, we all thought that was the end of it. Everybody, that is, but old Dr. Bruce. And me. For boys my age, like old, wise men, have instincts; intuitions. And him and me—we both smelled a you-know-what in the woodpile.

One morning in June I was walking up Seventh Street from the wharf where I had seen the *Queen City* put in to pick up a

great cargo of work pants made by the convicts up at the prison.
I was just passing Dr. Bruce's little office when he appeared in
the doorway with a sheet of white paper in his hand and asked
me to come in. When he was in the rocker behind his desk and I
in the chair on the other side he held the paper up.

A letter, he said. It arrived in this morning's post.

I see, sir.

It is postmarked from a town called Natchez downriver in the
state of Mississippi and it is signed with your Uncle Hildreth's
name, he said calmly, lighting up a long, dark Marsh Wheeling
stogie. The letter says he is well off, prospering in a new job, has
saved up enough money to head west, which he plans to do by
the time this letter arrives and adds that it is useless to send the
Law to Natchez after him because he won't be there anymore.
He will be westering. With a new name, a black beard, and a
whole new identity.

I'm mighty glad, I said. To know he's alive and well.

Dr. Bruce puffed slowly, thoughtfully on his stogie, whose
pleasant smell filled the little office.

Yet, he said. There are two things amiss here. There is more to
this than meets the eye. In the first place, it is unthinkable that
a man of the Christian caliber of Hildreth Cresap would ever
walk down a steamboat stageplank and onto the landing of a city
such as Natchez. For it as foul and iniquitous a place as Sodom or
Gomorrah. And I know whereof I speak for I was once there
briefly—during the War Between the States—when I was company surgeon under Longstreet in the Army of the Confederacy.

He paused, puffing on his stogie and rocking slowly.

I said there were two things amiss here, he went on. And here
is the second.

He paused, pondering, rocking, puffing hard.

This letter is signed by your uncle, he said. But it is not in his
hand.

He paused again.

I know your uncle's hand quite well, he said. A fine Spen-
cerian script. While this letter is written by someone scarcely
literate.

Is that all, sir?

No, boy. There is a third troublesome element here.

And what is it, sir?

I cannot tell you, he said. Yet. Not until I lay hands on all my facts. And I have the premonition that I will have them before the leaves of autumn turn and the pawpaw in the hollers go black from first frost. Stick by me, boy. We'll fish the truth out of this mud hole soon, unless I miss my guess.

And we did. Now it is mid-July. It is a night too hot for sleep and there is a full moon to boot and full moons always make me nervous as a girl till somehow I'm half-tempted to take a sip of Aunt Jane's paregoric for my nerves. But I didn't. Aunt Jane she keeps a close eye on the level of liquid in that blue glass pharmacist's bottle for she knows of the weakness for stimulants that runs through the Cresap line for generations back. But I gave up the notion of trying to sleep. I got out of my small four-poster bed, shinnied out of my flannel nightshirt, got into my worsted, checkered shirt, pulled on my linsey britches and tiptoed barefoot out of my room and down the staircase of that old house and out the front door. That house of Aunt Jane's was older than Mount Vernon and I wondered how I'd gotten out without waking her since nearly every step you take in that old place sets some piece of wood or other talking. But I did.

I stood a long spell in the yard, staring down the pasture, beyond the little orchard, at the house of Uncle Hildy. Nobody in Glory had gone near the place all that summer. Not even to clean up the blood and gore. They were scared of it, I reckon. But not me. And something seemed to whisper to me from the Other Side to go down there. Now. This moonlit night. Whispers from the lips of someone I had loved and who had loved me. Maybe my dead ma or pa. I got halfway down the slope when the wind rose from the funky, muddy old river—twanging in the cattails with frogs—and the wind gently stirred my hair, like the soft stroking of invisible and gentle fingers. The moon lay above the glimmering river like a great ripe casaba melon. It made things almost bright as noonday. I walked toward the fence

round the house and still was not scared. My heart was beating
fast but not from fear. From what then?

And presently I was pushing through the crumbling wood gate
on its whimpering, rusty hinges and standing in the yard where
once, out of sheer meanness, Aunt Jo had got mad at Uncle
Hildy over something and whilst he was in town, fetched a meat
cleaver and cut the heads off all thirty of his prize white leghorns
and heaped them there in a bloody heap for him to come home
and find. I tell you she was a caution—old Jo was.

As I stood there the wind quickened. And suddenly I was
aware of something I had never sensed in that yard before in all
the times I'd been there. It was perfume. A smell so sweet it
almost made you sneeze. A smell like somebody had gone to
Stone and Thomas store in Wheeling and bought a half dozen
bottles of the most expensive French perfume there is and then
come back and sprinkled them empty all along one side of that
bloody and deserted house. I poked around a good while before I
found what made it. It was a plant—a kind of vine of some breed
or other—with pale white blossoms. One look told me it wasn't
any plant I had ever seen growing in the bottomlands or back up
in the creeks and marshes and hollers in the hills where grow the
orchid and dwarf iris and lady slipper and bird's-foot violet. This
was a plant, I knew, from nowhere near our part of the country.

In the bright moonlight I ran all the way up the dusty river
road to Glory. To Dr. Bruce's house. I hammered only twice on
the big brass knocker before I spied, through the frosted glass
panels on either side of the white door frame, the bobbing gleam
of his oil lamp as he came hurrying down the steps. I knew he
wouldn't be mad. He was used to being roused out of bed at all
hours of the night and morning before dayrise. He opened the
door, his blue eyes keen and alert, and looking at me.

Come in, boy, come in, he said.

He had on a blue velour bathrobe and red carpet slippers, and
he led me into the library and lighted the oil lamp in the middle
of the library table. Its yellow shine gleamed on the row after row
of soft leather books which lined the walls of that room.

Now what brings you here at this hour of the night, Dan'l boy? he asked. Is it green apple colic or just the solemecholies?

I stared at him a little wild-eyed, I reckon.

Somethin' queer's agrowin' down there, I said.

Something queer, he said smiling. Is growing down where, son?

Down along the back of Uncle Hildy's house, I said.

He studied me a spell.

What species of plant is it, boy? he asked. Or don't you know?

I don't know, I said. I only know I never seen one like it. Not even in the seed catalog. It's a breed of vine with dark green leaves and white flowers. Flowers that give off a sweet smell strong enough to make you sneeze. Like real dear-costing perfume.

Yes, he said. I know it now.

He paused.

And spreading its scent all the stronger this night of the full moon, he said then. The moon which draws forth its sweetness tenfold.

He rose from his chair and stood staring at me.

Trachelospernum jasminoides, he said.

Beg pardon, sir?

The Confederate jasmine, he said. There can be no question. A plant from the deep southern states. And not native to our hills and river bottomlands.

He paused and smiled.

And you know as well as I, boy, he said. That there is but one thumb green enough to have planted that seed and made it grow to maturity within a space of months in these strange, northern climes.

I felt the little hairs the barber always misses standing up on the back of my neck.

Maybe it was the wind, I said. Blowing through the eaves of that old, bloody house, but I fancied I heard a voice, sir, whilst I was standing there breathing in the smell of that white flower.

And what did you fancy this voice said to you, boy?

Avenge me, I answered. And then it was quiet for a spell and the wind rose and the smell grew stronger, sweeter and then the voice spoke again.

And what did it say this time, son?

Seek and ye shall find.

I was sweating around my neck and trembling a little, not with scaredness neither but with excitement for I knew, as did Dr. Bruce, knew that things were coming to the Justice he said would come if we bided our time and waited long enough.

Am I crazy, Dr. Bruce? I asked.

Certainly! he cried. All ten-year-old boys are crazy—if they're worth their salt. It's only ten-year-old girls that are sane and practical minded. Otherwise the human race would have died out long ago. Still—

He smiled me a kindly smile.

—still that doesn't mean that you did not hear a voice, Daniel Cresap. Even a voice from what Shakespeare's Coriolanus called that world elsewhere.

And having left me now to ponder this cryptic utterance I heard him sprinting up the staircase to his bedroom to get into his clothes. He was used to that—being a doctor. So it didn't take him long. In an instant he appeared in the library doorway in his old Rebel boots and wearing his gray alpaca suit with the long frock coat, from the right-hand pocket of which protruded the earpieces of his stethoscope, and on his head his white summer planter's hat.

He bade me follow him quickly out through the kitchen door and out to the stable beyond which stood his summer house—his gazebo, he always called it—and I watched as he hitched his roan mare to his surrey and then turned to me.

Climb up, boy, he said. We must be on our way. For I think we can end all this before dayrise. And then proceed to the matter of Justice. Yes. There will be a Justice before this matter is played out.

Again I obeyed and he gave a flick of the reins and we were on our way.

Are we going down to Uncle Hildy's house? I asked.

Not quite yet, boy. There are pieces still to be fitted.

Then where are we going, sir?

He did not reply but drove the surrey up Pike Street and rounded the corner to Morning Alley till he came to Mr. List's General Store. Mr. List lived in a three-room flat above his store. He was a bachelor and cranky as could be. But when he poked his head out the window, after we had knocked a good five minutes, and saw who it was, he soon came down and let us in. He struck a light and lit the oil lamp which hung over his counter.

If it was anybody in Glory but you, Dr. Bruce, he said. I'd have told them to go to tarnation and come back in the morning. But I know you'd not be here at this infernally late hour if it warn't a matter of importance. Now what can I do for you, sir?

On a certain Saturday last April, Dr. Bruce said. Hildreth Eugene Cresap came to town from his farm downriver. He came to your store that morning. It is known that he purchased from you a hatchet. Later in the day, it is believed by some, he used that hatchet to murder his wife Josephine.

Yes, I remember, I remember, murmured the storekeeper. A tur'ble thing. Just tur'ble.

That, sir, said Dr. Bruce. Is a matter of opinion. But never mind arguments over it. I have come here tonight to find out what else Mr. Cresap bought from you that Saturday morning last April.

I'd have to go in the back, said Mr. List, a crafty look on his face. And fetch down my ledger of sales for the whole month of April. And my wheels—they're a little rusty at this hour of the night, Doctor.

Well, perhaps this may grease their axle a little, said Dr. Bruce.

And he fetched from his snap-purse a silver cartwheel dollar and set it spinning like a bright silver top in the lampshine by the cashbox.

Mr. List looked shifty and sheepish when he did it but he waited till the coin had stopped spinning and lay flat, stared at it a second, then plucked it up and dropped it into his cashbox.

Then he disappeared into the back with his oil lantern and returned, after a good long spell of fussing around, with a large,
canvas-bound book. He laid it on the counter between us and,
opening it, leafed through the stained pages till he came to the
entry. He cleared his throat with great self-importance.

On the morning of April third of this year of nineteen and
one, he said. Hildreth Cresap came here and bought—in addi-
tion to a new hatchet of the highest quality—the following other
items: a twist of sweet tobacco, a box of Poolock stogies, two
cans of Honest Scotch snuff for his missus, two quarts of
Breathhit County Kentucky Bourbon, a dozen oranges and three
boxes of lucifers.

Is that all, sir? asked Dr. Bruce, a little disappointment in his
voice as he leaned his fists on the counter and peered forward
down at the page of the open ledger.

No, snickered Mr. List. He did buy four other items. And I'm
half ashamed to tell you what they was, sir. For me to sell them
at all wasn't entirely honest. For they are useless in this part of
the country.

What, sir, what? cried out Doctor Bruce then. What were
they, man?

Four packets of seeds, said the storekeeper, sheepishly.

What species of seeds, man, what genus and species! snapped
Dr. Bruce, impatiently.

Mister List got red in the face, chuckling foolishly.

When the Burpee salesman come last winter to take my bulb
and seed orders, he said. He finagled me into buying a dozen
packets of seeds of a plant that won't even sprout in these parts. I
was ashamed when I bought them and I was ashamed when I sold
them four packs to Mister Cresap. Since any gardener with a
grain of sense knows that plant don't grow no further north than
Georgia—if that fur.

I know, said Doctor Bruce. They were the seeds of *Trachelospernum jasminoides*—the Confederate jasmine.

Mister List's jaw dropped a good two inches.

How did you know that, Dr. Bruce?

Never mind how, said the doctor, even more impatiently.

Simply tell me this. Did Hildreth Cresap put those packs of seeds
in his market basket with the other commodities and comesti-
bles?

Why, no—come to think of it, said the storekeeper. He
didn't. He looked at me kind of foolish and said his wife would
laugh him out of countenance if she found those seeds in with
the other truck.

One question more, said Dr. Bruce, excitedly. And then you
can go back to your bed. If Hildreth Cresap didn't put those seed
packets into his market basket where did he put them?

Mr. List was stumped for a minute, his face bowed, his forefinger stroking his jawbone as he pondered back, remembered
back. Then he looked up brightly.

I mind now! he cried out then. He stuck them in the pocket
of his shirt—a blue linsey shirt if I recollect!

Come, Daniel boy! cried Dr. Bruce, seizing me by the sleeve.
We're on our way again.

To the house downriver now? I asked timidly as he whipped
the mare at a brisk canter up Morning Alley and then down
Lafayette Avenue toward his home on Seventh Street.

Not yet, he said. Soon. But not yet.

In an instant he had driven the surrey up his driveway and he
was out of it and hammering on the door of the small building
where dwelt his two black servants: Coy and Lee Jim. He ordered
them to fetch two spades and a big canvas tarpaulin from the
barn and follow his surrey in the buckboard downriver to the
Cresap house. Coy and Jim Lee looked at each other in the
bright moonlight and their white eyes rolled with fear. Maybe I
looked scared, too. But I had my two lucky pieces in my britches
pocket—my buckeye and my Indian bird-point arrowhead—so I
knew that nothing of misfortune could befall me.

When we got out to the old house the moon had slipped
round to the dark side of the house and the blossoms of the plant
showed vividly in its light. Doctor Bruce called Coy and Lee Jim
to fetch their spades and the canvas tarpaulin and bring them
over. He pointed.

Dig here, boys, he said. But do not harm the plant. Remove it carefully from the earth—taking care not to miss any of its roots and then lay it gingerly on the floor of my surrey yonder. Is that clear? It must be kept alive!

Both nodded, though plainly scared out of countenance.

And then, said Dr. Bruce. Keep digging till you find what I know is buried there. And when you come to it, take it out, wrap it in that tarpaulin and put it in the buckboard.

He looked at me then.

Are you still game, boy? he asked me. It may not be a pleasant sight—what they'll find beneath that plant. Are you sticking, boy? Because what you will see will be the beginnings of a Justice. Or perhaps I should say the ending of one Justice and the beginnings of another. And, at last, the end of it all.

They'll find a corpse, won't they? I asked.

That is so, boy.

The corpse of her, I said bitterly. Old Jo. And I sure won't mind seeing that. Even if it's all hacked up and rotten. She couldn't look or smell any worse dead all this time than she did when she was alive.

But it isn't the body of her, he said, laying his big hand on my shaggy head.

Someone wanted us to believe that, he said. From the first. From the day of the murder. And someone wanted to impress it on us even more when they mailed that letter from Natchez. The letter signed by Hildreth.

The letter that was not in his hand, I said. Yes, I recollect. But there was a third thing you figured out that morning, sir—a thing you wouldn't tell me then but said you'd tell me when the time was right.

I paused.

Is the time right now?

Yes, he said. It is right now. The third thing I would not tell you then was that the handwriting was not that of a man at all.

A lady's handwriting, sir?

No, he said. Not a lady's. A woman's. And scarcely that. She scarcely deserves to be called a woman. For a woman is, at least, human.

He paused.

I am trying, he said. To break this to you easily as I can, boy. So let me tell you first that the hand that penned that absurd letter was the same hand that hacked to death the man whose body my boys are disinterring yonder beneath the jasmine plant. The same hand that went then to the barn, fetched a spade, dug a shallow grave, and shoved the body into it. No—not shoved. No—

He smiled, wrily.

Not shoved, he said again. *Planted* is the word I want. Because in burying him there she did not know—this murderess—that there were four packets of seeds in the pocket of his linsey shirt. Never realizing that when she planted that body there she was also planting seeds which the body and green thumb of the only man who ever lived in these hills and bottomlands could make sprout and put up shoots and flourish and set forth blossoms in one season. And in an alien and intemperate clime where no one else but he could make them grow.

Coy and Lee Jim had reached the body now and were loudly singing a spiritual called "Nobody Knows the Trouble I've Seen" to keep up their nerve as they hauled the mangled and decayed thing out, wrapped it in the tarpaulin, and carried it to lay in the buckboard. I could endure having seen—as I did in that bright moonlight—what she and a summer underground had done to him. But I could barely endure the scent of Old Mortality which cut acridly now through the sweet and pungent fragrance of the Confederate jasmine which had brought about a Justice. Yes, a Justice, as Dr. Bruce had said. But it was still not ended.

The people of Mound County—out of their own pockets—got together enough money to hire the Pinkertons to track old Jo down. It took them two years but they got her. She was in Memphis, Tennessee—Madam of a house of ill-fame of such low degree that the price of an hour with a woman there was fifty cents. Worn-out, sick and no longer pretty hookers all ended up in old Jo's house. Soon after she was brought back to Glory she was tried for murder in the first degree. And, since it's a Mound County tradition never to send a Mound County murderer to the

Glory gallows—old Jo drew a life sentence. But she didn't serve
it for long. In the autumn of 1907 she died in the prison infir-
mary of paresis. Syphillis of the brain.

She'd have been buried in Potter's Field if it hadn't been for
Dr. Bruce. He had other notions. He purchased a plot of land in
Glory cemetery far out at the edge of the grounds where the
caretaker doesn't bother much to cut the grass. And instead of a
stone at her head he planted on her mound the Confederate
jasmine. That was to be her marker. Her memorial. No headstone. Nothing else. A Justice, as Doctor Bruce said to me one
day when we came there to look at it the month before he died.

A Justice, he said, and led me away.

And here's the strangest part of all. It flourished. Just as
though Uncle Hildy was there to tend it. It spread. There's a
great tangle of Confederate jasmine all over old Jo Lindsay
Cresap's grave to this very day. I guess even the ghost of Uncle
Hildy's fabulous green thumb still has its power. But it doesn't
smell the same. The night I first smelled it there in the moonlight when the wind whispered words from Beyond in my ear
there on the dark side of that sad and bloody house it smelled
like some rare and lovely perfume on a pretty girl's bare shoulders, maybe at some fancy-dress ball at the Schenley Hotel in
Pittsburgh with Victor Herbert leading the orchestra. But not
now. It smells different now. Cheap. Lowly. Tawdry. Like some
miserable dime-store toilet water that an old bawd would wear,
remembering happier days. Or an old madam of a house of low-
degree where old bawds go to die.

CHECKER-PLAYING FOOL

Why do windows full of sunset always look so tired, and
windows rosy with dawn always appear refreshed and new?
—Davis Grubb, notebooks

If there was ever anything in the world that Jessie Steptoe was
proud of it was his checker playing. In a lot of ways he didn't
have much good sense, but in the checker-playing line he was
A-1. Jessie was champion of Harrison County and most of the
other counties in the state and some of the counties in Kentucky. Jessie was a man who would rather play checkers than eat
when he was hungry. He could play the game drunk or sober and
once he beat a man from Mingo County three games hanging by
his legs from a tree in Dick McCracken's apple orchard. You
never saw such a checker-playing fool in all your born days.
There wasn't nobody in the home town that ever beat him nor
heard tell of anyone that did.

It seemed like Jessie had been champion checker player since
anybody could remember, but I guess he got started on account
of he was jailer at the county jail and checkers is a lonesome
man's game. Jessie and Sheriff O. T. Hamrick used to play checkers till morning and when old Mr. Sun shinnied up over
Pinickinick Hill and come splashing in the jail house windows
Jessie would go fix coffee and eggs to feed the prisoners and then

him and O.T. would have a bite their ownselves and play one
more game. I guess you don't know how quiet and lonesome it
gets in a little town at night when you can't hear nothing but the
click of pool balls in the Recreation on Pike Street and maybe
when the wind is right, the far-off lonesome voice of the old
Queen City blowing her whistle twelve miles down river below
the Devil's Elbow. I reckon if you did then you'd understand how
come Jessie Steptoe took up the checker-playing habit in that
little office of his in the lonesome jail house at the bottom of
Twelfth Street.

Jessie was a kindly turned soul as far as that went but what
with his winning checker games all the time he wasn't exactly
what you'd call a modest man. In fact sometimes when Jessie'd
just got back from winning a checker tournament somewheres a
body could hardly stand to be around him he was so windy. The
people all liked Jessie but at the same time they knew that pride
cometh before a fall and someday there'd be a day of reckoning
for Jessie, too.

Well, one night around eight o'clock when the sun was going
down Jessie heard O.T. coming up the stairs bringing a prisoner.
When they come in the door Jessie looked up and seen O.T.
standing there with one of the strangest-looking prisoners Jessie
had ever laid eyes on.

Lock him up, Jessie, says O.T., shutting the door behind him.
Judge Garvy says give him ten days for stealing apples out of Dick
McCracken's apple orchard.

The prisoner is standing there looking sad and miserable and
scraggly as a groundhog that's been killed and hung up to dry. He
is tall and skinny and don't look like he's been fed since he was
born. Besides that Jessie can see that he is walleyed so's you can't
tell if he's looking up your nose or in your ear or out the window
behind you. Jessie gets up and stretches like a dog and shakes the
sleep out of his shoulders. He fetches down his big ring of keys.
Him and the new prisoner cross the hall and while Jessie is
standing there hunting for the right key old O.T. is sitting in
Jessie's chair peeling himself one of Dick McCracken's big, juicy
Northern Spies. When Jessie locks the new prisoner in his cell

and comes back in the office O.T. is cutting the apple in quarters and laying them out all neat in a row on Jessie's desk.

Dick's apples is sorty dry this year, Jessie, says O.T. with his mouth full. And they don't have the flavor they did last fall.

Jessie looks at O.T. eating the apple. Jessie knows it is one of the apples that the stranger stole. But both him and O.T. know you can't put an apple back on the tree once it's pulled. O.T. takes another quarter of apple in his mouth and chews it thoughtfully.

Have much trouble bringing him in? says Jessie.

O.T. can't answer Jessie because his mouth is full of apple.

Don't look like he could put up much of a fight, says Jessie, wishing O.T. had brought him an apple to eat.

O.T. has the other two quarters of the apple in his mouth now, working on it with his new teeth, and he can't answer Jessie this time neither.

Pretty quiet sort of feller, says Jessie.

O.T. swallows a big load of apple and nods.

Ten days of coolin' his behind in a jail house ought to cure him of stealin' Dick McCracken's Northern Spies, says O.T., looking all stern and bloodthirsty like he was a wild west sheriff that had just drug in Billy the Kid by the left ear. O.T. was a kindly turned sort of man but he got tired of bringing in drunks and wild women all the time. You could tell O.T. really appreciated an apple thief now and then to sort of bust the monotony. He stood up and hitched his big red thumb in his belt buckle and waved his fat finger at the ceiling.

It's time we learned some of these ornery scalliwags from Ohio they can't just come across the river and steal apples whenever they've a mind to, says O.T.

He walks over and fetches down his Stetson off the hat rack and gives it a good brushing on his sleeve.

I'm going down to Red Cottrill's, Jessie, says O.T. Red fell off a yard engine in Fairmont today and busted his leg. I'll be back later.

A little checkers tonight, O.T.? says Jessie with that sly, cocky little twinkle in his eye.

When I get back, Jessie, says O.T. and shuts the door behind him.

Jessie goes over and sits down in his old swivel chair and puts his number tens up on his rolltop desk. The window blind flops a little when the easy night wind blows up Twelfth Street from the river. A fly is buzzing and bumping around on the ceiling near the dusty thirty-watt bulb. These are lonesome sounds to Jessie. He listens to the click of the pool balls in the Recreation up on Pike Street. He can hear the putt-putt of the ferry starting back across the warm, dark river toward the Ohio side. Jessie lights up his old beat-up briar and puffs a while. Directly he looks out the doorway across the hall into the cell where the new prisoner is. The new prisoner is lying on his bunk staring square at Jessie with that walleye of his. Jessie studies him a minute trying to figure out if the stranger is looking at him or at the hoochy-koochy girl on the calendar over the watercooler ten feet away. When Jessie looks at one eye it's one thing and when he looks at the other it's something else. It's the sort of thing that is calculated to get on a man like Jessie's nerves a little. Jessie figures for a minute whether he'll get up and shut the door so the stranger can't lie there staring at him that way. But Jessie is lonesome. He listens to the sounds of the small-town river night till he can't stand it no more. Directly the stranger rolls over on his back and drags out a mouth harp. He shakes the tobacco out of it and lets loose on a couple of real low-down mean ones. Then he starts in to playing himself a tune on the mouth harp real soft and lonesome there in his dark cell. Jessie listens till he can't stand it no more.

Where you from, stranger? he hollers out real loud in that dry, crackly voice of his.

Matamoris, says the stranger. He goes to playing his mouth harp some more.

How'd you git acrost?

Ferry, says the stranger.

How come you stole them Northern Spies out of Dick Mc-Cracken's apple orchard? hollers Jessie.

Got hungry for 'em, says the stranger.

Ain't they no apples in Ohio? hollers out Jessie.

No free ones, says the stranger, going right on with his mouth-harpin' in the lonesomest kind of way.

I guess you don't know about Dick McCracken, says Jessie. He don't stand for no one foolin' round his Northern Spies. You should have stole the Baldwins. Dick don't put much store in them.

The stranger don't have no answer for that one. He just goes on playing his mouth harp in that sneaky, lonesome way. And by this time it's plain to Jessie Steptoe that the stranger is not a man of many words.

Been right damp these last few nights, says Jessie, lighting up his pipe again.

The stranger don't say nary a word. Just goes right on playing.

Good night to sleep, says Jessie.

The fly buzzes and races around the thirty-watt bulb, batting its fuzzy head against the ceiling. Jessie puffs on his pipe for dear life. He is doing some thinking. Nine times out of ten when you come across a prisoner that don't open his mouth much more than this one you've got a man that knows his way around a checker board. The idea is working on Jessie's mind and the lonesome sounds are working on it, too, and Jessie is puffing on his pipe till the smoke dims the light like a white morning fog.

Play checkers? Jessie hollers out directly.

Some, says the stranger.

Care to play a couple, hollers Jessie.

Don't mind, says the stranger, putting his mouth harp back in his pocket.

Jessie hops out in the hall with the big iron ring of keys and unlocks the door. Jessie don't bother to take down his holster and his big thirty-eight Smith and Wesson to set them handy to his arm on the desk. Jessie don't figure there's much danger to playing checkers with nothing more dangerous than an apple stealer. Jessie fetches down his prize inlaid checkerboard he won at the big checker tournament in Wheeling fifteen years ago. The stranger draws up a chair and directly Jessie is setting up the markers. Jessie is happy. His face is pink and contented. Jessie takes the red and the stranger gets the black. Jessie looks across at the prisoner sitting there staring at the checkerboard with his walleye. Jessie can't tell if he's looking at the checkerboard or at the spitoon in the corner by the hat rack. It makes Jessie a little nervous but it don't shake his confidence none. He stretches out his skinny fingers and makes the first move. Whenever Jessie Steptoe makes the first move in a checker game he sort of flicks his elbow out in a little fancy way that lets you know that Jessie is a sure enough checker-playing fool.

Now the stranger studies the board for a spell with his walleye and then he studies it with his other eye and then he makes his move. By the time he'd made his third move Jessie got so wild he almost dropped his end of the checkerboard. The prisoner's walleye was like the eye of a witch and his good eye was worse. They chased Jessie's red markers all over the place, jumped them, ran circles around, over, and under them and then drug them feet first off the board. When the game was over the sweat was running off Jessie's face and he was shaking like he'd run fifty miles stark naked in January. The stranger had beat him all the ways there is to beat at checkers and a few new Ohio ways throwed in for good measure. Jessie sat there for a minute swallowing and grinning all his teeth at the prisoner and mopping his head with his handkerchief.

I declare, he squeaks out directly. You play a right good game.

The stranger don't say nary a word.

I could tell, says Jessie, you was a first-string checker-playing man when I first laid eyes on you.

Care for another? says the prisoner, cool and dry, his good eye looking at Jessie's nose and his walleye staring at the watercooler like the eye of a prophet. Jessie didn't even bother to answer, he was so busy setting up the board again. His hands was shaking so bad he dropped half the markers on the floor.

Now, says Jessie, studying a while before his first move.

The prisoner tilts his head and fixes his walleye on the board just as cool as a cucumber and jumps two of Jessie's markers. From then on Jessie was a broken man. He played like he'd never seen a checkerboard before in his whole life. When the game was over Jessie got up and put his checkerboard back on top of his rolltop desk. Then he went over and stared out the window. Directly he come back over to the desk and knocked out his pipe and stuffed it again and lit up. Then he went back to the window and stood blowing white clouds of smoke out into the soft night air.

Reckon you won't say anything about this around town, says Jessie. The boys think I'm right smart of a checker player and if it was to leak out you beat me two games I'd be in for it.

The prisoner never said a word. Just sat there in the straight-backed chair with his hands on his knees, his good eye twinkling at Jessie and his walleye admiring the hoochy-koochy calendar on the wall.

You won't, will you? says Jessie, clearing his throat and loosening the collar around his neck. He could hear O.T.'s horse laugh and the other laughs when they told how the walleyed prisoner beat Jessie, the champion checker player, two games.

Well? says Jessie, feeling the cold sweat on his skin although the night was warm.

No answer.

Now listen, Jessie says at last, going over to the prisoner and staring wildly first into his good eye and then into the other.

You busted out, see! hollers Jessie. When I wasn't looking! I dropped my keys in the hall and you got 'em and busted out. Now git on out of here. Git on down to the river and jump on that ferry and go back to Matamoris and forget you ever heard tell of Dick McCracken's apples.

The stranger is staring at Jessie's vest with his good eye and grinning fit to kill. Jessie looks down at his vest and his blood turns cold. The stranger's eye is looking at Jessie's gold stem-winder and his big gold-link chain. Jessie swallows hard and snatches out the watch and chain.

Here! croaks Jessie, shutting his eyes and gritting his teeth together. You Ohio checker players sure drive a hard bargain! Take it! But get on back to Ohio right quick now before O.T. gits back. I'll tell him Dick McCracken was up here and withdrawed the charges!

But now the prisoner's walleye is running up and down that
fancy inlaid checkerboard on the corner of Jessie's rolltop desk
and his good eye is sliding in a mighty thirsty way up and down
Jessie's brand-new bottle of Kentuck whisky on the other corner
of the desk.

Great God a'mighty! hollers Jessie, shutting his eyes again and
clapping his hand to his sweaty head.

You Ohio checker players drive the hardest bargain I ever
seed! But take my checkerboard and the whisky, too. Now get
on out of this jail house and light out fast for Ohio. O.T.'ll be
back any time now.

Jessie falls back in his swivel chair and watches the walleyed
stranger stuff his bottle of whisky in his coat pocket and tuck his
watch and chain in his vest and stick his prize inlaid checkerboard under his arm. He don't say a word when he goes. He just
grins at poor old Jessie for a minute, gives a good-bye wave and a
wink with that walleye of his, and hustles out the door and down
the steps. Jessie lies back in the chair with his head hanging over
the back of the chair and his tongue hanging out like a hound
dog. He listens till the stranger's fast shuffling footsteps are gone.
After he'd gotten his sense back Jessie started figuring out what
kind of a story he'd tell O.T. when he come back. He decided
he'd tell him Dick McCracken had come up and said he didn't
put much store in his Northern Spies this year since they was so
dry and he had withdrawed the charges.

Directly Jessie went over to the window for a breath of air and
looked into the street. For a minute he couldn't believe his eyes
and the next minute he was so mad he thought he'd jump clean
out the window and bite a chunk off the sidewalk. Up on the
corner under the streetlamp by the Recreation stood O.T. and
Dick McCracken and the walleyed stranger taking big swigs of
Jessie's whisky and laughing till you could hear them clear across
the river in the new champ's home state.

THE HORSEHAIR TRUNK

> The drama with Christ and Mary Magdalene should be the
> last word regarding not only sexual but *any* kind of
> tolerance.
>   But apparently, it isn't.
>
> —Davis Grubb, notebooks

To Marius the fever was like a cloud of warm river fog around
him. Or like the blissful nothingness that he had always imagined death would be. He had lain for nearly a week like this in
the big corner room while the typhoid raged and boiled inside
him. Mary Ann was a dutiful wife. She came and fed him his
medicine and stood at the foot of the brass bed when the doctor
was there, clasping and unclasping her thin hands, and sometimes from between hot, heavy lids Marius could glimpse her
face, dimly pale and working slowly in prayer. Such a fool she
was. He could remember thinking that even in the deep, troubled delirium of the fever: a praying, stupid fool that he had
married five years ago.

You want me to die, he said to her one morning when she
came with his medicine. You want me to die, don't you?

Marius! Don't say such a thing! Don't ever—

It's true though, he went on, hearing his voice miles above
him at the edge of the quilt. You want me to die. But I'm not

going to. I'm going to get well, Mary Ann. I'm not going to die. Aren't you disappointed?

No! No! It's not true! It's not!

Now, though he could not see her face through the hot blur of fever, he could hear her crying—sobbing and shaking with her fist pressed tight against her teeth. Such a fool.

On the eighth morning Marius woke full of a strange, fiery brilliance as if all his flesh were glass not yet cool from the furnace. The fever was worse, he knew, close to its crisis, and yet it no longer had the comatose quality of darkness and mists. Everything was sharp and clear. The red of his necktie hanging in the corner of the bureau mirror was a flame. And he could hear the minutest stirrings down in the kitchen; the breaking of a matchstick in Mary Ann's fingers as clear as pistol shots outside his bedroom window. It was a joy. Marius wondered for a moment if he might have died. But if it was death it was certainly more pleasant than he had ever imagined death would be. He could rise from the bed without any sense of weakness and he could stretch his arms and he could even walk out through the solid door into the upstairs hall. He thought it might be fun to tiptoe downstairs and give Mary Ann a fright but when he was in the parlor he remembered suddenly that she would be unable to see him. Then when he heard her coming from the kitchen with his tray of medicine he thought of an even better joke. With the speed of thought Marius was back in his body under the quilt again and Mary Ann was coming into the bedroom with her large eyes wide and worried.

Marius, she whispered, leaning over him and stroking his hot forehead with her cold, thin fingers. Marius, are you better?

He opened his eyes as if he had been asleep.

I see, he said. That you've moved the pianola over to the north end of the parlor.

Mary Ann's eyes widened and the silver spoon shook in the glass of amber liquid.

Marius! she whispered. You haven't been out of bed! You'll kill yourself! With a fever like—

No, said Marius faintly, listening to the voice of himself as if it were in another room. I haven't been out of bed, Mary Ann.

His eyelids flickered weakly up at her face; round and ghost-like; incredulous. She quickly set the tinkling glass of medicine on the little table.

Then how—she stuttered. Marius, how could you know?

Marius smiled weakly up at her and closed his eyes, saying nothing, leaving the terrible question unrelieved, leaving her to tremble and ponder over it forever if need be. She was such a fool.

It had begun that way and it had been so easy he wondered why he had never discovered it before. Within a few hours the fever broke in great rivers of sweat and by Wednesday Marius was able to sit up in the chair by the window and watch the starlings hopping on the front lawn. By the end of the month he was back at work as editor of the *Daily Argus*. But even those who knew him least were able to detect in the manner of Marius Lindsay that he was a changed man—and a worse one. And those who knew him best wondered how so malignant a citizen, such a con-firmed and studied misanthrope as Marius could possibly change into anything worse than he was. Some said that typhoid always burned the temper from the toughest steel and that Marius's mind had been left a dark and twisted thing. At prayer meeting on Wednesday nights the wives used to watch Marius's young wife and wondered how she endured her cross. She was such a pretty thing.

One afternoon in September as he dozed on the bulging leather couch of his office Marius decided to try it again. Some-where on the brink of sleep he knew the secret lay. If a man knew that, any man, he would know what Marius did. It wasn't more than a minute later that Marius knew all he would have to do to leave his body was to get up from the couch. Presently he was standing there, staring down at his heavy, middle-aged figure sunk deep into the cracked leather of the couch, the jowls of the face under the close-cropped, white mustache sagging deep in

sleep, the heart above his heavy gold watch chain beating solidly
in its breast.

I'm not dead, he thought, delighted. But here is my soul—my
damned, immortal soul standing looking at its body!

It was as simple as shedding a shoe. Marius smiled to himself,
remembering his old partner Charlie Cunningham and how they
had used to spend long hours in the office, in this very room,
arguing about death and Ingersoll and the whither of the soul. If
Charlie were still alive, Marius thought, I would win from him a
quart of the best Kentucky bourbon in the county. As it was no
one would ever know. He would keep his secret even from Mary
Ann, especially from Mary Ann, who would go to her grave with
the superstitious belief that Marius had died for a moment, that
for an instant fate had favored her; that she had been so close to
happiness, to freedom from him forever. She would never know.
Still, it would be fun to use as a trick, a practical joke to set fools
like his wife at their wit's edge. If only he could *move* things. If
only the filmy substance of his soul could grasp a tumbler and
send it shattering at Mary Ann's feet on the kitchen floor some
morning. Or tweak a copy boy's nose. Or snatch a cigar from the
astonished teeth of Judge John Robert Gants as he strolled home
some quiet evening from the fall session of the district court.
Well it was, after all, a matter of will, Marius decided. It was his
own powerful and indomitable will that had made the trick possible in the first place. He walked to the edge of his desk and
grasped at the letter opener on the dirty, ancient blotter. His
fingers were like wisps of fog that blew through a screen door. He
tried again, willing it with all his power, grasping again and
again at the small brass dagger until at last it moved a fraction of
an inch. A little more. On the next try it lifted four inches in
the air and hung for a second on its point before it dropped.
Marius spent the rest of the afternoon practicing at it until at last
he could lift the letter opener in his fist, fingers tight around the
hasp, the thumb pressing the cold blade tightly, and drive it
through the blotter so deeply that it bit into the wood of the
desk beneath.

Marius giggled in spite of himself and hurried around the office picking things up like a pleased child. He lifted a tumbler off the dusty water cooler and stared laughing at it, hanging there in the middle of nothing. At that moment he heard the copy boy coming for the proofs of the morning editorials and Marius flitted quickly back into the cloak of his flesh. Nor was he a moment too soon. Just as he opened his eyes, the door opened and he heard the glass shatter on the floor.

I'm going to take a nap before supper, Mary Ann, Marius said that evening, hanging his black hat carefully on the elk horn hat rack.

Very well, said Mary Ann. He watched her young, unhappy figure disappearing into the gloom of the kitchen and he smiled to himself again, thinking what a fool she was, his wife. He could scarcely wait to get to the davenport and stretch out in the cool, dark parlor with his head on the beaded pillow.

Now, thought Marius. Now.

And in a moment he had risen from his body and hurried out into the hallway, struggling to suppress the wild laughter in his throat that would tell her he was coming. He could already anticipate her white, stricken face when the pepper pot pulled firmly from between her fingers and cut a clean figure eight in the air before it crashed against the ceiling.

He heard her voice and was puzzled.

You must go, she was murmuring. You mustn't ever come here when he's home. I've told you that before, Jim. What would you do if he woke up and found you here!

Then Marius, as he rushed into the kitchen, saw her bending through the doorway into the dusk with the saucepan of greens clutched in her white knuckles.

What would you do! You must go!

Marius rushed to her side, careful not to touch her, careful not to let either of them know he was there, listening, looking, growing slowly into one tall blue flame of hate.

The man was young and dark and well-built and clean-looking. He leaned against the half-open screen door, holding Mary Ann's free hand between his own; his round, dark face bent to hers, which was filled with a tenderness and passion that Marius had never seen there.

I know, the man said. I know all that. But I just can't stand it no more, Mary Ann. I just can't stand it thinking about him beating you up that time. He might do it again, Mary Ann. He might! He's worse, they say, since he had the fever. Crazy, I think. I've heard them say he's crazy.

Yes. Yes. You must go away now, though, she was whispering, frantic; looking back over her shoulder through Marius's dark face. We'll have time to talk it all over again, Jim. I—I know I'm going to leave him but— Don't rush me into things, Jim dear. Don't make me do it till I'm clear with myself.

Why not now! came the whisper. Why not tonight! We can take a steamboat to Lou'ville and you'll never have to put up with him again. You'll be shed of him forever, honey. Look! I've got two tickets for Lou'ville right here in my pocket on the *Nancy B. Turner*. My God, Mary Ann, don't make me suffer like this—lyin' abed nights dreaming about him comin' at you with his cane and beatin' you—maybe killin' you!

The woman grew silent and her face softened as she watched the fireflies dart their zigzags of cold light under the low trees along the street. She opened her mouth, closed it and stood biting her lip hard. Then she reached up and pulled his face down to hers, seeking his mouth.

All right, she whispered then. All right. I'll do it! Now go! Quick!

Meet me at the wharf at nine, he said. Tell him that you're going to prayer meeting. He'll never suspicion anything. Then we can be together without all this sneakin' around. Oh, honey, if you ever knew how much I—

The words were smeared in her kiss as he pulled her down through the half-open door and held her.

All right. All right, she gasped. Now go! Please!

And he walked away, his heels ringing boldly on the bricks, lighting a cigarette, the match arcing like a shooting star into the darkness of the shrubs.

Mary Ann stood stiff for a moment in the shadow of the porch vines, her large eyes full of tears and the saucepan of greens grown cold in her hands. Marius drew back to let her pass. He stood then and watched her for a moment before he hurried back into the parlor and lay down again within his flesh and bone in time to be called for supper.

Captain Joe Alexander of the *Nancy B. Turner* was not curious that Marius should want a ticket for Louisville. He remembered years later that he had thought nothing strange about it at the time. It was less than two months till the elections and there was a big Democratic convention there. And everyone had heard of Marius Lindsay and the power he and his *Daily Argus* held over the choices of the people. But Captain Alexander did remember thinking it strange that Marius should insist on seeing the passenger list on the *Nancy B.* that night and that he should ask particularly after a man named Jim. Smith, Marius had said, but there was no Smith. There was a Jim though, a furniture salesman from Wheeling: Jim O'Toole, who had reserved two staterooms—three and four.

What do you think of the presidential chances this term, Mr. Lindsay? Captain Alexander had said. And Marius had looked absent for a moment (the captain had never failed to recount that detail) and then said that it would be Cleveland, that the Republicans were done forever in the land.

Captain Alexander had remembered that conversation and the manner of its delivery years after that and it had become part of the tale that rivermen told in wharfboats and water-street saloons from Pittsburgh to Ciaro long after that night had woven itself into legend like river fog into the morning sun.

Then Marius had asked for stateroom number five and that had been part of the legend, too, for it was next to the room that was to be occupied by Jim O'Toole, the furniture salesman from Wheeling.

Say nothing, said Marius, before he disappeared down the stairway from the captain's cabin, to anyone about my being aboard this boat tonight. My trip to Louisville is connected with the approaching election and is, of necessity, confidential.

Certainly, sir, said the captain, and he listened as Marius

made his way awkwardly down the gilded staircase, lugging his small horsehair trunk under his arm. Presently the door to Marius's stateroom snapped shut and the bolt fell to.

At nine o'clock sharp two rockaway buggies rattled down the brick pavement of Water Street and met at the wharf. A man jumped from one and a woman from the other.

You say he wasn't home when you left, the man was whispering as he helped the woman down the rocky cobbles, the two carpetbags tucked under his arms.

No. But it's all right, Mary Ann said. He always goes down to the office this time of night to help set up the morning edition.

You reckon he suspicions anything?

The woman laughed, a low, sad laugh.

He always suspicions everybody, she said. Marius has the kind of a mind that always suspicions and the kind of life he leads, I guess he has to. But I don't think he knows about us—tonight. I don't think he ever *knew* about us—ever.

They hurried up the gangplank together. The water lapped and gurgled against the wharf and off over the river lightning scratched the dark rim of mountains.

I'm Jim O'Toole, he said to Captain Alexander. He handed him the tickets. This is my wife—

Mary Ann bit her lip and clutched the strap of her carpetbag till her knuckles cracked and the bones shone blue through the flesh.

—she has the stateroom next to mine. Is everything in order?

Right, sir, said Captain Alexander, wondering in what strange ways the destinies of this furniture salesman and his wife were meshed with the life of Marius Lindsay.

They tiptoed down the worn carpet of the narrow white hallway, counting the numbers on the long, monotonous row of doors to either side.

Good night, dear, said Jim, glancing unhappily at the Negro porter dozing on the split-bottom chair under the swinging oil lantern by the door. Good night, Mary Ann. Tomorrow we'll be on our way. Tomorow you'll be shed of Marius forever.

Marius lay still in his bunk listening as the deep-throated whistle shook the quiet valley three times. Then he lay smiling and relaxed as the great drive shafts tensed and plunged once forward and backward, gathering into their dark, heavy rhythm as the paddles bit the black water. The *Nancy B. Turner* moved heavily away into the thick current and headed downstream for the Devil's Elbow and the open river. Marius was stiff. He had lain for nearly four hours waiting to hear the voices. Every sound had been as clear to him as the tick of his heavy watch like a hard gold heart in his vest pocket. He had heard the dry, rasping racket of the green frogs along the shore and the low, occasional words of boys fishing in their skiffs down the shore under the willows. Then he had stiffened as he heard Mary Ann's excited murmur suddenly just outside his stateroom door and the voice of the man answering her, comforting her. Lightning flashed and flickered out again over the Ohio hills and lit the river for one clear moment. Marius saw all of his stateroom etched suddenly in silver from the open porthole. The mirror, washstand, bowl, and pitcher. The horsehair trunk beside him on the floor. Thunder rumbled in the dark and Marius smiled to himself, secure again in the secret wing of darkness, thinking how easy it would be, wondering why no one had thought of such a thing before. Except for the heavy pounding rhythm of the drive shafts and the shrill chatter of the drinking glass against the washbowl as the boat shuddered through the water, everything was still. The Negro porter dozed in his chair under the lantern by the stateroom door. Once Marius thought he heard the lovers' voices in the next room, but he knew then that it was the laughter of the cooks down in the pantry. Softly he rose and slipped past the sleeping porter, making his way for the white-painted handrail at the head of the stairway. Once Marius laughed aloud to himself as he realized that there was no need to tiptoe with no earthly substance there to make a sound. He crept down the narrow stairway to the pantry. The Negro cooks bent around the long wooden table eating their supper. Marius slid his shadow along the wall toward the row of kitchen knives laying, freshly washed and honed, on the zinc table by the pump. For a moment he hovered over them, dallying, with his finger in his mouth, like a child before an assortment of equally tempting sweets, before he chose the longest of them all, and the sharpest, a knife that would shear the ham clean from a hog with one quick upward sweep. There was, he realized suddenly, the problem of getting the knife past human eyes even if he himself was invisible. The cooks laughed then at some joke one of them had made and all of them bent forward, their heads in a dark circle of merriment over their plates. In that instant Marius swept the knife sound-lessly from the zinc table and darted into the gloomy companion-way. The Negro porter was asleep still and Marius laughed to himself to imagine the man's horror at seeing the butcher knife, its razor edge flashing bright in the dull oil light, inching itself along the wall. But it was a joke he could not afford. He bent at last and slipped the knife cautiously along the thread-bare rug under the little ventilation space beneath the stateroom door. Then rising, so full of hate that he was half afraid he might shine forth in that darkness with the colors of hell, Marius passed through the door and picked the knife up quickly again in his hand.

Off down the Ohio the thunder throbbed again. Marius stepped carefully across the worn rug toward the sleeping body on the bunk. He felt so gay and light he almost laughed aloud. In a moment it would be over and there would be one full-throated cry and Mary Ann would come beating on the locked door and when she saw her lover—

Marius lifted the knife with an impatient gesture and felt quickly for the sleeping pulsing, throat. The flesh was warm and living under his fingers as he held it taut for the one quick stroke. His arm flashed. It was done. Marius, fainting with ex-citement, leaned in the darkness to brace himself. His hand came to rest on the harsh, rough surface of the horsehair trunk.

My God! screamed Marius. My God!

And at his cry the laughing murmur in the pantry grew still and there was a sharp scrape of a chair outside the stateroom door.

The wrong room! screamed Marius. The wrong room! And he clawed with fingers of smoke at the jetting fountain of his own blood.

TALLY VENGEANCE

I believe that we—that mankind—are staggering in the remotest outskirts of infancy.

I don't believe man was started with eviction from Eden.

I believe man was sent forth with the riddle of reaching it, and though we are light-years from its portal, we are getting there quickly.

—Davis Grubb, notebooks

Her real name wasn't Vengeance. It was Natalia Lazarevitch when she and her man came down here from Mingo Junction in the spring of 1919. But ever after that night last September when she left Glory on the west-bound evening train she was Tally Vengeance. As I recollect it was old Colonel Bruce who started them calling her that. Though—even without the name—it was vengeance the people would remember her for. Still, it was more than just vengeance: I saw it as a brand of indestructible pride; something straight-backed and high-chinned without being stiff-necked. That, too, and a stealthy, peasant patience, as well. And, of course, that breed of wild, stoked slag-pile burning femaleness you don't often run into in the preacher-scared and custom-shackled life we've fashioned for ourselves here in the Republic. Maybe back in the old-world Serbia where Milosh Lazarevitch brought her from, Natty wouldn't have stood out as anything wonderful or dangerous. Or even peculiar. For all I know, the women in those Balkan states are all like Natty. If they are, God help the kings: It's no wonder they're always getting into wars. Because when that woman got done working out her notion of justice here in Glory you'd have thought Halley's Comet had gone through the roof of the First M.E. Church and thrown off enough cinders to set fire to the business district, the Elks Club, and half the respectable homes in town.

Let me be the one to tell you about Natty Vengeance. Because you'll never hear it from her. The Lord only knows where she went when she caught the ten o'clock west-bound that cool September night—or where she's at now. And even if she was still here, her own voice couldn't—even if it would—tell you what Natalia Lazarevitch was and how she got that way or did what she did and why justice seemed to her something more precious than religion, respectability, and personal pleasure. Or, for that matter, even personal safety. Natalia Lazarevitch couldn't tell you these things: she was a Serbian and couldn't talk more than a half-dozen words in English. And maybe, being the kind of woman she was, she never knew what made her do things anyway. Women like Natty do most of their thinking in their hips; they are moved about upon this earth by the silent—and sometimes dangerous—logic of the womb. I've only come across two or three like that in my day: females without enough brains in their heads to know how to pluck feathers off a chicken, but with all the mother-wit and knowledge of a genius down in the hunches and instincts of their glands. And there's never any sense asking that kind of woman why she did something. Because her reason for it has to travel all the way up from her hips and by the time it gets to her vocal cords there's not a bit of truth nor a grain of sense left in a word of it, not even to her. But there's still another reason you'd never get the facts about Natty from her own voice. She'd never tell you. Not in Serbian, English, or Choctaw Indian. Natalia Lazarevitch would consider the reasons she did what she did to Glory as something that was simply not a damned bit of your business.

Well, that was something else I admired about her. Spiritually,

I mean. Because I'm like that, too. My life—past, present and future—my sins, my business, ambitions, failures, good luck and bad, my pleasures, wounds and disappointments; the good side of me and the ornery side—I look on them as all mine and strictly private. I feel beholden to no man to tell him why or how or when I ever did anything. So if you're inclined to want to know everything there is to know about Henry Winemiller, you just better go ask some of these other big talkers here in town. The only trouble is you'll soon find out they don't know much more about me than you do. I don't mean to say I'm hiding any great, dark secrets. On the other hand, every secret I do have is personal and private and I'm not about to spend a great long while blathering about myself like quite a few of these voices of Glory I've been hearing.

My old mom, God bless her memory and keep it ever green— she died of consumption when I was a boy down in Braxton County more than fifty years ago—she was like that. So I started life not saying much. And a man doesn't run a barbershop in a town like Glory for thirty-seven years without improving the swiftly vanishing art of keeping his mouth shut. Lord knows, if I ever started talking about the things men tell me whilst they're cranked back in the chair I wouldn't be safe from my own razors. It puts me in mind of a stogie-roller in Wheeling once who ran in and told a priest he'd got a little sixteen-year-old dime-store clerk in the family way. He said he figured it wasn't too black a sin since the girl was illegitimate herself and so that kind of finagling around couldn't make much difference to her anyway. Well, directly here come the priest tearing out of the confession box. And he like to thrashed the clothes off that poor dude. I guess I won't have to draw any pictures for you to tell who that little girl's secret father was. I'm not telling that to knock anybody's religion. I'm just talking about big mouths.

Naturally, I'll tell you as much about myself as you need to know; enough so what I tell you about Natty Vengeance makes some sense. As a matter of fact, there's not much to tell about me that's very interesting. I'm fifty-seven, sober and single, have all my teeth, live in a nice little room over my barber shop in the two-story building which I own, and I hire one extra barber, Densel Yoho. I shave, cut hair, renovate toupees, sweep the shop myself, and chew a little plug tobacco. Since I keep my mouth shut, except to spit, I keep my ears open, in order to hear. On the mug shelf on the wall by the deer-antler hat rack you can read—in letters of rainbow hues and gold-leaf script—the names of Apple County's most substantial men. They are Glory's bankers, investors, farmers, fruit growers and mine operators, lawyers and doctors, real-estate leaders, mill owners, stock speculators, preachers, small children, two bootleggers, five or six steamboat captains and a heavy-set lady Girl Scout leader from a certain town down the river whose face hair I shave—with the blinds drawn, after sundown—twice a month. The bootleggers come all the way down to Glory from a certain city for their shaves because, it's my guess, it makes them upset having their faces covered with towels where they can't watch the passing cars in their home town. The bankers and business leaders give me two bits and a dime extra when Densel Yoho gets through with the whiskbroom, and the bootleggers get the same shave and the same haircut and leave me with a twenty-dollar bill in my hand. But I'd sooner have real-estate men or mine owners in my chairs. Because many's the time while I'm shaving a lawyer and Densel's cutting a banker's hair and maybe there's a state senator over by the window, waiting his turn and reading *Grit* or *Pathfinder* or *Iron Age* and they'll get to chatting a little about good healthy stocks on the Wheeling or Pittsburgh exchange and directly the senator'll drop a word about some stock that's going to get a lot healthier after the next session of the legislature.

So—every now and then—Densel Yoho and his brother Layhew take over both chairs for a few days whilst I take a little business trip up the Ohio. My big mouth never earned me a plugged nickel in my life but being a barber has taught me that my ears are worth more than my shearers, though you'd surely not guess it to look at me. Most folks in Glory think I'm worth about as much as the clothes on my back. Well, I guess a lot of them will be in for a good surprise when I kick off one of these days and a few of them gather up in Case Resseger's law office

and hear him read off the will of Henry Winemiller, Glory barber. I expect it will make some folks sore. And I'll reasonably
guarantee it'll make a lot more a good deal sorer when Case gets
to the part where I leave half of it to young Marcy Cresap's TB
sanatorium and the Apple County Health Association. Whilst
the other half I plan to leave—Well, now never you mind about
that. I've talked a good deal more about myself than I ever
should have.

Natalia Lazarevitch—Tally Vengeance—that's the one I want
to tell you about. But where do you start in to tell about a
woman like that? You could study that woman eight hours a day
for years—you could watch her hang out a Monday wash or kiss-
ing her children with their towheads and red-scrubbed faces out
on the door stoop when the first bell rang at Central—you could
stare at Natty Vengeance till your eyes fell out and never know a
bit more about what it was she had than you did before. It was
looks, all right: She had them. But it was more. Sometimes you
might see her kiss her man good-bye before he went whistling up
to Lafayette Avenue with his lunch pail full of good things she'd
fixed him, on his way to work in the Benwood mill. You'd see
him get that kiss and think about the things in that lunch pail
that her hands had fixed and put there and you'd feel a little like
not opening the shop that day and going up to the Elks and
spend the day getting drunk. Sometimes I'd look out the window
and see her pass on her way up Seventh Street and the comb and
scissors would start to shake a little in my hands for a second or
so. You'd look at her and feel it. Yes, that's what I'm trying to
say. It wasn't a thing you could see or hear—it was a feeling.
Any man raised in the country, around animals, knows what it
is. The way they feel things; well, there was a little animal in all
of us feeling the big animal in Natty Vengeance. Like a spoor,
maybe. Or the thing creatures scent when they're in heat. Yes,
heat's what it was. It was like that Natalia Lazarevitch was always in heat—a proud, fine bitch who wouldn't ever give so
much as a look at the whole, wild, sniffing, whimpering pack of
feisty mongrels she led behind her through the streets of Glory
all that year, and the whole pack tumbling pell-mell on top of

each other, sometimes snapping at each other and getting kicked
or run over by cars or maybe just dropping on the sidewalk out of
plain exhaustion: It never mattered.

By God, I still don't know what she had. I've been with a lot
of women here and there, now and then. When I go up the river
to Wheeling or Pittsburgh it's not all business. Once in a
while—but never you mind about me. It's Natalia Lazarevitch
I'm talking about. This thing she had. By God, I don't know. I'll
bet if any of those scientists ever figure out what it was that
woman had it's a cinch, within a year, they'll be passing laws
against it. Because it was a community problem, a real public
disturbance in Glory when Tally Vengeance came up Lafayette
Avenue to Kroger's every payday. Because there wasn't a man
within looking distance—even the oldest—who didn't catch his
breath a little and feel the old springtime of his poor, dead youth
stir inside him and then rise up like Lazarus from the tomb.
Every man wanted her. And every woman in Glory hated every
man for that. Though they might all just as well have stopped
the wanting or the hating either one. Because there was only one
man in Natalia Lazarevitch's life—that whole time she never
looked at any man but her husband.

Milosh Lazarevitch made good money at the Benwood steel
mill. Natty always used to cut his hair for him—I guess—it sure
looked it—and I reckon he shaved himself. But once a year he
used to come up to my barbershop—June twenty-eight, rain or
shine—and have a shave and a haircut and a slicking-down with
a tonic nobody but him ever asked for—I'd bought it from a
Parkersburgh drummer fifteen years before and been stuck with
three bottles of it. It had stood back in the corner on the marble
shelf so long it was so dusty and fly-specked and greasy you could
hardly make out the fancy label: Ellwell's Authentic Louisiana
Jasmine. And when he'd had the works Milosh would go marching proudly off home to his Natalia and the two kids, smelling
like the parlor of a Polack whorehouse on payday night. Then
later on that evening you'd see the four of them up at Spoon's or
Charley Seat's soda fountain whispering and giggling together—
in Serbian, I reckon, because some of the Glory ladies said they

weren't ever able to pick out so much as a word Natty ever said.
And they'd be sucking orangeades through straws and directly
they'd all troop out licking double-scoop ice-cream cones and go
down to the Grand Theater and have a big time whistling for
Tom Mix or crying for the Gish girls or hissing Monte Blue,
though the Lord knows what they thought the shows were about:
Even the kids couldn't read the titles yet. Milosh would be
dressed up in a big stiff black suit that looked like cardboard, like
one of those suits they put on convicts after they get through
hanging them and put them out for public viewing up at Peace's
Funeral Parlor. Natty would have on a big-brimmed leghorn
straw hat with a bunch of celluloid cherries and a shiny rayon
dress with a big flower pattern of six or eight different colors—
and this was something else the women of Glory couldn't forgive—the loudest, commonest dress off the nigger racks at
Ganz's Store and yet when Natty put it on it didn't hide a thing,
it made everything she had, in fact, look a little better; you'd
have thought it was the fanciest, good-taste, twenty-five-dollar
New York City dress from Steifel's up in Wheeling.

I think the Glory women hated Natalia for her hair a little bit,
too. Because it was thick and the deep brown glossy color of a
polished buckeye and she braided it in a sort of chestnut crown
around her head; it must have fallen clear to the backs of her
calves when it was undone: a whole lifetime of hair, you might
say, and there was hardly a woman in Glory that year who hadn't
had her hair cut to what they called a "boyish bob" or else had it
cut page-boy style with bangs in front like Colleen Moore. No,
indeed, Natalia Lazarevitch's hair didn't help her popularity
much among the Glory wives. When Natty was alone on the
street I used to look out the window, and, I swear, she always
gave me the idea she was tall. Though she wasn't as tall as
Milosh; she came just about an inch or two above his shoulder.
Then I figured out one day it was because of the way she walked,
straight-backed as one of Remington's Indians and with her
white, round chin held back and a little smile sort of teasing
around the corners of her pink, full mouth. Since then I've seen
that smile in my recollections—yes, I'll be honest, I see it some

nights in dreams—and I try to figure out what she always seemed to be smiling about. But I'm never sure. Sometimes I guess she was thinking it was only two hours or five hours till the Wheeling streetcar dropped Milosh off at Twelfth and Lafayette and she was smiling to think how he'd look when he ran down the yard under the big willow beside their little house on Water Street. But I never knew for certain.

Sometimes I'd think she was laughing at the other women but I know it wasn't that—not, at least, in the beginning: She never noticed them. Or else she just felt good and was smiling at the goodness of being alive and being the kind of wild, full woman she was in whatever sort of a day it was, beneath whatever sort of sun or cloud. More often I thought it wasn't any good kind of smile at all; that maybe it was the little cruel grin of a woman who is waiting for an injustice to happen to her—and who knows it's got to happen because that's how the world's made—and who knows how she'll get even because that's how she's made. Maybe. By God, I don't know yet. And when I'd get done with every damned fool answer a man could think up for the thoughts behind that smile I'd start getting all sore and American and hot under the collar and tell myself: Well, by God, she ought to be smiling. Because she's a citizen of the greatest republic on earth. And she's living in the finest state in it and has a nice little home for her family in the valley of the prettiest county in the state. And her kids are going to school and growing up in the swellest, nicest town in the county. Though I'll grant you I couldn't imagine any part of the U.S.A. not looking pretty good after Serbia.

Hell, I'd never even heard of the place till Natalia Lazarevitch and her man Milosh came to town. Some nights I couldn't sleep and I'd lay there awhile listening to the electric fan and the kids roller-skating down Seventh Street and I'd start thinking about Serbia. Serbia, I'd say it over to myself a couple of times in my mind and sometimes I'd say it out loud in the dark, Serbia. And I'd try making up pictures of it in my mind, the way I imagined it looked over there where Natalia was born. And sometimes it was so real in my mind it was like looking at a colored photograph on a new calendar or sometimes I'd start adding a little to it: a palm tree here, maybe a quaint little jungle-type cottage there till it seemed as elegant to me as an expensive hand-painted oil picture. I used to get really artistic up there in the room, in the dark, in my thoughts about Serbia. Serbia, I'd say to myself till I fell asleep, Serbia. But after I was asleep I wouldn't say Serbia any more. I'd say, Natalia. And twice that summer I got disgusted with myself and the barbershop and had Densel Yoho call in his brother Layhew and take over both chairs while I went to Pittsburgh for a weekend. And it wasn't on business either; it wasn't any hot market tip I was chasing. And both times I came back to Glory worse off than when I left it.

I'd stand in the dark awhile by the lonesome depot and smell the warm river night and hear the rattle of Hook Madden's telegraph key back in the station and listen to the lonesome cry of the evening west-bound way off now, down among the river hills. And I'd walk up Seventh Street under the big trees and know I'd have to go up to the room directly and lie there with the worst old hangover in the world and wanting to burn my BVD's because they smelled like disinfectant and some poor, cheap, Soho, Polack girl's perfume. Through the open window I'd hear old Mrs. Tigglebeck's Victrola whining and squawking away across the street and the fan would whine on in the dark and I'd stare at the little square of light the window made on the ceiling over the big framed picture of Mom and try not to think about it. I mean Serbia. Mrs. Tigglebeck's Victrola keeps going till sometimes ten o'clock of a night and the sort of records she plays are just what you expect. She must not own but four or five and being the sort she is—an old, morbid-minded whistle-tit who never misses a single funeral on Glory Hill plus every time they hang a man with no family to claim him and have to bury him down back of the smelter in Potter's Field—as I say, it's no surprise that her two favorite records are "The Wreck of the Shenandoah" and "The Death of Floyd Collins." Half the nights I had to listen to those damned things I felt like heaving a shoe across Seventh Street.

But the second Sunday night when I got back from Pittsburgh

I was glad to hear that old Victrola: that's how blue I was; glad for anything to listen to, something with words to keep my mind off Serbia, anything to keep my thoughts away from the woman in the house down on Water Street, smiling in her sleep, clasped in big Milosh's arms, and all her grand hair, thicker than ropes of carved mahogany laying dark all round her on the white pillowcase. So I laid there thinking about all those gallant Navy lads and their brave commander out in Ohio that night, plunging to their doom in that awful line-storm. And I thought about the time we'd all heard a sound from the air like a hundred motorcycles and run out in the middle of Seventh Street and see the big silver *Shenandoah* floating right over Glory, so close you'd wonder how it could clear the hills across the river. And when the other record commenced I killed a little time thinking about Floyd Collins, poor boy, dying that way, trapped in his Kentucky cave. But I still couldn't get sleepy somehow and I still had you-know-who in the back of my thoughts and directly the old woman put on a Two Black Crows and I listened to that for a spell, though I knew all the jokes by heart, and directly that got me to thinking about the darkies up Misery Hollow by Parr's Mine. And, naturally, darkies got me to thinking about hunkies and they set me thinking about Slovaks and spics and the next thing you know I was right back to Serbians again.

Well, next morning I felt just terrible and everybody else in Glory must have been feeling the same way, too, because nobody came in for so much as a mustache-trim before ten o'clock. I just sat there on the chair by the window, bluer than ever, and stared at the hair tonic ad on the wall over the cash register that said: IT'S TOO LATE FOR HERPICIDE, and listened to Densel stropping his razors. Densel Yoho and his brother are two of the best damned barbers in the Ohio Valley but Densel's mind goes off on a strange, disordered tangent every six months or so. He gets these seizures, so to speak, and comes to work in a baseball uniform, cap, cleated shoes, catcher's mitt and all, and just stands around chewing gum and grinning till I send him home and call his brother Layhew. Later in the day you'll see Densel up in the middle of Seventh Street by the courthouse, squatting and punching his glove, his eyes bright and his jaw working faster, waiting for the ball. I can always tell when his spells start coming on: He's moody and nervous for a few days and then he buys four or five packs of Fan Tan Chewing Gum up at Charley Seat's candy counter. A normal, intelligent person can make a sensible remark to Densel when he's like that and he'll come back with a fool answer that'll make them wonder if he's got all his buttons. Layhew takes over Densel's chair for a few days then and directly Densel seems to get it all worked out of his system because he'll show up for work in a couple of mornings, bright as a pin and starts fetching his towels and stropping his razors like he hadn't been anywhere but home overnight; I don't think he remembers what's been going on because he's never been back more than two hours till he asks me how my trip was. Well, that morning I was sitting there staring at the bald head of the man who was too late in the Herpicide ad and still thinking about what I'd been trying to keep from thinking about all night.

Densel, I asked, though I should have had better sense; he had that moody scowl on his face and I could smell the Fan Tan a good ten feet away. Densel, where is Serbia at? In the Balkans—that's where Serbia's at, isn't it?

I have my fears about that, Henry, I have my fears, said Densel, chewing faster and not even bothering to turn around. Gehrig, Lazzeri, and Koenig never looked better, I'll grant you. But them aching legs of Jumping Joe Duggin could ruin Huggins's whole infield combination this summer!

I just sat there, disgusted, and stared at the twisted suspenders on Densel Yoho's big fat back.

Call Layhew! I shouted before I stormed out and slammed the door behind me. You hear me, Densel? You get Central on that phone right this very minute and have her ring up Layhew and you tell him to get right over here. You hear me, Densel? I'm going up to the Elks Club for a drink.

I've always made it a hard rule never to take a drink till the sun sets. But a man can just stand so much. And yet sometimes when he's stood all he can stand, he finds out he can still stand a little more. Because when I came back to the barbershop I found out Densel not only hadn't called Layhew but had left the place empty with three men waiting for shaves and gone home to put on that damned baseball suit of his. So that I only had but the one chair working till long after lunch; Layhew had to come upriver all the way from Captina.

I didn't eat my supper at the hotel that night. I went down to Joe Lowrey's Restaurant on Lafayette Avenue. When I thought about what I planned to do that evening I felt like I didn't want a lot of people I knew sitting across the dining room from me, watching me, and maybe guessing what was really in the back of my mind. It was a fine June evening with a little breeze from the river. As soon as the sun went down I hurried up past the courthouse toward Tomlinson Avenue. The little hairs on the back of my neck still had that tingly feeling like a lot of folks were staring at me. There weren't any people in the Glory Public Library except Miss Aurora Twigg, the librarian, and a couple of little girls looking at magazines in the back. I felt uneasy, though, when Miss Twigg looked over her eyeglasses and smiled at me. Books, a whole room full of them; I guess it was books that made the place smell queer like that: musty and close and queer, like somebody's old trunk. I'd never been in the Glory Public Library until that spring night; not once in my whole life.

I don't mean to say I'm not a reader. And I'm not just talking about newspaper and magazine reading either. Up in my room I've got a whole shelf full of those little blue books from Haldeman-Julius out in Kansas. I've been sending away for them for years—just little blue paper books and most of them only cost a nickel and I've read every one of them from the one on bee culture to Judge Lindsay on Free Love. Just the same I felt nervous in the library that night with Miss Twigg looking at me and smiling. What's she grinning at? I wondered. Does she know what's really there in the back of my mind? I told her I wanted to see some sort of a geography, one with maps in it and not just U.S.A. maps or state road maps. Finally, I just come out straight and said I wanted a map that showed the Balkans. And having gone that far I said real quick: Serbia. So she smiled again and said it was an atlas I needed, not a geography, and she went and fetched this big flat dusty book and found the place for me and went away and left me there at the table. Well, a map's a pretty dull thing to look at, usually, except for the colors or if you're planning a motoring trip somewhere. But I'm not ashamed to say that when I saw that map that showed Serbia it was like a love letter. Through the dead, musky air of that breathless room, quiet except for the little girls whispering over their *Literary Digest* pictures in the back, I could almost smell the lilacs that grow in the backyard of a certain house on Water Street. I could fairly see the color of a spray of them against dark hair roped in thick coils and almost too thick to take the tooth of a comb. Serbia was there right at the tips of my fingers and I moved them all around its different counties like some torn-up patchwork quilt: Croatia was blue and Slavonia was river-green and there was pink Montenegro and bright orange Bosnia and one called Herzegovina that was faded violet.

It just shows you how little you know, I thought silently. For I always thought the Balkans must be islands. Warm islands somewhere off near the coast of India, maybe. Palm trees and warm days and cool nights with the winds blowing lilac through the window screens. But it's not islands at all. It's up near Hungary so it must be cold. It's not islands like I thought, at all.

Gracious, Miss Twigg whispered, hurrying toward me with another book and laying it flat on the table she commenced leafing through the pages. Gracious, she said. I gave you the old one without thinking, Mister Winemiller.

The old what, ma'am? I said.

The old atlas, Miss Twigg said. The 1910. The one before the War.

What war? I asked, like the worst ignoramus in the world; because I really didn't know what she was saying.

Why, the Great War, she said, smiling, her eyes bright with natural surprise. Here you are, Mister Winemiller. The Balkans. 1920. Yes, *here* we are.

Her finger pointed; I looked at her hands, how thin they were with a little, old-timey engagement ring—her mother's, I reckon, because Miss Twigg wasn't married. Her hands looked

clean but dusty, like your fingers get from handling moths, only
it seemed like it was all over her hands, on the backs of them,
among the pale blue veins. Dust of books, I thought. I followed
her fingers as she pointed. It said Jugoslavia.

But where's Serbia, please? I said, and felt like a lot of things
were going wrong somehow.

Oh, I'm afraid it's gone, Mister Winemiller, she said. Just simply gone. Just swallowed up in the treaties. Clemenceau and
poor, dear, late President Wilson and those other fine, earnest,
weary souls. Mister Winemiller, did you ever notice what a star-
tling resemblance Lloyd George bears to our own dear Deacon
Ambers?

But I wasn't listening to her somehow; she's a good-hearted
soul and mighty well educated but I always get a little nervous
around people that whisper all the time.

But where did it go? I asked, still like a dunce, not getting
wise to any of it.

Pardon? whispered Miss Twigg. Where did who go, Mister
Winemiller?

Serbia, I said. I'm afraid I don't understand maps very good,
Miss Twigg.

Swallowed up! she whispered, with a little flutter of her fingers
over the table, flinging them over the outline of the vanished
states like a flurry of dusty pigeons. Gone! she whispered again.
Absorbed. Digested. Ah, the Great War changed so many
things! Only today I saw poor Mister Rogerson down at
Kroger's—his boy, you know; his only son. But then why should
I be telling you about the War, Mister Winemiller? You, who
served in France with the AEF—you, who saw Europe first hand!
Still, you might like to read up—to recollect a little. Wait now.
I have just the right books for you.

And she tiptoed off among the big shelves of musk and gloom,
still whispering to herself, and left me alone there, staring at the
place where Serbia was but wasn't any more; staring dumb and
thick-headed. And getting sorer by the minute. I felt like running out and catching the next Wheeling streetcar and jumping
off right in the middle of Benwood or McMechen and giving

some people a piece of my mind. I felt like going up there and collaring all those Hunkies and Polacks and Slovaks and Slavs and Montenegroes and Serbians. I just want to get hold of them all and holler: What the hell's wrong with you people? Haven't you got any pride? Haven't you got any patriotism? I just looked at a map and listen, you dumb bohunks, you know what? Your countries—they aren't there any more. You hear that, you dumb Serbians? There ain't no Serbia? How come you let a damned fool thing like that happen? Hell, we've had better than a hundred years of wars in the U.S.A. but, by God, you can still find it on the map. No wonder you people have to scratch a living out in the mines or sweat the marrow out of your bones in the steel mills. You don't deserve any better!

I just felt like taking both those map books and throwing them out in the middle of Tomlinson Avenue. But directly I commenced to cool off; I sat down and leaned my elbows on those maps and thought about it. I knew I didn't give a damn about the rest of them: the poor fools up yonder in the steel slums south of Wheeling. It was Natalia I was thinking about. If I was mad it was because of her; if I felt sad it was from thinking how a woman like her must feel. I mean how it must be to be proud of a place you come from and then suddenly it's not there any more.

Directly here come Miss Aurora Twigg back with a great, huge stack of books in her arms. She put them down in little heaps and I looked at her hands again. Covered with dust, like moths leave behind. Dust of books, I thought. Dust of kingdoms.

There now, cried Miss Twigg softly in a choky, pleased little whisper. There, Mister Winemiller. The whole history of the Balkans.

I sat there a spell looking at the three piles of dusty, musky books that covered now the quilt squares of the maps. I felt real grateful to Miss Twigg for her time and trouble but I didn't want to read any of those books. I don't think I could have even made my hands touch them. They disgusted me. There was something unclean about them. They were dusty like Miss Twigg's hands and the dust seemed like it was in my throat, choking me. I thanked her and ran out of there.

Lordy, it was hot on the bed in my room that night; the fan didn't seem to move the air at all. But I was so busy thinking I hardly noticed; thinking and looking out at a few stars I could see through the screen in the corner of my window. I thought about a lot of stuff, trying to grasp it all, trying to read some kind of map of things that I was on, before something got signed by beaten kings or winning presidents or neutral God; hurrying to find the shape and meaning of me before they all signed something and brought a new map out, and me not on it anywhere anymore. There wasn't many sounds outside in the street that night; I guess it was the heat. Miss Tigglebeck's Victrola was still; she must have gone to bed early, or was back in her little kitchen drinking death-black coffee and reviewing all the obituaries, ax murders, and fatal auto wrecks in the Glory *Argus* and the Wheeling and Pittsburgh papers.

Around midnight I heard Densel Yoho. He wasn't bothering anybody; he never does when he gets these simple spells. He was somewhere out yonder in the dark; I judged him to be up near the courthouse corner, squatting right out in the middle of the trolley tracks, spitting in his mitt and punching the leather with his fist every now and then. Play ball! he'd holler out from time to time and then he'd squint and focus hard down the deserted street, or else scan an eye along the star paths of the big June velvet night for a long, high one out in left field. But, hell, who's got the right to say what's real or empty fact, I'd like to know? Densel's desperate ball game out in the empty street—the old woman fighting each night, with flirting flattery, to charm away the black drummer whose overdue visit has got her hypnotized with dread—some poor, dumb Serbian's pride in a country canceled out by ministers and kings: a homeland long since scissored off the map—and me up there in my room with my fool fingers dreaming they feel the thick weight of dark and wondrous hair. Well, who's the crazy one, I'd like to know!

I laid there sweating on the bed in my BVD's, my hands behind my head, and thought about the rest of the sane and sensible folks in Glory. Well, I couldn't keep from chuckling out loud. I swear, there in the close, hot dark I could feel all of it out there in the night: the wanting, the hating that was going on. I could feel it like a thickness in the air: all the men out yonder in Glory asleep in their beds and just scheming and dreaming for the means to get at that woman in ways real nice and cozy. And all the wives beside them, dreaming and scheming of ways to get at her themselves—but in ways not quite so nice and cozy. Which ones of us all were the fools, I'd like to know. Who were the crazy ones that night in Glory? I heard Densel Yoho cuss and throw his glove down with a loud smack against the bricks; directly he commenced hollering at the umpire. When I dozed off he stopped hollering, but he was still arguing in a low, choked, hopeless voice. I could half hear him in my sleep, in my dreams of Natalia's hair: those bright braids thick as carved wood; poor Densel was saying it was the Black Sox Scandal all over again. He was saying the game was crooked—fixed from the start.

Well, maybe it was. Because the very next morning Marcy Cresap came in my barbershop asking for money. She waved at me with a smile and went over to Holly Withers, who was waiting his turn, and asked for a donation. She had an old blue coffeepot in her hand; it sounded like there was about six or eight dimes and nickels in the bottom. Marcy knows I like her. And she knows my barbershop is a good place for soliciting donations, especially when both chairs are busy and there's two or three fellows waiting their turn. A barbershop is a place where few men like to look cheap.

Who's it for this time, Marcy? I hollered across to her.

I remember I was shaving A. K. Pyle's neck and I knicked him a little when she told me.

It's for Mrs. Lazarevitch and her two children, Marcy said. Her man was killed at the Benwood steel mill this morning.

Just then a young blond-haired boy named Filipovitch went hurrying up Seventh Street; when he saw Marcy through the window he came tearing inside. He undid a big safety pin from the pocket of his blue work pants and tugged out a wrinkled wad of greenbacks and stuffed it in Marcy's coffeepot. Then he whipped off his cap and gasped when he saw John Grimm and A.K. and the police chief Holly Smithers and all those important Glory men there. He swallowed fast, his pale blue eyes bugging out, and clutched his cap against his shirt, striking a kind of pose like a fellow about to make a speech he's already done six or eight times that day.

That there money's from the men in Mike's crew, Miss Cresap! he cried in a tight kind of singsong voice. I was there and seen it happen!—when Mike Lazarevitch got killed! We'us all jist so nervous—Oh, it was somethin' jist ter'ble. The superintendent—he sent the whole shift home for the day! Holy Jesus, and please excuse me for cussin' thisaway! But it was jist somethin' ter'ble, folks! Mike—he was up there on the walk above the crucible and he leaned accidental and the wood rail on the scaffolding—it busted! And down came Mike a'fallin'! Holy Jesus, and he never even reached that hot metal! And, for God's sake, please excuse my cussin'. Down come Mike a-fallin' and when he come about fifteen foot from the blazin' top of that molten steel—Mike he just disappeared. There'us jist this little blue flame and a puff of smoke!—Whissshht!—Mike he jist disappeared in the middle of the air! Never even had time to give out a yell. Jist—whisshht!—and Mike was gone! Holy Jesus, and please excuse my bad talk but it was jist somethin' ter'ble to see! And that there money, Miss Cresap, that there's from the boys that worked with Mike! For Miz Lazarevitch and them two kids! A hundert seventy-six dollars and eighty-three cents! Holy Jesus, Miss Cresap, I thank you and excuse my bad talk, one and all, God amighty!

And he tucked his cap on inside-out and backed off, stumbling and blushing through the door, and run off hard up Seventh Street. Directly John Grimm opened his alligator wallet and gave Marcy a twenty-dollar bill and so did Holly Smithers and Claude Wayman, and A. K. Pyle coughed and fetched around in his snap purse and come out directly with a five, folded up small so nobody'd think he was tight. When Marcy come round to me with the coffeepot I rang open the cash register and turned my back on them all so's they couldn't see what I was giving. I wasn't about to have them know. And I'm not about to tell you either.

Well, Milosh sure had a queer funeral. Way up on the side of the hill above Benwood, far up beyond the last, dirty slum-house privy where something green, at least, grew—though nothing much more than goldenrod and polkweed and a few skinny sumacs. A queer sort of funeral with all those Serbians and Polacks and Hunkies standing around plus a few valley Americans: me and Marcy and Tadd Cockayne and his boy Albert and old Doctor Cecil. And they had this preacher from the South Wheeling Orthodox Church: an old man with a beard like the picture of Walt Whitman in Judge Peabody's library. A strange sort of feeling you got, standing there with him praying and sprinkling and making signs in the air, like it was all happening on some foreign hillside and not in Mound County, at all. He did his preaching in Serbian and then some in English for the ones who had forgot or never knew and talked in a high, proud voice about Milosh Lazarevitch who had fought bravely with his brothers and sisters against the Turks and the Austrians and then come to America and become a good American without forgetting his brave heritage.

Right in the middle of it Mabel Peabody come up the dirt road in her 1922 Pierce Arrow with old Miss Tigglebeck in the front seat beside her and they parked a good distance off, watching and listening while the preacher, his white beard blowing in the hill winds of that fair June morning, said Milosh Lazarevitch was now and for everlasting in the high company of his people's undying heroes: Saint Sava and King Marko and the holy Prince Lazar and somebody named Stephen Dushan—a mill-worker friend of Milosh's, I reckon. No, I'll not soon forget it: the queerest sort of funeral, without even a hearse or county coroner's ambulance to bring poor Milosh up there, but instead of that a big, muddy, six-ton Garford truck with WHEELING STEEL CORPORATION stenciled on the cab, and a cheap, black wreath on the windshield. While looming up in the truck bed was this gigantic mass of cold steel with Milosh in it—six or eight tons, I reckon, if it weighed a pound: a great, enormous cone: ragged

and ugly as the meteor they got up in the museum at Pittsburgh.
And somewhere in it—I guess that's how they figured—was
whatever ashes of Milosh Lazarevitch that didn't go up in that
little blue flame when he fell.

Natalia's dark eyes had watched, proud and brave in her
bloodless face, above the smooth cheeks that looked soft as blossoms above her chin and then seemed to tighten and gleam
where the scrubbed skin stretched over the flat, high bones; and
her broad bow mouth with its full underlip was not shaking, it
didn't seem even tight like women's mouths when they don't
dare cry, though the little smile didn't play in the corners that
day. And all she ever did that even seemed close to grieving was
to shut her big eyes gently when the twelve mill workers, struggling the huge mass out of the truck and down the makeshift
ramp of girders, let it go, at last, with a single-voiced shout and
let it plunge with a ponderous rumble into the enormous company grave.

My! *That* lady sure is a cool cucumber! I overheard Mabel
Peabody exclaim to Miss Tigglebeck when the services were over;
Marcy and me were just walking past her car.

Were you watching her face, Nevada? Mabel went on. She
never shed a single, solitary tear. Not that I'm really surprised: a
woman of that sort—and a foreigner besides. I declare, Nevada,
I don't know how I ever let you wheedle me into driving you up
here to witness this common spectacle!

Ah, now, Mabel, said Miss Tigglebeck. There is some grief
that's past all tears. And it's true, dear—the poor thing is a foreigner, and foreign ways are strange, sometimes beyond our understanding. Still—just look yonder, Mabel: her two fatherless
little waifs!—see how the one tries to hide her eyes with her
bonnet brim! Look how the other tugs at the black fringe of the
mother's shawl, trying to stuff it in her little mouth to staunch
the sobs! Ah, the poor soul—widowed with those two little girls!
And so far far from the land of her forebearers! Mabel, whatever
shall she do?

Well, that's sure not a hard one to answer, sniffed Mabel Peabody, glaring out the window at Marcy and me. She can always go back where she came from!

Marcy was pulling at my sleeve, but by that time I didn't care; I shook loose and walked through the tall grass right over to that Pierce Arrow running board, and stuck my head in the window.

'Be a little hard to go back to go back to Serbia, wouldn't it, Miss Peabody? I said, with an educated smile.

And *why* would it, Mister Winemiller? she shouted, backing away from me a little.

Because—it's—not—there—any —more—is why! I said.

Then, tipping my hat politely to Miss Tigglebeck, I turned on my heel and went off with Marcy Cresap, who drove me back to Glory.

And so it commenced. A week passed—then two—and by the last week in June it didn't need a mastermind to guess what most of Glory was up to. I lathered and shaved men daily while they smirked and hinted at the mention of Natalia's name; I trimmed some mighty important heads and watched their faces through the snip-snapping scissor blades and saw their winks and gloating leers and knowing, wiseacre nods. And after I'd whisk-broomed them off they'd tarry awhile by the door, whispering and chuckling Natalia's name behind their hands and the big gold lodge rings would twinkle as their fingers twitched in ornery anticipation. Nights when I'd have my supper in the hotel dining room I'd see the women's smiles and hear their whispers, too: The Glory ladies had their plans for Natalia, as well. What with the little wife sitting right across the tablecloth from them, the men kept their mouths shut now, though—from time to time— one of them would get a dreamy look and stare out the plate glass window into the mists that rose from the river in late June's moonlit dusk, and smile a little smile, and pick their teeth behind a hotel napkin, and ponder what the next move should be now.

Because the first move had already been made for them. I mean Milosh's death. Natalia didn't have a penny to her name. When Marcy Cresap told me that I couldn't hardly believe it. I asked her about the hundred seventy-six dollars and eighty-three cents the men in the mill chipped in. I asked her about the coffeepot money, too, and Marcy said Peace's Funeral Home had taken all of that for Milosh's sandstone marker and she still owed money to the steel company.

What for? I said.

Well, said Marcy, her eyes flashing a little behind her spectacles. It seems that hill above Benwood where they buried Mike is company owned. Maybe some day they plan to expand—they'll build a plant there or dig a mine—Lord knows. Meanwhile, they use it for that. For burying. There's half a century of men up there who died in the mill. Some just got old and wore out; some had accidents. When a man dies like Mike died they always bury the whole thing that he fell into. Henry, I guess there must be better than a dozen eight-ton chunks of steel stuck into that smoky hillside. The company's sentimental that way. It's just lucky she doesn't have to pay for all that steel Mike spoiled. As it is, they're only charging her for the worth of the land where he's buried.

She chuckled and turned her head away real quick; I could see an angry mist in the corners of her eyes.

Up at the funeral home last week, Marcy said, Tom Peace's boy made up a real good joke. It was the day they ordered Mike's marker from the stonemason down at Marietta. Folks all over town are still chuckling over it—the cute motto Tom Peace's boy said they ought to use on Mike's tombstone.

What was it? I said.

Rust in Eternity, Marcy said.

But I guess that wouldn't have been worth Glory's trouble. Natalia couldn't read English; she'd have missed a good joke like that. And so Glory went about getting at her with jokes she could understand—even if they weren't quite as funny as the one Tom Peace's boy made up. A woman doesn't need to understand English for her and her kids to get along, but she's got to eat, she has to pay the rent, there's a gas bill every month and doctors send bills, too; there's the week's groceries to buy at Kroger's every Friday and children's clothes don't last forever. One night toward the end of June I was awake as usual, thinking about Natalia, and I couldn't figure it out to save my life. It just seemed too queer to have an answer: all these businessmen in Glory making it so hard on her—all these men who were itching so bad to get on her good side. Well, I know I'm a fool but I didn't have to strain my brain much figuring that one out. It was plain as daylight that somebody was putting the screws on every one of those men: the doctor, the grocer, the real-estate fellow, the clothing-store keeper, the nabob up at the gas company, the shoestore owner, the dentist, the steel company secretary, the tombstone contractor and all the rest—though I'm not mentioning a one of them by name. Yes, somebody was putting the screws on them to put the screws on Natalia. A whole little chattering bunch of somebodies, to be exact—and every single somebody among them wearing a skirt!

However tender—or however ornery—a businessman in Glory might have felt toward Natalia Lazarevitch that spring, can you just imagine now him giving her credit or, worse still, money and coming home that night to anything less than a household full of nagging, married hell? So by the end of that month Natalia's back, at last, was flat against the wall. To my knowledge there was but one Glory merchant who went down to the little house on Water Street with any sort of suggestion. Natalia sent the children out of doors and fetched in an old one-eyed Croation miner's widow—a bone-setter by trade—to stand by the stove and tell her in Serbian what the man had come to tell her in English. Well, it sure was a nice little plan, all right: Natalia was to get a whole year's supply of groceries and all she had to give him was a whole year's supply of something else. I remember that night well—I rented a bottle of leeches from Seat's Drug Store and fixed up both this certain party's eyes pretty good, but his nose was bad for months; even though, I declare, it did look sort of scenic and grand the way it went from deep violet and baby blue through all kinds of green and orange and tan and finally ended up in a finale of pale yellow ochre, like the sunset in the Maxfield Parrish picture that hangs over my washstand.

Though she hadn't really hit back yet. She wasn't Natty Vengeance yet. Natalia Lazarevitch could have fetched a black iron skillet up side the head of every big man in Glory and not even touched them the way Natty Vengeance would touch them in due time. Was fated to. Yes, something in me will always believe it was fate: every bit of it. There was something fixed and irresistible the way people went through their movements from first to last: beginning with Milosh, the day he fell, clean till the night Natty Vengeance left Glory behind her forever.

Marcy Cresap saw what was happening: the men in Glory sick with the fever of wanting Natalia, the women of Glory hating Natalia, not because the men were sick, but because it wasn't them that got them that way; knowing they couldn't anymore get a fellow fevered-up that way than they could raise a thermometer stuck up a corpse on Peace's cooling table—hating Natalia Lazarevitch as only women can hate woman, whilst hounding their men, day and night, to drive her off the brink of Glory. Marcy saw all this happening; she fought it the way she fought everything like it in Apple County—not ever hating the haters, just hating the hate. But even Marcy couldn't change it now. Because, by this time, Natalia was mad.

She couldn't get work and she wouldn't take charity. And one sweltering June morning a delegation of ladies of the Glory Associated Charities came smiling down Water Street to Natalia's kitchen door with three apple crates full of old winter clothes, several cans of lard and two big bags of flour. Well, charity from that quarter didn't surprise me a bit; if there's one thing women can never resist, it's a good, close sympathetic look at someone they're destroying. And what is even the best of charity but the bared backside of contempt, cheaply perfumed and offered for a kiss?—the last insult scared winners ever seem able to cook up against spunky losers.

And it was work Natalia wanted, to keep herself and the two little girls together. She'd asked at the glass plant, the back doors of Glory's restaurants and cafés, the aeroplane factory, the two hotels, the enamel works; she'd gone from house to house offering herself as housemaid, cook, washer woman, grass cutter. Nothing. Meanwhile, though she had enough to eat for a while from the little cellarful of things she'd put up the fall before, the rent was due. And the gas bill. And the rest of the bills. So she tried selling a few things from her cellar shelves: mason jars of apples and spiced pears and green beans and queer, strange Balkan eggs—sleek and velvety things—boiled for two days in olive oil, Serbian style. But, of course, no one ever bought so much as a single jar of fruit, or an asafoetida bag, or a sheep's-milk cheese, or a posy of wild flowers from the stuff she hauled rattling behind her, in the old child's wagon, through Glory's leafy streets. And, before long, men who'd worked with Milosh in the steel mill—Serbians from Natalia's own outlandish abolished hills—came courting and asked honorably for her widowed hand in marriage. But she drove them away with shouts as wild and final as if they'd been Glory Rotarians with something less permanent in mind. And folks started wondering why she didn't just pick up and go somewheres else—a place like Steubenville or Weirton or even back to Benwood, to the old battleship-gray frame house where she and Milosh had lived and had their kids before they came to Glory. But it was too late for that now; something had got hold of that woman's mind that was fiercer than pride or getting-by or even just plain survival. Natalia Lazarevitch was mad. And here's a funny thing: that wisp of a smile was back in the corners of her mouth again: the smile-ghost nobody'd seen since they buried those six tons of Milosh up on Benwood hill.

I'm not ashamed to say I laid awake those nights—sweating with scared notions that one of those big, laughing mill-hands would finally win her. Or that maybe she'd just give up, at last, and run off with the kids somewhere new. But she didn't. Though, before long, I was to wish to God she had; before many weeks I was to curse myself for ever being thankful she was still there. But, you see, by now she had to stay. They could have tractored her house down and set fire to the ruins and rubble and she'd have stayed; she'd just have taken her kids and her three laying hens and her two sheep and gone out to sit under the big willow, while that ghost-smile kept on teasing the corners of her mouth, like little licking flames. Because Natalia Lazarevitch still had something she planned to do with Glory before Glory was done with her. And I guess I was the last man in town to know she'd already commenced doing it.

There's one big trouble to living a life like mine: I mean, following a trade where you have to keep your mouth shut for thirty-seven years. And that is, once you ever do start talking about things, there's no shutting up. Lord, when I think of some of the things I've told you, it makes me wonder if my senses haven't left me—I've owned up to stuff I wouldn't have even whispered to Mama's picture up there in the dark of my room. So I might as well tell how I laid awake every night of those last weeks in June scheming for some way to get round Natalia. Well, I know—every other male in Glory was awake scheming that himself. Only, God help me, I wanted the crazy, wild she-devil for my wife.

Falling in love, like mumps, is better off having while you're a boy; it's mighty disorganizing when it hits you in the fifties. Like a butcher's sledge, it slams you between the eyes and before you know it you haven't got the judgment of a reasonably dumb fourteen-year-old.

One night in the hotel dining room I caught myself mumbling out loud during my peach pie and saw a few people staring at me, curious naturally, and realized suddenly what I'd been saying. I'd been working out the sort of speech I'd say if I went down to Water Street some June evening and proposed. And had half a mind to go do it right then and there. Not knowing yet that the time had come when it was way too late for that; never guessing that Natalia's queer, dark vengeance had already begun.

I snuck into the library; I just had to go there that night. Because it was the only place in Glory that had Natalia's picture: the only likeness I could think of that I could look at whenever I wanted and touch with my hands. For me the beautiful colors of the map in that old dog-eared, out-of-date atlas was a picture of Natalia Lazarevitch; the only one I had—a face that crazy kings and crook-ministers couldn't ever treaty out of being. Let them repeal the maps; let them scrape and ink out, paint over and reprint the shapes of all those queer Hunkie homelands—they still couldn't embezzle away the tough pride of some people. And with all their monkeying around, they couldn't ever change the smiles in the corners of some women's mouths.

The library was just the same as the first night I came there: Miss Twigg was fussing around with her little cards behind the desk, the two little girls in the back were whispering together still; it was like nobody'd even gone home since then. Then Miss Twigg spied me.

Ah, Mister Winemiller! she cried with a hushed gasp. So you *did* come back for some more books, after all!

No'm, I said. Just to look something up. In the atlas—the *old* one, that is.

Oh, dear, now! Miss Twigg whispered. Dear, dear now! What shall we do! It's busy, I'm afraid.

Busy, ma'am?

Those two little ladies in the back, she said, *they're* looking at it! But I suppose they'd be just as happy looking at magazines.

Miss Twigg held a dusty hand up to one side of her mouth and leaned closer, whispering softer still.

Poor little things, she said. Before their father died they used to come here often of an evening. But now they're here every night. Till closing. Then I see them from my bedroom window— wandering the streets long after I've gone home—sometimes they sit yonder on the courthouse porch till past midnight. I don't think the mother wants them home evenings. Heaven only knows why not—they're such little dears. That *strange* woman—

What woman? I said, though something in me knew already.

Why, Mrs. Lazarevitch, Miss Twigg gasped softly through her fingers, and seemed to breathe out little puffs of book dust when she spoke. The foreign woman down on Water Street. The *widow*, she added, then bit her lip and glanced away quickly as if she'd just said a word that ladies shouldn't use.

Children! she chirped brightly, and fluttered off before I could stop her. Mary—Sophie! Come let me give you the new *Delineator* to look at! It's simply full of pretty pictures. And there's a splendid new Butterick dress pattern! Has your mama taught you to sew yet, my dears? No—I suppose she hasn't. Still, there's lots

of colored pictures, so come now, my lambs. Mister Winemiller
wants to use the atlas and I'm sure two well-mannered little
ladies won't mind giving it up!

I looked behind me at the door but it was too late to run. I
just seriously felt like hiding somewhere amongst those dusty
bookshelves before I'd let those two children of hers see me there
and maybe recognize my face and know what I'd come there to
look at. Sophie pouted but little Mary just smiled bashfully and
stuck a finger in her mouth when Miss Twigg spread the new
magazine on the table before them and shoved the atlas to one
side. Then she turned, smiling, and beckoned to me with her
fountain pen. So there was no way out of it for me; I had to go
sit in the chair right next to those two and make some kind of
show out of it. So I went back there and sat down somehow and
just stared at the tops of my clammy hands on the open page
before me without even knowing what it was. And to make matters worse, the oldest girl, Sophie—Mary was the shy one—the
bold one, Sophie, she spoke to me.

My, I jist love maps, she whispered, looking around at me
with big, frank, friendly eyes. Don't you? I reckon—next to
movie shows—there's nothing I'd rather look at than maps.
Don't you? When I git old enough to git a job at the glass factory
that's the very first thing I'm gonna buy me!—a map book just
like that there one.

I cleared my throat and I must have been purple with shyness;
I've given a lot of Glory children their first haircuts and spent
thirty-seven years learning how to talk to them, but these were
her children and that was her map under my hands. I just felt like
my tongue was an old shoe.

Of course, she went on in that bold, hoarse whisper, I don't
plan on working at the glass factory more than a month. After
that I'm going to be a movie actor like Norma Talmadge. Next
to Mama, Norma Talmadge is the gorgeousest lady I ever did see.
I think she's gorgeouser than Clara Bow. Don't you? I just know
I'll get to be a real famous movie actor. Because I'm always pretending I'm somebody else. I reckon that's why I just love map
books. Because I'm jist always pretending I'm somewheres else

than where I'm at. I can jist sit and look at maps for hours and
hours—can't you? I jist sit there looking at maps and dream I'm
far far away.

I sat there staring at the backs of my big hands. But I had to
smile and something tight inside me seemed to burst and spill
and run all through me till it warmed my clammy fingers.

Don't you? the bold child Sophie was saying suddenly, her
fingers laid with lonesome friendliness upon my sleeve.

Sure, I said. You just bet your life I do.

Me, too! whispered Sophie loudly. Oh, me, too! I'm jist dyin'
to go there!

I sat quiet a spell; I wondered how a man could break the news
about something like that to a child without breaking her heart
as well.

Suppose it's not there anymore, I said.

You're jist kiddin' now, she laughed, and even shy Mary had
to giggle at my foolishness.

No, just suppose, I said. A body can't be too sure of things in
such a world as this. Things change. Sometimes they go away.

You're jist kiddin', she laughed, more tickled than ever, and
Mary had to stick her little fist in her mouth, rocking with
sneezy, muffled chuckles.

Places don't go away, she said scornfully. My, you sure are an
awful kidder.

Sometimes they do, I said. I'm a good deal older than you and
I know about these things.

Where to? she whispered, with great, huge, solemn eyes, a
little scared-looking now. Where could places go?

Nowhere, I said. Things like wars come. And when the war's
over the place isn't there. It's just gone. So there's nothing left
for the men to do but make the maps over. And old maps—like
this one—they don't mean no more than pictures in a fairy-story
book. D'you see?

She looked so puzzled and sad I wished I hadn't tried to explain; her big eyes shone with lonesome sadness, half sore at me,
and the little smiles that played in the corners of her child-
mouth, they were gone. But I kept on anyway; I had to let her
know the way things are.

So if you got dreams of going back, I said firmly, either you or your sister—or your ma—if you're fixing to go back to Serbia—

That ain't Serbia, she said, cocking her head with puzzlement at me. I never said a word about Serbia. That there's a map of Texas! That's the place I always pretend I'm at!

I looked down suddenly, feeling strange, foolish feelings, and looked at the map of the U.S.A. under the heels of my big, dumb hands.

When they got the war done, she begged, in a half-scared whisper and tugged at my sleeve, was Texas gone?

I shook my head and queer thoughts made me tremble; I shook my head no real hard again and slapped my hand on the map.

No, by golly! I said out loud. The war never changed nothing on *this* map! And no war never will!

With a little sigh of glad relief the child clambered across the arm of my chair and leaned on her elbows, turning the thumb-marked pages of the atlas till she found what I wanted.

There! she said, with a stab of her finger on the page. That there's Serbia.

And she leaned closer—frowning, searching—her breath so close that it stirred the little hairs on the back of my hand.

And that there, she said, with another finger-jab, that's where my Mama was born and there's where Papa was born and that's where Uncle Danilo got killed fighting the Turks and that's where—

And she kept on pointing and talking and I looked at the queer names on that queer map of No-Place-Any-More and thought about the people she was talking about who had vanished just as totally and the towns that hadn't even mattered much when they were there, queer-named towns where nobody of any importance ever did anything important enough for anybody to take notice of and how they'd all so soon been forgotten; a beautiful land it had been, but I kept thinking: Whatever had such lost, outlandish flyspecks on a canceled map ever done that touched a single human life in Glory—or changed a soul in the whole great U.S.A., for that matter—except to send a woman out of its ragged obscurity to change the life of me? I looked at all the meaningless, lost, queer names of them as they passed under the little girl's finger; the sad small towns where nothing, but Natalia, ever happened: Travnik and Topola, Pruska Gora and Dubrovnik and Zagreb. And Sarajevo.

Suddenly on the first stroke of the courthouse striking nine, Miss Twigg tapped her little iron bell and tiptoed back, still whispering, to tell us it was time to go. The two children ran off ahead of me into the pearly river mists.

Wait now! I hollered boldly. You kids leave me walk you safely home. It's too late at night you going down there to Water Street in such a fog as this.

But I could barely make out their small shapes in the corner lamp post's smothered bloom of light.

Good night! cried brave Sophie. Good night, mister!

You go home now! I hollered, stern as if I was already their father. You hear? Go straight home now!

We dasn't! sang out shy Mary, with a sudden, sorrowful boldness of her own. Mama don't let us never come home till after the clock's struck twelve! Mama don't—

Hush! I heard brave Sophie whisper in the mists.

—Mama don't finish entertaining her gentlemen till twelve! shy Mary finished, heedless.

Hush, I said, you little fool! cried Sophie in a rage, and I heard the smart smack of a slap and off they scampered somewhere, small Mary wailing and Sophie scolding, deep in that white woolly wilderness of night.

And so it was that I first came to know—what most of Glory had known already: how, in that desperate, queer last week in June, Natalia Lazarevitch had started selling her favors for a price. I tell you I took it hard. I thank the Lord I'm not a drinking man or, I tell you, I'd have been a goner. As it was, I had Densel and Layhew take over both chairs whilst I took off a week out of town to pull myself together. I couldn't have stood the sight of Pittsburgh just then, so I took a trip over to Uniontown where the Methodists were throwing a big spring Tri-state Revival. I went religiously four nights in a row and watched while the world-famed evangelist made kindling wood out of four perfectly good kitchen chairs. But the night he hollered out in front of three thousand people: Women, cross your legs and close the Gates of Hell! I got up and walked right back up the Sawdust Trail and went out of that tent disgusted with everything—chairs, Methodists, women, hell and myself—and went back to the tourist home and laid on the bed listening to the delighted ladies who'd commenced singing "Beulah Land"—with crossed legs, I reckon. I thought out things pretty thoroughly those last few days there, away from Glory. I knew that nothing had happened back there that could ever change my mind about Natalia. I knew she could put out for money in every town between Aliquippa, Pennsylvania, and East Liverpool and I'd still want to marry her. What had me really stumped was why she was putting out to the very men in town she hated worst. Until I remembered something else; Natalia was mad. And when a woman like that gets mad she's not about to give up nor give in either; she's more likely working on some female scheme to make a man wish, before she's done with him, that he'd been born a gelding.

So June came to its end. And then commenced one of the strangest summers Glory'll ever have to remember. For me it seemed the saddest since the one when Mama passed over. But just about everybody else in Glory seemed to be having a pretty good time. The men had Natalia when they wanted her. The women had her where they wanted her. Their tight-lipped mouths showed the Christian victory of seeing her beauty forced to be what they'd all suspicioned it was meant for from the first. They'd seen her upstart Hunkie pride forced into public prostitution. And no woman ever minds immorality in a town when immorality is the price of justice.

I guess I could have gone crazy without much trouble that summer if it hadn't been for Marcy Cresap dropping in for a chat now and then. And when nightfall came there were two folks in all of Glory who befriended me, listened to my yowls, talked back, kidded me a little, prayed some and scolded a lot. One was old Miss Tigglebeck and the other was Densel Yoho. Nights of laying up there in the old room, evenings with nothing to do but think, and the dark ceiling like a moving picture screen with

pictures of Natalia and all those men—sometimes I'd get scared
I'd turn dog-mad and go running down to the house on Water
Street. So I'd go sit in Miss Tigglebeck's front parlor and drink
Postum and listen to her Victrola. And for a while I'd forget my
own miseries thinking about that poor boy trapped in that Kentucky cave and about gallant Captain Lansdowne and all the
young lives doomed on the *Shenandoah's* last trip that night. I
got so I even worked up a little interest in Miss Tigglebeck's
scrapbooks of obituaries and the murder of the little Parker girl
by the fiend in California and whether Harding's death was natural or not. Miss Tigglebeck would come up now and then with
some first-rate little nature note she'd gleaned from Headstone
Footnotes, the curiosity column in *Evergreen Memories,* the
American Mortician's Monthly, or maybe a comic remark from
Cript Quips, their joke department. I'd drink Postum till I was
half sick and sleepy and listen to Vernon Dalhart whining away
on the machine: One dark, September mor-ning—the ear-th was
fa-a-ar be-low; the migh-ty Shen-en-doah. . . . And I'd shut my
eyes and I could just see her, the way she used to come gliding
low over Glory—just clearing the courthouse trees, it seemed,
and the way you'd feel cool for a minute in that long, gigantic
shadow that flitted over the streets and up the building fronts
and across the back lots. It doesn't sound like much to you,
maybe, but it kept my thoughts away from Natalia for a while.
And when I didn't have Miss Tigglebeck I had Densel.

That Densel Yoho is a tough one to figure out. He's as kindly a
soul as you'd ever went to meet and forty weeks out of the year
he's as bright as a new dollar. He only has these baseball seizures
once or twice a year; I guess all that fuss over Babe Ruth's world
record last season was the reason he had three. When he's got
that uniform on, Densel hasn't got the sense of an epileptic ape.
But once he's got it all worked out of his system he comes back
sharper than ever. His brother Layhew is a boob by comparison.
When Densel gets over one of his fits he hides his glove and suit
and baseball shoes somewhere in the boardinghouse he lives at
and comes back to work. He never remembers a thing he did.
But he looks as refreshed as if he'd spent a week's vacation out in

Kansas at Doc Brinkley's clinic. I don't know where he learned it
at, but Densel's got a strong philosophy about women. That's
how I first got round to confiding in him my feelings about
Natalia. Pretty soon we got to eating supper together every night
at the hotel. Afterward we'd pick our teeth a while and have an
extra cup of coffee and then go down on Lafayette Avenue for a
few games of balkline or three-cushion at Leaky Waldorf's Crystal Billiard Lunch.

Aw, stop your sweating, Hen, said Densel one cool August
evening. That woman'll straighten out directly. She's busy working on something, that's all.

It'll wreck her, I said. Her constitution won't take it. It'll kill
her, Densel.

Constitution! said Densel. *Kill* her. Why, Hen, putting out six
or eight times a night don't tire a woman like that as much as
you'n me sweat over a game of rotation pool. You listen to me,
Hen. That woman'll straighten out directly. And she'll quit putting out. Because she'll never be worth a damn as a hustler. It's
just not her speed—she's too hot-blooded for it. Hustlers is like
nuns, Hen—scared to death of a real good loving. So they both
have to get as far away from it as they can—someplace where,
most of the time, there's nothing around but a bunch of other
women. That woman's not like that—she's a hot-blooded devil,
a real one-man-er. He sure had himself a female—that poor
bohunk that married her. I'll bet it wasn't hot steel that killed
him at all. He likely went up in smoke just thinking about what
he had waiting home for him. The poor, dumb Polack. They
should have buried the bed and not that hunk of pig iron—

He wasn't a Polack, I said sternly. He was a Serbian.

Polack, Serbian, Lesbian, whatever, said Densel. That's not
what I'm talking about. I'm talking about that woman. She's just
hustling now because it's part of her scheme. Lord, when I think
of those damned fool men, he sighed, and chalked his cue.
Those poor, damned fool men.

Well, in your judgment, what *is* her scheme? I said.

I don't know, said Densel. You don't know. These fool men in
Glory don't know. Their wives don't know. And I'd lay even

money she herself don't know. The only thing in that woman's thoughts is getting even. One day she got the word Revenge in her head, and, from then on her head didn't have no more to do with it—the rest was all juices and glands and instincts. She's not thinking, Hen. She's *feeling*. When that kind of woman starts thinking she ends up doing something stupid.

I leaned on my cue and sipped a little of Leaky Waldorf's near-beer; I gazed out the gloomy, dusty poolroom window at the yellow light from Tadd Cockayne's gooseneck lamp still burning in the *Argus* office. All I could feel was that awful doom of ruin I felt so sure was waiting for Natalia somewhere up there in the weeks and months ahead. I heard a steamboat blow her lorn lament; like some cry of a nightbird's fatal omen.

They'll get her, though, I murmured. Can't you see that, Densel? In the end, *they'll* get her.

Who? said Densel. Who'll get her.

Them, I said. You know these married women in Glory—all those wives. Don't tell me they don't know. Don't tell me they don't give a hoot: their husbands slipping down to Water Street. Every night—the minute the sun's down and the fog's up. Oh, don't think they don't know, Densel.

Densel stuck his cue back in the rack, chuckled and tossed a quarter on the felt.

Sure they know, he said. They know that woman's putting out. They know she's gone to hustling. And what do you reckon that makes them do, Hen?—shed a charitable tear for one of their fallen sisterhood? And a bohunk sister at that.

Serbian, I said. I sure wish you'd try remembering that fact, Densel. Natalia is a Serbian. A mighty proud people. And without any map anymore, I added, in a slightly superior tone. Except the maps of our own Apple County.

Serbian, said Densel. Whatever. I'm talking about women now and they don't make any maps of that. Whatever. Because it don't matter a bit: whatever breed or denomination she is or they are—that's not what I'm getting at. I'm talking about that woman on Water Street putting out and every other woman in Glory knowing she's putting out. And glad she's putting out because putting out's what they've always wanted her to have to do since she and the poor, dead bohunk first come here from Benwood with the kids. Don't you see it, Hen?—the way they're all settling back now to enjoy it for a spell: the sight of her crawling in the ditch of harlotry and disgrace. Just wanting what they always wanted: to see her stuck-up, god-awful, terrifying beauty have to crawl. And have to put out for a living. Even if it's their own men that are getting what she's putting out. They'll watch her for a spell, see her get what they reckon is coming to a working-stiff's wife who dares walk with her chin stuck back that way and her eyes crackling with pride the way hers always done. You know. Like the queen of something. Maybe that's what she was back there. Queen. Of Serbia. Or Timbuctoo or China. Whatever. Because it don't matter where. What matters is here. In Glory. What matters is the way she held her head up on Friday nights when she come into Kroger's on the dead bohunk's arm: the way she always looked like she was getting ready to smile but hadn't quite started yet. All that, Hen, plus that god-awful femaleness that didn't leave nothing safe around it after it walked past.

Just coming here to Glory in the first place—wasn't that enough to get them sore, Hen? Instead of staying up in Benwood or McMechen or Mingo Junction with the rest of the Polack steelworker trash? Wasn't it enough? And then behaving like she was some sort of a sixth-generation, English, valley-born, Legion Ladies' Auxiliary, dame of the DAR, Methodist preacher's wife and beauty-contest winner at the Panhandle Peach Festival, to boot? It was too much, Hen. By God, it just wouldn't do. So they had to work it round and wait till life whored her down to humbleness. And now they'll enjoy that for a spell. And when they get tired of playing with the mouse they'll eat it. Except that I'm betting on the mouse, for some queer reason. I'm betting that by the time the cat figures it's time to get ready to move, the mouse'll be having herself a regular cat church-barbecue! In a way it's almost sad, Hen—all them women tonight up there in Glory—they're just sort of mesmerized in the spell of their own reflections. Now, there's nary one them doesn't know

that woman's finagling around right this very minute with somebody's husband. But do you reckon there's one of them whose
pride would let her own up that it's hers? The party lines are all
humming tonight, Hen, but they're all talking about somebody
else!

We had long since left Leaky Waldorf's; we'd talked all the
way down Lafayette and up Seventh. The way Densel's voice
carried through the fog when he got worked up, I was half-scared
some woman would overhear. Miss Tigglebeck's light was out, I
noticed with disappointment. But I talked Densel into staying
out a while longer and we went and sat in the dark in the barbershop and Densel had him a sip from the hair-tonic bottle we
kept disguised between the bay rum and the Herpicide.

Densel, how'd you come to know so much about women? I
asked, though maybe I shouldn't have done it.

By staying shut of them, he said.

Never had a gal? I said, and shouldn't have asked that either.

Got one now, he said. She taught me all I know about 'em,
Hen.

How'd she teach you? I said.

By being dead for fifteen years, he said.

And then he sat studying the lights in the river mists beyond
the glass and cleared his throat and took another big swig from
the hair-tonic bottle.

I loved her, he said. But I never understood her. Not when
she was around. She loved me, she teased me, let me have my
way with her, then run off with a laugh and married a harvest
hand from Braxton County, died in child-bed, and left me fifteen
years to figure it all out. No, not all, by God. Not all. I still get
stumped by women when I'm around them. When I'm alone it's
all as plain as daylight. But when you're around them it's no
good ever trying to figure them out and it's purely fatal to try
outguessing one. Don't ever try it, Hen. Not even with the
dumbest woman ever born. You'll lose if you do—just like those
poor dudes are going to lose. When the bohunk woman gets
done, it'll be them that suffer. Even the wives—they'll be winners in a way. Because they belong to the same team, the same

breed; the bohunk woman will get her revenge in a few months and the wives will be enjoying theirs for years to come. Yes, it'll be the men that'll pay the piper. Because the game was rigged against them before they ever started. They're out there tonight—taking their turns at the house on Water Street—thinking they've got their wives and the bohunk woman both outguessed. That's a mistake, Hen. Don't ever make it. When it comes to the love game every woman born is a genius. That's because they invented it. Every bit of it: the rules, the prizes, the penalties. They invented everything from doing it to the words that's used to do it with to the dunce stool you get sent to if you don't do it their way. Don't ever try to outguess a woman at *that* game, Hen. You might as well go try to tell Edison how to change a light bulb!

He glared around him suddenly in the twilight from the streetlamp; for a minute I thought he was going to fetch the bottle for another swig but he merely cracked his knuckles one by one and glared at his faint reflections in the mirrors.

By God, Hen, said Densel Yoho. Sometimes I think I've got them all figured wrong, though. Sometimes I ain't sure of any of it! Not them—not males—none of it: not even Life. Sometimes I think it's all something—something bigger! Fate! We're all just shuffled thither and yon—men and maids alike—moved round by something none of us can do a God-damned thing about. Like a game, Hen—that's what it is. Some sort of a dirty game that somebody's fixed! It's— It's—

For a minute I thought Densel was almost remembering something; I wanted to seem obliging.

I know, I said. Like the Black Sox.

The which? said Densel.

You know, Densel, I said. The Black Sox. That big baseball scandal here a while back—

Why, now I never did hear tell of that one, said Densel, and sat studying his hundred reflections a while longer.

And please don't never mention that damned game to me, Hen, he said directly. I never seen a baseball game in my life and I don't care if I never do. I couldn't tell you the difference between a touchdown and a punt. And a few weeks from now, Alec Pyle and John Grimm and the rest of them fanatics will be setting up there at the Elks with their ears glued to that damned Atwater Kent and coming down here afterward to get shaved and I'll have to listen to nothing but baseball talk for the rest of the summer. So just kindly don't never mention the name baseball around me, Hen.

He stared off, kind of grumpy and baffled for a bit, but then his face brightened; I guess he thought he was changing the subject, though I could fairly smell the Fan Tan gum and neat's-foot ointment in the air.

Say, Hen! You never did say! he cried with a genial grin. How was your trip?

Well, that was the longest summer I can remember in Apple County since the year of Mama's last sick spell. Those two summers were a lot alike; they both ended on the same sort of September evenings: nights with that same first feel of fall; twilight all dusty with sundown and goldenrod, and green smells of the hay harvest blowing in the wind from every ridge and river meadow. It was on that same kind of autumn night when Mama passed over that Natalia Lazarevitch caught the west-bound out of Glory. I'll long remember those nights; they both left me waiting, heartbroke, puzzled, maybe hoping, maybe just watching, for a long whiles after, for someone who might be coming back. Or maybe only waiting for another such September night to come, when I could ride west-bound out of Glory, too, and someone nice up the line, in some sweet, grassy, little hick-town depot, hunting for my face along the dusty day-coach windows. That kind of fall evening.

Though it all commenced in the morning—a Monday, it was: Labor Day. All the men in town were home having their day of rest: taking down porch swings, mowing lawns, or changing furniture around in the parlors. A few events had been announced for the holiday. Major Tinkum was going to stunt his Curtis Jenny over the Ohio River and his wife Cayce was going to walk the wing. Murph "Mile-a-Minute" Mooney, former Glory High track star and popular free-lance Christmas card salesman, was going to race a seven-foot Lithuanian all the way down river to McKeefrey. And that night there was to be a concert by the prison band.

Around noon I was all alone in the barbershop, dressed up like a fop—and a fool, too, because I didn't even plan on taking in the band concert. Still, maybe it was a hunch made me spruce up a little that morning. For I had just finished combing my hair down flat and neat when I spied the three of them coming up the deserted sidewalk on the other side of Seventh Street: Natalia and the two little girls. They marched right across the street, too—making a big racket, talking and joking about things, and pulling that half-busted old child's wagon behind them—till directly they stood right out front, staring through the window, waiting for me to come unlock the door.

You close, said Natalia, with a flirty shrug. Aw, sure! I bet you close! Everybody close today. Sure!

And she chuckled deep inside.

Even Natalia! she laughed. I close today.

Well, yes, I am closed, I said. Yes. And no. In a way no. And in another way yes.

I cleared my throat, scratched my neck, commenced over.

Yes, I said. I just this minute opened.

She smiled like the sun; it brought back summer, a-hurrying.

Yes? she cried. You haircut Sophie?—Mariya? You haircut them kids pretty like you haircut my Milosh on Saint Vitus Day?

Well, I couldn't say a word for a minute. Because somehow I couldn't get it through my head: Natalia there, what she was saying, me there looking at her—none of it seemed real. She didn't understand my stillness either. Because she looked worried a minute, then gave a rich laugh and fetched a dollar bill out of her patent-leather purse and waved it under my nose.

Pay cash haircut, she cried, smiling. No credit. No pay-later haircut Sophie—Mariya. Pay cash. Credit bad thing this here town!

And she swung her slant-eyed, savage stare off up the empty morning, while a smile turned in the edges of her mouth like

flame curls burning paper, and the look those eyes gave Glory, it
was a whip that bit but made no sound.

No credit! she shouted softly in that milky voice and laughed
and I saw the painted fingers on her flowered hip digging the
round flesh, warm beneath the flimsy of her frock. Natalia
Lazarevitch!—only one in this here town say: Okay, credit!
Okay—sure! Pay later!

Then she turned her high chin round and set that stare on me,
looking hard and deep for a spell, and then the look came kind-
lier; she had that kind of eyes: hard like agate now, cold as river-
ice, and then—in a twinkle—soft as big, wet marigolds. She
smiled, seized Mary's fingers in one hand, Sophie's in the other,
and herded them through the open doorway. Now as she bent,
first from one to the other, laughing and whispering low, fast
words in Serbian, I couldn't keep my eyes off her hair: those
braided coils, that thickness like the good grain of clean-turned
wood, but the color—well, how can I tell you?—I've seen it
somewheres in country kitchens long ago: that smoked-gold
gleam like copper kettles get—a sooty glitter; and something like
the color of the twined and toasted loaves of that queer, shiny
bread they sell in Hunkie mill-town bakeries. It was all I could
do: keeping my hand back; my fingers ached with wanting to
touch that hair.

But it was the hair of little Sophie I found presently beneath
my hands, while shy Mary waited her turn, sucking a pink thumb
now and then and, each time, Natalia, murmuring some low,
strange word, would gently strike the plump fist from her lips,
then settle back to watch my handiwork, while—once now and
then—shouting some teasing, foreign words at Sophie and
Sophie'd answer back and then all three would laugh. My hand
shook some; I'll not deny that those were the two slowest, care-
fullest haircuts I ever gave. Can you wonder?—with her right
there, not eight feet away; so close I could hear her breathe and
the rustle of her clothes when she moved and, each time she'd
laugh, I'd look in the mirror and see her bright lips leap like
redbird wings and fly back from the white flash of her teeth; I'd

see those fine, small bosoms spring and jump in her common, gaudy dress at every gasp of almost-weeping laughter—Lord, you could feel that woman's heat like standing against a round stove in a store!

And I've cut children's hair by the hundreds in my thirty-seven years—it wasn't that. It was her watching me work, watching the scissors and comb in my fingers and looking out to make sure I did it pretty, the way she said I haircut her Milosh: special, de-luxe, nothing but perfect would do. You'd have thought they were young princesses that came and clambered up to sit straight-backed on the child board in my barber chair that day: the little, laughing, whispering daughters of a queen; some empress from a land too wild and beautiful and queer to put on maps, and not ever in the coarse and common colors of this poor schoolbook earth. Yes, I had to work slow, careful—my hands shook so, with her watching, but even if she hadn't had eyes to watch me, even if she'd been blind as old Ransome, the piano tuner, just her there—being—that would have made me tremble. And under my fingertips the fair, clean hair—fine as milkweed floss—of bold Sophie and the shy Mary and me knowing that each of them was a smaller piece of her, until at last they got to seem all one, all Natalia, and me the man to head that footloose home. Every time I breathed the whole damned barbershop seemed filled with them; it reeked of the scrubbed, washtub immaculateness of them all: that smell of cleanness, starched cloth, girl-smell—a crazy kind of musk and yeasty sweetness, like a walking bake-shop smell that went with them where they went. Till, as I say, they seemed mixed up in one: soap and clean hair and the fresh-ironed gingham of cheap dresses that had been washed too often because she would sooner have them shabby rags than not be just as clean as the pink-scrubbed skin beneath the darned and threadbare sleeves and rickrack hems and the little girl necks like bobbing flower stems in collars raggedy as wornout valentines.

And I was hopping mad on top of that—just perfectly furious thinking what I'd say if somebody like A.K. or John or Holly Smithers or maybe some of their wives was to show up right then

and make some smart remark; I kept on having these imaginary
conversations between them and me—they'd say something cute
about me having that common harlot in my place and cutting
her children's hair and then I'd think up a comeback to that and
end up throwing them all to hell out in the middle of Seventh
Street anyways. In a way, I was half-disappointed nobody like
that did show up; I sure had some snappy quips, real sarcasm, if
ary one of such as them dared open his yap. But nobody came.
And it's just as well they never, I reckon. It took me long
enough to get done as it was and I drew it out a little extra
anyways, wanting to please her, wanting to keep her there a spell
more. And I never gave two better child haircuts, if I do say so.
And when I was done, Natalia clopped over, like somebody
who'd never got the hang of walking in those high spike-heels;
she scrambled her fingers in her shiny violet purse and fetched
out some money.

How much cost? she said.

I waved my hand and got red-faced; I stared down at the little
wisps of pale curls round my shoes. I couldn't bear stepping on
them.

Nothing, I said softly, and shook my head and still couldn't
look up at her.

She was quiet a minute and I didn't have to see her dark eyes
to know they were blazing.

How much? she whispered, sore as hell. One dollar? Two
maybe? How much cost haircut my Sophie—my Mariya!

I just shook my head and stared at her high-heel blue shoes
and the slim ankles in the white cotton ankle socks.

Free, I muttered. I done it free, that's all.

She jammed two wrinkled dollar bills in my hand and stood
back with a little snort of scorn.

Free? she laughed, and said some more words in her own queer
tongue and the little girls both laughed. Free! she mocked. No
such thing as free in this here town! No free, mister! And no
credit! Natalia Lazarevitch—she only credit in this here town!
Here! Take!

And she waved another green dollar bill an inch or two from the tip of my nose.

More? she sneered. Four dollar maybe?

And that's right when I got mad and snatched the dollar out of her fingers and crumpled all three of them up and threw the ball of green money in the cuspidor.

Not four! I shouted. Not three neither! Not a goddamned one. Haircuts for grown-up adults is a quarter in this shop and kids is twenty. But I meant them two as a gift. And it wasn't meant as barter neither. I reckon there's nothing now you've got I'd want much to swap for, lady. Why, they really got it smeared all over you, didn't they?—A.K. and John and the rest of them!—they really made you stink a little with their greed, lady! Why, you don't even know the face of common kindness any more. I guess you must have sold them bastards a little more of yourself than you reckoned to!

Bold Sophie stared and shy Mary sucked her thumb. And Natalia's eyes narrowed, searched, got wider then, and darker, deeper somehow: older than some queen's eyes remembering her dead king's ways or the real ways of any man—she'd been so long away from that, I guess, she'd clean forgotten how to judge a gesture's honesty or filth. But suddenly the old softness swept back in her eyes: wet marigolds lit up again by sun. And she shrugged and gave a queer, sad laugh and clattered off, beautiful and foolish in those high heels and dime-store anklets, and went to the marble shelf behind the chairs and commenced lifting the tonic bottles, one by one, and raising each one to her nose with gingerly and childlike carefulness, sniffing the tops before she put them back. I smiled and went right to the back where I kept them: the three bottles of the tonic that nobody but him ever wanted. When I handed it to her she took it, sniffed, sniffed once more, than a third time, harder, and her dark eyes burned like altar candles.

Hah! she cried. This one! Sophie—Mariya!—come! Hey!

And she doused their bowed, obedient heads—Lord, it made me think of some wild, foreign baptism!—and fetched a comb and doused their bright hair some more with the stuff and shy

Mary took a deep breath, smelling, smiling, while bold Sophie only smiled a little—in her mouth's corners—her mother's smile, and stood still and straight and awful proud while Natalia's strong hands worked the comb and patted and laughed, straightening a lock here or a stray stand there, and cried a little and stroked hard with the brush, sniffing and laughing some more and crying some more and then murmuring things in Serbian which somehow sounds like both. With the brush in the right hand, the comb in her left she stood back then, cocking her head, judging her work and presently gave a grunt that it was right. Then Natalia shut her eyes and drew her head back, breathing in deep—smelling, I reckon, the unearthly, god-awful sweetness of that Elwell's Authentic Louisiana Jasmine—and her long nostrils flared like a mare's does, and I watched a little pulse beating in the tall, milky column of her throat while she kept on smiling a spell more—smiling harder, it seemed, at some thought that went roaming back—and then two wild tears sprang swimming out and hung in the brush-thick lashes of her clenched lids. But right away she flung her eyes open wide, shook her head fast and laughed a shout and went running at the two little girls, waving the hairbrush, threatening and hollering, jolly and teasing.

Outside! Go! Go! Outside now! she shouted, whacking their bottoms and hurrying them shrieking and laughing out the door and down the steps. And you *wait* now! You hear, Sophie!—Mariya! You wait now! I come. You hear!—*wait* now!

And she came back and stooped and picked up the green wad of money where I'd thrown it like an old quid, stared at it in her fingers, shrugged, chuckled, and stuck it back inside her purse. Then she turned and came over and stood in front of me, close to me, and studied my face real careful all over; her eyes were still wet; dark—the way it looks inside a great pine forest after a rain—and I knew it was a dark of kindness, and I have prayed since that it was, maybe, something more.

Now, I give *you* something, she said and touched my cheek with a finger.

Sure! I give *you* present now, she cried in a low soft voice. I give you thing I never give one man since my Milosh—

Natalia gave a thoughtful sigh while her queer, dark eyes searched my old, silly, American face and I could feel her slow breath against my chin.

—Not even man I do bad thing with, she whispered, savage, and lifted her fingers to touch my other cheek. Never! Not one man in this here goddamn town! I never give *this* thing! Oho, never! I give this thing only my Milosh. Now—I give you.

And Natalia Lazarevitch held my head in all her fingers while she lifted her face and gave me one soft, slow kiss across the mouth.

Some days go and you never know what happened to them. The summer Mama passed over—it was ten o'clock in the evening—and I couldn't tell you what I did till sunrise of the next morning; it was the look of the daylight told me Mama was gone. A thing happens to you—a death, a wonder—and you look round directly and it seems like two minutes has ticked off but it's really hours, months, maybe years that's gone. That day—that's how it was.

Around sundown Densel Yoho came tearing up to my room, two steps at a time, all out of breath, and sat down, panting, with both hands on his knees, in the cane-bottom chair by my bed. He didn't even look at me lying there on my back; he just stared wild at the worn place in the dusty oriental rug.

Well, it's happened, he said. She waited all this while—the whole summer. Didn't I tell you, Hen? She bided her time and then, by God, she struck like lightning. Didn't I tell you she was feeling it all out, waiting, biding her time, Hen?

What's happened, Densel? I asked quietly.

Her. That one. The Hunkie widow, he said. Serbian. Whatever. Her and them two little girls—Hen, they've rung every doorbell in Glory this afternoon. By God, they really made the rounds, hauling that kiddy wagon behind them like a chariot of fire!

What the hell are you talking about? I said, sitting up on the bed.

Her. That Serbian. Or whatever, he said, smiling. Woman
amongst women. A justice amongst men. Lord God, Hen! Nigh
every doorbell in Glory—there's hardly a one she's missed. Her
and the littlest one, Mary—up on the porches, ringing the
bells—or knocking on the screen doors. Polite knocks, too. Get
that, Hen—easy, genteel knocks. Polite; but businesslike. It was
a spectacle long to remember: her and the littlest one up there
on all them porches, knocking, ringing, one house after the
other. Whilst the oldest gal—what's her name?—the one they
call Soapy—her standing out front on the sidewalk, by the kiddy
wagon, reading from that big cloth-backed ledger book—calling
out the party's name, how many services rendered, the total bill
due. Three dollars at one place—nine or maybe twelve dollars
owed next door. A few lucky ones like A.K. and Doc Stribbler
headed her off and paid her before she got as far as the porch
steps. Cash, too. And when they give her a big bill the gal Soapy
made change from a stogie box full of greenbacks in the kiddy
wagon. Then her and the little one would go on to the next one.
And whatever amount the gal Soapy found in the ledger column
she'd holler out that number. And that was it. She could have
asked three times that much and got it, too—they'd have paid
just to get her out of sight before the little woman saw. But she's
honest. Not a penny more nor a penny less—she only asked for
what she'd earned—hard earned. One of the wives would answer
the door now and then. Quite a few ladies screamed, fainted,
went into hot flashes and sinking spells. And whenever that happened, why, her and the little girl Mary went and sat politely on
the porch steps to ride out the storm. Sooner or later the man of
the house come running with the cash. Anything to get her out
of the little woman's sight.

I laid back down on my pillow, sick-hearted, picturing it:
those proud, strong hands held out like a common bill collector,
that brave face shamed.

John Grimm had a light stroke a little before three o'clock,
Densel went on. His missus phoned Holly Smithers and de-
manded he rush right over and put the woman under arrest.
Holly knew better. He was next page in the ledger. He came

simpering and soft-soaping out the front door before she got near
his porch. He figured to wheedle and bluff her off his lawn. She
turned and said something in Hunkie—or whatever talk to the
big girl. And she—what's her name?—she, Soapy, she reached
in that old wood wagon and fooled around amongst a big pile of
souvenirs and directly she come waving something over her head
like it was Flag Day. A pair of initialed BVD's. I reckon Holly'd
left them down in her bedroom once—probably one of them
nights when Tacky Bledsoe used to go down Water Street on the
city motorcycle to fetch Holly home drunk in the sidecar.

This town has crucified that poor woman, I groaned, staring at
Mama's picture in the pale light of early fall evening.

Crucified her! Densel said. Why, Hen, how so? I'd say Glory
has shared with that ignorant immigrant the homely business
creed on which the Republic is founded. It has opened to her the
golden pages of the thrifty Christian principles on which the
Home is built. And don't never fancy she's such an ingrate as to
let those lofty lessons go by unlearned—unprofited—unappreci-
ated! It was credit, don't you see? They taught her that one word
from the beginning. They shoved that word in her face like an
empty dinner plate—they nailed it to her wall like a sheriff's
eviction paper—and then they whipped the rags off her babes'
backs with it. Well, that's one word in English she learned good
enough to savvy its meaning and worth and, I guess, learn how
good it makes you feel to accommodate somebody and tell them
there's no hurry about paying. Even when they held out cash-in-
hand, I bet she told them to fold it again and stick it back in
their vests and pay later. Credit. The one word they taught her
good. Good enough to give credit to them who didn't even need
it nor ask for it—credit, what's more, to them very same ones
who'd not given her credit for a soup bone nor a loaf of stale
store bread for her kids' supper. So that's how she's been putting
out to them all summer long—on credit. Well, what's being
more American than how she done? Or Christian either? I
mean, to give them sanctimonious tightwads the kindly terms
they wouldn't give her. How's that for turning the other cheek?
Oh, Hen, the beauty—the naked, lovely justice of this day!

Lord, I don't see how this town can afford to lose a woman like that. She's a living symbol for our children. If Glory has a bit of sense they'll make her stay—they'll draft her if they have to! She could give speeches every few weeks to the Lions Club and get up and talk at a few Rotary luncheons. And then, maybe, every Sunday or so, she could give a little chat to the Christian Endeavor or the Methodist Women's Bible Class or maybe even take over old man Toombes's pulpit and preach the regular sermon—offhand, I'd suggest something on the Golden Rule. Then maybe they could pay her off with a few good hot chicken-pie church suppers. I reckon she'd enjoy a good meal or two after the lean summer she's spent. Not that she appeared exactly puny or run-down up there in town this afternoon. When it comes to nourishment, a woman like that—

Whatever kept her from starvation—God knows, I muttered, staring at the cracked, old wallpaper on my ceiling.

As I was commencing to say, never you mind about a woman like that starving, said Densel. A woman like her—just never you mind. I reckon the old Hunkie miner's widow give the little girls their meals. And you can bet she wasn't in much danger this summer of getting throwed out of her house for any back rent. If Harp Follansbee had so much as whispered eviction in that woman's ear he'd have been blackballed by the Moose, castrated at Kiwanis, and shot by a Legion firing squad.

God knows, I went on, heedless. God alone knows what kept her strength up all these weeks.

Outrage, I reckon, Densel said. The body heat of hate. God knows—you're right, Hen: God *does* know. And sometimes it must just scare Him a little—looking at that wild rib he took out of Adam. God looking and seeing a woman like that, with a wildness like that—burning inside her like a coke oven. Well, Hen, you remember all them talks we had this summer—down at the Crystal, under the billiard lights—nights I told you about that wild, crazy female ferment I could watch working inside that woman like too much yeast in a bottle of warm homebrew. Don't you understand it yet, Hen?—how a woman like her can hibernate inside herself like a bear in a cave and live off the burning fat of her own wrath, and sleep, curled up, throughout whatever. And live on little else but that. Just holed-up there inside herself like a winter bear, sucking on that big, bitter paw of her instincts' own sweet vengeance and the long, little justices of time. And not minding all the slow while it takes neither, knowing when spring comes she'll uncurl, thaw out and go eat. And square up for a few things while she's at it. It's something they've got and we don't, Hen. I mean natural patience. We don't have it and we never will. I mean the kind of patience—like body fat—that nature gives women because they're the only humans that ever really have to learn how to *wait* for things.

Densel sat a spell, staring. Then he gave a queer, bitter little chuckle, pulled his folded, sweaty handkerchief out from under his collar and commenced cooling his red face with a cardboard fan from Tom Peace's Funeral Parlor.

Yes, it's been quite a day, Hen. Quite a day, said Densel Yoho. They canceled the foot race to McKeefrey, called off the band concert at the prison, and that damned fool aviator's wife has been up there walking that aeroplane wing for the past three hours and not a living soul but small boys has come out to wave at her. Quite a day. It looks like quite a night, too. A lot of the boys tonight will have to sleep in their cars. Some others has packed up and taken the streetcar to Wheeling to spend a few days. And I understand the Mound Hotel and Tomlinson's both is sold out and quite a few army cots has been loaned to the Elks and the Legion by the Red Cross. For a Labor Day spectacle I'd say it has even beat the one thirty years ago when they brought Bryan to the camp ground to do the Cross of Gold.

Densel cracked his knuckles nervously, one by one, and glared at the Maxfield Parrish picture over my washstand.

Makes a fellow glad he's single tonight, eh, Hen? he said directly.

No, I said. It don't particularly.

Densel was still a while more, brooding worse, and we listened to the west-bound blowing for Glory somewhere up the harvest-smelling dark.

Hen, I know what you're feeling, Densel said. You got a bad

case on that woman. I've always known that, Hen. I thought maybe if it was me that broke the news about what she done today and how she done it—how she come through it all just looking elegant—the only one amongst them all not looking common nor whipped. Hen, I didn't want you hearing it from some of them boys in the shop tomorrow morning. The way they'll tell it—now and for years to come. Ugly and ornery and mean. Some wise guy even made up a new name for her already—Tally Vengeance—but it'll never stick, Hen.

No, I know. It won't stick, I said. She's Natalia Lazarevitch. Serbian. Lady.

Whatever, said Densel. Anyways, I guess you ought to know now that her and them two little girls is down at the depot waiting to go. That's her train blowing now, Hen. I thought maybe you might want to go say good-bye or some such thing.

I done that already, I said.

Anyways, he went on, in a soft, furious voice, like he was working himself up to a quiet rage again at the way everything is. Anyways, Hen, I just thought my coming up here and telling you and talking all this fool talk for a while—Hen, I figured it might help ease the hurt. But it don't—does it?

Nope, I said; my breath was all played out somehow, I couldn't say another word to Densel—not even thanks.

Densel picked up the cardboard fan again and sat glaring at the funeral parlor ad printed across it in thin, black letters.

Still, by God, it was *that*, he said, with a soft, bitter chuckle and his voice was like he was talking to himself now. Something kind of glorious—something kind of beautiful and fierce moving amongst us here for a while. By God, it was *that*! Like somebody for once had beat the crooked wheel! Like they'd finally won the game in spite of the fix—the eternal, goddamn fix!

Densel got up and swung his arms a little, flexing his muscles, loosening his joints; he cursed under his breath and went off toward the door.

I'm going down to Charley Seat's before he closes, Hen, Densel said, without turning around. I'm all out of gum. Charley's got the only gumrack in Glory that stocks my brand.

I listened to his footsteps down the stairs; I sort of envied him.

So now I've blabbed it all and it'll get back to Glory sure as hell. Still, I don't care. When a man's in my trade and has to spend thirty-seven years of his life keeping still I reckon he's entitled, just once, to out-talk everybody else in Glory. So, I don't care how many people know what I said or how sore they get or how many customers I lose. I've got me a nice nest egg laid away. I'll get by just fine. And when my will is read, half goes to Marcy Cresap's TB Sanatorium—that's for Mama. And the other half—well, never you mind who that's for! Though, I reckon by now that's no secret to you either.

Natty Vengeance is still around Glory—in name, in whispered memory, sometimes in laughter, sometimes in awe. It was Natalia Lazarevitch went away that soft, fall night. And who knows?—well, the B. & O. runs east-bound through Glory, too. And if, one of these nights, Natalia Lazarevitch should come back and I'm not around anymore to wave hello or cut her children's hair or ask her what I always wanted to but never could figure out how, I just want her to be all right. I mean, I don't want her ever again having to take those two children and go dragging a busted kiddy wagon up cool, rich streets just to get whatever her flesh and spirit tells her it happens to cost to stay alive on this earth a little while and still not stop being beautiful and mean and Serbian and unbeaten and proud and female. Just because a queen has her country stolen off the maps is no reason to have to go wandering away like that with two sleepy-eyed princesses, three one-way tickets, a pasteboard suitcase full of rags and only one or two hundred dollars just to get her somewhere, anywhere, up the line. Somewhere, someday I want Natalia Lazarevitch to be a real winner in the little while of her life.

Play ball! yells Densel way off up the summer darkness of the Glory streets; there's a wind in the leaves and his voice is almost faint.

I get real mad about something all of a sudden. I run to the window, move the electric fan off the sill, pull in the window screen, and poke my head and shoulders out into the dark. Over my head I see the fixed, still stars in the windy autumn night; but they don't faze me one bit.

PL—AY BA—LL! I yell in a voice so loud you'd think I was hollering it at the world.